Praise for the *Vampire Earth* novels

Choice of the Cat

"David Valentine is a true hero. . . . I found myself rooting for him on page one." —SF Site

Way of the Wolf

"A winner. If you're going to read only one more postapocalyptic novel, make it this one."
—Fred Saberhagen, author of the *Berserker* series

"I have no doubt that E. E. Knight is going to be a household name in the genre." —Silver Oak Book Reviews

"[If] *The Red Badge of Courage* had been written by H. P. Lovecraft." —Paul Witcover, author of *Waking Beauty*

"E. E. Knight has managed to create a compelling new world out of the ruins of our existing one. It's a major undertaking for a new author. . . . He does it with style and grace, and I would highly recommend checking out the book as soon as you can." —Creature Corner

"It was obvious to me within the first few pages that Knight knew how to write. . . . Valentine is a complex and interesting character, mixing innocence with a cold-hearted willingness to kill. . . . Knight brought the setting (a future, apocalyptic United States) to vivid life. . . . The setting drew me in. . . . His world is well-constructed and holds together in a believable fashion. . . . Compelling." —SFReader.com

TALE OF THE THUNDERBOLT

BOOK THREE OF *THE VAMPIRE EARTH*

E. E. Knight

A ROC BOOK

ROC
Published by New American Library, a division of
Penguin Group (USA) Inc., 375 Hudson Street,
New York, New York 10014, USA
Penguin Group (Canada), 10 Alcorn Avenue, Toronto,
Ontario M4V 3B2, Canada (a division of Pearson Penguin Canada Inc.)
Penguin Books Ltd., 80 Strand, London WC2R 0RL, England
Penguin Ireland, 25 St. Stephen's Green, Dublin 2,
Ireland (a division of Penguin Books Ltd.)
Penguin Group (Australia), 250 Camberwell Road, Camberwell, Victoria 3124,
Australia (a division of Pearson Australia Group Pty. Ltd.)
Penguin Books India Pvt. Ltd., 11 Community Centre, Panchsheel Park,
New Delhi – 110 017, India
Penguin Group (NZ), cnr Airborne and Rosedale Roads, Albany,
Auckland 1310, New Zealand (a division of Pearson New Zealand Ltd.)
Penguin Books (South Africa) (Pty.) Ltd., 24 Sturdee Avenue,
Rosebank, Johannesburg 2196, South Africa

Penguin Books Ltd., Registered Offices:
80 Strand, London WC2R 0RL, England

First published by Roc, an imprint of New American Library,
a division of Penguin Group (USA) Inc.

First Printing, March 2005
10 9 8 7 6 5 4

Copyright © Eric Frisch, 2005
All rights reserved

Cover art by Koveck

 REGISTERED TRADEMARK—MARCA REGISTRADA

Printed in the United States of America

To John and Laura Anne,
for getting me to the next level

Glossary

Aspirants: Teenagers, often sons and daughters of those in a particular caste, who travel with the Hunters and perform assorted camp functions.

Bears: Hunters and the most fearsome of the Lifeweavers' human weapons; warriors who go into a battle-fury resembling that of the berserks of old. The Bears are proud to take on anything the Kurians can design.

Cats: Trained by the Lifeweavers, these Hunters act as spies, saboteurs, and assassins in the Kurian Zone. Some work in disguises; others work openly.

Dau'wa: "Forward-thinkers"; the minority of Lifeweavers (mostly concentrated on the planet Kur), who used vital aura to become immortal, i.e., vampires.

Dau'weem: "Backwards-thinkers"; the majority of Lifeweavers, who eschewed use of vital aura to become immortal.

Golden Ones: A Grog variant, more verbal and organized than the more common Gray Ones. Fawn-colored fur on their shoulders blends to white on their bellies.

Gray Ones: The most common kind of Grog, an apish humanoid with thick plates of gray skin. Marginally intelligent, though quick to adapt to human tools and weapons.

Grogs: Any of the multitude of creations the Kurians have designed or enhanced to help subjugate man. The term *grog* is in general use for introduced life-forms, but properly belongs just to the humanoid variants. Grogs come in many shapes and sizes; some are intelligent enough to use weapons.

Hunters: Human beings who have been enhanced by the techno-magic of the Lifeweavers to cope with the spawn of Kur.

Interworld Tree: An ancient network of portals between the stars, the doors of which allow instantaneous transportation across the light-years.

Kur: One of the nine planets of the Interworld Tree. A great storehouse of touchstones was found here; it was a center of Lifeweaver science and learning. Later it became a renegade world when the Kurian Lifeweavers began to use vital aura to extend their lives, touching off a civil war that has spilled over to Earth.

Kurians: Lifeweavers from the planet Kur who learned how to indefinitely lengthen their lives by absorbing vital aura. They are the true vampires of the New Order.

lifesign: Energy given off by any living thing in proportion to its size and sentience. The Reapers use it, in addition to their normal senses, to track their human prey.

Lifeweavers: The ancient race who discovered the old Pre-Entity Gates between the Nine Worlds.

Pre-Entities: The Old Ones, a vampiric race that died out long before man walked the Earth. From their knowledge, the Kur learned how to become vampires by living off of vital aura.

Quislings: Humans who assist the Kurians in running the New Order.

Ravies: A virus the Kurians distributed to break up the social order of man, allowing them to take over more easily.

Reapers: The Praetorian Guard of the New Order, they are in fact avatars animated by their Master Vampire. They permit the reclusive Kurians to interact with humans and others, and more important, absorb the vital aura through a psychic connection with the avatar without physical risk. Reapers live off the blood of the victim, while the aura sustains the Master Kurian. Also known colloquially as Capos, Governors, Hoods, Rigs, Skulls, Scowls, Tongue-Tong, Creeps, Hooded Ones, and Vampires.

Touchstones: Record-keeping technology used by the Pre-Entities and discovered by the Lifeweavers. Touchstones hold anything from knowledge to memories; the data is accessible by a sentient being's touch. This can be dangerous for less-developed minds, such as humans'.

vital aura: An energy field created by a living creature. Sadly, humans are rich in it.

Wolves: The most numerous caste of the Hunters. Their patrols watch the no-man's-land between the Kurian Zone and the Free Territories, and they also act as guerrilla fighters, couriers, and scouts.

From the east to the west blow the trumpet to arms!
Through the land let the sound of it flee;
Let the far and the near all unite, with a cheer,
In defense of our Liberty Tree.

—Thomas Paine, "The Liberty Tree"

They sailed away for a year and a day
To the land where the bong-tree grows.

—Edward Lear, *The Owl and the Pussy-Cat*

Chapter One

New Orleans, January, the forty-eighth year of the Kurian Order: Formerly glorious in its decay, under the New Order the city transformed from an aging beauty into a water-logged corpse. Much of the Big Easy rots under a meter of Mississippi River water—save for the old city's heart, now protected by two layers of dikes. The rococo facades of the French Quarter, once browning into a fine patina, fall to pieces in quiet, unmourned. The stately homes of the two great antebellum periods, pre-1861 and pre-2022, have vanished under a carpet of lush kudzu or riverside saw grass. As if the flooding and years of neglect were not enough punishment, New Orleans suffered a major hurricane in 2028: a titanic storm that rose from the Gulf like a city-smashing monster in a Japanese movie. No FEMA, no insurance companies showed up afterwards to clean and repair the storm-battered city. What was destroyed stayed destroyed; the inhabitants found it easier to shift to still-standing buildings than to rebuild.

But the mouth of the Mississippi is too important, even to the reduced traffic of the Kurian Order, to be given up entirely to nature. The metropolis, both the section behind the dike and the Venice-like portions of the flooded districts, still support a mélange of denizens from all across the Gulf of Mexico and the Caribbean. Counting those living among the lakes, bayous, and in the Mississippi estuary, New Orleans boasts a population of over two million—a total that few other cities known to the Old World can match. The rich harvests of seafood, fish and game of the swamps, and mile after mile of rice plantations feed the masses concentrated at the sodden bend in the river.

The Kurian Order encourages fecund populations. A Kurian lord must breed his polis to supply him with enough vital aura, for only in feeding on the energy created by the death throes of a sentient being can he revitalize his immortal lich. The Masters of New Orleans have no regrets about its silenced music, its smothered culture, its reduced cuisine, or its broken history. Healthy, mating herds of humans, kept from escape and from the clutches of rapacious competing Kur, are the only form of wealth that matters.

For the human race, living to see another year is now the paramount pursuit in a city once known for its sensual diversions.

Though the Easy Street was only a waterfront dive, it was *his* waterfront dive, so Martin Clive took pride in every squeaky stool and chipped mug of his saloon. From grid shielded-electric lights to sawdust-covered floor, he loved every brick of it.

His customers, on the other hand, he could take or leave.

Not that he didn't need them. Clive's herd of cash-bearing cows, properly milked, provided for him. Clive surveyed the noisy, smelly Thursday-night crowd as the winter rains poured down outside. Safe behind the badge sewn to the money vest he seldom took off—even to sleep—and in the ownership of the biggest bar on the dockyard district of the dike-hugging waterfront, he passed his time and occupied his mind in sizing up the men as they talked, smoked, and drank. The few women in his bar were there on business, not for pleasure.

Clive perfected a three-step practice of evaluating customers over the years, now so ingrained that he did it unconsciously. Separating the "payers" from the "bums" came first. Knowing who had the cash for a night's drink and who didn't had been second nature to Clive since before he acquired the establishment. Distinguishing "gents" from "trouble" was yet another specialty. As he aged, and passed the responsibility of serving out drinks and rousting the "bums" and "trouble" to younger, stronger men, he took up a third valuation: that of predicting the remaining life span of his customers.

Clive looked at a bent longshoreman, hook over his shoulder and a pewter mug of cheap beer at his lips. The man had drunk, smoked, and wheezed out a few hours in the Easy Street six nights a week for the past ten years. Clive had watched him age under grueling physical labor, rotgut alcohol, and bad diet. If the longshoreman could stay in the good books of his crew chief, meaning handing over kickbacks out of his wages, he could probably spin out as many as ten more years if he stayed out of the hold. Sitting two seats down from him, a merchant sailor drank plain coffee, sixty if he was a day, dye rubbed into his hair to darken it in an effort to look younger. Soon no captain would hire him on, no matter how sober and upstanding a character he might be. He was due for the last dance within a year or two. On the next stool, a boy kept an affectionate eye on the aged sailor, perhaps a relative, perhaps just a shipmate. The boy did not drink either, and with hard work and a clean nose could expect to live another fifty years as long as he kept indoors after nightfall.

Over at a warm corner table, a young officer drank with three of his men. The officer was a welcome combination of "payer" and "gent," to the point where Clive bothered to name him. The officer was "the Major" to Clive, and the Major always ordered a good bottle and never complained about the cheap whiskey substituted inside. That made him a fine payer. The Major and his men rarely caused trouble; therefore, they qualified for genthood. They wore the mottled green uniform of the Carbineers, one of the horsed troops of paramilitary Cossacks who kept civil order and patrolled the streets of New Orleans.

Maybe in other city establishments the Major threw his

weight around, took food and drink without paying, and had his uniform silence objections. But not in the Easy Street. Clive had friends at the top of the city's food chain.

Clive learned in his youth that if you were in good with Kur, you could thumb your nose at the Port Authority, the Transport Office, even the police and militia. With Kurian patronage, he bid for ownership of the moribund Easy Street. A whiff of anything going on in the bar that Kur wouldn't like, and he picked up the phone. Clive wore his third ten-year badge on his chest, not due to expire for six more years, and he was certain of acquiring another. The badge put him off-limits to the Kurians' aura-hungry Hoods — well, mostly — and brought him peace of mind that muzzled any protest from his conscience.

The inner door of the entry vestibule opened, and Clive heard the wind and splatter of the rain pouring down outside in the moment before his doorman swung the outer portal shut. Clive liked the rain. It drove customers indoors and flushed the filth from the city's gutters.

A stranger stood silhouetted in the door.

The man didn't remove his raincoat. Clive took a closer look. A coat could conceal any number of unpleasant accoutrements. The Easy Street's owner relaxed when he caught a glimpse of uniform under the coat's heavy lapels. The flash of navy blue and brass buttons revealed the stranger as a Coastal Marine. From the fit of the coat and the good though mud-splattered boots Clive judged the man a payer. But something about his face made Clive reserve judgment on whether this man would be trouble or not.

The marine was tall and lean, but not remarkably so in either aspect. Clive put him in his mid-twenties: he had the narrow, crinkle-edged eyelids of a man with a lot of outdoor mileage, and the bronze skin of someone with a hefty dose of Indian blood. The stranger walked with a trace of stiffness in his left leg, not a false limb but perhaps an old injury. He was good-looking in a clean-shaven, sharp-jawed way, judging from the looks exchanged by a pair of whores keeping each other company at the end of the bar. Shining black hair hung in wet tangles, a ropy opal mane thrown back over his collar. A thin white scar traced his right cheek from the outer corner of his dark eye to his chin like the path of a milky tear.

With a moment to get a good look as the marine moved, Clive judged the man to be wearing a pistol at his hip, then the capped tang of some kind of knife appeared as the entrant turned. Clive knew how to spot weapons, long coat or no.

The new customer glanced around the room. His gaze flicked from the massive fireplace at the west end, big enough for a barbecue, to the game tables at the east.

The marine froze. Clive followed his gaze. Before he could determine whom he had recognized, the scarred stranger approached the bar nonchalantly. Clive guessed he had recognized the Major, for the table in the corner had gone quiet. Probably some old quarrel over a girl, or a smuggling deal gone bad. The Coastal Marines, with their mobility and lack of supervision, were notorious black-marketeers on the coast stretching from Galveston to the Florida Floods. Intrigued, Clive looked across the bar to the Major's table. The gents had their heads together. Clive's nose, after years of smelling the various aromas of a saloon—tobacco, liquor, sweat, urine, sawdust, and vomit (usually in that order)— was not as straight as it once had been, but he smelled trouble.

"Tea and rum, if you've got either," David Valentine said, dripping from head to foot on the sawdust-sprinkled floor. His coat trapped the wet of his shirt better than it kept the rain out.

"Got both, Coastie."

"The hotter, the better," he said, pulling his hand through his slick hair again to get it out of his eyes. The gesture gave him a chance to look at the corner table. A silent mental alarm had tripped a switch in his nervous system, warming

him better than any fire. Details stood out: florid printing on
the bar bottle labels, the meshed ranks of gray hair on the
barman's arms, a blemish on a prostitute's neck, footsteps
muffled by the sawdust scattered on the floor, the rancid
smell out of a spittoon.

The officer leaned across the corner table to speak to his
men. Valentine trembled as his mind raced.

"You cold, Marine?" a whore asked, brushing a wet lock
of hair behind her ear. Gold lamé and blond hair covered
what little skin she didn't have on display. "I got a way—"

She'd been attracted by the uniform. Ironic, because its
thick, high-quality fabric and solid brass buttons repulsed
him every time he put it on. Whenever he looked at himself
in a mirror, he saw the Enemy looking back out of his own
eyes.

"Some other time, perhaps." Valentine turned away from
her.

His conscience hammered at him until his eyes shone wet
with more than rain. *Fool! Lazy, irresponsible fool!* Over a
year's worth of preparation, service to the Kurian Order
under a false name, all turned to shit and flushed. Just because he'd been tired and felt like coming in out of the
weather.

Valentine racked his brain for the name, picturing the
hawkish face in the hammock that summer in the Yazoo
Delta during his training in Free Territory. Lewand Alistar, a
freshly invoked Wolf six years ago and posted missing, pre-
sumed dead. So the Reapers hadn't killed him after all. Perhaps he had been captured and turned; perhaps he had been
planted in Southern Command as a spy who saw his chance
to get away clean. Whatever put him in a Carbineer's uniform in New Orleans was immaterial. The fact remained
that mutual recognition occurred.

Valentine remembered Alistar as a quick-witted, active
comrade. A hot mug of spiked tea arrived, and Alistar chose
that moment to rise and take up his coat. Valentine blew into
the steaming crockery. Alistar's companions shifted their

chairs around. They pretended to watch the barmaids and hookers, but all three heads were pointed at Valentine.

Valentine heard Alistar move behind him. He readied himself to turn and fight, should the footsteps approach. But the Quisling left the Easy Street in a hurry. Typical of Alistar—not heroic but smart. No wonder he wore a major's cluster in the Kurian Zone.

Valentine needed to get out of the bar, too, without being impeded by Alistar's comrades, who he guessed had been ordered to keep him from leaving. He reached into his pocket, wadded a ball of money in his hand. He raised his mug in a come-hither toast to the whore who had approached him.

"Interested in a little fun and a lot of money?" he asked, his rough voice low.

"Always," she said, smiling at him with a decent, if tobacco stained, set of teeth behind compound layers of lipstick. "My name's Agri. Like as in agreeable to anything."

Valentine thrust the money into her shirt, pretending to feel her up. "Glad to hear it. There's a hundred and then some, Agri. Which girl here rubs you the wrong way?"

"Huh?" she said.

"Quick, or a man. Who don't you like here?"

She dropped the attitude at the quiet urgency in his voice. "Umm, there's Star," the woman said, leaning out to look around Valentine's wide shoulder. "The head of hair with gold earrings. She's always breaking in and screwing my work up."

He followed her gaze. "Which one is she, in the pink?" he asked, spotting a prostitute with a mass of wavy hair framing her face like a lion's mane. "Okay, I'm going to go talk to her. I want you to start a fight, fast."

"And that's all I gotta do?"

"Make as big a scene as you can. Yes, that's all."

"Shit, Marine, I'd do that for free."

Valentine turned away from her and moved to the darker woman in a hot pink half-top. "I've heard you're quite a woman," Valentine said, raising an eyebrow suggestively. The whore cocked her head and smiled welcomingly.

"That's my up, you bitch!" his paid prostitute shrieked.

Noisy, even better, Valentine thought.

Star reacted with a speed that would have done credit to many of Valentine's former comrades in the Wolves. She planted herself, lowered her hips, and spread her arms.

The two women fell to the floor, fighting bobcats spitting and hissing at each other. A ring of hooting barflies formed around the combatants. Valentine backed through the crowd, snatched a hat off of an unattended table, and moved out the door before any of Alistar's soldiers had a chance to push through the crowd to guard the exit.

The conditions could hardly be worse for tracking a smart man in the crowded—and dangerous, thanks to prowling Reapers—city with a two-minute head start. Night, rain, and the rickshaw-cluttered streets all conspired to hide his quarry. Visibility nil—the big bosses never bothered much with public lighting. Most men would not have had a chance.

David Valentine was not most men. He was a Cat, one of the select specimens of humanity called Hunters trained by the Lifeweavers to fight against the abominations of their vampiric brethren, the Kur. The Kur controlled most of the planet, and the regions that remained outside their grasp, like Valentine's adopted home in the Ozarks and Ouachitas, owed much of their freedom to the sacrifices of the Hunters.

The Hunters, outnumbered and weak compared with the Reapers and the other creations of the Kur, relied on enhanced senses, physical ability, and tight mental discipline. The last was of paramount importance. The Reapers, the Praetorian Guard of Kur, tracked human prey by reading lifesign, psychic auras sent out by sentient beings.

Valentine needed to wash the fear from his mind. At the moment he was alone among enemies, surrounded by thousands who could gain a ten-year badge protecting themselves from the Reapers by pointing him out as an enemy of the New Order. And somewhere in the rainy darkness, a man whom he knew to be no fool was hurrying to ring the alarm bell.

Alistar would not just run to the nearest phone. He had no idea if Valentine was working alone, or with others who might have picked up a surreptitious signal and followed him out of the bar. Valentine remembered him as a man who liked to be in command. It was possible that he would get a posse of his own Carbineers together, to better take the credit for his coup in capturing or killing one of Southern Command's "terrorists."

The barracks of the Carbineers would mean a long walk, too much time wasted. But Valentine knew from months of working the port that a contingent of them guarded their supply warehouse by the docks. Some of Alistar's men would be there.

It was only a guess, but as good a guess as he could make. Valentine ducked through an alleyway and broke into a sprint down a road parallel to the one Alistar probably took. Even if he had guessed wrong, the farther he got from the Easy Street, the better.

He loosened his coat to run. If anyone saw him, pounding down the center of the near-empty street, splashing through puddles, they might mistake him in the wet and darkness for a Reaper. His sprint did not end at the hundred-yard mark; he called on his reserves, and they answered, propelling him through the night with legs and lungs of flame. Astonishingly, at least to anyone who did not know what a Hunter was capable of, his speed increased.

The warehouse he sought was in an old, brick-paved part of town. Garbage lay in heaps on every corner, and better than half the buildings were fire-gutted shells. Empty, glass-less windows gaped out at the street like skulls' eyes when they were not boarded up.

One closed-up window wore a freshly spray-painted skull with a heart around it. According to the graffiti of New

Orleans's streets, someone just lost a loved one to the Reapers within.

Any of the empty buildings around might contain a prowling Reaper. This was one of the districts of the city where it wasn't considered healthy to be out after dark, even for a man in uniform. He relaxed his mind, let his vision blur, tried to feel for the cold, hard spot on his mind the Reapers sometimes made.

Sometimes. He prayed his psychic antennae were working tonight.

He pulled up at a noisome alley, partially blocked at one end by a stripped car turned on its side. Its gutters served as the local populace's latrine, judging from the smell. Hand tapping at his pistol butt, Valentine cut down the alley and back to the main thoroughfare. Alistar was a former Wolf, and there was every possibility of him scenting Valentine before seeing him without some kind of masking odor.

A *thunk* and a metallic clatter sounded from one of the broken windows, hitting him like a shot. He spun, crouching against the half-expected leap as he drew his revolver. His keen ears picked up the sound of the skittering, scrambling claws of a fleeing rat within.

Valentine edged sideways down the alley, gaze flicking from paneless window to window until his heart slowed again.

He paused in a deep well of darkness under a fire escape, reholstered his gun, and drew a stiletto from his boot, nerving himself for what he had to do. Killing in battle, with bullets cracking the air all around and explosions numbing his senses was one thing. Premeditated murder of a fleeing opponent required an entirely different side of his persona. It was a version of himself who had killed helpless men in their Control Tanks in Omaha; blown a bound policeman's head off with a shotgun in Wisconsin; and knifed lonely, frightened sentries on isolated bridges. Cold-blooded need provoked those killings, but his sense of exultation in the deeds bothered his conscience more than the acts themselves did.

Valentine heard footsteps over the steady patter of rain, coming from the direction he expected Alistar. Two people hove into view in the middle of the street, walking together under some kind of tarpaulin sheltering both from the weather. Not his quarry then, but—

One was definitely pulling the other along. The insistent guide was about the right size and sex. Clever. Trusting his hunch, Valentine collected himself for a leap. As he crouched, the analytical side of his brain appreciated the irony of Alistar using a woman as camouflage, paralleling his own subterfuge in the bar. The tarpaulin provided just the right touch of shape-concealing cover. He probably grabbed her out of a doorway, tucking himself under the improvised umbrella with her and ordering her to accompany him. Alistar had always been cool in a crisis.

As they passed, not seeing him in the rain and dark, Valentine leapt. His standing broad jump covered five meters, ending in a body blow that caught Alistar in the small of the back. The two tumbled down, the man ensnared in the wet canvas.

The girl screamed out her fright, and Valentine heard her stumble and right herself. He paid no attention, concentrating on getting his knife to the Quisling's throat. The man struggled in the folds of the tarry material like a netted fish.

He straddled Alistar, pinning his chest and arms with the full force of his body weight and muscle as he cut open the tarp. The stiletto dug into his former comrade's neck, eliciting a squeal. "Dave, no! Wait!"

Valentine paused, not moving the knife either farther in or back. He had not been called Dave since his days as a recruit.

"Not what you think," Alistar said as his face drained to white. "You think I wanted this? You remember how it was, we got separated. . . . The Reapers were after us. One got me, picked me up. They took me all the way back to Mississippi. After questioning, it was join 'em or die. Never really joined though, never really joined. That's why I ended up in this rear-area pisser, didn't want to fight against y'all. You have to believe me. I met a girl, got married. We've talked about running—every chance we get alone, we discuss it. Lois wants out."

"You could have contacted me in the bar, then. Quietly. What did you run for?"

"I—I got scared."

"Looked to me like you were running for help."

"I didn't tell the guys you were with Southern Command. I said we fought over a job. You threatened you'd kill me if you ever got the chance. I ducked out to go get my wife, I was going to have her go in there and talk to you. Make you see our way. Lois's honest—you can tell just by talking to her. I knew you could always read people, Dave. You'd be able to get us out."

Valentine listened with Lifeweaver-sensitized ears for anyone approaching to investigate. He let Alistar speak.

"We can be ready in an hour. Hide out wherever you tell us. I dunno why you're here, but maybe you need some advice about how to get away." Alistar paused. "Or not. Any way you want it. Just trust me—give me a chance to prove it."

Valentine put himself in Alistar's shoes. The summer of his eighteenth year, had their roles been reversed, could he honestly say he would not have followed Alistar's path, given a choice of death or grudging service? But how grudging? He wore a major's cluster, after all. Perhaps he wore other insignia.

He shifted the knife and used his right hand to pull open Alistar's raincoat. On his old comrade's breast was a row of little silver studs, projecting out of the green uniform over a shining five-year badge. Valentine knew that each stud represented five confirmed kills of enemies bearing arms, and the badge probably gained through turning over friends, neighbors, or comrades to the Reapers.

Alistar read his fate in Valentine's eyes and opened his mouth to scream for help. Valentine shot his hand up to Alistar's throat, crushing cartilage and blood vessels in a granite grip. A sound like a candy wrapper crinkling and an airy wheeze was all that came out of the Quisling's collapsing throat.

"Would've let you go another time," Valentine said, fighting his friend's final paroxysm. "But what I'm here to do is just too damn important."

Valentine got up off the corpse. Emptying his mind, quieting his thoughts with the aura-hiding discipline of the Lifeweavers had a succoring side effect: it kept him from thinking about what he had just done. He carried the corpse off to the stinking alley and went to work with quick, precise motions. Using his knife, he tore a ragged hole just below Alistar's Adam's apple, then picked up the twitching body and held it inverted. The warmth of the draining corpse nauseated him. He watched the blood mix with the rain on the cracked and filthy pavement, and stood shivering from wet cold and nerves.

Between the injury and the confused girl's story of a flying assailant out of the shadows, assuming she was brave enough to go to the Authorities, there was a chance that whoever found Alistar's body would conclude a prowling Reaper had taken him, draining him of blood with its syringelike tongue.

Valentine had seen enough Hood-drained bodies to mimic the injury and disposal of the corpse. He stuffed Alistar in a debris-filled window well. The Reapers usually concealed their kills so as not to disturb their human herds. But an investigation blaming the death on a Reaper feeding was too slender a thread on which to hang the success of his mission.

It would have to start tonight.

Chapter Two

The City Center of New Orleans: No matter what his or her status in the Kurian order, a human has to consider the risks before going abroad after dark, even at the busy city nexus of road and rail lines. At night, the vital aura of any sentient being shines bright and clear to the senses of a Reaper, drawing it and the Appetite that sees through the avatar's eyes. The Reaper, tall, thin, and cloaked, grabs its victim in a bruising grip and buries its long tongue in the food's neck. Sharp teeth keep its hold while the tongue searches out the wildly beating heart.

The "last dance," as the locals call it, leaves the victim emptied of blood. The rich fluid is absorbed into the Reaper's rudimentary digestive system, and life aura is transferred to the Kurian Lord animating the Reaper. The Kurian is a puppet-master working the million synaptic strings of the Reaper's nervous system. Rumor has it that the pain and fear of a victim enhances the Kurian's appreciation of aura. Reapers have been known to stalk and play with their food, even dragging it away to the Master's refuge for a cleaner "connection" for the draining transfer. What torments might be added, flavoring the aura like seasoning on a meal, do not make for pleasant speculation.

Valentine's night began with a call on the Station Rooms. Too comfortable to be called a prison, and too regimented to be called a hotel, the Station Rooms housed wives and families of the men at sea. In Imperial Roman tradition, the families of the men serving the Coastal Patrol remained under watchful house arrest until the sailors' return. The freedom from the Reapers provided by naval service required some kind of guarantee that the men would fulfill their duties, and with their usual efficiency, Kur settled on hostage-taking. While it was well-fed, curtained hostage-taking, the implicit threat remained no matter how bourgeois the surroundings.

With the grisly scene in the alley playing over and over in his head, Valentine wanted nothing more than a few hours' sleep, perhaps with a stiff drink to help him calm down. He could obliterate it all in the arms of a woman easily enough, but whores weren't to his taste even if he'd had the time. He had been up since well before dawn, making his way by boat and foot to the rendezvous at the outskirts of the city. Once again, the dozen Wolves had not shown, making them nine days overdue. He'd lingered as long as he dared among waterlogged ruins under the old water tower, its rust-scoured letters leaving only the vaguely menacing block capitals ORWOE still legible on its sides. Once back in the city, he'd bought an okra-and-rice dish from an open-air diner, not trusting meat that had flies buzzing around it in winter. It began to rain, and on his wet and weary journey back to the ship he'd decided to stop for a drink at a strategically placed waterfront bar his marines spoke well of: the Easy Street.

Now, chances were that the hunt was on and he was the game afoot. He would have to put into effect the plan he had been considering since the Wolves had turned forty-eight hours overdue. Phony repairs to the ship could only be stretched out so long, no matter how imaginative the chief engineer was in his delaying tactics. The captain had shown symptoms of apoplexy at being told the *Thunderbolt* would be laid up another few days, waiting for parts. Further postponements might mean a change of personnel in the form of a new chief engineer, which would be more fatal to the mission than the nonarrival of the Wolves.

Valentine's thoughts kept returning to details of his encounter with Alistar. The gleam of the wedding ring on the dead man's hand—how much of the story about his wife was real? Valentine wished he could meet the woman, and in an overwrought fantasy imagined the two of them having a conversation in private, where he could confess his regrets about her husband's death and the bitter choices, tonight and six years ago, that had necessitated it.

The rain slackened as Valentine approached the Station Rooms. The name came from the proximity of the building to the train station, an odd location for mostly naval dependents. As he neared the entrance, he walked loosely, mimicking the purposeful stagger of a man full of drink.

A sentry stood just inside the barred doors, rather than at his usual post on the first step. The rain had driven him into a minor dereliction of duty, but the Station Rooms contained nothing of value, and what security there was concentrated on keeping the Coastal Patrol families indoors at night.

Valentine rapped on the glass between the added-on bars, a relaxed smile on his face. "Hey Ed, open up, eh?"

The sentry, whose nameplate read HINKS, P, shrugged and spread his hands helplessly. "It isn't Ed, Mr. Rowan, sir, it's Perry."

Valentine raised his eyebrows. "Ed sick? He always has the duty Friday nights."

"He does, but this is Thursday, sir."

"Look, Perry, let me in, will you? I want to see my wife."

"Mr. Rowan, sir, you know the rules. Overnight visits have to be okayed beforehand."

"Coursh I know that," Valentine said, "but I don't want to shtay overnight. Jusht an hour or two. You know. Ship's ready for shea, parts came in, and we leave in the morning. Have a heart—it's a three-month out."

"Mr. Rowan sir, you're listed as active duty. You should be at your ship tonight, not ashore."

"Have a heart," Valentine repeated. "Jush don't log me. You don't catch the shit for letting someone in, and I don't catch the shit for vishiting."

"Be a little difficult for me to explain when you leave."

Valentine summoned a belch. "You've got the midnight to four, right? I'll be out by three. Not logged in, not logged out."

"Sorry, sir, what if you get delayed?"

"Look, call Mrs. Rowan. She'll promise you I'll be out by three. You know her—if she made the promise to you, she'd see to it I got out in time. It's a three-month out, for chrissakes."

"What about the desk?"

"I'll bullshit my way past. I've got an understanding with Turnip. Thesh captain's bars are good for more than just a spot at the front of a ration line, eh?"

"Sir, maybe that's the way they do things up in the Great Lakes, but not here."

Valentine held his breath, forcing his face to color and his tone to harden. "Do they stand their watches indoors here?"

Hinks blanched. "Aww, Mr. Rowan sir, have a—"

"Heart?" Valentine finished.

The guard looked inside the Station Rooms. "Okay, Mr. Rowan, three a.m. You're not here by three-oh-five, I'm phoning up. Okay? Mr. Turner isn't at the desk anyway. Reading in the john again. You wanna report someone, you should start with him."

"Forget about it, Ed, errr—Perry. You're a good egg. I'll bring you back a bottle of rum or something, how'sh that?"

"Just be out by the time my shift ends, or I'm perishable."

"Hey," Valentine slurred, "I promised, right? Just a quick visit, and we ain't spending it talking."

The guard opened the door. "Mrs. Rowan's some lady, sir. I hope I get some rank and get a chance to take my pick."

"That's the shpirit, Perry," Valentine said, coming in out of the rain and wiping his hair back. "One way to move up is to do favors for higher ranks. Maybe I can get you into the Coastal Marines. Quick advancement. Dishipline isn't too hard, if you do your job."

The sentry shook his head. "Like my outfit just fine, sir.

Going ashore and attacking a blockhouse full of outlaws
ain't my idea of a career."

David Valentine waited for the sentry to unlock the inner
door, and moved across the stained carpet to the stairs. The
night manager's desk was empty, as Hinks predicted. Most
of the lights were off, and the remaining elevator that still
worked was always shut down at night when the hotel
closed up to conserve electricity. Valentine smelled soap and
heard splashing water coming from the basement: someone
was doing laundry in one of the slop tubs there.

He climbed to the top floor, remembering the intolerable
heat of their arrival that summer, the last in a series of moves
as he performed his duties as a Quisling Officer. His real
home lay in the hill country of Arkansas, Missouri, and
Eastern Oklahoma, on free soil, though since being recruited
as a Cat, he'd hardly spent six consecutive months there. For
the past year, he'd been dragging Duvalier all around the
Gulf Coast, worming through the Kurian Order, obtaining a
commission and a promotion under a dead man's name and
background provided for him by Southern Command—it
made him feel like a maggot in a corpse.

Though the Station Rooms predated climate control and
therefore had fair-size windows, the bars prevented residents from escaping to the fire escape to nap out the heat.
The bars and windows were the only part of the Station
Rooms inspected and kept in prime condition. Elsewhere the
paint was peeling, the walls were dimpled, and the plumbing fixtures were maintained in a condition that shifted back
and forth between inoperative and barely functioning.

Valentine reached the chipped wooden door to "Mrs.
Rowan's" apartment. He knocked softly, using a three-and-
two rap to identify himself, three soft and two loud. The sole
lightbulb in the hallway faded for a moment and then
brightened; New Orleans's patchwork power system was
having its usual nighttime irregularities.

The door opened, revealing an attractively angular face under short red hair sticking out in all directions.

"You're out late," Alessa Duvalier said, still half-asleep. She wore an oversize yellow T-shirt of tentlike proportions, which was coming apart at the shoulder seams. "What is it?"

He ducked inside and flicked off the light. To his Cat-eyes, the room remained lit and as detailed as ever. There was just the usual color-shift that came with low-light vision.

"I was recognized." He used old American Sign Language to convey this information as he said for the benefit of the microphones: "Baby, we're out tomorrow. Last chance for ninety nights." They'd found a bug when they'd first moved to the Station Rooms months ago, and asked for a different room—complaining, with justification, about bedbugs. Management moved them to the stifling top floor, and a Coastal Marine widow, Mrs. Kineen, took an empty room next to them the same day.

Duvalier woke up fast. "Somebody made you? How?" she signed.

He flopped down on the bed as soon as he got his coat off. He let out an occasional moan as he told her, spelling out some of the words with his fingers. They'd had training in sign language before setting out from the Ozark Free Territory, and though they practiced, Valentine's usually quick-acting brain faltered after the long day and the encounter with Alistar.

The woman who'd taught him to be a Cat sat in her chair, folded herself up so her chin rested on her left knee, and rocked the bed with her right leg so the headboard banged the wall they shared with Mrs. Kineen.

The room smelled of cloves and walnuts. Duvalier had picked up intestinal parasites in her travels, perhaps as long ago as their trek into the Great Plains Gulag when she first recruited him three years ago, and was dosing herself again in an effort to flush them.

"This week has been nothing but bad news," she signed,

interrupting the tale when he began to describe his disposal of the corpse. "Laundry-room intelligence says there's been a lot of new faces in town. Troops moving in. Some say a push into the Tex-Mex borders; others say it's Southern Command's turn again. I know the train station's been busy. Lots of cars taking on supplies coming in from the Gulf Coast and moving west. This didn't turn into such a dull assignment after all. I've been able to watch the station and pick up a little." She peeked out the window. "Hope you can get going soon. Southern Command needs to know details."

"I don't think the Wolves are going to show," he decided. "I'm going to have to go with it and improvise. Figure out a way to oust Captain Saunders and get control of the *Thunderbolt*—"

She let out a yelp, faintly orgiastic, and winked at her partner.

"You'll improvise yourself right onto the Grog gibbet," she signed. Valentine never tired of admiring her quick, dexterous fingers. They were the first thing he'd noticed on her when she bandaged his former captain on Little Timber Hill. "Who will help you?"

"The crew."

"Quislings?" She added the question mark with her sharp eyebrows.

"They wouldn't be in the Coastal Patrol if they didn't like being away from the influence of Kur."

"All the more reason for Kurians to pick the men for loyalty. Remember what you had to do to get your commission down here, and then the promotion to captain."

"Don't remind me," Valentine signed. Elaborate fake papers showing his service record in the Great Lakes took him only so far. For the past year, Valentine had put his manifest talents to the service of Kur, assembling a good record in a rear area before being offered a promotion in exchange for "more active duty." He had seen men shot, hanged, or given over to the Reapers without batting an eye. And more.

He'd learned the reason for the elaborate groundwork

only a few months ago, once he had received his commission on the *Thunderbolt*. Ahn-Kha appeared afterwards, bearing his detailed orders. In twenty-four hours, he memorized the instructions, based plans on the objective, and destroyed the letters, maps, and drawings. Since then, he concentrated on making friends in the crew and learning all he could about the Caribbean, and particularly Haiti.

"So are you ever going to tell me?" Duvalier asked. "Once you're at sea, it couldn't hurt for me to know." She stopped the headboard-thumping with her leg, waited a moment, then started again with renewed vigor.

"You know better. If you were really in on it, I'd have your opinion every step of the way. But I can't risk the Kurians finding out if it goes amiss."

Amiss. The word was a kind of shorthand between them. A euphemism for "capture, torture, and death."

She climbed on to the bed next to him, lay close so she could breathe in his ear. "We're good together, Valentine. Hope they haven't tasked you with a one-way trip. Some things shouldn't even be tried. Like turning that crew. We should blow and get out of here. The mission is down the drain, and Mountain Home needs to know· about this buildup."

"Taking the ship's not the half of it," he whispered back, feeling his skin tingle at her scent. "Or I should say that's not your half of it."

She rubbed her hand through his damp hair. "David, I know I had the easy part this time. Maybe old Ryu thought I needed a rest. I got to look around, safe behind my ID, then disappear after you ship out. But now my stomach's hurting, and you have that never-say-die look like in the Dunes. You didn't come up here for a good-bye."

Valentine smiled in the darkness. "No. I have to ask you a favor. It would make my job easier if you could get some of the other wives and families out."

She quit toying with his cowlick.

The room waited in silent darkness. His sensitive ears

could not even pick up the sound of her breathing. "How many families?" she finally whispered.

"As many as you can. Make contact with the pipeline, and have them help guide you all out."

She sat up, pulled her knees up to her chest, and thought before she started signing again. "Val, that involves getting about a hundred people out of New Orleans. On my own. I've no gear, no weapons but a skinning knife. Lots of kids, so I need transport for everyone and food to last us out of the KZ. It can't be done."

Valentine signed back: "Of course it can't be done. Since it can't be done, I don't think the Kur will be expecting it."

"No one expects me to step off a thirty-story building either. But if I do it and give everyone a big, effing surprise, that doesn't mean much when I hit."

"The only way I have a chance with the men is if they think there's hope for their families."

"Valentine, full abort. Set all this back up somewhere else. Mexico. There's got to be plenty of transport—"

"And blow a year's worth of work. It's the ideal ship. Who'd 'ave ever thought I'd get assigned to a gunboat? I figured we'd have to settle for a troop trawler full of men. If we get her, there's hardly a ship in the Carib that can say boo to us, plus she's seaworthy in case of bad weather. She's not some coast hugger."

"Good arguments in favor of a bad idea."

"Didn't you say you had made friends among the women? That a lot of them were discontented?"

"Who wouldn't be?" she signed back. "We get out of this building only twice a week when you're away, and even then it's to a fenced-in market. I'm sick of this place, too. If it weren't for the danger to some of the people I've met here, I'd torch it as soon as you're out of the harbor and vanish. They'd think I maybe . . . Whoa there . . ."

Valentine could almost feel her brain revving up. "You know, if you got everyone out and rigged some kind of explosion . . ." he suggested.

"Don't have the tools to collapse the building," she signed, "but this is an old structure. Set a fire somewhere hard to put out but not immediately dangerous, the authorities evacuate everyone, and I have someone from the pipeline who knows just where to be, and when. Maybe they would have a few people around to make sure we don't wander off, but they wouldn't expect an organized breakout. I can handle them."

"Be careful who you tell," Valentine advised. "I'd just let a couple of trustworthy people know. Wait until the absolute last minute to spread the word."

"Who taught who this game, Val? I was keeping myself alive in the KZ while you were still running with the Wolves, if you recall."

"Keep yourself alive. The Cause needs you. So can I count on you? Think about it while I sleep."

"I'll do it—if I can get the pipeline to open. You can tell your men that. Guarantees aren't my style. I like to bug out if things get hairy. I think you're headed for a noose, or maybe a long drag through the ocean back to the nearest port. Getting a mutiny started won't be easy. I've never heard of that being done before."

"All the more reason for it to work, they won't be expecting—"

She cut him off with a forceful thrust of her hand. "Oh God, don't start on *that* again!" she said, this time aloud. Then they smiled at each other. What would Mrs. Kineen make of that?

Valentine dreamt of the Ozarks. A fall breeze rustling a million leaves all around, cool streams running in the morning, the sounds of fish splashing as they jumped—

He felt Duvalier shaking him by the shoulder. The hour's rest was not nearly enough, but it would have to do. "Last chance, Valentine," she signed after handing him his coat. "Full abort, plenty of reason to justify it. I don't like the feel of this, not at all."

His doubts had also rested, and returned refreshed. *No! Ignore them!* "I'm not happy about it either. But if you knew more, you could see that I don't have a choice. This could turn the tide."

"You and your coulds." She hugged him, nuzzling her chin against his chest. Duvalier was seldom affectionate toward him, their bond exhibited more through ribbing than rubbing. Though he was attracted to her, she had a wall around her he couldn't break. Sometimes she lowered the drawbridge. Tonight was one of those moments.

"I grew up in Kansas," she whispered in his ear. "I don't know tides, except that they're caused by the moon. Oh, and a king tried to do something about them once but couldn't. In the end, the tide always wins. It's too strong."

He turned the risks over in his mind, then unholstered and tossed his heavy .44 service pistol on the bed along with the spare ammunition he carried. He'd hide the loss somehow. "No," Valentine signed, after buttoning his coat. "It's not too strong. The tide wins because it doesn't give up."

The look of relief on Perry's face made Valentine forget the gruesome events of the night. For a moment.

"See, Perry, I told you so," Valentine said, pointing to the clock. Its plain face indicated 2:40.

"You're a man of your word, sir. Thank you."

"No, Perry, thank you," Valentine said, smiling and waiting for the outer door to open. "I'll see you in three months."

"I hope so, Mr. Rowan. Word has it my unit's going to rotate out. They're saying West Texas, which is fine by me. I've had it with the humidity around here. I got mold allergies something terrible."

"Mobilizing for something big?" Valentine asked nonchalantly, looking out at the rain.

"Like I'd know. 'You'll find out when you get there,' is what we get told." The guard drained a cup of cold coffee.

"Enjoy the sun. I've got to get back to the ship before the captain gets up."

"Me savvy."

Valentine plodded into the rainy night, his hands thrust deep into his coat pockets. He had a good hour's walk ahead of him. The *Thunderbolt* sat moored well to the east in New Orleans's expansive but underused dikeside riverfront. High seas trade was not something the Kurians encouraged. They seemed so uncomfortable with oceans that Valentine wondered if Kur itself was not arid. Most of their sea traffic was made up of barges and tugs, hugging the coast as they moved from port to port in the shallow waters of the Gulf of Mexico.

Fear brought him out of his thoughts. A cold tingle ran down his spine. . . . There was a Reaper somewhere behind him in the fog.

Valentine stepped faster, shutting down everything in his mind except the animal reflexes required to keep moving, a fish swimming quietly and straight to avoid the prowling shark.

And he'd given his gun away to Duvalier. All he could fight with was the short service knife at his belt. Not enough steel to bite through a Reaper's neck—his sword was back at Ryu's hall with his other possessions.

The street was empty, almost unlighted. Doors and windows all around were buttoned up for the night.

He felt the cold spot growing as it came up behind. Its booted feet clipped along in the drizzle somewhere behind. He tore off his raincoat. Perhaps it would hesitate to attack a uniform.

A massive figure appeared out of the mist ahead of him. *Ahn-Kha! Thank you, God.*

Solid as the *Thunderbolt*'s icebreaking prow, ugly as commandment-breaking sin, and the closest thing he had in the world to a brother, the Grog waddled down the street.

He heard the footsteps following halt as the Reaper read the newcomer's lifesign.

Ahn-Kha carried a great boat hook across his shoulder and wore a brown Grog Labor Brigade sash across his chest.

Like a bull gorilla, he used his arms as well as his legs in his slow, deliberate stride. Rain matted his fawn-colored fur and dripped from flexible, batlike ears. Ahn-Kha bore a face like some stony nightmare leering off a cathedral at travelers below, but his steady eyes, black-flecked with irises the color of a healthy acorn, could only be called "gentle."

Valentine clasped hands with Ahn-Kha. "Careful," he breathed, gesturing behind with his chin.

He heard the Reaper approach, and Ahn-Kha straightened to his full eight-feet-plus, planting the boat hook solidly before him like a pikeman.

Valentine met the yellow-eyed gaze, touched the side of his hand to his eyebrow, and lowered his head, the usual salute to a representative of the Kurian Order.

The Reaper responded by throwing its hood back over its scraggly-haired scalp and striding off into the night.

Valentine didn't relax until the cold spot on his consciousness faded. The Reaper probably could have killed the both of them, but perhaps the Kurian animating it was more risk-averse than most, and didn't wish to damage his living tool for the extraction of vital aura.

Ahn-Kha put the boat hook over his shoulder again.

In the three years since Valentine had met Ahn-Kha, he had learned to rely on him for thought as well as thews. Years ago, Ahn-Kha's people, the Golden Ones, had been brought with the other species, labeled alike by much of mankind with the epithet *Grog,* across worlds to help the Kurians with the conquest of humanity. But even the Golden Ones had been betrayed by Kur when they were no longer useful. Thanks to the pair's chance meeting, the Golden Ones were again thriving along the west bank of the Missouri River around Omaha.

"My David," Ahn-Kha rumbled, his bass voice sounding as if it echoed from a deep cave. "I began to worry when you did not arrive by the time we darkened the ship. I feared something might have happened to you, and I made for the

Station Rooms. Is all well?" The Grog did a neat turn on one of his hamhock fists and walked beside Valentine.

"Yes and no, old horse. Someone recognized me tonight, in a bar. He's dead, but unless his men were born stupid and got worse, they'll be looking for me. We're going to have to set off with the dawn, before the Kurians can organize a manhunt."

"What about the men? Have they arrived?"

"No. We may have to go with the crew we have."

"And the captain and the executive officer? Perhaps you plan to have them both meet with accident?"

"I'm going to try to turn the crew."

Ahn-Kha snorted. "Maybe a few brave hearts will try. Not enough, my David, not enough."

"I'm going to promise them a new life with their families, if we can make it back to the Ozarks. Duvalier is going to get their wives and kids out."

"If she can manage that, the fates themselves fight on her side. But without the promised Wolves, I do not see how we win the ship."

"When we're at sea, I'll try Lieutenant Post first."

"The man's a drunk, my David, or he would be in command of the marines instead of you."

"Yes."

"How will you explain their absence to the captain? You told him the Coastal Marines were supplying a team of scouts, showed him fake orders."

"We'll use your Grogs. I'll tell him your laborers can perform the job. Besides, the men like having a few Grogs around to do the dirty work. Will they do what you say?"

"They're Gray Ones—brutes. They obey me; it is easier than thinking. On paper, they are a combat-ready team, but I've never seen them shoot. When they are done working the ship, they were supposed to be moved inland. But a request from the Coastal Marines would outweigh such a trifle. The Kurians have many to take their place."

"Better get them ready as soon as we reach the *Thunder-*

bolt. I'll have a word with the Chief, and we'll be under way by dawn. The radio is going to break down, as well. We can't be too careful."

The *Thunderbolt,* tied up to the dock, did not live up to her name. She looked like the swaybacked old icebreaker that she was, new coat of paint and polished fittings or no. Her 230-foot length had a high prow, a deep well deck, and her castle amidships. Just below the bridge in the bow was the five-inch gun, her main armament. On the other side of the castle, a twenty-millimeter Oerlikon looked like an avant-garde sculpture under its protective cover. Valentine's marines were responsible for it and the four 7.62-millimeter machine guns in action. They lay ready to be placed in the mounts on either side of the ship, more or less at the corners of the upper deck of the square main cabin.

As she was now configured, she carried four commissioned officers and seven warrant officers, supervising divisions of forty-five Coastal Patrol crewmen and thirty-four Coastal Marines. Usually she patrolled with a higher proportion of CP, fewer marines, and more space for all concerned, but she had been modified to carry troops this trip. The captain had made no secret of their mission. A nest of "pirates and terrorists" on the island of Jamaica had been bold enough to trouble the continental coast. The *Thunderbolt* and crew was to "capture, scuttle, or burn" the pirates' ships and destroy their base. The gunboat had little to fear in return: she could stand off and sink the pirates in their harbor or on the sea, for the sail-driven brigands had no gun to match the five-inch cannon, and nothing short of naval gunfire, mines, or torpedoes could penetrate the icebreaker's hull.

Whatever her hoped-for glories, the *Thunderbolt* looked dismal enough in the predawn gloom as she waited in her berth. A light burned at the entry port at the end of the gangway, and a glow from the bridge revealed the outline of the officer of the watch.

Valentine and Ahn-Kha walked up the gangplank.

A duty officer came to attention. "Mr. Rowan, sir," the CP said with just enough briskness to prove that he had not been sleeping. The man did not acknowledge Ahn-Kha.

Valentine looked forward and aft. Ahn-Kha's labor team lay in a snoring heap at the stern. Frowning, he turned on Ahn-Kha.

"If your gang is going to sleep like that on deck, you might as well get them some bedding," he said. "You have permission to get it out of ship's stores."

"Sir, thank you, sir," Ahn-Kha said, giving a quick bow.

The duty snorted. "Hope they wash it afterwards. We got enough bugs already."

For'ard, Valentine saw the red glow of a cigarette. The Chief sat on a stool, his legs up on the rail and an ankle comfortably cradled in a machine-gun mount, watching the rain fall. In a complement of more than eighty, Valentine's confidants consisted of the Grog next to him and the Chief by the rail. He moved forward. Obviously the Chief was waiting for him to return.

"Good evening, Captain Rowan," the Chief murmured as Valentine approached. The Cat paused and rested his elbows on the rail, looking out at the drizzle. Chief Engineer Landberg, like Valentine, had a strong dash of Native American blood in him, giving his title an ethnic twist which he bore with good humor. Though not a tall man, he had a wide wrestler's torso supported by pillarlike legs. Unlike his body, his face was soft and rounded, a textbook example of the kind of face described as "apple-cheeked." The Chief had been an informer for Southern Command since his youth, but until this run limited his service to simple intelligence-gathering.

The rain had washed the air clean of the usual fetid river odors. All Valentine could smell was the vaguely metallic tang of the ship, new paint, and the Chief's burning tobacco.

"What's the matter, Chief, can't sleep?" Valentine looked

back over his shoulder. The sentry probably couldn't hear them over the weather, but no sense taking chances.

"No, the sound of rain on this biscuit tin keeps me awake sometimes, so I just come up and watch it fall."

"How's that fuel pump coming? I'd really like to get under way. The men are getting anxious."

Landburg looked up, swallowed. Valentine gave him a nod.

"They are, huh?"

The engineer pinched his lower lip between thumb and forefinger when overhauling a problem. He would pull out his lower lip then release it so it hit his upper lip and teeth with a tiny *plip*. "Well, I reckon good news shouldn't wait"—*plip*. "I got sick of waiting on the part, so I found something I could modify with just a little machining. I'll try it out right now, if you want"—*plip*—"and we can let the captain know if it works. These delays have been driving the old man nuts."

"Good work, Chief."

Valentine exhaled tiredly and left the Chief to finish his tobacco and thoughts. He was committed now. By this time tomorrow, he would be at sea, with only Ahn-Kha and the Chief set against the captain and crew, backed up by the Kurian system that controlled them. Were it not for the rock-steady support of Ahn-Kha, as imperturbable as a mountain, and the Chief's wily aid, his quest would have foundered long ago.

He climbed one of the metal staircases running up the castle side to the bridge and asked the watch officer to call him at dawn, and retired to his shared cabin. Originally only he and the captain were given their own cabins, but after he saw the crowded conditions on board, he invited Lieutenant Post to share his cabin. Post got quietly drunk each night, duty or no, and Valentine felt for him after hearing some of the gibes hurled with casual viciousness by the other ward-room members.

He looked down at Post, a sleeping ruin of what must

once have been a physical archetype of a man. His six-three frame didn't fit on the bed, from his salt-and-pepper hair to rarely washed feet, breathing in the restless, shallow sleep of alcoholic oblivion. As usual, he hadn't bothered to undress before turning in, and would attend to his duties tomorrow in a wrinkled uniform, permanent stains marking the armpits and back. Post ignored even the captain's comments about his appearance, but in some fit of contrariness shaved each morning after Valentine had once privately mentioned over coffee that he would have a terrible time keeping his marines clean shaved if his lieutenant sprouted three days' worth of stubble.

Valentine sat on his untouched cot and began to remove his shoes. Above him, a railed shelf held his meager collection of books. Father Max's gilt-edged Bible—the old Northern Minnesota priest had raised him after his family's murder, and died of pneumonia while he was training Foxtrot Company. The Padre had willed the aged tome to him. It had arrived while he and Duvalier were seeking the Twisted Cross on the Great Plains. Next to the Bible were his battered old Livy histories, brought down when he first joined up with the Cause eight years ago. He owned copies of Clausewitz's *On War* and a Chinese Army translation of Sun Tzu, volumes he'd had to study at the military college in Pine Bluff, Arkansas, as he'd been studying for his commission. His American Civil War histories were next: Sam Watkins's *Company Aytch* and Frisch's *Lincoln: Leadership to Liberty.* Then came his little collection of fiction. *Watership Down,* its yellowed pages stitched together and ironically rebound in rabbit skin—given to him as a welcome-home gift by the craftsman, a Wolf named Gonzalez who'd survived their ill-fated courier mission to Lake Michigan in 2065. Next to it, and in much better shape, was a recent hardcover of the complete set of the *Sherlock Holmes* stories. Then there was his latest acquisition, a copy of *Gone with the Wind* bought at a New Orleans bookstore. He'd seen his fellow infiltrator Duvalier reading it last year while he was undergoing Coastal Marine training in Biloxi, Mississippi. Shocked to find her so deep into such a brick of a book, he'd made some comment about the four-color cover. "Ever read it?" she asked. When he admitted that he hadn't, she told him not to offer an opinion out of ignorance. Sensing a challenge when he heard one, he sat down with it his first free day, intending to mock it and her—but within twenty minutes was so captivated that he went out and treated himself to a bottle of cognac to enjoy with the epic.

The rest of the shelf held mostly unread Kurian propaganda and service bulletins.

There was a quiet knock at the door.

"Naturally," Valentine said to himself and two hundred pounds of alcoholic stupor a leg's length away. He rose and opened the door.

A twelve-year-old boy in a uniform two sizes too big for him stood in the corridor. The crew called him and his twin brother Peaone and Peatwo, being identical twins sent to sea in the care of their uncle, one of the petty officers. The captain, sick of not being able to tell them apart, flipped a coin and had all the hair shaved from Peaone's young head. Under a messy shock of sun-white hair, Peatwo looked up at Valentine with piercing blue eyes.

"Sir, the captain's passing the word for you, Mr. Rowan. He wants to see you in his cabin."

"Tell the captain I'm coming."

"Aye aye, sir," Peatwo said, turning and moving six feet up the passageway toward the captain's door. The captain was not the sort of man to just knock on the wall or come himself.

Valentine retied his boots, wishing he had had just five minutes out of them. He walked the short distance to the captain's cabin. He smoothed out his uniform unconsciously and knocked.

"Come," a sharp voice answered.

Captain Saunders fancied himself a species of tough old seahawk, but to Valentine, he seemed more like a rather aged rooster. The heavy wattles hanging under his chin were hardly hawklike, and the full head of gray hair that was the captain's pride and joy was brushed up into a bantam's pompadour. Perhaps something hawkish flickered in the stare of his hard hazel eyes, between which a beak of a nose matching that of the mightiest of eagles, if not a toucan, arched out in its Roman majesty.

"You passed the word for me, sir?" Valentine asked. The captain was in one of his work-all-night fits, and Valentine tried his best to look alert.

"Ahh, Captain Rowan. Are the marines ready to go to sea?"

"Of course, sir."

"Good. You'll be glad to know we'll be leaving in the morning—the fuel pump is repaired. I had to light a fire under the Chief, but if properly motivated, the man can work wonders."

Valentine blanked his expression. He looked around at the small day cabin. The captain sat behind a massive desk that must have been brought in sections, then reassembled. It dwarfed the other chairs in the room. A few pictures, all of Captain Saunders in various stages of his career or of ships he had officered, decorated the walls. "Glad to hear it, sir. The waiting has been hard."

"It's finally over. Keen to get to sea, I hope? Ready for the smell of burning sail?"

"At your order, sir. One thing though, sir. I still haven't had any luck finding a reliable team of rangers. Something must be going on inland. I've tried through channels and I've tried out of channels, but all I can find are kids or old men," he said, more than half-telling the truth for once. "The Grog labor team is a combat squad on paper. I'd like to just keep them, sir."

"What about quartering them? We're crowded enough— the men won't share with Grogs."

"We can rig some kind of shelter in the well deck, sir. Tents would do."

Captain Saunders thought for a moment. "Very well, they can eat the leftovers. Stretch the stores. I understand Grogs aren't too particular. Put that foreman of theirs in charge of squaring them away. I'd like to depart at dawn, and you'll be welcome on the bridge at six a.m. We'll take her out right after breakfast."

Close to two hours of sleep! Valentine sagged in relief. "Thank you, sir."

"One thing, though, Captain Rowan. I'd like you and the exec to do a final weapons inventory. You'll do your marines and the small arms locker, and he'll cover the heavy weapons. Wouldn't want to reach Jamaica and find your men's rifles had been left dockside by accident. 'For the want of a nail,' am I right?"

"Yes, sir." Valentine said, the prospect of sleep evaporating like a desert mirage. "Speaking of small arms, I had to give over my revolver for barter for some parts the Chief needed. I'll need a new pistol from the ship's arms."

"Rowan, you have to learn to throw your weight a little more. Greasing palms with your sidearms . . . Still, if it helped get us to sea, I'm grateful. Anyway, get that inventory done. That was item one, business. Item two is pleasure: I'd like your company at dinner tonight. A tradition of mine, to celebrate the beginning of what we all hope will be a successful cruise. Mr. Post is invited, too, of course. Number One uniforms, please. That will encourage your lieutenant to clean himself up."

"Yes, sir. Thank you, sir," Valentine said.

"That's all for now. See to your men, Rowan."

"Aye aye, sir." Valentine shut the cabin door softly behind him and began his day's work.

He hardly noticed the ship pulling away from the dock and moving downriver, so busy was he with final preparations. The executive officer, Lieutenant Worthington, started on the heavy weapons inventory then begged off as the engines were turned over to attend to duties on the bridge.

Valentine, who had little to do with the actual handling of the ship, was glad to be rid of him and offered to finish Worthington's part of the barely begun job. The exec, though two years older than he, had not seen much action and assumed Valentine to be a man of vast experience, to be a captain of marines in his mid-twenties. He had the annoying habit of wanting particulars of the various real—and faked—incidents in Valentine's "Captain Rowan" dossier. Valentine did not wish to discuss the faked events out of fear of slipping up on some detail, and the memories of the real incidents seen from the sidelines in the service of Kur troubled him too much to want to talk about them for the entertainment of a callow fellow officer.

Inventory and inspection done, he just had time to change into his best uniform before dinner.

Naturally, the dinner began with a toast over the cloth-covered folding table that had been set up for the meal. Worthington raised his glass of wine, an import brought all the way from Western Mexico. The captain and exec sat opposite each other, stiff in their crisp black uniforms, the captain's solid-gold buttons engraved with illuminati eye-and-anchor. Valentine and Post in their brass-buttoned navy blue filled the other places on the square table.

"The *Thunderbolt,* Queen of the Gulf," Worthington intoned as they raised their glasses. Saunders sipped with a connoisseur's thoughtful appreciation; Post drained his glass in a single motion; Worthington barely tasted his. Valentine took a welcome mouthful, grateful just to be off his feet.

The wine hit him hard, and he fought to keep from falling asleep in his soup. A winter salad followed. The captain and the exec did most of the talking, discussing the pilot's navigation of the treacherous, shifting sandbars at the mouth of the Mississippi and the balance of the stores on the ship. Valentine was content to eat his main course, a fresh filet of Texas beef smothered in onions and mushrooms, in exhausted silence. Post, who had been encouraged by Valentine to mend his best uniform and press it to celebrate the freedom of being at sea and away from the humid air of New Orleans, finished the bottle and started on another of less illustrious vintage.

"Captain Rowan?" Captain Saunders's voice broke in through the mists of Valentine's fatigue.

"Sir?" Valentine asked, looking to his left at the captain.

"Lieutenant Worthington asked you a question. About the Grogs?"

"My apologies, Lieutenant," Valentine said, bringing himself back to the dinner with an effort. "I'm not myself tonight. What was the question?"

"Seasickness, Captain Rowan?" Worthington asked, a smile that was half sneer creeping across his face. "We're still on the river."

"Probably."

"I just wanted your opinion on Uncle's Grogs," the exec continued. "We were really hoping for some rangers for the inshore scouting work." The men on the ship called Ahn-Kha "Uncle," and Ahn-Kha was too well mannered among their enemies to correct them. In the Ozark Free Territory, he would have flattened someone who could not be bothered to learn to pronounce his name correctly.

"Uncle says that they are combat trained. I'll vouch for his word."

"It's your responsibility, of course," Captain Saunders said.

By now Valentine knew that the phrase was Saunders-speak meaning that if the Grogs failed in some way, the blame would be passed to Valentine.

"I'm sure we can keep them busy on the ship," the exec said. "I've never had any experience with Grogs in combat. I've heard they leave something to be desired."

"Properly armed and with a decent leader, I'll put them up against anyone," Valentine said. "I've seen them in action, once they sink their teeth into a fight, the only way to stop them is to kill them." He did not add to the speech that his experience mostly came from fighting against the Gray Ones, rather than with them.

"But as scouts, Rowan, as scouts?" the exec asked.

"Like dogs who can shoot guns. Fine marksmen. Good eyes and ears. Not a whole lot smarter than a dog, though. Decision making isn't their forte; they'll come back and hoot at you to let you know they've found something. Uncle can make more sense out of their tongue than I can."

"Very well, Captain Rowan," Saunders said. "That settles my mind, knowing you are confident in the matter. I'm sure they'll be an asset."

The rest of the evening passed in the captain telling stories to his captive audience. Valentine leaned back in his chair, keeping his eyes open while his brain turned itself off. He shifted his gaze to Post, who had restricted his conversation to a few polite phrases during dinner. His lieutenant remained silent, failing to murmur appreciatively at Saunders's yarns. Post finished the second bottle of wine before turning to the brandy.

Chapter Three

The Caribbean: An empty, brilliant blue sky is mirrored by an equally blue sea. The gunboat has left the rainy gloom of New Orleans behind her, pushing her hardened prow southeast into the Gulf under the power of her eleven-foot propeller at a steady ten knots. Diesel–electric engines provide the motive force for the propeller, giving her a throbbing, piston-driven heartbeat and sending sky-staining wisps of black carbon into the air from the central smokestack. Below the exhaust she leaves behind a trail of churned water over a mile long, flanked by the low waves of her wake.

The gray ship with her bleached white decks flies no flag, letting her armored bulk identify her, leaving the mouth of the Mississippi coasters and fishing ships scattered, parting like an antelope herd with a lion trotting through. The smaller boats fear an inspection shakedown or impressment of valuable crew. But once in the Gulf proper, only a two-mast schooner approached, and even that turned tail and put the wind to her quarter before binoculars and telescopes allowed positive identification.

The Kurian Masters of the Earth are not a sea-minded race. They avoid blue water and leave its security and commerce to their Quislings. There are few armed vessels anymore. The old navies of the world have been broken up for scrap and spare parts. The great tankers, merchant ships, and passenger vessels now lie in their last moorings, giant rolling stones come to barnacle-encrusted rest as the world fell apart. A few have been put to other uses: agricultural workers in what is left of Florida after the Great Wave that washed across it in 2022 go home from oyster beds, crab farms, and orange groves each night to cruise ships, living in cramped squalor under the last vestiges of the vessels' glitzy luxury of former days.

As the sea is out of reach of the Kurians and their Reapers, a loose Confederation of the Waves exists, nomadic oceangoing caravans of anything from a few sailing ships to hundreds, visiting land only in the most unoccupied areas for supplies. But the sea is a cruel provider. She takes her toll in lives, as well, probably more than the same number of people would suffer under the Kur. Some of these bands have turned pirate, raiding rather than trading for necessities the sea and isolated coastline cannot provide. When their depredations become too troublesome, an armed ship is sent to deal with the menace. While they have little use for it, the Kurians won't let a trifling thing like the sea stand between them and vengeance.

It was the third day out, and life on the plodding *Thunderbolt* had already turned into routine. The first light of dawn saw the Grogs hosing down and cleaning the decks. They devoured their morning fare with work-sharpened appetite. The cook, his mate, and the officers' steward then cleaned up the kitchen and prepared the meals for everyone else. The men tolerated the presence of the Grogs on the ship, especially since they took on so many of the petty labors, but drew the line at eating with them, or indeed sharing the same space. Grogs in tight quarters smell (even to noses not sharpened by the Lifeweavers) like a kennelful of mating ferrets, so they lived on deck in shelters rigged to the bulkheads of the forward well deck.

With their routine duties and weapons drill done, Ahn-Kha gave them leisure to fish. The rod-and-reel obsession began when a pair of flying fish broke the surface, leaving furrows in the calm ocean in their dash away from the ship.

The Grogs hooted until Ahn-Kha reported that his team wanted to know if the "sea chickens" were good to eat and how they could catch them. Both Valentine and Ahn-Kha were strangers to deep-sea fishing, so he asked around the crew until one old bluewater man, less fastidious than the rest as to who he associated with, descended to the "Grog deck" to teach them how to use the ship's store of fishing poles and reels. Afterwards, the Grogs spent every spare moment fashioning lures, rods, and reels. Valentine prevailed on the captain to slow the ship to a crawl for an hour a day, when the garbage would be dumped overboard and the Grogs, wild with excitement foreign to human fishermen, pulled in all they could catch. It was just as well, for Grog appetites could tax the ship's stores on the three-month patrol.

Valentine's particular responsibility was the Coastal Marines. The Coastal Patrols looked on the marines as only one rung above the Grogs on the evolutionary ladder, and a short rung at that: gun-toting, useless ballast for most of the trip. Valentine put the rivalry to good use, organizing physical contests between them. Races around the deck, arm-wrestling matches, and boxing contests occurred each night, giving the two sides a chance to scream their lungs out supporting their contestant and abusing the opponent. Not all the diversions were physical; singing and musical entertainment were often a spontaneous part of the after-dinner leisure hours. As Valentine stood next to the Oerlikon on the aft gun deck, listening to the music produced by an improvising group of players and singers, he almost forgot these men were technically his sworn enemies. Under different circumstances, he might have been ordered to sneak aboard the ship and plant a bomb that would blow musician, wrestler, and fishing instructor to bloody shreds. All the while, a long line of stormclouds on his mental horizon, came the worries about what he had to do and how to go about doing it.

Valentine felt for the sailors. The captain believed himself an expert disciplinarian, when in fact his rules verged on pointless sadism. He had an elaborate system of uncomfortable punishments for the last man out of his bunk on a watch, the last man on deck for inspection, the last man in line at mess call. Since physics required someone to be last, Valentine thought the practice cruel: spending a watch-on-watch at the top of the old communications tower without food or water for being shoved out of the way coming up a hatchway improved no one. Of course, the captain's distemper was exacerbated by the ship's radio breaking down after leaving port. Valentine pointed out that their orders demanded radio silence until the pirates were dealt with, so the loss of communications made no difference, but Saunders just grumbled out his familiar "want of a nail" liturgy again.

The executive officer was even worse. Wishing to emulate his captain, thereby showing himself fit for command, Worthington out-Heroded Herod in his punishments.

Valentine and Post kept their marines busy, and as far from the eyes of Saunders and Worthington as the ship would allow.

Valentine felt nervous, bottled up. If he'd been on land, he would have quartered logs and chopped kindling, but there was no firewood to cut on a gunboat at sea. After they grabbed a quick dinner with the marines, they returned to the cabin and undressed. Valentine picked up one of his lieutenant's bottles and sniffed the mouth. It smelled like rubbing alcohol stored in an old boot. "Will, why do you do that to yourself?"

The two officers kept to first names when out of uniform.

"I'm still trying to figure out why you don't."

Valentine marked the tiny blue veins crisscrossing Post's nose and forehead. "Maybe I want to live a few more years. The way you're going, your liver will abandon ship or you'll get drummed out. Either way, you'll be finished."

"Hear hear," Post agreed, refilling his glass, his thick features under the salt-and-pepper hair taking on a red flush. "I figure you for the type to step into the shower, close the curtain, and blow your brains out with your service revolver. The system's rotten, and you know it same as I."

Post either trusted Valentine or did not care about being turned in. Either way, from their first days sharing a cabin, they began to tentatively express to each other unorthodox opinions about their Kurian masters. But neither had yet expressed it so directly.

"Did you lose someone, Will?"

"I was married once, yeah. Close to six years ago now. That's why I tried so hard for officer—it helped us get better housing. But it all went wrong." He took another gulp. "Not worth talking about. You're lucky, your wife gives you someone to live for. Not sure I even want to live for me anymore."

Valentine nerved himself for the plunge. "She's not my wife, Will. The license is forged."

Post looked up at him. "Yeah? What, you pretending for some reason? Might as well get married, that way you don't need false documents to get your allotments. If it goes wrong, just toss her, plenty other officers have done it, hasn't hurt their careers one bit."

Valentine opened the door briefly to check the corridor. He shut the door to their cabin again and sat down on the bed opposite Post. "Will, everything about me is faked. Her, my commission and service record from up north, even the name 'Rowan's not my own. My name is David Valentine."

Post turned over in his bunk, lying on his side. He put the bottle on the floor between them and took another sip from his glass. "Okay, you've got a false name. I don't get it. What is it then, an escape attempt?" Post asked, also lowering his voice. "Damn elaborate one. You'd better pick the right island—go to the wrong one, and the residents will eat you alive. I mean that literally."

"I need the *Thunderbolt,* and I'm going to take it," Valentine said. He let the words sink in for a moment. Post's face rippled from blank astonishment to incredulity, then back again to astonishment as the idea took hold.

"The original plan was to try with a small group of men I would bring on board," he continued. "That didn't work out, so I'm going to make do with what's already on the ship. The Chief is on our side, and so is Ahn-Kha, the Grog foreman."

"Our side? Whose side is that?" Post finally asked, his liquor-lubricated train of thought finally leaving the platform.

"Southern Command. I work for one of the Freeholds, the one in the Ozarks and Ouachitas. And I'd like you to join us, if you'll risk it."

Post reached for the bottle and took a drink, ignoring his glass. "The sun's gone to your head, Dave. What are you going to try to do, turn the crew? They didn't get this job by being unreliable. Plus they have families back home to think about."

"The families will be taken care of," Valentine countered. "It's in the works right now. In a few more days, they'll be on their way out of the KZ. One of our Cats is on the inside."

"Cats?"

Valentine's hypersensitive ears searched the adjoining rooms and corridor. Someone moved through the passageway, and he paused before continuing in his low monotone. "It's a nickname, I guess. It's a long story, but the Kur and the Grogs aren't the only ones here from Elsewhere. Earth is part of a larger war, and other worlds are involved. The Kurians are what you might call a faction of a people called the Lifeweavers.

"Their society split thousands and thousands of years ago when the Lifeweavers on a planet called Kur discovered how to become immortal through . . . I call it vampirism. They've been at war ever since. Way back then, the Kurians came here, and the Lifeweavers picked some people to hunt the things brought over from Kur. They explained to the primitive men that they were placing the spirit of Wolves or Bears or Lions or what have you into the warriors they chose. I still don't know what they do exactly or how. All I can compare it to is turning on something inside you, like a light going on once you close the circuit. There was a hiatus lasting about six thousand years when the Lifeweavers won and Kur's transportation network got closed down. We turned into a civilization in the gap. Then they came back, and the Lifeweavers appeared again to help us."

Valentine looked at Post. He wondered if his lieutenant thought him a lunatic, or simply an imaginative liar.

"I've heard rumors," Post finally whispered. "Weird stuff about men who can become invisible, or breathe water, or wrestle a Reaper to the ground. Is that what you can do?"

"None of those," Valentine said, smiling. "I can see and hear better, and they did something to quicken my reflexes. But that doesn't help me with this, at least now. The best hearing in the world isn't going to help me take this ship. But you could."

Valentine felt relieved for some reason. Something had felt wrong in keeping up the pretense in front of Post. Having a man he instinctively liked believing him a tool of the Kurians grated.

"I'm not the only discontented one, just the only one that shows it. But you tell most of the men what you just told me, they'll claim they're in with you and two minutes later go straight to the captain. Claim the Terrorist Bounty. It's big enough to live on for years, if you catch a real one."

"Post, in the KZ the 'rest of your life' is whatever the Kurian in charge wants it to be. In the Ozarks, you're not livestock, you're an individual. Part of a community. It's not Old World, at least not in material terms. But the old beliefs are there. Life has value."

"Some community," Post said thickly, his rotgut kicking in. "I've heard you folks are so hungry that when winter comes, you live off the dead."

This was not the first time Valentine had heard that grisly rumor. He was happy to gainsay it rather than cite invented facts to support it. "Not true. I will say we don't eat as well as a lot of folks in the KZ, but then we're not being fattened for the slaughter, either. I'm offering you a way out of all this, Will. A real escape—not like the bottle you're using now. More, a chance to fight back. You'll be with men and women working to smash the system."

Post picked up the nearly empty bottle and looked at the mouth in a sidelong way, as if it were playing some kind of tune only he could hear. He shut his eyes and opened them again, staring straight at Valentine.

He stood up, a little unsteadily, and extended his hand. "It ain't going to work, Dave. But maybe you won't die alone."

They shook on it.

A long moment passed, and Post sat back down in his bunk. He wiped his face, turning the gesture into a long, thoughtful pull at his chin.

Valentine slipped back into his pants and shoes and left the cabin for a moment, passed the word for the officer's steward to bring some sandwiches to his cabin. He stepped out onto the afterdeck, felt the engines through the rail. The Grogs were hurrying to finish up their duties, looking forward to an evening's rest, and off-duty marines and sailors lounged around the deck, playing games of card and dice, or sitting absorbed in wood carving, reading, or just talking. He smelled the men's dinners below, the sea air, and the oily smell of the diesels.

When he returned to the cabin, Post had his footlocker open and was unwrapping a burnished steel pistol from a terry-cloth rag. A matching gun lay on his bed.

"I wasn't planning on moving this minute," Valentine said, shutting the door behind him.

"Hope not. I'm too drunk to shoot straight. Thought you might want something to replace that .44 wheelgun you lost. Some mementos of my bright and shining youth."

He handed an automatic to Valentine. Its straightforward lines and large, businesslike grip made it instantly identifiable. "A Colt 1911 model?"

"One of the variants. Got a .45 shell that should stop just

about anyone, good and permanent. Bought this pair fresh out of Officers' Training."

Valentine tested the slide. The weapon was in fine condition.

"Take one, Dave. It shoots faster than that revolver ever could."

"Happy to," Valentine said. Post also presented him with magazines of freshly loaded ammunition for the weapon. "Are the bullets reliable?"

"Better than most," Post said. "Not service issue—they come from a gunsmith in the old town. He's a good man, as long as you treat him right. I heard that a major went out one time, threw his weight around to get a free gun, and damned if his pistol didn't misfire just when he needed it."

The sandwiches arrived, accompanied by a gumbo soup made of the scraps of the fresh meats brought out of New Orleans. They pulled out a mini-desk between their bunks and ate in thoughtful silence, mopping up the remnants of the soup with the ship's fresh bread. For the first time since Valentine started eating with Post, his lieutenant did not wash down his meal with half the contents of one of the iodine-colored bottles.

"Can you tell me what you need the ship for?" Post asked.

Valentine had committed himself, and if he could trust Post with his life, he could trust him with the few details that he knew. Ahn-Kha would take over if he were killed, but if by chance both of them—

"I'm to find a stash of old weapons. I don't know what kind. Then I'm supposed to get them back, either going through Galveston or farther south by Mexico. That's the reason for the armed ship: it's supposed to help at the island, and then make sure nothing can challenge us on the way back. There's a man in Southern Texas who'll take it from there."

"Why don't they tell you what it is?"

"I think the danger is that if the Kurians found out about it, they'd either take it themselves or destroy it."

Valentine heard someone in the passageway outside, and held up his hand for silence.

"Where is it?" Post asked after Valentine had dropped his hand.

"Haiti."

"Haiti?" Post choked. "Jesus, I figured it was the old naval base at Guantanamo. Sir, Haiti's hell's own greenhouse. It's pretty fuckin' big, and I've never heard of anyone getting inland out of range of the ship's guns and coming back to tell about it."

"I know roughly where on the island I'm supposed to go. There's some kind of traitor in the Kurian organization there who'll teach us about it. I know it will be bulky—that's why we need a ship and so many men for the job."

"There's an awful lot of *ifs* in your plan, if you don't mind me saying, sir."

"I know."

"I'm not asking you to follow me inland. I was counting on you to run things on the ship until I return."

"Sir, you want a weapon, think about this ship. She's well armored, carries a good-size gun, and you could put enough men on her to shut down water traffic from Louisiana to Florida."

"Any other time you'd be right, Will. But they tell me that whatever is waiting on Haiti is something that could really change the equation between us and the Kurians. Don't you think the risk is worth a chance to make a difference?"

"Some difference. Seems to me, the difference will be the one between being alive and being dead. Not that I really care," he added. To his credit, Valentine thought, he did not sound convinced of the last.

From that dinner on, Valentine did not see Post take another drink. His lieutenant suffered unvoiced agonies in silence, driving himself to keep up an appearance of stability in front of others, only to flee to the head or the cabin when the shaking in his hands got to be too much for him. Valentine never asked him to quit drinking; in fact, with the mental strain he was more than a little tempted to try the contents of the squared-off bottles himself after retiring at night. Valentine found a growing new respect for Post that replaced his previous feelings of pity. He admired his lieutenant for keeping the pretense of normality despite the torrents of sweat pouring out of him and God-knew-what other torments to his body.

The next evening Valentine arranged for a meeting in the arms locker with the Chief, Post, Ahn-Kha, and himself, purportedly to determine which weapons Ahn-Kha's Grogs would carry in their duties. The captain had suggested a brace of dusty shotguns, captured in some action long ago and forgotten. After viewing the weapons in question, Valentine asked that the Chief take a look at them and see if the ship's machine shop could bring them back to usability. Thus the conspirators were able to get a half-hour or so of privacy within the ship for a meeting of their group. Squeezing Ahn-Kha's bulk into the room proved to be only the first difficulty in a long line of challenges before them.

"We should make landfall off Jamaica tomorrow afternoon or early evening," Valentine began. "The captain plans to head straight into the harbor they are thought to use the next morning. God knows what might happen in the fight, so I think we have to move before then."

"How about we go into action and rig a shell to blow in the bridge during the fight?" the Chief suggested. "The crew will think the pirates just got a lucky shot, and Mr. Rowan assumes command. Looks legit."

"Who knows what damage the explosion would do?" Post asked, sweat running from his hairline under the hot work-lamp. The marine was balling his hands into fists and rubbing them against his thighs under the weapon-strewn table.

"Maybe we go aground. So much for the *Thunderbolt*. I doubt the pirates would fix her up and take her to Haiti to oblige us."

"Yes, and we might not get both. The exec will probably be at the main armament. I think it's better if we do it before. Offer the men an alternative to the fight," Valentine said. "Freedom. That's a powerful persuader."

"Cut off the head, and the body will be yours," Ahn-Kha said, quoting a Grog proverb from his place, squeezed between the rifle racks filling up one whole end of the room. "We have much of the head of the ship here. We remove the captain and Worthington. Then we let the petty officers know who is in charge. They will do as they are told."

"Ahn-Kha is right as far as the captain and exec go," Valentine agreed. "But I want to give everyone else a real choice. We assemble the crew and give each man the option: join us, or be put off the ship in a boat with food, water, even weapons. They can take their chances on Jamaica or try to sail for the coast. All they have to do is go north—they'll hit Kurian territory soon enough."

"Will you tell them why you need the ship?" the Chief asked.

"Can't risk it until the captain and the exec disappear with the crew that want to follow them. I have no idea how long we would be on Haiti. The last thing we need is him trying to hunt us down."

Post shook his head. "You'll lose half of them. Maybe more. We might not be left with enough to keep this bucket moving."

"I think a lot of them signed on for sea service to get away from the Reapers. You can tell by their talk, their interests. They're free spirits, not conscripts."

They hashed out the rest of the plan while working on the shotguns. They decided they would let a few subordinates they felt could be trusted know about the plan at the last minute. Post felt that he knew two marines well enough to say they would follow him, and the Chief insisted that his engine-room crew would sign on to a man. Ahn-Kha said the Grogs would do as he ordered; few of the humans on board could even make themselves understood to the creatures beyond simple instructions.

They would take the ship in the dark after making landfall at Jamaica. The captain planned, as soon as he got his bearings, to move east along Jamaica's north coast and arrive at the pirate bay with the dawn. Around midnight, Ahn-Kha would go below and guard the arms locker with his Grogs, also controlling the nearby hatches to the engine room and generator room. The Chief would kill the power when this was accomplished. Post and the marines he hoped to recruit would go to the small store of "ready arms" on deck, and mount machine guns fore and aft covering the main decks from the gun platforms. It would be Valentine's job to take the bridge, doing whatever was necessary to keep Captain Saunders and Worthington from issuing any orders. With that accomplished, Valentine would assemble all hands on the deck and offer them their choice.

There was some dispute over what to do with the captain and the executive officer.

"You'll probably have to kill them, sir," Post predicted.

"I'd rather not. I'll get a pair of handcuffs on them and toss them in the motor launch. Or the lifeboat, depending on how many of the crew decide to go with them."

"It will come to killing," Ahn-Kha said. "They will turn the crew against you, if they can."

"Handcuffs and gags, then. I don't want their blood on our hands unless it is a matter of us or them."

Valentine spent the next day lost in his duties, so much so that he did not go up on deck as they caught their first sight of the blue Jamaican coast. In preparation for the next morning's activities, which he hoped would never be carried out, he and his NCOs attached reflective tape to the backs of their green-and-black camouflage battle-dress. Someone joked that Irish, a Coastal Marine corporal in their complement, should form his into the shape of a bull's-eye, since he'd managed to get himself shot four times in the course of his duties, and even Post laughed. At the midday meal, Ahn-Kha and the marines held an informal meeting in the crew's mess, where they went over the destruction the *Thunderbolt* was to visit on the pirates. Saunders hoped to reach the harbor before midnight.

His imagination continued to get the better of him as the afternoon wore on. It seemed the entire ship crackled with electricity, so tense were the men and their officers in anticipation of the fight tomorrow.

"I hope the Chief is doing better than I am," Post reported, joining Valentine at sunset at the ship's starboard rail. They watched the thickly forested slopes of Jamaica slide by like a rolling backdrop in a stage play. Post still trembled, and his shirt was soaked with sweat, but his face seemed more animated and his eyes brighter. "I tried sounding out a few of the men, but I chickened out at the last moment. I just couldn't bring myself to say what we're planning, the moment didn't seem right. I kept thinking about a Hood at my throat, got so as I could almost feel teeth. About all I was able to do was warn them to be ready for anything. Sorry, Dave."

Valentine shrugged. "Too late to worry. I talked to Ahn-Kha and the Chief—we're going to switch the time to twenty-two hundred. The men are supposed to be assembled an hour later, ready to climb into the boats for the landing. That way Ahn-Kha leading his Grogs to the arms locker won't seem so unusual—they're supposed to go ashore first anyway."

They forced themselves to act normally at dinner with the men. Valentine sat with one group he called his "deadeyes," the four best marksmen in the culled company. Post ate with the noncommissioned officers at the other long table in the galley. Though he had no appetite, Valentine forced himself to eat mouthful after mouthful of the traditional preaction steak and eggs. The beef was stringy and tough, but even the *Thunderbolt*'s indifferent cook's mate could not ruin the eggs. Valentine forced himself to have seconds on the latter, washing it down with glassfuls of faintly orange-tasting sweetened water that he guessed to be some concoction trying to pass as orange juice. He joked with the men, listening to service stories and telling a few of his own, like the time a supply officer fed an entire harem of young women in the loft of a marine warehouse, which grew into a thriving bordello over the years. When caught by a visiting inspector, he argued that pimping a whorehouse fell under his duties, since one of his official responsibilities was listed on his duty sheet as "recreation procurement officer."

With dinner finished, the marines broke off to leave the galley to the sailors, and Valentine retired to his shared cabin.

He looked around the close, bare room. A single locker held all his clothes, and a footlocker, the rest of his belongings. He spent an hour in a long shower and shave, and changed into his heavy cotton battle-dress. The combat fatigues, acquired from a tailor in Mobile when he first entered the Coastal Marines, were a tiger-stripe mix of black and dark green, spotted here and there with blotches of dark gray. Heavy pockets hung like saddlebags from the side of each thigh on the pants, but the short officers' tunic held only insignia and an expanding map pocket and a pencil-holder on one sleeve. He unlocked his chest and began to take out his equipment. He laced up his boots, traditional black service models, the leather softened and oiled by a year's wear and care. His final wardrobe item was a nylon equipment vest with heavy bullet-stopping pads slipped into the liner and compass, flares, first-aid kit, matches, and whistle distributed amongst the pockets. Post's .45 pistol went to his hip holster. He sank a machete into the sheath strapped across his back hanging over two canteens. Finally, he extracted the one item he brought out of the Ozarks, his old Soviet Russian PPD model submachine gun with the drum clip. It was a heavy-barreled, formidable-looking gun, restored by an old friend and given to him the summer he became a Cat three years ago.

Slinging the gun and drawing comfort from its familiar weight, he made a slow circuit of the *Thunderbolt*'s central superstructure. Ahn-Kha had the Grogs gathered on the well deck, talking to them. The Golden One looked up at Valentine and cocked his ears up and forward, giving his broad head the momentary aspect of a bull: his friend's equivalent of a thumbs-up. The gesture went to Valentine's nerves like a fast-acting sedative. He looked out at the nearly empty aft decks and turned the last corner on the rectangular walkway. Post stood at the foot of one of the stairways going up to the bridge deck, idling next to the arms locker holding the machine gun for the forward mount.

Valentine squeezed past and gave him a nod. "Ready?" Valentine asked.

"Getting there. Sure makes you feel alive, doesn't it. Like the whole world's been turned up. Sounds, smells, everything. I never noticed all the waves before. A million of them—"

"Just take it easy, Will. Wait for me to go up the stairs— then get the gun. You checked it, right?"

"Yes, it's fine."

"Just a few minutes longer. Ahn-Kha's still talking to his team. They haven't gone below yet."

Post gripped the rail, the tendons in his forearms rising up under his tan skin. "You know why my wife lit out, Rowan—er, Dave?"

"I might be able to guess. The system?"

"The system," Post said. "She and I had a difference of opinion about it. She left. I eventually came round to her side, but only after her stuff had two years' worth of dust on it."

Post looked out at the ocean and the sinking moon. Valentine thought he saw the man's lower lip tremble.

Valentine leaned over, knocked his shoulder against Post's. "One way or another, you'll be clear of it soon."

"First, got to get rid of this shit," Post said, tearing off his tunic. Buttons flew, clattering to the deck and falling with barely audible *plop*s into the ocean. Post stood in his stained undershirt for a moment, as if coming to a decision. He wadded up his uniform coat and fed it to the all-consuming sea.

"If I'm going to buy it, I don't want to go in their colors."

"I'll get you a different one when we get back to free soil, if you'd like," Valentine said. "Just try to live to claim it. I hope the exec doesn't come down those stairs and see you like that. He might have a few questions about your tunic."

"I'll pick him up and send him to look for it. He's a bottom-feeder if there ever was one.

"Could you do me a favor, Dave? If I don't make it, maybe you can look up Gail in the Free Territory. She would have headed that way—it's an easier trip than going across Texas. She's probably using her maiden name, Gail Stark. Tell her . . . just tell her about this."

"Can do, Will."

"Thanks, sir."

"See you at lights out."

"Good luck, Dave," Post said, offering his hand.

Valentine shook it and went forward to look down at the well deck. It was empty. Ahn-Kha and his Grogs were already on their way to the arms locker and engine room. A nervous thrill sparked up his spine, bristling the hair at the back of his neck.

He chambered the first round in his gun and lightly ascended the stairs to the open deck just behind the wheelhouse. As his head broke the level of the upper deck, he listened with "hard ears" to voices from the bridge.

"And when is this supposed to happen?" the captain said from somewhere on the bridge.

"Early in the morning, sir. The ship's power will be cut off, and that's when they'll take the ship," Valentine heard a high-pitched voice say.

"It makes no sense," Worthington's voice exclaimed.

"They will be ashore by then, Grogs and marines, and Rowan will be with them."

"Can't argue it, there's something afoot, that's for certain," Saunders said. "Damn, there always was something about Rowan I didn't like. Haven't I said so time and again, Lieutenant?"

Worthington changed the subject. "I've already alerted the master-at-arms," he said. "I didn't know which marines to trust. Dortmund is bringing an armed guard up now, and he's—"

Valentine's worries cleared, as they always did when planning gave way to doing. All his questions were gone: it had become a matter of killing everyone on the bridge, and somehow holding the wheelhouse and upper deck through the coming confusion. The moon had disappeared below the horizon, leaving the ship lit only by the stars and its few running lights.

"Halt!" Valentine heard a voice boom from the bottom of the staircase. "Unsling your weapon, sir, and don't touch anything but the sling."

He turned to see Dortmund, three sailors lined up behind him, pistols pointed up at him. While he had been concentrating on the bridge, Dortmund had reached the bottom of the stairs without Valentine noticing. Valentine thanked God that Dortmund hadn't shot first and questioned later. He obeyed the instructions, going so far as to crouch to put the gun on the stair below his feet, and readied himself for a leap—

—when the loud, deadly rattle of a machine gun roared from behind the sailors, filling the night with noise. Dortmund's men fell forward, jerking spasmodically as if swept off their feet by an electrified broom. The hard plinking sound of bullets ricocheting off metal stairs and walls punctuated the sound of the slugs tearing through flesh, a noise that reminded some part of Valentine's mind of eggs thrown against a wall. The four-petal blossom of the machine-gun's muzzle flare lit Post's snarling features as he fired the support weapon from his hip, using a thick leather strap to help him wield it.

One sailor went overboard with a cry; the others fell at the bottom of the stairs.

Valentine retrieved his own gun before they hit the deck. Blood had been shed, and his hopes of a simple seizure of the ship were cut down as brutally as Dortmund and his henchmen. He peeked over the edge of the deck above, only to be met by a burst of bullets that zipped out to sea past his ear. Worthington was no fool; he had armed himself before going to the captain. Valentine had to get down to Ahn-Kha and his Grogs, so he would at least have a nucleus of armed men to command.

The lights died, and Valentine felt a change in the ship's motion. The Chief had level-headedly proceeded with the plan upon hearing the firing above.

Valentine backed down the stairs and joined Post, where his lieutenant covered the starboard side walkway from the base of the stairs.

"What the hell happened?" Post said. "Where did Dortmund come from?"

"One of the ship's boys overheard something and went to the exec. We've got to get to the Grogs."

The ship's public-address system squealed into static-filled life. "All hands, all hands, this is the captain speaking. . . ."

Valentine grabbed Post by the arm and pulled him into the stairwell leading into the bowels of the ship, almost jerking him out of his shoes with the force of his movement. Two shots rang out from the top of the stairway, cutting the air where they stood seconds ago, as Saunders's voice continued.

". . . Captain Rowan of the Marines, Lieutenant Post, the Grogs, and an unknown number of others are attempting to mutiny. They are to be shot on sight. All hands to the aft deck, all hands to the aft deck."

"Make a hole, damn it! Make a hole!" Valentine barked,

exiting the stairway with Post in tow, waving his submachine gun to accentuate the threat as they pushed back
sailors popping like magical rabbits into the narrow passageway. Somewhere around the T-junction corner ahead he
heard Ahn-Kha's bellow, barking out orders in the Grog patois. The captain's voice continued to issue orders over the
PA, including one to the dead Dortmund to report to the Oerlikon. An emergency light bathed the corridor in harsh shadows. Valentine turned a corner and caught sight of a knot of
Grogs standing behind a small, bright spotlight pointed
down the corridor. He shielded his eyes.

"Ahn-Kha, it's me and Post! Cut that light for a second."
The two men hustled toward the improvised barricade.

A pistol fired from the darkness behind them, and Post
grunted. He sagged against Valentine, who turned and fired
up the passageway. Ahn-Kha leapt forward with apish
agility, blocked the floodlight with his bulk, and put his
mammoth arm around Post's chest. The machine-gun clattered to the steel floor, but Post gripped the strap as Ahn-
Kha dragged him backwards. Valentine backed down the
corridor, but whoever fired stayed safely around the corner
of the intersection at the end of the hall.

He reached the Grogs outside the arms locker. Ahn-Kha
had improvised a barricade of mattresses and a wooden
door, which the muscular Grogs still worked to construct as
they shifted a beam to let them pass. Ahn-Kha carried Post
into the arms locker and gently stretched him out onto the
floor. Valentine knelt beside his lieutenant, who had blood
staining the undershirt across his chest.

Post groaned and coughed. "I can taste blood," he said.

Valentine found the wound, high enough on his chest to
nearly be at the shoulder. He grabbed a first-aid kit off the
wall and found a compress within. He applied the dressing
to the softly pulsing hole. Noticing blood on the floor, he
gently lifted Post and found another hole opposite.

"Good news, Will. It went straight through."

"Watch . . . out. The captain'll have the marines on you in a minute."

"Most of them won't be armed. All they'll have are whatever guns are scattered in the ship."

"Stern. He'll send men down the hatches." Post was pale with pain, but still thinking clearly enough. His bravery gave Valentine heart.

"We've blocked everything off," Ahn-Kha said from the doorway. "The Chief is welding the access hatches shut."

A Grog hooted and fired toward the T-intersection forward. The shotgun blast sounded like a grenade explosion in the confined area of the metal passageway.

They heard a clatter around the shadowed corner of the T-intersection facing the barricade. Ahn-Kha knelt behind the mattress-shielded door, the pump-action in his hands looking like a child's toy.

"Mr. Rowan?" a voice called down the hall. "It's Partridge. I've got Went and Torres with me. What's happening, sir?"

Valentine exchanged a look with Ahn-Kha, and mouthed the word *marines*. "I don't have time for the whole story, Party. But everything the captain said over the intercom is true. Post is with me. We are trying to take the ship."

"What're you talking to him for?" a voice said from around the right-hand corner of the intersection.

"Shut up, See-Pee. It's our officer," Valentine heard Torres growl.

"You planning on going into the Blue, sir?" Partridge continued, ignoring the byplay.

"Something like that. It's a life away from the Reapers to any man who comes with me."

"You move, and I'll shoot you down," the unknown voice from the right side of the T-intersection threatened.

"Hey, what're—," Partridge began, but the sound of shots cut him off. Valentine heard four shots in rapid succession, and the three marines appeared in the corridor, Torres and Went holding the wounded Partridge between them.

They squinted in the glare of the spotlight, holding up their free hands. Torres had a revolver in his, and Went a rifle.

"Bastards! You killed Delano!" someone yelled from around the corner as the marines approached the barricade.

Ahn-Kha plucked the wounded man over and bore him into the arms locker, and put him down next to Post. Valentine helped the other two. Torres followed Partridge, who had blood already soaking through the right side of his uniform.

"We're with you, Mr. Rowan," Went, one of Valentine's deadeyes, said once they were safely behind the mattresses again. "When we heard the announcement, Party, he said, 'Who'd you rather take orders from, Saunders or Mr. Rowan?' I grabbed my match rifle, and Torres got Corporal Grant's pistol, and came to see what was happening. That bastard Delano fired first, sir, and we shot back. Everything's dark and confused. I heard firing forward. I think everyone's shooting at each other."

"I'm glad you're here, Went. I want to be straight with you. This is not going as I planned. It's us, the Grogs, and the Chief and a few of his men. We're outnumbered about eight to one."

The corners of Went's mouth twitched back into something that, if not a smile, was at least a wry grimace. "Leastways the guns are here." He peered over the edge of the barricade. "They won't take me alive. I'm not going to get delivered in handcuffs to some Hood."

The hatch to the generator room at the bottom level of the ship opened, and the Chief's face looked up at the assembled Grogs and men. "Tight as a drum, they're going to have to blow a big hole in the ship to get at us from down here. Captain's going to have an interesting time commanding the ship without engines."

"Good work, Chief," Valentine said.

Valentine heard a commotion down the hall and sought out the location with hard ears. The captain was speaking to someone, demanding a report. Saunders did not care for the answers, he began to yell. "That's all? And you let men *join* them?"

"They shot Delano, sir, and he had the only gun right then."

"You've got a wrench in your hands—you should have bashed some skulls in with it. Out of my sight!"

After a moment, Valentine heard Saunders's voice raised again, this time projecting from somewhere along the starboard-side corridor.

"The attempt on the ship has failed, Rowan. You know it, and I'm sure it's starting to dawn on those deluded enough to follow you."

"We're ready to wreck the engines, Captain, if we come to believe that," Valentine called back.

"You're a dead man, Rowan, and so's your pet drunk. But I'm offering an amnesty to whoever turns you in. I'll hush all this up. Like it never happened, long as they frog-march you and Post out."

Valentine looked over his shoulder; Torres and Went were both looking at him. He read doubt in their expressions, but whether it was doubt in him or doubt in the captain's promise he could not say. He slowly placed his gun on the floor, butt end pointed at the marines. "Takers?" Valentine asked softly.

Went blanched, but Torres just smiled and shook his head. Partridge groaned something from his position on the floor of the arms locker.

"What was that?" Valentine asked Torres, who knelt beside the wounded man.

"'Tell Captain Saunders to go fuck himself,'" Torres repeated for the wounded man.

Valentine picked up his gun. "We put it to a vote, Captain, and it's unanimous: Go fuck yourself."

"You'll all bleed, you renegade bastards," the captain swore.

"Tell me, sir," Valentine shouted back. "What happened

to the last captain that failed in a mission because of a mutiny? I heard Kurians ordered—"

"By Kur, Rowan, I'll make it so hot for you, you'll wish you were in hell. I'll keelhaul you. You'll beg me to let you die, renegade!"

Torres disappeared into the arms locker and returned, scooting up toward Valentine with something in his hand. Valentine recognized the can-shaped object as one of the ship's grenades. "Play much pool, Mr. Rowan?" Torres asked, putting two fingers into the ring atop the explosive.

"Not my game, Torres," Valentine whispered back.

"Can I try a two-bumper shot?"

"Be my guest."

Torres pulled the pin and listened for the hiss. Valentine saw a thin wisp of smoke appear from the central fixture that held the fuse. The marine stood and, with a left-handed sidearm throw, sent the grenade spinning down the corridor, whirling like a gyroscope toward the voice of the captain. Valentine kept his head up long enough to see it bounce off the bullet-marked wall at the crossbar of the T-intersection and heard it hit again somewhere in the corridor corner leading to the starboard passageway.

There was just enough time before the explosion for cries of "Grenade!" and "Look out!" to be heard, before an orange flash lit up the corridor.

As the ringing noise faded from their ears, Valentine felt the sweat running down the skin over his spine.

"About time for the captain to try something really stupid," Valentine predicted grimly, hearing voices yell back and forth from both sides of the intersection. He hated the thought of what was coming.

The captain obliged him. The loyal sailors and marines of the *Thunderbolt* tried to take the barricade with a rush. One of the machine guns from the upper deck appeared around the portside corner and began firing blindly toward the barricade. Valentine and Torres knelt behind the mattress-reinforced door, while the others took cover in rooms off the main passageway. Valentine heard the bullets hitting the door with a chunking sound, but the mattresses slowed down even the large-caliber shells enough so they failed to do more than dig into the solid wood.

When the gun's belt ran out, the corridor filled with screaming attackers trying to rush the barricade under the cover of a few pistols in the front ranks. The spotlight lit them up with unearthly clarity, ghostly faces white and straining. Ahn-Kha lifted the machine gun Post had dragged with him, and firing from his shoulder swept the corridor, cutting down the attackers running at them two abreast. Valentine added short bursts from his own gun. They flung the men down into bloody heaps well before the hopeless attack reached the barricade. A pair of men dodged into the dark laundry room, only to be hurled out again by shotgun blasts from Ahn-Kha's Grogs waiting within.

The charge was bloody but brief, and when it was over, Valentine counted eleven dead and wounded heaped in the corridor, lying in a thin lake of spilled blood under spattered walls. Only their blood penetrated the barricade, seeping in under the mattresses and door, until its odor overwhelmed even the cordite in the air.

Valentine sank to his knees, reloading. "Last thing I wanted. This is not what I wanted," he heard himself saying over and over again, waltzing on the edge of hysteria.

Ahn-Kha placed a reassuring hand on his shoulder. "Steady now, my David," the huge Grog said. "Better them than us."

A figure arose from the bloody heap in the corridor, pushed up by an arm and his one good leg. The marine tried to take a step back toward the intersection when he slipped on the slick red liquid pooled on the floor, falling full on his injured leg with an agonized scream.

"Would you help Cal before he bleeds to death?" Valentine shouted down the corridor.

"You won't shoot?"

"No, for God's sake. Get him, would you?" Torres added.

The tacit truce allowed a pair of sailors to pull the wounded men away around the corridor. Ahn-Kha placed a new belt in his machine gun, closing the receiver with a determined slam.

"Partridge died," Went reported. "Sorry, Mr. Rowan. And I think Mr. Post is in shock."

Valentine crawled into the locker and felt Post's pulse. It was weak but steady, his breathing shallow.

A half-familiar burning smell tickled Valentine's nostrils. He looked up at the ceiling, where smoke began to flow from an air-supply vent. He moved to the hatch to the engine room. "Chief, looks like they're burning something in the ventilators, can you do anything about it?"

"Yeah, I noticed," the Chief called back. "I'm turning off the fans now. The access to the smokestack is welded shut—otherwise, I could shunt it out of there. It'll get smoky, especially if they burn something in the stairways, too."

"How about reversing the fans?"

"We'd have to rewire them. We're just going to have to cough for a while, I think."

The squawk box crackled to life. "Last chance, men," the captain's voice gloated. "We've got some fires going in the ventilators, and we'll be dropping bits of fender tire on for good measure. It's going to get unpleasant down there in a few minutes, if not lethal. Anyone who comes to their senses will get mercy. Too much has happened for it to get covered up now, but I'll do what I can."

"Why can't you shut him up, Chief?" Went yelled as Torres solemnly laid his tunic over Partridge's head.

"It's on an emergency battery up on the bridge. I could cut the wires, I suppose—"

Ahn-Kha wrinkled his nose. "Disgusting."

Valentine began to cough at the harsh smell of burning rubber filling the room, causing his eyes to water.

"Try this," the Chief said, passing Valentine a damp rag.

Valentine imitated the Chief and his men by tying the

cloth over his mouth and nose. He did not notice a difference.

Eyes watering in the noxious burning-rubber smell, Valentine tried to come up with a plan. If all else failed, it was his duty to at least deprive the Kurians of the *Thunderbolt.* He could have the Chief open the scuttle to the ocean, and let the sea take the ship and his mission with her. Perhaps he and Ahn-Kha could even survive the swim to the Jamaican shore. . . .

Something hit the side of the ship with a resounding thump. A slight sideways motion rocked the *Thunderbolt,* barely enough to make a man unsteady on his feet. Had they run aground, or drifted into a reef? A second later, Valentine heard firing from above.

Valentine looked up at Ahn-Kha. The Grog's hornlike ears were twisting this way and that, listening to the confused clamour from above. Valentine recognized the sound of voices shouting, almost cheering together, intermixed with the gunfire. He and Ahn-Kha exchanged questioning looks.

"It has to be the pirates," Valentine said.

"Aww, shit, just what we need," Went said, his voice sounding strangely pitched owing to a set of improvised noseplugs.

Valentine hopped up to join Ahn-Kha. "You're exactly right, Went. It is just what we need. Men!" Valentine said, raising his voice and calling down to the Chief and his men below. "Let's make some noise. Yell for help, everyone!"

They all looked at him for a moment, uncomprehending. Valentine took a choking breath. *"Heeeeelp!"* he howled down the corridor.

Torres and Went began shouting, as well as the Chief and his men in the engine room. Valentine yelled until he saw spots in front of his eyes, taking unpleasantly deep breaths of smoke-tainted air. Ahn-Kha outdid all the men, bellowing loudly enough to rattle cups in the galley. Ahn-Kha's Grogs joined in, beating metal tools against the pipes and walls, adding a metallic clamor to their combined voices.

He held up a hand for silence. "Kill the spotlight," he ordered. Torres turned the switch at the back of the lamp, incautiously putting his hand on the light's housing and burning himself. Torres swore.

"Quiet there," Valentine said, listening to footsteps in the corridor. Two sailors came around one end of the intersection, a marine from the other, holding their hands up.

"Don't shoot Captain Rowan!" the marine, a corporal named Hurst, begged.

"Mr. Rowan, we're giving up to you here," a CP petty officer added.

"Okay, come forward. Keep your hands in view, men," Valentine said, nauseated from the burnt-tire smell. "What's happened up top?"

"Dunno for sure, sir," Hurst reported. "The exec had me watching the engine-room escape hatch, in case y'all came up that way. All of a sudden we got small-caliber fire. Sweeping bad, sir. There was a ship alongside, and a boat, too, come up in the dark while everyone was busy. Nilovitch got hit, couldn't do anything for him, so we came below. Had to jump over the smoke fire they had going, heard a lot of shouting and shooting behind me. Figured it was a good chance to throw in with y'all. Then we saw these two," he said, gesturing to the *Thunderbolt* sailors.

"My David," Ahn-Kha said, but Valentine was already reacting. Lights appeared from the T-intersection.

"Get over here, men," Valentine said, and he and Went helped them get over the barricade as Ahn-Kha pointed the machine gun down the passageway.

"In there," Valentine ordered, indicating the hallway behind the barricade leading to the aft storage lockers. "Torres, keep an eye on them."

He heard voices coming from the two joining corridors. "Musta been back here," one of the voices said. A few shots still sounded from forward.

"Hello?" Valentine called down the hall. "If you're looking for the people yelling for help, you found them."

The voices hushed. Valentine hardened his ears, searching where his eyes could not go.

"Mebbe a trap," someone muttered around the corner.

"If it is, you can tell the commodore you avenged me. Quiet now, I need to listen," a female voice said. "Hello back," the unknown woman added, a bit more loudly. "This ship is in the hands of the Commodore's Flotilla, of Jayport, Jamaica. I offer you a chance of surrender with fair treatment. Why were you calling for help?"

The owner of the voice stepped around the corner, and all that Valentine could make out in the smoke and darkness was that she was a tall woman. An equally tall man joined her, and at a motion from her hand he opened a kerosene lantern and held it up, revealing the two of them. They both wore loose cotton shirts, cut as pullovers with deep V-necks, dark culottes topped with a sash and gunbelts, and boat sandals. She had dark hair pulled back from her face and handsome, large-eyed features showing Latin blood in her golden complexion. The man behind her was ebony-hued, eyes narrowed suspiciously as he searched the men on the barricade, a revolver in his other hand.

Valentine thought it best to match her and hopped over the barricade, though he took care to land on his good leg. "Ahn-Kha, tell your pair in the laundry not to fire. It's over."

Ahn-Kha barked something out, answered by grunts from the darkness of the laundry room. Valentine moved forward to meet the two at the intersection. She looked at the bodies, and Valentine saw her reading the story in the carnage.

"Surrender might not be the right word, but we won't trouble you."

"You in a position to cause trouble?"

"Not if you play fair by us. My name is Valentine, out of Southern Command in the Ozarks. God knows how I could prove it to you, though. Our plan was to take the ship, but"—Valentine indicated the barricade behind him—"it went rather wrong. Help us, and you'll have my thanks, and my word that we will not harm you or the *Thunderbolt* further."

"You are a long way from Mountain Home, Valentine," she said, showing a better knowledge of his land than he would have guessed. "My name is Carrasca, First Leftenant of the *Rigel*."

"What's happened to the rest of my crew?" Valentine asked.

"A few were killed. Someone from the bridge fired a machine gun into us, and more were shot off the superstructure, but most surrendered. I see your men are better armed than the rest."

"We had the arms locker and engine room, about the only thing that went right tonight. You picked a good time to board."

"Lucky for both of us. Can you clear out that mess in the corridor? I need to send men down to watch the engine room."

"Nobody is going to sink her," Valentine said.

"It is my responsibility to make sure of that. I'm sure you can understand."

Valentine stepped aside as more of the *Rigel*'s men entered, nodding to Ahn-Kha. The Grog gripped the door of the barricade and lifted it aside. Carrasca gave orders, briefly and to the point. Valentine admired the way her men were in control, even in the confusion of a fight. Whoever these pirates were, they had a discipline different from, and superior to, the fear-inspired one that dominated the *Thunderbolt*.

The defenders from the barricade huddled in a silent little group in the arms locker, like children unsure of a new teacher.

Valentine decided a gesture was in order, if nothing else to preempt the orders that would soon be issued from their captors. "Can we get the fans on, Chief? Our friends here put the fires out. Let's get some air down here. Turn the power back on, and start the engines, if you please."

The Chief pushed his stunned men into their positions. "Sir, tell these islanders not to keep pointing their guns around, will you? The fingers on all these triggers are making me nervous."

Carrasca leaned over the hatch. "Bierd, have your men watch their weapons." She turned back to Valentine. "I'm sorry, but for the safety of your men, you'll be put under guard. Could you bring your men up on deck?"

The diesels coughed into life, and Valentine felt the roll of the ship change as the propellers began to bite.

"C'mon, men, up on deck. I've had enough of this air. Let's get these bodies up, too."

The sailors, marines, and Grogs started the grisly work of clearing up the corpses. Valentine picked past the remains of a burning pile of tires and rags, following Carrasca to the stairs.

The intercom buzzed to life again. "Congratulations, men," a deep voice with a singsong musical intonation announced. "Thees is Captain Utari. D' ship is ours. Fair shares all round."

As the pirates cheered, Valentine felt the rudder turn the *Thunderbolt*'s vital tonnage toward Jamaica.

Chapter Four

Jayport, Jamaica. February: Like Malta in the Mediterranean or Singapore on the Krai Peninsula, Jamaica is the key to the waterways around her. Dwarfed by larger neighbors — Cuba to the north and Haiti to the west — the mountainous little island of blinding white sand and lush green hills sits like a tollboth in the center of a network of water routes around her. North is the passage between Cuba and Haiti leading to the coast of Florida and the Bahamas, west is the Yucatán channel off the coast of Mexico, and to the south is the Latin America coast. Far to the east lay tiny island chains and cays that mark the boundary like a lattice curtain between the Caribbean and the Atlantic proper.

In the days of the great buccaneers Morgan, Blackbeard, and Captain Kidd, the legendary pirates of the Caribbean pillaged French and Spanish possessions in the New World, spending their loot in the sinful dens that the seventeenth-century Babylon, Port Royal, boasted. The latter-day freebooters of Jamaica are after no such glittering wealth. Their desired booty is limited to food, medical supplies, technology, and shipbuilding materials.

The latest ruler of Jamaica rests near the old center of Kingston around the great southern bay. But the Kurian's realm extends only to the foothills of the Blue Mountains. These peaks, named for their color as seen from the sea, give the island its serrated spine that resembles a sea serpent resting in the Caribbean. Outside the Kurian's land, isolated coastal communities live in the primitive conditions *of the Arawaka Indians Columbus discovered, building huts of thick grasses and banana leaves, or of mud and thatch. A few are lucky or powerful enough to control one of the pre-2022 buildings still standing after the titanic wave that washed across the Caribbean, followed by foundation-shattering quakes and roof-ripping hurricanes.*

In Montego Bay, a bloody-handed sea lord rules with a brutality that would curl Morgan's mustache, and among the central mountains, an unnamed band of killers, thought to be the remnants of some drug kingpin's gang, leave piles of severed heads along the jungle trails to warn trespassers away. But for the most part, the Jamaicans are a gentle people, taking the bounty nature sewed in the rich volcanic soil of the island and the surrounding sea and sharing what little they have with the generosity of people who have known hunger and misfortune between periods of plenty.

One bay to the north, however, is an exception to the rule in a number of ways. The pre-2022 buildings are in as good a repair as local materials can make them—though one wave-gutted, multistory hotel stands untouched in its beach-front location—and hundreds of white bungalows of wood and thatch show the best example of what can be created out of clay, leaves, and coconut coir. Two thick palisades of wood run for miles from the high hills to the west to a great oval bulge along the flatter ground south and east, bordered by fields of rice and corn with the jungle cut back from the walls.

Sailing ships now dot a broad concrete pier that at one time berthed cruise ships. At the end of the pier is a gray-and-rust ship, a relic of the Old World dominating the center of the bay like a castle's keep. She sits separated by thirty feet of water crossed by a floating bridge leading to a portal in her hull big enough to drive a truck into. She is a strange sort of ship, four decks of superstructure crowded over the bow, and perhaps a hundred yards of what used to be flight deck broken only by the housing for the ship's off-set stack. At the top of her aerial stack, a white flag with a

red cross alternately ripples and droops in the shifting noon-
time air.

Farther out in the shallow waters of the bay, on a calm
day it is easy to see the outlines of sunken shipping, now en-
crusted with coral, forming an underwater, unbuoyed wall
guarding the seaward approaches to the dock. At the south
end of the great concrete pier, a gate stands beneath a guard
tower, allowing passage of landward trade, as well.

This is Jayport, refuge of the Commodore's Flotilla. Its
history, a story too long to be recounted here, goes back to
the last days of 2022, when two ships of the Royal Navy and
a liner full of refugees came here and established the float-
ing hospital. But this flotsam and jetsam of the world-that-
was eventually formed an alliance with a band of island
mariners. Now their combined children roam the Caribbean
from the Texas coast to Grenada, raiding off the Kurian
Order just as their English forebears plagued the Spanish
Main and French Colonies.

Standing on the *Thunderbolt*'s bridge, David Valentine
watched as they approached the Jayport harbor. The ship
threaded her way through the reefs, unmarked save for two
points where the surf splashed up against the coral obstruc-
tions projecting just past the surface. A fishing trawler led
the way, like a pilotfish swimming before the gray bulk of a
shark, and behind came the graceful pyramid of wood and
canvas, the three-masted clipper *Rigel*. She had shortened
sail to keep position behind the plodding gunboat.

Valentine squinted his eyes against the glare of the sun.
The light refracted off the armored glass of the bridge, glittering with spiderwebs of cracks from the bullets of last
night's fight. Carrasca, the officer in charge of the prize
crew, watched the *Thunderbolt*'s progress from the wing
projecting out of the bridge deck over the ship's side, her
black hair now untied and fluttering in the landward breeze
like a pennant. She watched the course of the *Thunderbolt*
as carefully as if she did not have a guide through the reefs

protecting the port. The pirate at the wheel wore a sleeveless, cut-at-the-knees jumpsuit, his thick legs planted wide on the deck. The helmsman looked as if he spent time fighting tiller ropes, rather than the hydraulic rudder of the *Thunderbolt*.

"This reef is a bastard," the helmsman commented to Valentine. "The gap likes to silt up—many's the time I've heard a scrape going over it."

Valentine moved outside the enclosed wheelhouse and joined Carrasca on the starboard side. He looked down at the forward Grog deck, where the other surviving "loyal" hands of the *Thunderbolt* sat in an apathetic bunch under guard. They remained under the supervision of the chief petty officer, a frog-faced toady of the captain named Gilbert. The captain had never been found, dead or alive, and Worthington had been killed with the crew trying to load the main gun just below the bridge.

Valentine could still see the wine stain of his former wardroom mate's blood on the wooden planking. Somewhere to the rear, Ahn-Kha and the men who joined Valentine's fruitless attempt to take the ship were already scrubbing the decks clean after laying out the corpses in a neat row. By tradition they should be sewn up in their bedding, but the cloth was too valuable to waste in such a fashion. The fourteen men who had died last night would leave the world as naked as they came into it.

"Nice breeze," Valentine commented, watching Carrasca's wind-whipped hair. Had he reached out his arm, he could just have touched the longest strands.

"We call it the Doctor. It usually blows all day. Then there's the night wind off the island, it's called the Undertaker. It doesn't smell as good, but it'll keep you cool." Valentine enjoyed hearing her speak. There was something of the music of a Caribbean accent mixed with Hispanic pronunciation.

"Pretty view," Valentine said, applying it both to the woman and the island, though he kept his eyes on the bay.

He was used to the coastlines of North America: flat expanses of beach, wood, and marsh. On Jamaica, the hills rose right out of the ocean like a green wall.

"Yes. You'll want a hat. The sun is strong, even this time of year."

"What's that big ship in the center?"

"She's the hospital. Once was the Royal Fleet Auxiliary *Argus*. She's been here my whole life; I was born in her. So were a lot of the men you see around here."

"How many people do you have?"

"A census isn't one of our priorities. There are the townspeople and plantation families proper. I'd guess around seven hundred or so. Then there are the ships' crews. You could add in the folks inland and along the coast, fishermen, and a few free spirits who come in with a hold full of grain or pork when it suits them. Oh, and the rum distillery. You might say that they're allies of ours, even if their product goes out on Kurian ships, as well. Maybe six thousand people could call Jay home."

"Jay? Does that refer to Commodore Jensen?"

She looked away from the ship's bow for the first time. "You've heard of him?"

"He's not the most popular man up north. They're starting to take Jayport seriously in the KZ."

"KZ?"

"Kurian Zone. My former employers."

"Ahh, I see. We call it Vampire Earth."

Valentine smiled, his first unforced smile in days. "Lurid."

"Saying the name is inaccurate?"

"I wish. Our maps show this island as Kurian controlled—Vampire Earth."

"Most of Jamaica is theirs—or his. We call him the Specter."

"Friendly terms?"

Her mouth writhed. "No. We're no lackeys of his. As

long as we don't bother him, he leaves us alone. Better for us."

"Better for the Specter, too."

She crossed her arms, and looked him up and down. "Just like . . ." The sentiment trailed off. "Would you like to meet Commodore Jensen? I suppose he'll have to decide what to do with you and your men, in the end."

"I'd be grateful if you could arrange a meeting, if you think you can."

Her lips parted, revealing white teeth as she smiled. "I'm sure of it. I'm his granddaughter."

The ships docked and began to disembark wounded. Valentine said a quick good-bye to Post as attendants carried him and the other injured off and placed them on wheeled litters. The attendants then pushed the litters toward the hospital ship, which in proximity dwarfed even the bulky *Thunderbolt*.

Then the Jamaican soldiers, then prisoners, and finally sailors came down the gangway Valentine had last climbed a week ago in New Orleans.

Valentine, with nothing to do but wait, watched Jayport's inhabitants. They were for the most part black-skinned, long-limbed, and healthy looking. A messenger boy received a hollow wooden tube from an officer on the *Rigel* and sprinted off toward the shore like a runner in a relay race. He wondered which building held whatever passed for government headquarters among the low, whitewashed buildings clustered around the bay. Fishing shacks and a few hung nets dotted the beach.

Valentine felt the odd sensation of standing on a firm surface after days at sea. Some of the Grogs sat down hard, holding their heads in their hands at the motionless feel of terra firma. He enjoyed the brassy sunshine—the climatic changes still echoing from the cataclysm of 2022 that cut the amount of sunlight north of the tropics were not so noticeable in the central Caribbean. Farther down the dock, the "loyal" hands of the *Thunderbolt* squatted on the bare concrete surface, slapping at flies hardy enough to venture out this far from shore. Some glared in his direction, some looked to him plaintively, but most just contemplated their surroundings with a fatalism bred by a lifetime in the KZ.

Dockside idlers examined the *Thunderbolt* from behind a rope line that divided the captured ship's part of the dock from the landward extension, where a few armed men in white T-shirts and khaki shorts that looked more like school uniforms than police kept locals and new arrivals apart. Men bearing platters of fruit followed by graceful women with tall wooden tumblers of water were allowed past the line, and they began distributing the island's bounty to Valentine's men and prisoners alike.

"Enjoy, mon, enjoy!" said one, handing out bananas and halves of coconuts.

"No worries, mon! Spring water for now, maybe some rum later," added a woman, her voice bringing out the cadenced phrases more as if she were singing than speaking. She exchanged a few words and a smile with a dockhand, but Valentine could make no more out of it than he could Ahn-Kha's Grog patois.

One man leaned toward a guard's ear, pointed at Valentine, and spoke. A few others craned their necks, and Valentine wondered what sort of dockside rumors were already floating around about the fight on the *Thunderbolt*.

Valentine tasted his first fresh banana—he'd had banana bread and a pudding mix in New Orleans, and there was no comparison—and followed it with the meat and milk of a coconut. He strolled over to Ahn-Kha and the Grogs, who were learning to peel their fruit before eating it in imitation of the humans. A knot of the Chief's men crammed down the colorful fruit with Went and Torres.

"What do they have in mind for us, my David?" Ahn-Kha asked, scooping meat from his coconut shell with his strong, flexible lips.

"We're safe for now. It seems they give the royal treat-

ment to prisoners. They'll try to recruit the captain's men, I
suppose. They don't know which category we're in. We're
not under guard, but I don't think those men at the rope gate
will let us just wander into town."

"They left you your weapons. They locked the rest back
up in the small-arms room. They are either very trusting or
very confident," Ahn-Kha mused.

"Either suits me, for now. We're lucky to be alive, old
horse."

"Your race needs to learn to greet every day with those
thoughts."

"There's something kind of old-fashionedly formal about
the way they've handled us. It's like we've stepped back
three hundred years or so. Like letting me keep my guns: a
captured officer used to be allowed to retain his sidearms in
the days when wars were fought by gentlemen against other
gentlemen. I'm half expecting an invitation to dinner, rather
than an interrogation."

The invitation to dinner arrived two hours later, waking
him from a shaded nap. Like humans, Grogs laugh to indi-
cate amusement, so when a barefoot sprout of a boy in
ragged white ducks and a straw hat arrived with a note from
the commodore requesting Valentine's presence at the Governor's House for dinner, Ahn-Kha laughed loudly enough
to send the flies fleeing in alarm. Carrasca arrived shortly
thereafter with an escort, announcing that they were to be
moved to more comfortable quarters. They formed up behind her, and the procession of visitors walked the pier toward town.

The wide pier reminded Valentine of an etching of
London Bridge he'd seen long ago in a book. Crowded with
buildings at the landward end, so much so that it resembled
a narrow street for the last hundred yards before it reached
the shore, the walkway was where goods from land and sea
traded owners. Two-story buildings, making up in floors
what they lacked in width and depth, overhung both the

street to the inside and the water to the outside, creating a shaded corridor leading toward the town proper. Carrasca explained that the twentieth-century dock was one of the best-built foundations in the bay, an important consideration on an earthquake-prone island. Valentine's men and their baggage were placed in a series of rooms above a clothing-reclamation shop, next to an empty storage room that would accommodate Ahn-Kha's Grogs. The prisoners from the *Thunderbolt* were placed alongside the dock in a permanently moored ship, where Carrasca assured him they would be well looked after. Valentine asked to see the wounded who'd been taken to the hospital ship, and Carrasca wrote him a note that would get him on board. He and his men were free to move about the pier as they wished.

"But you might not want to be too visible," she warned. "A lot of characters come into port. We're sure we get spies sent by the Kurians now and then. Once a small fishing ship blew itself up at the pier—perhaps you noticed the big patched-up crack. We depend on trade too much to deny access to the pier to strangers. But even men such as you whom we assume to be friends are not allowed in town, and are searched before going on board the *Argus*."

Of all the choices Valentine had faced in the last twenty-four hours, the most unexpected was deciding what to wear to dinner at the Governor's House. With the message he had in mind to say to the commodore, he preferred looking like an ally rather than a castaway. Going in his full Coastal Marines uniform would be inappropriate—he no more represented the Kurian Order than the Zulu nation. Lacking anything else presentable, he wore his tailored uniform trousers and good boots, topping it with a simple white shirt. He washed and combed out his thick black hair and drew it back into a tight pigtail. Torres completed the ensemble with the loan of a short black jacket and a strange combination of sash and cummerbund, an item common to what passed for aristocracy in his native part of Texas. Valentine's long arms dangled from the sleeves of the jacket, but he at least looked properly dressed.

One of the ubiquitous messenger boys—this one had shoes on his feet—arrived at the rooms to escort him off the dock as the sun went down. The breeze had reversed itself with the cooling of the land. What had Carrasca called it? The Undertaker. It smelled of the decay on the seashore rather than the clean ocean.

The boy led him past another watchman's post on the dock and into the first of Jayport's streets. An open carriage rocked back and forth on a heavily patched turnaround at the base of the pier; a single horse shifted impatiently in the traces before an elderly driver. The old man's white hair and whiskers framed a round black face; he gave Valentine a look more like that of a suspicious police officer rather than a taxi driver.

Carrasca waited for him in the carriage, wearing a neat blue uniform tunic with her hair in a tight bun at the back of her head. Oddly, the uniform made her even more feminine, thanks to her wide, dark eyes and portrait-perfect face. The thought crossed his mind that perhaps Carrasca—or the commodore—wanted to make as good an impression on him, mirroring his own efforts in securing proper attire.

Valentine assumed the attitude of one who took her presence there, in a cushioned and polished carriage, as if it were the most natural thing in the world.

"Good evening, Lieutenant," he said with a perfunctory bow that seemed to suit the occasion. "Does this mean you are doing me the honor of being my escort to dinner tonight?"

"Thank you, Mr. Valentine. My duties on your former ship were such that I could be spared for an evening." She opened the tiny door to the carriage, and Valentine primly took the seat opposite her. The corner of her mouth flickered up, and he answered with a raised eyebrow that dissolved their playacting pretenses. She giggled and he snorted.

The driver called out a low "move on," and the carriage

lurched into motion as the horse started off at a brisk walk, iron-rimmed tires squealing on the mix of cobblestone and tar.

"Actually, Valentine, your presence is a bit of a coup for me. For a people whose ships travel a thousand miles in every direction, you'd be surprised how cut off we feel out here. We get shortwave contact sometimes, but it's usually passive—we've been burned a couple times by talking over the radio. The only people we really trust now are the Dutchmen to the south."

He could smell her now, a mixture of soap, a coconut-scented lotion, and a hint of perfume blending with the warmer female scent escaping out the collar of her uniform. The animal in him wanted to tear open the tunic, pull her head aside, and let his lips explore her neck, his hands those round, high breasts beneath. . . .

Madness. He regained control of his thoughts, crated up his lust, nailed it down, and padlocked urges too long sublimated.

"Please call me David. We're both off duty, aren't we?"

Her pupils narrowed for a second, then widened again. "Maybe. You may call me Malia, if you like."

Valentine liked. "Gladly, Malia. So the commodore wants an interview?"

"He's always eager for news from the north. The people we pick up know less about the real story than we do."

"I might disappoint him," Valentine said. "I've been . . . I suppose you'd call it 'undercover' for about a year. My only current information is what the Kur are up to on the Coast between Florida and Texas. I'm sure it will be useful to him, but if he needs current news about events farther in than that, I'll be a dry well. Since I'm part of your triumph tonight, maybe you can tell me more about how you managed your ambush so well."

She shrugged. "I had little to do with it. Your captain's mission wasn't a secret, though if you ask me, they sent out too small a force even if everything went right. This town has grown in the last few years, grown a lot. It's funny how word of a haven gets around—we have mariners showing up from all points of the compass looking for shelter. We've even started another settlement farther along the coast at Port Maria to help accommodate the newcomers."

"Jamaica can provide for you all?" He looked at the few wanderers on the main street. The Jamaicans made up for the drab streets and whitewashed buildings by dressing in brightly dyed colors: deep reds, brilliant yellows, and heavy purples.

"Rich soil and richer waters." She waved to a young couple out for a stroll. "But back to your ship. Your captain did not keep his mission a secret. We have a spy or two in most of the major ports on the Vampire Earth. They tell us when something worthwhile is shipping for the most part, but we heard about your—or *their,* I mean—plans while you were still outfitting. Just because the *Thunderbolt*'s gun could sink anything we have afloat didn't mean we couldn't do something about you at sea. One of our cutters kept watch at the mouth of the Mississippi, waiting for you to come out, and then it raised every sail when it saw you, and beat you here by two full days. A coastwatcher told us of your landfall by radio. We need to keep an eye on Montego Bay and the west end of the island all the time as it is.

"We knew you were moving up the coast, so we went out to meet you on it. I had a motorboat full of men, cut low, it would be hard to see. We were heading out for you from the time the moon went down. When we heard the shooting and saw the gun flashes, Captain Utari brought the *Rigel* out and put the extra men in the boats. Your captain was foolish to hug the coast like that."

"No one was expecting you to come after us. It turned out for the best. Or at least, I hope it will. I need the ship, Malia."

"I can't imagine what your Southern Command would do with a gunboat, other than sink it trying to get it back up the

Mississippi. I promise you we will make better use of it. You have enough problems, judging from the shortwave we get."

"What's that?"

"Battles, shortages. It seems that nothing but bad news ever comes from the north."

"We're still standing. That's something. So you made for the *Thunderbolt* when the firing started?"

"Yes. We expected it to be a lot worse. We had an inflatable boat full of explosive we were going to use as a last resort. All the confusion you caused made the difference; otherwise, I expect it would have been a lot bloodier."

"It was bloody enough," Valentine said. "If it weren't for you and Captain Utari, I doubt I'd even be alive now. I'm in your debt."

Her voice turned colder than any winter Jamaica had ever seen. "Then pay us back by leaving us alone. We do not need more trouble from Vampire Earth. We have problems enough."

The carriage moved up a slope, clusters of white buildings giving way to trees and lush ferns. Valentine smelled the rich aroma of green growing things all around and felt newly invigorated in the cooler night air. "Aren't you afraid some cruiser is going to show up and get your town under its guns?"

"We're pretty sure they do not bother with big warships. Our worry has always been a strong landing force. We've also heard rumors about some kind of Grog that takes to the water—that's one of the reasons you saw armed men on the docks. It's well for us the vampires don't organize themselves properly."

"It's their weakness," Valentine agreed. "They're about as cooperative as a cave full of rabid rats. They can't see past the next infusion of aura."

"Aura?"

"Do you call it something else here? It's what the Kurian Lords live off. Kind of an energy created by sentient beings. No, strike that—it's generated by anything that lives, but

it's just hundreds of times richer when it's created by an intelligent being."

"I thought they drank blood," she said, puzzled.

"Their Reapers do, but the Reapers are just puppets,
walking and talking tools for the dirty work of killing.
There's some kind of mental link between the Kurian Master and his Reapers. The Reaper feeds itself off the blood,
yes, but its Lord gets the energy we call 'vital aura.' Either
way, your calling it vampirism is correct, even if it sounds
kind of . . . poetic."

"Not a pleasant subject for conversation on such a beautiful night, David. We're almost there."

There emerged out of the palms and night. The Governor's House turned out to be a substantial building con-
structed on a flat prominence jutting from the steep hill, or
small mountain, just west of the town. Behind it, somewhere
in the forest, the wooden wall wound down from a watch-
tower at the top of the hill. The building itself was fashioned
of cut and whitewashed stone with a red clay roof, remind-
ing Valentine of an old Spanish mission he'd seen on the
Texas coast. The driver waved to a pair of white-shirted police at the entrance to a flowered courtyard and wheeled the
carriage around a fountain in the center of the circular drive.
The horse seemed to know the routine better than the driver,
and it stopped before the door at the tiniest murmur.

"Thank you, Jason," Carrasca said, patting the driver on
the shoulder. "We will be several hours, so be sure to have
your dinner."

"I'll see to the horse first, but thank you, miss."

Valentine stepped out of the carriage, and held the door
open for his escort. "Miss?" he asked, as the driver moved
off.

"Jason taught me to ride and drive. I grew up here. He's
as much of a fixture of the place as the commodore. His father saved my grandfather's life way back when. He's a bit
of everything: bodyguard, driver, interpreter. He knocked
together my first boat, a little clinker-built toy I learned to

sail. He also made that," she said, pointing to a flag that fluttered from a corner bell tower on the building, built to cover the door as well as the road coming up the hillside from the sea. "It's dark so you can't see it. Our flag is half blue and half green, with a sun in the center, kind of like the old French sun-king design. Do flags mean anything anymore?"

"Flags? They're not much used up North. Maybe nobody in the Free Territory could figure out what color represents survival. I'll have to have a look when it's lighter."

Valentine's night vision could pick up the emblem, even if the colors were muted, but he said nothing. The physical gifts of the Lifeweavers aroused suspicion in some people, as if he were no longer human. To this woman at least, he wanted to be a man rather than some kind of curiosity.

He sometimes wondered what exactly the Lifeweavers did to their human creations. The nearest thing he could compare it to in human experience was puberty, a sudden shift into an entirely new body type, complete with changed abilities and desires. Would any of it be passed on? His own father had been one of the Lifeweaver's elite, but apart from a remarkably healthy childhood—despite several bad falls, he had never broken a bone, nor could he remember a serious illness—he had not been the most athletic of the young men growing up around him. Only his ability to sense the presence of a Reaper, as a cold shadow appearing on the fringes of his consciousness, distinguished him from the others in the Lifeweavers' service.

"Mr. Valentine?" Carrasca said, calling him back to the present from his contemplation of Jamaica's night sky.

"Sorry, my mind wandered," he said, turning to the door she held open for him.

"That's the only way it ever finds anything," she said, following him into the wood-paneled entry hall.

A boy took them down the hall to another plant-filled courtyard. Valentine paused at the tile surrounding the door at the other side. Each piece had been painted with delicate tropical blossoms.

"Beautiful," he said.

Carrasca turned. Her eyes arced up and across the span of tiles around the portal. She looked oddly wistful. "You like them? That's my work. I spent a few years obsessively painting. When I was a teen."

"I was an obsessive reader. I was—"

He had started to talk about his parents, his brother and sister, but stopped himself. He needed to watch his mood tonight.

She took a step closer, lowered her voice. "Orphaned? I know."

"Same with you?"

"The same."

Valentine read the hurt as if he were looking in a mirror. He extended the crook of his elbow, and she took his arm. "What can you do?"

She gave him a gentle squeeze with her forearm. "Go to sea. That's what finally worked for me. But let's change the subject. Tonight's a state dinner."

And they passed down a hall to a dining room. The furniture in the Governor's House, richly covered and well carved, did not match—the collection was perhaps pieced together from various recovered antiques on the island.

The man standing in the dining room did not match the elegant furniture either: a stumpy, tanned man bristling with energy and heavy white sideburns. The latter first traveled down his jaw, then turned up to join his mustache. He was broadly, powerfully built, and stood with the ready stance of a judo sensei. Perhaps because of the thickness of his chest, his arms seemed stunted by comparison, dangling afterthoughts on his barrel frame like the forelegs on a *Tyrannosaurus rex*. He stood beside a sideboard, over which a hand-inked map of Jamaica hung in a gilded frame. Behind him, pairs of French doors opened out onto a balcony filled with fragrant white jasmines and red ixoras. According to Carrasca's account, her grandfather had served as an officer in the Old World's Royal Navy, which had to put him close to his seventies.

"Sixty-eight, my son, sixty-eight," he said, turning to the young people. He slapped his broad belly, the gesture cracking like a pistol shot in the enclosed room. The expanse of stomach, which hung out from a gaily colored shirt over suspendered canvas trousers, did not ripple from the impact, demonstrating still-firm muscle beneath. "Everyone always wonders that when they see me, but are too polite to bring it up. Thought I'd save you the trouble. Am I right, Leftenant?" he asked, buttoning his shirt to preserve some formality at the meeting.

"And they always guess 'not a day over fifty,' sir," she said, suddenly transformed into a young girl amused at her grandfather's antics.

"The next question, at least to any young man who sees the two of us together, is where did she get her height and her looks?" Jensen said, apparently reading Valentine's mind again. "Maria—my daughter—was even shorter than I was, may she rest in peace. It's her father's doing. Tall, handsome Cuban man he was, hair like yours—Mr., Mr.—"

"Valentine," Carrasca supplied.

"That's the problem with age, my son, and it's a real bugger. What happened thirty years ago is bright as the island's sun, but what you talked about just this morning disappears into a fog. But there was more to Eduardo than looks. As brave and as sharp as they come. Also dead, by the way. Should fair fortune be with you and you see long service, Valentine, you'll see too many of the best ones die."

Valentine's memory, always too ready to parade the faces of the women and men he had known and lost, rose to the occasion. Jensen gathered as much from the expression on his guest, and he changed the subject.

"Let's eat, the cold dishes are already served," the commodore said, moving to a chair. "Come down by me, you two, no sense shouting at each other over twelve feet of table. That American President Eisenhower used to take dignitaries out on his back porch and talk to them, said he 'got a better measure of the man' or some such. I do the same thing over the dinner table. Cook tells me the chicken turned out well, and no one does a glazed ham like he does. Cook!" Jensen bellowed through the wall. "We're ready when you are."

By the time they were seated, one of the picture-frame-like carved panels on the wall opened, and the sweating cook appeared with a tray. He began to arrange dishes before the three: chicken swimming in orange sauce, some kind of peppery-smelling stew, corn and potatoes surgically carved and neatly arranged. A second man followed, bearing a thick ham glazed with slices of pineapple and something that looked like black cherries.

The three began to help each other to servings from the varied dishes, as the cook poured wine into glass goblets, the only matching dinnerware on the table.

"Captain Utari doesn't know what he's missing. I invited him, but then he hates this sort of thing. There's no sailor like him, but he refuses to do anything with shoes on, or eat anything that can't be bitten off the tip of his knife. Or maybe he just has a superior sense for the ridiculous. But as I'm fond of saying, this Port wasn't just founded to preserve life, but to—"

"—preserve a way of life," Carrasca finished, reaching across the table to pat the commodore's hand.

Valentine sipped lightly from the wine.

"Don't like it? It's a bit harsh, I know, but I get tired of rum and brandy," Jensen apologized. "Jamaica's a second Eden as far as I'm concerned, except for the wine. Don't know enough about it to tell you why. Years ago we had some pretty fair stuff from the old hotels and resorts, but it's been used up over time."

"I wouldn't know. Haven't had many chances to drink it. What I've had has been from dandelions or blackberries. This is rather good—in comparison."

They spent a few minutes eating under the anxious eye of the cook. He hovered like a teacher watching his pupils take a make-or-break exam. Valentine, who usually disliked the feeling of having too much of anything: alcohol, food, or even leisure, ate heartily until he heard his innards groan in discomfort.

Valentine raised his glass. "May I offer a toast? To the bounty of Jamaica, my hosts, and especially to the author of the best dinner I've had in years," he said, dipping the goblet in the cook's direction.

"I second the motion," Carrasca said, eyes reflecting flickers of the candlelit room.

"Hear hear," added the commodore through a full mouth.

Fresh fruits and a sweet, milky pudding identified as flan finished the meal. The commodore enjoyed a private dessert, a toasted marrow bone. He went to work on the contents with a miniature fork, and Carrasca turned to him expectantly.

"Young man," Jensen began, sucking unabashedly at the bone, "my granddaughter tells me you tried to take the gunboat."

"Had matters taken a better turn, we would have gone straight to Haiti."

"Valentine, there's nothing on Hispaniola but death. Are you looking for allies in the islands? You wouldn't find any on Haiti who'll help you up north. They have miseries enough."

"Or here," Carrasca said, her eyes turning hard. "We had a group of you Freeholders arrive before, when I was sixteen. Marched them through town and everyone cheered. They gave us lots of talk about guerrilla cadres and hit-and-run raids. Uniting the different parts of the island to go after Kingston. All they managed to do was get some of our inland people killed and a lot of families on the other side of the Blue Mountains hanged. There wasn't any cheering when they left. If you think the people of Jayport—"

"Nothing like that," Valentine said, startled at her sudden

turn in temper. "I'm looking for a weapon, not allies. I'm not asking you or anyone to fight Reapers."

"Malia," her grandfather said, "the reprisals weren't Mr. Valentine's fault any more than they were Major Hawthorne's.

"Forgive my granddaughter," Jensen added, turning to Valentine. "After the aborted uprising, they wiped out one of our settlements up in the mountains. That's where her mother died," he said, clamping his mouth firmly shut and looking at Carrasca. "My great mistake."

"Not yours, Granddad," she said. "You saw the uniforms, counted the guns, heard Hawthorne's promises. Believed in him. He knew the kind of words to use. Even on Mum. She was a widow, Mr. Valentine, and—"

"Let's not bore our guest with family business," Jensen said. He looked at his granddaughter for a moment, as if trying to summon her mother's features from Carrasca's shapely face, then turned back to Valentine. "You need that ship you were on, the gunboat, to get this weapon?"

"Get it and get it back to the mainland. We needed something big enough to carry it, a ship that could anchor off the coast long enough for me to find it and load it, then be able to go back unchallenged. The *Thunderbolt* is as large as they come in the Caribbean these days."

"You're wrong," Jensen said. "The Dutchmen down south have an old cruiser still working, God knows how. I think it used to be an American ship, too. It could blow the *Thunderbolt* in half, but the Dutchmen are on our side. In fact, I was planning on feeding your gunboat with their diesel fuel."

"Was?" Valentine said, sensing an opening.

"Mr. Valentine, I'm looking for a weapon, too. We are growing here. It's getting harder and harder to support the people we have. Always more coming in, not always the sort we need, but still mouths to feed. I've never been much good at turning needy people away. The best land, at least for planting, is on the south half of the island. It's not just my people I worry about; it's my ships, as well. This harbor is worthless in a real storm. But if I could get old Kingston, take it somehow from the Specter—that's what we call that trumped-up devil running things there—a lot of our problems would be solved. A real harbor with a real shipyard, though it's run to ruin like everything else, would mean a lot to us. Just that every time I've tried"—he nodded in his granddaughter's direction—"it's gone wrong."

Jensen stood and went to the map of Jamaica above the sideboard. He extended one of his short, thick arms and pointed to the coastline.

"The Specter has it pretty good. He's about as secure in his position as he could be. Lives on a sort of estate, in a castle, no less." Jensen pointed at a black square just off a crescent-shaped bay on the southern coast, west of Kingston. "They say he sometimes appears on the walls, to watch the women work his fields or see a new wagonload of the condemned come up the road, bound for the killing hole."

Just right for a Kurian, Valentine thought.

"He's jealous of his lands, always worried about another of his kind moving in. He has his Black Guard—that's those Reapers you call 'em—and he keeps a good-sized regiment of Asians to keep the rest of the Jamaicans down. Those are the Horsed Police. Then the Chinese and Indians in turn run the Public Police—more thugs, mostly a rabble, that organize the farms and labor using the hard end of a club. Same old game: elevate an ethnic minority to a position of privilege that said minority knows will disappear if the ruler does, then give a lot of brutes a little power. He's got informants everywhere . . . even within my palisade, I expect. Kind of reminds me of a web with a fat spider sitting in the center of it, sensitive to vibrations at the edges. We try to enter the web, we get stuck, there's just not enough of us to get to him, even with the guns we've been stealing and stockpiling. Years before Major Hawthorne arrived, my son-in-law once tried to recruit some of the gangs in the mountains, but they killed Eduardo for his trouble. We can do what we want in the water around Jamaica, but that doesn't do much for us. He can get everything he needs from the land and the southern shoreline and the occasional armed trade ship. About all we've managed to do is keep his brothers and sisters from showing up to run other parts of the island, like maybe ours on the north coast or the Cockpit Country in the west."

"I suppose he never leaves that castle," Valentine said, looking at the scale of the map.

"We've never heard of it, if he has," Carrasca said.

"That's usual for a Kurian. Their Reapers act as eyes and ears. No need to risk venturing out," Valentine said. "They stay in their holes with just their servant or two ever seeing them. Immortality turns you into a recluse, evidently."

But this one likes to have a look around, now and then. Is he too secure for his own good?

Now that he knew more about the island's situation, he saw the chance of an answer. Maybe not even a chance, maybe more of a prayer. "Sir, I'll take your analogy about the web one step further." Valentine felt his skin flush, not from the wine, but from his quickening pulse.

"Don't let me stop you. I'm listening."

"His organization also has the weakness of a spider's web."

"What's that?"

"If you kill the spider, the web falls apart in a matter of days."

Even Cook paused and looked at Valentine.

"My son, I would say it is impossible," Jensen finally said. "The Specter lives in a bloody fortress, a real rock castle. It's about as old as the British flag on this island, and he's got it fixed up. Word is he stays in some cave beneath it. A dozen or so years ago, some of the Jamaicans on the other side got the same idea as you. Thirty of them swore a blood oath: they'd kill him or they'd die trying. They'd managed to get a key to a back door, thought they'd sneak in and do him in. They got together a few guns—the rest had fishing spears and machetes. Two of those Black Guard Reapers caught them on the approaches, and they died, to a man. Of course, the Special Police tried to round up their families, but I'll say this for the Jamaicans: they know how to keep a secret better than anyone I've ever heard of. Offers, bribes, even using torture they got only a name or two, and still there was enough of a delay for their children to head for the bush. Captain Utari lost his older brother in the attempt, by the way. That's how we ended up with him in our orphanage."

"Then what did you mean, you *would* say it is impossible?"

Jensen looked at Cook, suddenly uncomfortable. "This is going to sound like utter bollocks, Valentine, but I want to tell you, nevertheless. There's a woman living inland the Jamaicans go to for advice. Sort of a witch, she is, at least to them. They call her Obay. Over six feet tall, and they say she has four breasts. According to the stories, she once suckled four infants at once, her top two breasts thrown over her shoulders to two tied to her back, and then two to the front, and they grew up to be the four great headmen of the free inlanders. They really exist, by the way, they're known as the four Kernels, though I suspect what they really mean are Colonels. She holds festivals at the solstices and equinoxes, when they go to her for predictions. An oracle she may be, I'm thinking now," he paused, perhaps for dramatic effect, but more likely out of embarrassment. "At the last one in December, she said a man would come from the sea, a Crying Man. This man would rid the land of the Specter."

Valentine reached up to his face, and felt the old scar moving up from his chin to the level of his eye.

"I forget the rest," Jensen said. "How did it go, Cook?"

The cook cleared his throat. "The Crying Man would bring a storm in flesh, and a storm in metal. His eyes would see to the end of a long straight path, and at this path's end would come our salvation."

"What was your ship called, the *Thunderbolt*?" the commodore asked. "Thunderstorm? Thunder in metal?"

"Yes," Valentine said. "But the rest is a leap. I might be able to do it, but not because of an oracle. I have certain . . . abilities . . . that the Jamaicans who tried before lacked. To do the job, I'll need the ship back, on loan for a short cruise round the island. If I can get rid of the Specter, break his hold on the island, would you return the ship and crew to take me to Haiti and back to the coast? Afterwards you could keep her. I'm sure you'd find her useful."

"Valentine," Jensen said. "If you can do this, I'll give you the ship and a team of men who'd sail with you across hell's lava ocean in a powderhulk, no fear."

"That's what I'm counting on. No fear."

The party broke up after midnight. It turned out Jensen was a fan of mah-jongg, and he insisted on teaching Valentine. The driver from the carriage, now formally introduced as Jason Lisi, joined them to make the fourth. After the pieces were distributed, Jensen started telling Lisi Valentine's idea to oust the Specter. Valentine had to force his brain to do double duty as he explained his plan to Lisi while learning how to match up his tiles, when to call *kung,* and when a hand was over. Valentine asked about the depths in the waters off the southern coast of the island while keeping the ancient box-top from the mah-jongg set ready to remind himself what the bamboos and characters and flowers and so on were worth. He had a feeling that convincing the commodore to commit to his plan somehow rode on his ability to play the old Chinese game—easy enough to learn but difficult to play well.

He lost.

The experience left him drained. Jensen caught him rubbing his eyes and suggested that the party break up. "I'll think it over while I sleep," he promised Valentine. Valentine then accepted an invitation to stay in a guest bedroom.

The bedrooms all opened on the same balcony as the dining room. All had similar French doors open, inviting the soft night air. Valentine's room held the same cluttered hodgepodge of antiques—only the ticking on the mattress looked new. He found an old laminated "guest services menu" inside a nightstand drawer and relaxed, imagining the luxuries of a bygone age. Jasmine perfumed the air. What sort of assignations had transpired in the days when the Residence was just another luxurious rental property on Jamaica's sunny coast? He hung up his cumberbund and short jacket and tried to relax in bed, but his mind wouldn't let him sleep. He went out onto the balcony, barefoot on the cool concrete, and looked down at the moored hospital ship, the smaller *Thunderbolt,* and the town of Jayport.

Light still fell out the doorway from the dining room, though less than when they'd been shuffling tiles under the chandelier. Perhaps the commodore was an insomniac. Valentine walked softly to the edge of the light.

It was Carrasca, with her thick hair released from its confinement. She still had the mah-jongg tiles out, arranged in a three-tiered pile that looked like a Japanese castle. She tapped two of the tiles together as she stared at the arrangement, her lower lip thrust out in thought, a half-filled glass of wine on the table. Her wide-lapeled jacket hung on the back of her chair, and she'd partially unbuttoned her shirt. Valentine saw now that the shirt was far too big for her. Perhaps it had belonged to her father.

Valentine cleared his throat.

Carrasca glanced out the open doors. Then she jumped in her chair with a shocked gasp. Mah-jongg pieces skittered across the dinner table.

"Sorry to sneak up on you," Valentine said. He took a step into the light.

"Mother of— You frightened me."

Valentine noticed her arms were goose pimpled. "I'm sorry. Wrong of me to creep around my hosts' house."

"No, not that. Your eyes." She rattled out the words staccato.

"My eyes?"

She shivered again. "They were—glowing."

Perfect. You're the wolfman to her now, Ghost. "Glowing?"

"Like an animal's at night, a cat's. Sort of orange yellow. I've never seen a man's eyes do that."

"Maybe they caught the light just right."

"Maybe. Maybe my imagination, too. Long day," she said, her words returning to their usual genteel pace.

"Sorry about your stack. What were you doing?"

"You can play mah-jongg solitaire, too. You take the chips out of the bag and stack them in a certain way. The trick is to not look at the ones on the lower levels as you put it together. Then you pull them off in matching pairs."

"Didn't get enough after dinner?"

"I couldn't sleep. It relaxes me. My mind had too much to work on. This is like counting sheep."

"I'm sorry your parents came up in the conversation."

Some of the warmth that had been in her eyes earlier in the evening returned. "No. Oh, no, it wasn't that. You see, my grandfather talked to Captain Utari earlier. The commodore decided to let me captain the *Thunderbolt*. My first real command."

She led him out onto the balcony, and they looked down into the bay. The *Thunderbolt* looked like a toy ship.

"You're lucky Utari didn't want her."

She smiled. "He hates anything without a sail. Says there's no seamanship in engines."

"But you don't feel that way."

"You don't know sailors, David. My first real ship. My first command. I loved her even as we limped into the harbor." The light trickling out of the dining room played across her dusky features. "I can't wait to put her to sea again. She's the most beautiful thing I've ever seen."

Valentine could have said the same about the *Thunderbolt*'s new commander. He would have, if there hadn't been a hint of anxiety in her eyes as she met his gaze, wary against the return of that inhuman glow.

Chapter Five

The Specter's Lands: From the jagged course of Jamaica's Southern Shore to the spine of the Blue Mountains, the Specter's domain casts its invisible shadow over this sunny land. The Jamaicans somehow know when they walk within his borders; they grow nervous and sullen. No great wonder, for they have been returned to the slavery of three centuries ago. They work tiny plots of cultivated ground that form islands amongst the riotous growth of returned wild trees and grasslands. Viewed from a buzzard's eye high above, the topography resembles that of a tangle of grapevines, dollops of tended lands connected by one or two main roads. Smaller trails cut through patches of forest, with the vine's principal stalks growing out of what used to be Kingston. A few swaths cut in the red earth of the hills at the bauxite mines yield the makings of aluminum. This export is shipped north and west in return for the few technological necessities the Specter needs to maintain his control.

Slave labor, carried out at a dead slow pace, tends the fields in this, one of the most backwards and ill-governed of the multitude of Kurian Principalities. Organization is nil. Construction is moribund, maintenance haphazard. Technology, with the exception of the bauxite mines (under rust-streaked signs with the word JAMALCO sometimes still visible) and the guns in the hands of the Specter's Chinese Quislings, has slipped back into a stage somewhere between the Neolithic implements of the Arakawa Indians and the eighteenth century. It is not unusual to see the land worked by stone tools, before the slaves go home to rude huts lit by charcoal fires. The Jamaicans have resorted to an atavistic belief system filled with good-luck charms, incantations, and totemism to keep the Reapers from the door. Rocks or coral painted with designs in chicken blood can be seen on some doorsteps, below patterned threads of beads that sway in every window. Some families never eat after noon, in the not unreasonable belief that an empty belly makes the body less visible to the Reapers' senses. The Reapers, in the manner of wild predators, usually pick off the aged, the sick, or the few who try to flee. The Specter's cloaked avatars often lurk on the beaches and borders, taking those who try to escape over the mountains or into the cockpit country of the Northwest.

While the Reapers isolate and then kill individual troublemakers, any sort of mass disturbance is a matter for the Horsed Police and Public Police. With their intimidating combination of horses, dogs, guns, and clubs, the Specter uses them in one of the oldest tricks in the tyrant's playbook: that of keeping one race under control by using another. The Horsed Police are of mixed ethnicity: Chinese Jamaican and Indian Jamaican predominating. They control the more numerous but less disciplined members of the Public Police, little more than baton-waving bands of thugs, but effective enough in controlling the workers on their plantations. The great privilege of the Public Police is being allowed to use small boats to claim the cod, rock beauties, and parrotfish from the surrounding waters, though their better-fed families suffer nearly as much from the Reapers as the ordinary Jamaicans who work the crops and mines.

The Specter rests at the apex of this pyramid of power and fear, an engorged demigod swollen on the rich life aura of the island's fecund people. Cunning as a grave robber, for forty years he has jealously guarded his island paradise, turning down overtures of fellow Kurian Princes to join him on the island, and one attempt to wrest it from him by force. From a European-style castle overlooking a wide bay he feeds off one of the first discoveries of the New World as a maggot feeds off a corpse, decomposing anything he touches like a necroptic King Midas. With only the irritation of pirates to the north and a few scattered gangs in the mountains, hardly enough to threaten him even in the unlikely event that they united, one could wonder if he would have given the news that there was a Cat on the island much thought, so secure is he in his habits, behind his walls guarded by a thousand guns and the ferocious teeth of his Reapers.

It took all of three days for David Valentine to cross a 1,200-yard field. In fairness, the first day hardly counted: it had been spent surveying the estate's lands. The more rugged ground sloping down toward the bay turned into fields and orchards closer to the castle. A road servicing the Kurian's home wandered westward along the coast and eastward toward a settlement centered in the ruins of a beautiful Colonial Spanish square. The immediate lands beyond the castle's pebble-colored faces were filled with tobacco fields, stretching out from the walls like a green carpet. The distinctive odor tickled his sensitive nostrils as he allowed his nose a moment's play in the air from his perch in a palm. He had surveyed farms with staple crops, fruit trees, and livestock, but this was the first tobacco field he had seen since being dropped off by Utari's fast-sailing sloop.

The first order of business was to get a feel for the rhythms of the castle's lands, filling in gaps in the knowledge of local spies.

The Specter relied on his Reapers to guard the castle and the tobacco fields at night; Valentine had made sure of that after the second day's observation. Ordinary Jamaicans avoided the acres around the castle as if the air were toxic. Women dressed in neat cotton smocks or heavy black dresses worked the Specter's personal fields and orchards as their children played amongst the crops. Valentine guessed by the quality of their clothing and shoes that they were families of his Horsed Police. They worked in a curiously lack-adaisical, though not disorganized, manner. Valentine had seen many fields where the people under the Kurian thumb worked with the maniacal intensity brought on by knowing that whoever turned in fewer bushels at the end of a season would go to the Reapers.

The Reapers, with their innate ability to sense human beings by the lifesign they projected, could spot anyone approaching the castle at night across the fields. Thus had the brave Jamaican band died the night they came to kill the Specter. The men might as well have approached the castle shooting off Roman candles. At night a cluster of humans could be marked miles away by a prowling Reaper. Even a lone man would show up in the empty fields as if a spotlight were shining on him from one of the four corner towers.

But Valentine was another matter. The Lifeweaver training of six years as a Hunter had taught him to shield his lifesign through mental discipline, a practice of shutting down parts of his mind until he became intent as a prowling cat, thinking only of the furtive scratching of the rat in the drainpipe ahead. Once in the proper mental state, it was as if a skeleton wearing his body were performing on a stage, marionetted by invisible strings from himself somewhere in a balcony above. Jamaica's tropical growth and abundant animal life generated its own form of lifesign, masked him from the prowling Reapers, and allowed him to remain at the edge of the fields in comparative safety.

He had another ability, equally useful but less explicable, even to the seemingly all-knowing Lifeweavers who had selected and trained him. Valentine could sense a nearby Reaper, mirroring its own ability to detect lifesign, though his own senses were far less precise than those of the vampiric Reapers. He once described the sensation to Alessa Duvalier as akin to "feeling where the sun is with your eyes shut." Though to be more accurate, it felt more like a cold presence in his mind, the creepy alarm that most people experience sometime in their lives when they wake up suddenly with the fear that someone is in their bedroom. The ability was unpredictable: sometimes he could sense a Reaper moving on a wooded slope a mile away, but other times walk over one sleeping in a basement below him with only a vague feeling of unease. In the absence of any authoritative opinion, he formed a theory that his ability had to do with the mental connection between the Reaper and its Master Kurian, but like most theories, it was probably half-right at best. Anecdotal evidence suggested there were others like him. Stories filtered in from elsewhere about other Hunters with the talent, but he had never met one and compared notes.

From the uncomfortable cradle of a palm tree, he spent the second night concentrating on lowering his lifesign and sensing the Reapers' movements. For what the sense was worth—and the more precise evidence of eyes, ears, and nose during his observation—he determined that the Specter loosed two Reapers to prowl his lands at night. One watched from the castle tower nearest the road. As would be expected, they retired with the dawn before the first women appeared on the road from the old colonial town.

He spent the third day in a long, agonizing crawl into the tobacco fields. Burdened by Ahn-Kha's oversize gun and decorated with some of the broad leaves cut from the crop, he inched through the fields at a speed a determined beetle could pace.

The crawl, punctuated by drowsy half-naps in the shadow of the tobacco stalks, gave him time to reflect on his plans. It was long past the point where he could change them, but his mind was nonetheless plagued with worries that he barred from his nighttime meditations.

What if the *Thunderbolt* was delayed in its journey? Her diesels were reliable but so ancient, a breakdown could not be discounted. How long could he stretch his two canteens, one now containing only a mouthful of water or two, in Jamaica's heat?

He might be able to hide his lifesign from Reapers, but he

had seen lean brown dogs chasing and playing with the children as their families worked. Suppose one scented him and started barking? His cumbersome, single-shot Grog gun would be almost worthless in a running fight with the Horsed Police.

Could he get close enough to the castle so he could be sure of the leaf-sights on the rifle? Some unknown pirate of the commodore's command had looted the gun's telescopic lens, which would have allowed him to take advantage of its range. ("I'm sorry," Carrasca had said, "but any kind of optics are almost priceless here." A strict inquiry among the crew had yielded nothing but shrugs.)

He had spent two nights awake and taken only brief naps in the day. Suppose he fell asleep lying amongst the tobacco stalks on the most dangerous night of all? One vivid dream or a sudden awakening would reveal him to the patrolling Reapers, and that would be the end of him: even the toughest Bear would not challenge multiple Reapers alone at night.

Alone, with only fear to keep him company, he slithered beneath the tobacco leaves. He wished for the comfort of Ahn-Kha's presence. But Ahn-Kha was off to the east somewhere with his Grogs and some Jamaican friends of Captain Utari's, hiding from the comment their appearance would excite.

Post was resting in the old auxiliary hospital ship on the other side of the island, and the rest of his shipmates in the *Thunderbolt* were beyond the horizon. The Jamaicans could be trusted to keep secrets from the Police and the Specter's henchmen, but undoubtedly there were a few spies in the community. Suppose one should learn of their presence, and a hunt ensue?

Right now the Specter thought himself secure, but at the first word of a plot, he would retreat to his deepest hole guarded by the fury of a dozen Reapers, with his mounted men riding to his aid from every station for miles around. What then?

Valentine wanted to succeed, not just for the sake of regaining use of the *Thunderbolt*, but also for the aging commodore's hopes. There was more to his dream of a free Jamaica than space for his polyglot of buccaneers and refugees. A new freehold in the Caribbean in alliance with the Dutchmen to the south might mean much to the larger struggle.

His final plan had come to him only after hearing a description of the Specter's refuge.

"Some old British Empire mon build d' ting," Captain Utari explained, his cadence as rolling as the sea he traveled on, going on oral tradition and boyhood memory. "It 'twas like out of d' history book, high walls and towers at d' corner. For years 'twas empty, but de Specter, he brought it back and set it all up to his likin'. Dey say he do as much diggin' as buildin' an' it has basements an' catacombs beneath. You can see de ol' Devil at times, up on his balcony or the towers, watchin' us an' seein' to deem."

By *us* and *deem* the captain meant the Jamaicans and the Asian master caste the Specter had imposed upon them. On further inquiry, Valentine learned that the balcony faced the sea, looking out on a wide bay. The description transformed his vague idea into a plan. He talked it over, first with Ahn-Kha, and then with the Grog's refinements put a finished plan before the triumvirate of the commodore, Lisi, and Carrasca.

He stopped his crawl three-quarters of the way across the field. Any closer, and his view of the balcony would be disturbed. Captain Utari's description of the castle was accurate enough, though Valentine had always pictured medieval style castles as being much larger—he had seen pre-Kur houses nearly as big as this walled hold. But close up, he could see why the Specter chose this building for his lair. The towers, the narrow windows, the heavy stonework, even its grim, isolated location would appeal to a Kurian.

Nothing but the insects disturbed him during the long, drowsy day in the field. The sun sank, the stars emerged, and

Valentine removed his mind from his body. Again the Reaper patrolled the edges of the fields as another stood in the tower, its head turning this way and that like a watchful owl. A curious fit of optics made the stars around the figure dimmer as Valentine stared, as if the thing were drawing the energy even from the twinkling star field. The Undertaker blew fitfully off the mountains, neither as strong nor as pleasant as its daytime sibling. An afternoon rain shower had left him cold and even more uncomfortable rather than refreshed, and the omnipresent flies and ants took their turns at disturbing his self-hypnosis.

Dawn approached, and a heavier rain set in, something Carrasca had assured him was almost unknown at this time of year. Valentine cursed the rain, the poor visibility, and Carrasca's meteorological acumen at dripping length. But with the sun, the clouds thinned and dissolved, fleeing in a burst of sky-flaming color.

The Reaper retreated with the growing light of dawn. Valentine, muscles aching, fought the urge to rise, to try to gain a view of the bay that would allow him to see if the *Thunderbolt* approached. Her blockish ugliness would be a comfort to him, and if things went badly—what the commodore called "tits up"—the gunboat's cannon could throw the coastline into enough confusion to allow him to escape.

The women on their way to their day's work in the fields saw her first. Valentine watched them point and chatter, suffusing a warm wave of relief through his clammy body. He pressed Ahn-Kha's gun to his shoulder and checked the slide of the sight for the umpteenth time.

The gun rested in an improvised bipod, a screwed-together contraption the Chief designed to help him with the weight of the gun. He had tied lengths of creeper to the barrel, careful not to obscure the foresight, over the dingy and green leather covering Ahn-Kha had sewn over the barrel. The gnarled, shillelagh-like stock was built for the Grog's larger frame, but Valentine padded the end with canvas stuffed with sawdust so it fit snugly into the crook of his arm. He opened the bolt and slid one of the .50-caliber bullets into the breech.

At this range, even firing upward, Ahn-Kha's shells would have a nearly flat trajectory. Valentine breathed slowly and deeply. He'd heard that the Kurians could sense lifesign as easily as their Reapers, but precise information was scanty. With the waxing dawn he knew that detection would grow even more difficult: sunlight interfered with whatever waves humans emitted. He tried not to wonder what was transpiring in the dark castle. No doubt some daytime sentry had alerted his officer, who would have a look, then perhaps pass the word of the *Thunderbolt*'s arrival to one of the Specter's retinue.

Valentine bet his life, so to speak, on the Kurian coming himself. The Specter would wonder what the *Thunderbolt*'s appearance portended. The Kur of New Orleans might have told him that their ship would be operating in his waters, but would he trust their word? She could mean the arrival of an ally in his on-again, off-again war with the pirates on the north coast, or an attempt by some other Kurian to supplant him and take the plentiful aura-fodder of the island.

By the plan, Carrasca was to bring the *Thunderbolt* into the bay and put troops into her boats. The Kurian would be eager to see, from his faraway vantage, whether the approaching men would behave as friends or foes.

The fortress came to life. Valentine watched two horsemen gallop out from behind the castle, one riding hard for the town, and the other turning on the road west. As the riders galloped away, hanging on to their mounts' manes, three torsos appeared on the tower. They changed from silhouettes to figures in the growing light. One held a box with a high antenna waving back and forth in the confused airs that preceded the Doctor's offshore breeze.

Valentine hardened his eyes as the figures went to the edge of the balcony. He sighted down the barrel with his own telescopic vision. The view sharpened, detail springing to life as his visual sense came at his will. The three figures became individual portraits. One was undoubtedly a Reaper, hood pulled well over its head to ward off the morning sun, another a rail-thin black figure, perhaps a Jamaican. Between those two, a fleshy, sagging form emerged. The first Kurian Valentine was to hunt reminded him of a Buddha in flesh instead of bronze. Though the Kurians, like their Lifeweaver brethren, could appear as Eve's serpent or Abraham Lincoln if they wished. But this Kurian, for whatever reason, did not choose to put much effort into his human form. Hairless, with skin as gray as a corpse, it seemed to float to the balcony rather than walk. Valentine moved the rifle a fraction of an inch, putting the foresight squarely in the center of the Kurian's sagging chest. He placed his finger on the trigger and looked into the face of evil.

Valentine felt a shudder creep up his spine as their eyes met over the distance. The Kurian read him and his intent in a flash of thought. Valentine's mind clouded—he felt a rush of vertigo as if he were standing before an abyss. A kaleidoscope of color coalesced, filling his vision, a mental fog of chaos from which he would not return.

He squeezed the trigger as he felt his will fleeing. The recoil of the shot jarred his frame, startled him like a slap in the face, breaking the psychic link. As through a haze he saw a wound blossom at the Buddha statue's throat. The Specter's jaw dropped open in a silent, gaping scream even as the kick of the huge bullet flung it backwards, misting the back of the balcony with purplish fluid. But the disguise stayed. For a moment Valentine feared that even Ahn-Kha's bullet, big enough to drop an elephant, would not kill it, but then the head lolled. It sagged forward again, as if it were mounted on a rocking chair, and collapsed into something that looked like an umbrella with a bulbous octopus head at the top. Valentine heard a faint splat as it fell.

The Cat lay still, fighting the instinct to get up and flee. He knew his single shot would be hard to locate from any kind of distance. So he waited for the collapse he expected to begin.

The Kurian no longer animated the Reaper; the cloaked figure stalked the balcony to slay in animal panic. It seized the thin man by the throat, popping off the Jamaican's head even as its mouth sank against the neck. Blood fountained, sprinkling the Reaper, the rail, and the castle wall as the beast dragged its victim into the shadows.

While daylight lasted, Valentine had little to fear from the fiends now prowling the halls of the castle. With the link to the Kurian gone, the Reapers inside would mindlessly slay whoever remained behind the walls, and trouble no one until darkness came. Any Reapers wandering the lands of the Specter would probably do the same, grab a victim and retreat into a dark hole. Valentine felt a feral, id-tickling thrill at the thought of the fate of any of the Specter's Horsed Police sharing shelter with the vampires.

Eventually, and with proper organization, the masterless Reapers could be hunted and burned out of their holes. But that would have to come later.

He inched backwards among the tobacco plants. With chaos sitting in the Specter's throne, the Kurian's realm would totter and be ripe for the taking. It was time for him and Ahn-Kha to hasten its fall. As he crawled between the stalks, the freshly fed Reaper at the door to the balcony shielded its face from the morning sun and retreated into shadow.

"So this is the Crying Man."

If Obay was over six feet, it was by the width of an eyelash. Nor did she have four breasts. There was enough flesh beneath her woven robes—like Joseph's composed of many hues—on her to make it look as though she had an extra set. She had liver-spotted skin the color of milky tea and a crinkled forehead, with gray-black hair drawn back in tight braids. Obay walked with the help of two men—sons, Valentine soon learned—and a pair of canes.

The Specter had been dead for twenty-two hours, and his regime was melting away like ice in the Caribbean sun. Captain Utari had brought Valentine and Ahn-Kha to a trailside village with mountains blue green in the background, mottled by the shadows of clouds. Faint sounds of gunfire echoed from the direction of the main road to Kingston. Armed Jamaicans of every description, from a blue-eyed Scandinavian or two to glossy African, filled every piece of shade in the village. Most carried machetes and a smattering of old rifles. The smell of roasting pigs, horsemeat, and corn came from clay or brick ovens and oil drums used as barbecues. "Two of d' kernels bring d' men to Obay's call," Utari explained.

"Not enough. Not enough for the town I saw," Ahn-Kha said. He, the *Thunderbolt*'s Grogs, and Utari's men had been hidden on the outskirts of Kingston.

"More come every day. Don't forget our people, an' de city folks. We've waiteed for de day of liberation. When Obay make her promeese—"

"Her prediction, you mean?" Valentine cut in.

"A 'prediction' from Obay is a promeese, Cryin' Mon. You d' proof."

They went into a whitewashed brick house at the center of the village's only street, sixty or seventy feet of asphalt flanked by gravel roads. By the shaded windowlight Valentine met the Kernels under a brightly painted ceiling mural of crops and trees and birds and frogs. The owner of the house welcomed them with hugs before she and her family went back to bobbing before Obay. There was an oddly dressed retinue to either side of the oracle. One wore what looked to be the final remnants of a priest's vestments; the other had gold tassels and yellow braiding sewn to the shoulder of a sleeveless green dress army coat.

"Thank you, boys," Obay said, after recognizing Valentine. She extended a hand. Valentine shook it, touching a heavy ring on her forefinger with a jewel the size of a pea.

He took another look, trying to read the script, as Ahn-Kha engulfed her hand in his long fingers.

"Yale. I would have been class of '23," Obay explained,

sticking out her hand. The knuckles were enlarged with arthritis.

It was a pretty thing, but it looked like a man's. Valentine wasn't sure what to say, so he fell back on what his father used to ask the educated of the Old Order. "What did you study?"

"Pre-law. I buried the needle on my SATs."

"Essay T's?"

"S. A. Ts. Scholastic aptitude tests."

Valentine was flummoxed. "You had to do well on those to be allowed to learn? Sounds self-defeating."

"There's a long answer, but it's not important. Of course, it didn't hurt that my father was a vice president with General Mills. I started as a freshman with a major in Anthropology. Coddled rebellion. Then I got a taste of academics and college politics. I wised up by the end of my sophomore year. I switched to pre-law. With a history minor—I'd always enjoyed it, and you should take your share of fun those years."

"Never had the opportunity. Unless you count some classes at a shoestring war college. They didn't give out souvenirs."

Her sons helped her sit down on a bench. The assembly took their seats on chairs ringing the main room of the tiny house. Except for Ahn-Kha. The bench he tried let out such a groan that he shifted his buttocks forward to a comfortable squat with the bench as a backrest.

Obay looked down at her ring. "I was doing an internship in Boston when the Ravies hit. I ended up on a cleanup crew behind a guard unit. Loading bodies. Even martial law was breaking down—it didn't look like there'd be bar exams for a while. I saw the ring on a body—he had a suit worth a good three thousand dollars—and thought, what the hell."

"Boston's a long way from Jamaica."

"My father. Pulled every string with every man he'd ever known."

"Did he make it out with you?"

"He didn't even try. The airport was a nightmare. Gun battles between Boston Police and Massachusetts State Troopers and the National Guard. Nobody had orders. People crying, begging. I saw a man shoot himself right in front of his family."

She related her story without the shocked, vacant look that Valentine had seen on so many survivors of those days.

"I got flown down here with a bunch of children in a jet with enough fuel for a one-way trip. I guess there was a rumor that Jamaica was Ravies-free. A lot of the kids were sitting two and three to a seat. Babies crying. It was a frightening ride. The bombs were going off by then, and planes were dropping from the electromagnetic pulse. There was an army captain on board. Talked me and the kids through it. We ended up married just before I had my first boy."

She looked at the man in the vestments. Now that Valentine knew her face, he saw a hint of Obay around the son's eyes.

"Your visions are pretty accurate. A law firm could have used that, predicting a judge's decisions."

"Oh, that came later. Wasn't something I was born with. Given to me. I suspect you know a few Lifeweavers, too."

Valentine said nothing.

"One came to Jamaica. He had a small group of men—I suppose they were some kind of Special Forces. A mixture of Americans and British and Cuban soldiers, I think, going by the flags on the uniforms. The visit was brief; he was being chased."

The light broke through Valentine's doubts.

"I didn't understand much of what he had to say. I never even learned his name. Everyone called him 'the Brother.' It made him sound like a Mormon or an Amish or whoever that was that called each other that. Then I found out he was more like *The Brother from Another Planet.* He said I was going to be part of a new communications network. A biological one. They had me drink some kind of goop out of a tequila bottle, and I passed out for a few hours. When I came around, the Brother character was speaking in my head. Soon as he saw I was alive and getting his words without him using his mouth, he started glowing and told the rest 'Obey her.' Pointing at me, you see. Then he and the soldiers left. It made an impression on the kids. Everyone kept looking at me and repeating 'Obey.' Duane, my captain, had us go into a town in the mountains.

"Whatever he did to me, it didn't quite take, at least in the way you'd think telepathy should work. I get strange images now and then. Visions, pictures—sounds sometimes. Just had an audio last week with a lot of gunfire and explosions. The vision about you, it was a gray ship that seemed to be made of thunderclouds, and I saw your face, clear as I see it now. Your friend, Mr. Ahn-Kha, he was part of the clouds, too, with lightning in his eyes and fingertips."

"What do you see for the future?"

"Nothing from the Brother. But the men my sons lead will take care of their end, if your ships can help us with the garrison in Kingston."

"Dey come. Dey come tomorrow, Obay," Utari said.

"And then what?" Valentine asked.

Obay looked at the ceiling. The island's panoply absorbed her for a moment; then she returned her eyes to Valentine. "A new Jamaica. For all the factions, I hope and pray. With the Specter gone, even the Cockpit Country might see reason."

"And you?"

Obay played with her ring, twirling it on the shrunken digit between the enlarged knuckles. "Might end up using the old law studies before I die after all. What kind of constitution do you folks operate under there in the Ozarks?"

"They're landing now."

Valentine looked down from his perch on a rooftop water tower at Kingston in turmoil. Two days after the death of the Specter, the *Thunderbolt* and a pair of three-mast clippers sailed into the harbor as though in a naval show. All three ships were filled to overflowing with every willing man of the commodore's who could shoulder a rifle.

Faint booms came up from the docks. The *Thunderbolt*'s gun systematically blasted the harbor defenses. The posts were manned by the few troops still obeying orders under the Horsed Police officer. According to the Kernels, a Horsed Police officer named Colonel Hsei had tried to take control of the Specter's organization.

Valentine and Ahn-Kha, through their Kingston contacts, probably knew more about Hsei's struggle to assume the reins than the warlord himself. Formerly in charge of the city's garrison, the colonel managed to keep many of his troops together, even as the Public Police vanished into the countryside. Valentine had to admire Hsei's execution, if not his methods. A storeroom beside the regimental stables held the bodies of rivals and subordinates who failed to agree with his plan for Jamaica's future.

The same grapevine passed word to the inhabitants of Kingston that with the arrival of the ships, the north side of the island would finish the liberation of the south. The sons of Obay guided Valentine and Ahn-Kha to the city, and the Jamaicans filled rooms and streets with men and women eager to meet "the Crying Man" who had delivered them from the Specter. As they moved from village to city, time after time Valentine felt the touch of eager hands, as if physical contact with him somehow guaranteed their freedom.

Now buildings burned, and the clatter of hooves and echoing shots told the tale of the rising city. Ever since Valentine's arrival, machete and club had been matched against horse and gun, but without the Specter's organization and Reapers, Hsei's command had begun to crack. The booming arrival of the *Thunderbolt* and the commodore's flotilla turned confusion into collapse.

Valentine, Ahn-Kha, and a group of armed Jamaicans had occupied what in the late world had been a professional building of some kind. It was three stories of whitewashed brick, with broad balconies servicing the network of rooms inside. Until the Specter's death, it had been a barracks of the Public Police. Valentine chose it for its view of the city and of the main road north out of town. Equally useful for holding up reinforcements or Colonel Hsei's troops, its strategic location demanded occupation with what forces he could organize. The enthusiastic Jamaicans, led by men and women who had sprung seemingly from nowhere, had barricaded the highway before the building and lined the railings of the balconies with mattresses and furniture. Anyone trying to pass along the highway would hit the choke point and come under gunfire at a range that made skill superfluous.

Ahn-Kha looked out across the rooftops from beneath a straw hat and canvas parasol. Despite his fawn-colored fur and thick hide, he suffered from Jamaica's sun more than his bronze-skinned friend. They stood together on a tiny platform running around the edges of a rooftop watertower supplying the barracks.

"And the police, my David? How are they reacting?"

Valentine watched the *Thunderbolt* spit fire from her Oerlikon into a rusted crane, one of the harbor's few strongpoints still fighting. A body, ant-size at the distance, plummeted from the tower.

"They're running. Looks like they have a dock secured. *Polaris* and *Vega* are being tied up to the docks—they didn't even have to send in boats. It's almost over."

"But not for us."

The Cat turned his gaze to the captain's compound. "It looks like Hsei has seen enough. Two trucks are being loaded up at headquarters. Horses too. Hell, they're firing into the mob again. Wait—yes, they are coming this way. The informants were right—he's going to run north toward the mountain stations. Better get your Grogs to the windows."

The Golden One picked up his long gun and moved to the roof-access ladder. Valentine watched the column for another minute, just to make certain of its direction. Hsei's men had perhaps been unnerved. The group leaving the barracks was as much of a mob as the Jamaicans hurling rocks from the alleys.

He swung down from the water tower and jumped to the gravel-covered roof, careful to land on his good leg. The work ahead would be bloody; he hoped it would be brief. Allowing Colonel Hsei to escape into the countryside with even a nucleus of armed men might mean trouble for the commodore and the Jamaicans in the days ahead; it would take weeks to organize an occupation of the various stations, forts, and barracks strung out across the Specter's lands. In the meantime, others might rally around the colonel.

Picking up his old Russian-made gun with its drum clip, he hurried down to the first floor. Grinning Jamaicans all around brandished their weapons and called out to him in their local patois. He understood only a phrase or two.

"D' dundus comin', mon?"

"We cut dey bakra asses now!"

Valentine nodded to their officer and went out to the front of the building. He and Ahn-Kha walked the balconies, cutting a serpentine trail down to the first floor, nodding and clapping the Jamaicans on the shoulder. "Keep down and wait for the horn!" he said, over and over again until it became as much of a singsong as their greetings.

He looked out at the barricade from the first floor, where Ahn-Kha's Grogs waited, covering the street from the windows and doors of the front of the building. What had been a parking lot sloped down to the highway. Carts and wreckage had been arranged to force any traffic moving up the road to negotiate a hairpin turn. Valentine wanted the obstacle to look to be the result of accident rather than design, so Hsei would stick his neck well into the trap before it snapped shut.

Valentine knelt behind the walkway barricade and searched southward with his hard ears. He picked up the sound of diesels and hooves. He nodded to Ahn-Kha, who had been walking back and forth in front of his Grogs, grunting out orders as he moved along the sidewalk fronting the shuttered windows. Ahn-Kha picked up a tarnished circular horn, an ancient foxhunting relic from Jamaica's colonial past. It had been gathering cobwebs on the wall of the barracks until one of the Grogs decided it would make an interesting headband.

The first horses reached the barricade, galloping pell-mell up the potholed road. Some fools fired from one of the upper levels, but neither the riders nor the horses took hit or heed. A horse vaulted over the frame of a broken sofa, unseating its rider. Valentine let the others pass and chambered a round in the PPD.

The first of the mass of riders trotted into view, coming up over a rise in the road like ships appearing over the horizon. Behind the clattering riders came the grinding gears of the two trucks and the higher pitched farting of a motorbike. Ahn-Kha barked something to his Grogs.

"Wait for the signal," Valentine said, loudly enough so it would carry to the balcony above him.

"Wait," he repeated.

The riders approached.

"Wait."

The Horsed Police slowed their horses to a walk as they saw the obstacles.

"Wait."

Now he could see the trucks: beds crammed with equipment, furnishings, and loot. Women and children, probably families of some of the Horsed Police, rode atop and among the cargo. Corrugated aluminum welded over the doors and windows protected the driver and passenger. A motorcycle with a sidecar puttered before the big diesels, but the sidecar held only a mound of possessions rather than a passenger ready to fire the machine gun mounted there. More soldiers jogged amongst the mob, already panting and casting aside their weapons in an effort to keep up with engines and horses. Strained, anxious faces in a dozen different skin tones looked warily at the partially blocked road and to the buildings at either side.

The vanguard of horsemen did not like what they saw and called to their fellows, drawing rifles and shotguns from saddle sheaths.

Valentine nodded at Ahn-Kha, who blew into the circular horn. Its wavering wail filled the air.

Wide-shouldered Grogs filled the windows and doors of the first floor of the barracks. Valentine heard shots crack from above. Horses screamed and plunged as their riders turned tail, fell out of the saddle, or dismounted by flinging themselves to the ground.

Valentine dropped two uniformed Jamaicans shouting orders. The PPD chattered out its harsh coda as he aimed short bursts into the crowd. Ahn-Kha methodically fired his rifle into the aluminum-covered cabins of the vehicles. The .50-caliber rounds blasted thumb-size holes in the plating and slumped the drivers within.

Cartridges fell like brassy hail from the balconies above as the Jamaicans emptied their weapons into the mob.

The motorcycle roared to life. Its uniformed rider gunned it, expertly swerved around dying horses and between the barricades. The cyclist threw his hips off the saddle to counterweight the tight slalom. The colorful insignia on the rider's uniform tipped Valentine to his identity: Hsei. He fired a burst but missed the racing figure.

"Ahn-Kha! The motorcycle!" he shouted.

Ahn-Kha stood and took a round from his mouth. In battle, the Grog kept cartridges in his lips, tucked into his flexible ears, and between his knuckles. He closed the breech of his gun, sighted, and fired. The bullet's impact threw the rider bodily into the motorcycle's handlebars. The bike spun sideways and crashed.

One truck, its driver dead, went nose-first into the ditch at the side of the highway. Riders and cargo tumbled forward and out. The truck behind halted, dead horses blocking its path.

Jamaicans flooded the street, wielding improvised weapons. Some grabbed the unwounded horses and ran off, leading their prizes. Others leapt into the trucks, looking for booty. But most of the mob concentrated their energies on the hated Horsed Police.

"Cease fire!" Valentine yelled, fearing any more firing would do more harm than good. At a word from Ahn-Kha, the Grogs put up their smoking guns.

Years of death and brutal treatment resulted in ugly scenes in the street. Whole and wounded Horsed Police, their hands raised in surrender, fell victim to the mob. A few Jamaicans flung themselves over the wounded and protected them from the clubs and knives with their own flesh, but the mob merely sought other targets. Valentine heard women's screams and saw some of the Horsed Police's children caught up in the mob's fury. A child fell under a club, skull opened and yellow-gray brains spilling to the pavement.

He shouldered his way into the crowd, stepping over bodies of the dead and dying, and jumped on the cab of the second truck. He fired his gun in the air.

"Enough!" he yelled, putting every decibel his body could produce into the bellow.

Ahn-Kha grabbed a horse, threw off its saddle, and mounted. He led his Grogs into the fray. The spectacle of the strange, apelike creatures distracted the mob enough for Valentine to get their attention. Eyes turned to Valentine and the Grogs.

"Enough!" he shouted, forcing a grin to his face. "The time of death is over!"

The mob turned from rage to celebration. Jamaicans joined Valentine atop the truck, waving their arms and calling out to their fellows.

"Free!" "Death is dead!" "Death is over!" came the cries.

Something gave way inside the exhausted Cat. He stood in the celebrating throng, shaking with exhaustion and emotion. He realized his head hurt; the sun struck his eyes like knives. He summoned a few Jamaicans and began to carry the surviving wounded into the shelter of the barracks. As his hands grew sticky with sweat and blood, he thought of the clean sea.

Chapter Six

Hispaniola, April: The largest island of the Caribbean has a record of woe. The rugged land remembers only moments of peace in its long history of strife and sorrow. Rule by colonial aristocrats, despots, corporations, or military dictatorships made no difference to the impoverished inhabitants. The new boss, as the twentieth-century song said, was much the same as the old one. The passage of the Kurians across their green island made the rest of their unhappy past a mere warm-up for the horrors to come.

The island's role as one of the first gateways of the Kur's invasion shrank the populace from the millions to the thousands. When the Kurians arrived, their Reapers hunted down the Hispaniolans in even the most remote villages on their way north, south, and west. The few slaughter-shocked inhabitants of the island remember these years in oral tradition as "La Fiesta de Diablos."

The beauty of the island stands in contrast to the ugliness of its history. Royal palms tower over empty towns, vanishing under a carpet of leafy vines. Nature left to itself covered the eroded scars left by charcoal gatherers in a dozen years. Cackling colonies of birds flit from enormous palm to enormous palm over an ocean of lesser trees and creepers. Gulls and sandpipers congregate on empty beaches, nesting in washed-up fishing boats. Further inland, wild dogs and pigs hunt and root through new and thriving forests.

What civilization there is exists on the east side of the island, where the Kurian families rule a retinue of Quislings

from the gray ziggurat of the Columbus lighthouse. A few
coastal communities dot the perimeter of the island, sending
tribute to the Dark Lords in the east. Their combined
Reapers hunt farther inland, or land here and there along
the coast in search of auras. Perhaps something of the spirit
of Columbus has entered the Santo Domingo Kurians, for
they are some of the few who venture into the sea in ships in
their predatory wanderings along Hispaniola's long coast-
line. The appearance of the Kurian "Drakkar" sends whole
towns fleeing into the mountains.

It was not a bad storm; the Caribbean sees far worse during hurricane season. The spring storm lashing the channel
in between Hispaniola and Cuba made up in bluster for what
it lacked in size.

Valentine watched Captain Carrasca on the *Thunder-*
bolt's bridge. A knotted rope and a stick, in a curious mix of
hairstyle and seamanship, restricted her thick hair to the
back of her head. She stood next to the wheel, bending first
one knee and then the other as she rolled with the ship's
motion like a slow metronome, owlish eyes watching the
storm.

Since leaving Jamaica—gaps in the crew filled with the
commodore's sailors—Carrasca had taught Valentine a
good deal about the islands of the Caribbean: cays and atolls
where some found refuge, larger islands such as Cuba and
Cozumel, which fed the appetite of the Kurians. She knew
winds and weather, currents and courses, radio procedure
and sail setting; she spoke of them as easily as Valentine
could describe his old platoons in the Wolves.

"How's the rudder?" she asked the steersman.

"Biting fine. She's a heavy ship. All that steel in this old
ice-shover. Wouldn't care to ride this out in the *Guideon.*
We'd have to heave-to."

"She's working. We're shipping more water than I'd like.
The sea hasn't worked up much—I'd put it at three meters."

"Four sometimes, Cap," the steersman said.

"Any sign of the coast?" Valentine asked, trying to pierce the rain-filled darkness forward.

"By dead reckoning, it's there," Carrasca answered. "I don't dare get much closer. The best harbors are on the other side of the island, and we can't use them."

Cool and professional. The warm moment they shared that night on the balcony where she admitted her thrill at her command seemed like a childhood game of you-show-me-yours-and-I'll-show-you-mine. Now she just watched him every now and then out of the corner of her eye, as though checking the professional wall between them for cracks.

"Your ships don't land here?"

"Nothing worth landing for, except fresh water or firewood. We hit richer lands. Now Cuba, there's good hunting there, especially on the north coast and in the stretch between it and the Florida peninsula."

"My work is on Hispaniola—the Haiti side."

"I'll get you there. Nothing's going to happen until this blows itself out, Valentine."

"I'll try and sleep. Have me woken if this clears, please."

Valentine descended from the bridge, weaving past a mix of the *Thunderbolt*'s old crew and new shipmates from Jamaica. He went to his cabin, formerly shared with Post, who now lay almost recovered in sick bay, thanks to the skilled teams of Jayport's aged hospital ship. Sea air and sun were speeding his recovery, but the former Coastal Marine was still not up and around for more than a few hours a day.

Ahn-Kha was on the cabin floor. The quarters smelled of Ahn-Kha's horsey odor and vomit, the contents of the Golden One's stomach having abandoned ship when the storm started.

"My David, take out your pistol and put an end to my suffering," Ahn-Kha groaned. He lay on his stomach, with four-fingered hands clasped over his pointed ears.

"Carrasca says it won't last long, old horse," Valentine replied. The motion stimulated Valentine, if anything, though he longed for surcease of the endless sounds of rain, wind, and the ship groaning in the weather.

"It's a new hell each hour."

"What's that?" Valentine asked, dropping into his bunk.

"My people . . . say there are four hells. The theosophists need to add one more, the Hell of Motion."

Valentine placed his boots on the floor, tucked them away from Ahn-Kha's head in case the Grog decided to bring up another ten gallons of digestive matter. Best to keep his friend's mind on something else. "They left out a hell?"

Ahn-Kha lay silent, as if gathering his words and putting them into English. "The Golden Ones believe that you must be purified by Hell before gaining Paradise. There is a Hell of Hunger and Thirst, a Hell of Pain, a Hell of Illness, and a Hell of Loneliness. If you suffer deeply of these in your life, you are spared them after death, and reach Paradise that much quicker."

"That's a lot of suffering to reach Heaven."

"By our creed, 'Only through suffering do you grow a soul capable of understanding others, and appreciating the'—what is it—the word for grace of gods?"

Valentine thought for a moment. "Beatitude?"

"I must look that up as soon as I can open my eyes again. I've never heard it. English has too many words for some things, and not enough for others. You take too long in the telling. Your words can never match the music of our proverb-verse."

"I'll work through a King James Bible with you. It'll change your opinion."

"Arrgh. Those tracts, most of them read like the family history of a group of nomad *pfump*-raisers. One of your theosophists tried to instill in me a belief in my own soul, and me having tasted only the bitter surface of the Hell of Loneliness and Hell of Pain in the time before we met. The fool. As if Paradise could be gained by affirming the divinity of some human. Bah!"

"I've always thought there was more to it than that, my friend."

"My David, if you wish to learn the true path to Paradise, you must read of the Golden Ones' *Rhapsodies*. Then you will be steeled to torments that must be overcome before a joyful afterlife."

"'There are four and fifty ways of constructing tribal lays, and every single one of them are right,'" Valentine quoted.

"Then what is your opinion of your gods?"

"God? You mean Bud?"

"There is only one? I thought you had two or three."

"Depends who you talk to," Valentine said, sinking into his bunk. On his back, the ship's motion seemed to tilt him headdown first, then feetdown.

"I don't remember anyone calling your god Bub."

"Bud. It's from an old story the top sergeant from Zulu Company used to tell."

"Old stories are the best ones. The bad ones die young. Tell me about Bud."

Valentine sifted his memory. "The sergeant's name was Patel. He was built almost as broad as you, a helluva wrestler, too, and he always fought clean unless someone tried something. Then it was anything goes. But back to the story, before he was in the Wolves, he fought with the regulars, the Guards—"

"Yes, I've seen them," Ahn-Kha said from the noisy darkness. "Good guns, better uniforms, and the best food."

"They can fight when it comes to it. I think when Patel was with 'em they didn't have the nicest clothing. Especially where he was. He said it started while he was watching the ground south of Saint Louis. For a while there, it was trench warfare: the men and Grogs working for the Kurians were trying to blast them out of these hills with artillery. Got so there wasn't a tree standing, but the Guards just kept digging and digging. They'd build little caves of wood with tons of dirt overhead—they were called 'dugouts.' Anyway he was young, and he had this real nervous NCO running the dugout these twenty men were crammed into. The damn Grogs—sorry, old horse—the damn Kurian Grogs started building these rockets they were launching off of railroad rails, and they had enough of a bang in them to collapse a dugout.

"When those babies landed, Patel said it felt like someone picked up the hill and dropped it again. The concussion outside was enough to stop your heart. Well, this corporal starts to lose it—they're in there and it's dark and cold and wet, with the noise and smell of burnt flesh, and as if that isn't bad enough, it seems like any minute they're going to get blown to hell.

" 'Get friendly with God!' this corporal starts shouting. 'The time's coming, and you'd better know him! You gotta know God and be on a first-name basis with him to get into heaven. Hurry up, guys!'

"Of course, some of the men just tell him to shut up, but you've always got a joker or two who thinks a nervous breakdown is entertainment, so they start quizzing him.

" 'Praise Jesus!' one hollers, trying to egg him on.

" 'I'm talking about God, not Jesus!' the corporal says. He keeps looking at the ceiling of the dugout. 'Know him. Love him.'

" 'Okay, what's God's name, then?'

"The corporal doesn't even think about it—he says *Bud* right away. Some of the guys think this is just too funny to let go.

" 'Bud is my shepherd, I shall not want,' one starts to say. They start misquoting stuff like 'Praise Bud!' and 'Bud, bless this stewed rat, which I'm about to eat, and probably puke up again.' "

"Skip the food part," Ahn-Kha groaned.

"Well, after a couple minutes of humor like that, some old soldier yells, 'Shut your Bud-damned mouths, for Bud's frickin' sake.'

"The corporal loses it, says he's not going to stay in there with a bunch of blasphemers, and he heads out of the dugout with the shells and rockets still landing all over the hills. Patel thinks the corp is going to get killed, and so he goes out after him. Patel catches up to him thirty yards away and jumps on him, wrestles him to the ground in the trench, when one of those rail-rockets lands right on the dugout. Kills every man in there, either the blast or suffocation did them in. Patel and a bunch of others, even the corporal, tried to dig out the shelter to rescue them, but no luck. Sure enough, some of the bodies are blue, and this corporal starts pointing at the ones who suffocated and saying 'Bud's mark!' and things like that.

"Patel and this corporal get out of the trenches and are posted with a new unit in western Missouri in the bush-whack ground. This corporal seems sound enough most of the time, but now and then he points out the color blue and says 'the Hand of Bud,' or something like that. One day they're on patrol on a footpath and he just freezes, with his head cocked like a dog listening to a whistle. He says that 'Bud's whispering in my ear.' A couple of the guys pass him, maybe they thought he was taking a leak without bothering to use his fly, and go right into a tripwire that fires this harpoon through two men. Patel said he started to think that old expression about God looking out for drunks, children, and idiots might be true.

"After that, this corporal turned into the kind of NCO that stays behind to watch over the sick and the supplies. Until this one day, there's a beautiful blue sky. So he decides to climb a tree and look at Bud's handiwork. He falls asleep up there, no one knows where he is, they figure this time he's really flipped and run off into the woods. They don't even bother looking for him. Which is too bad, because if they had been dispersed, these three Reapers passing through the area wouldn't have caught all that lifesign in the camp. They went in and killed everyone but the corporal, maybe when he was in the tree talking to Bud, he didn't put out much more lifesign than a cuckoo clock. After that, the corporal pulled kitchen duty at an infantry training school by Mountain Home.

"Patel ended up joining some Wolves who were hunting the Reapers, he made himself useful when they caught up to the bastards, and ended up in Zulu Company.

"Funny thing is, every now and then in a tight situation, I'd catch Patel saying, 'Bud help me' or something like that. I don't think he really believed it, but Patel wasn't taking any chances."

The storm blew itself out overnight. Valentine arose and dressed around the slumbering Ahn-Kha. He checked Post, who slept with his familiar snore in the tiny sick bay.

The indefatigable Carrasca still stood on the bridge. She looked as fresh and alert as when Valentine had last seen her, rocking with the storm.

"That's Haiti, Valentine, dead ahead."

Valentine stepped out onto the wing of the bridge. Something loomed ahead, a heavy presence in the darkness. As the light grew, he could make out mountains coated in green.

"Why the white knuckles?" Carrasca asked, joining him in the open air.

Her words weren't in the cool captain's voice with its self-assured intonation. They tickled his ear like a playful finger.

Valentine looked down at the decorative wood top to the rail where his hands gripped the painted metal. He breathed out, half-laugh and half-sigh. "For over a year, I've been trying to get here in the right kind of ship."

"Worth it, I hope. The commodore thinks you're chasing a rumor. Said it reminded him of the years after the Kurians first came, where ships and men were lost looking for remnants of the old society."

"That's what my father was doing when he ran into a Lifeweaver. This chase is something the Lifeweavers put me on."

She put binoculars to her eyes and searched the coast ahead. "How much do you know?"

"There's something on that island the Cause needs."

She frowned. "The Cause. You sound like Hawthorne of the hasty retreat."

Valentine involuntarily stiffened. Now a row of ghostly bodies lay between them, friends Valentine had lost, talents the world had lost, in the sake of "the Cause."

"I'm sorry," she said, looking away. "You've proved yourself to Jamaica."

"But not to you?" Valentine asked.

"It's the same thing."

Valentine stifled a laugh. He might have said those exact words. Jensen and Carrasca had proved themselves to the Cause by letting him use the ship, the same thing as proving themselves to him. He took his hands from the rail and rubbed life back into them.

Carrasca broke the silence: "Why is it nobody's thought to go get this whatever-it-is until now?"

"We didn't know it was there. It was put there hundreds of years ago by a Lifeweaver. He lived in secret among us, with a few followers. He guessed what the Kurians were planning, but he only knew about the one door. He and his people were ready for what was coming on Haiti, but something happened, they were betrayed, and I don't think anyone survived. One of the followers kept a journal of some kind, more as a record of that Lifeweaver's teachings, but in it was a section about this weapon against them.

"Like a lot of places, there's a resistance against the Kurians. These Haitians are fighting without really knowing what they're fighting. They just know it's evil, and they're doing what they can to protect their own people. They found a cache of weapons in a cave, along with this diary. They made sense of it and somehow word got passed to us. I never knew about it—I just got orders to join up with the Quislings on the Gulf Coast with fake papers and background. I think they chose me because I speak a little Spanish and French. My mother was from the French part of Canada, and I was raised by a priest from Puerto Rico. It took me a year, but I got into the Coastal Marines and managed to get myself posted to the right kind of ship to bring it back. It's a year I wouldn't care to repeat. Now it's like life in the Ozarks is something out of my childhood."

"Is there snow there?"

"Sometimes, in winter. The mountains aren't big enough to be snowcapped year-round. Why?"

"There's a story the people here tell. They think if you go somewhere there's snow all the time, like the north pole, the Kurians can't get you. It's all mixed up with stories about Christmas now, that there's this place everyone is safe from them with plenty of food and electronic toys and no fighting."

Valentine watched a frigate bird float above, drifting on the air currents with only the tiniest alterations to its wing.

"If only. I grew up almost in Canada. It gets colder in the winter than you can probably imagine, and the Reapers still made it up there. They don't come in winter, but we're still not out of it. You go much farther north from there, and the land can't support many people year-round away from the coasts. Just not enough to eat. And the old-timers say the climate is strange now, summers are longer and hotter, but somehow winter is even worse. God knows how the Kurians managed it. There's no safe place, or if there is, they're keeping it to themselves."

She nodded. "Cape Haitian is ahead. What is the plan?"

"The plan is to sail into the port as bold as if we have the proverbial balls of the brass monkey. We have a contact in town who'll get in touch with me. He's on the lookout for a ship from the north. Not sure what happens after that. Maybe we pull out and land somewhere nearby on the coast, and he gets us in touch with the resistance. They load us up, and back we go."

"Will it be that easy?"

Valentine found a smile. "Somehow I doubt it."

*   *   *

The *Thunderbolt* rounded Cape Haitian and turned her prow to the town, a cluster of white and gray snuggled into a stretch of flat land with mountains towering behind. The vivid colors of the Caribbean struck Valentine once more: deep blues of the ocean; brilliant blues and whites above; and behind stretches of white sand a green so lush, it hypnotized.

Fishing boats, hardly more than canoes, rocked in the gentle swell. Tall, lean black men threw nets into the water and gathered them again. If they noticed the *Thunderbolt*, they showed no sign of it. As the ship approached, Valentine observed that the fishermen were either naked or wearing stringy loincloths. Wiry muscle glistened under the sun.

A boat with four oarsmen put out from the docks. Its splashing approach scattered seabirds bobbing on the calm surface of the bay.

"Dead slow," Carrasca called into the bridge.

"Dead slow, aye aye," the junior officer there answered.

The bulky ship coasted to a crawl. The small boat cut across the prow, as if blocking the larger vessel's entry. A man in a simple gray uniform stood and put a speaking trumpet to his mouth.

"Que bâteau?" Valentine thought he heard.

"What did he say?"

"What ship is that?" Valentine translated.

"I thought they spoke Spanish here."

"Creole French, mostly. Or a form of it. But you can get along in Spanish, too."

Valentine inflated his lungs. *"Thunderbolt*, New Orleans. May we anchor here tonight? We will buy food," he bellowed, hoping his French would be understood.

"What do you do here?"

"We chase pirates. Have any sailing ships passed?"

"No, not close. Not since before the last hurricane season."

"May we drop anchor?"

The man lowered his speaking trumpet for a moment, then raised it again. "For now. Our officer will come. Do not lower your boat until then."

"Thank you!" Valentine yelled back.

The same four-oared boat brought out the "officer." Valentine watched him make the transition to the *Thunderbolt* with a fair amount of agility. He wore a similar uniform to his underling, though with gold buttons and a brilliant scarlet sash beneath his pistol belt.

Valentine went to greet him.

"Monsieur speaks French?" the man asked. His features were exaggerated: strong cheekbones, a pointed chin, knife-like nose, wide eyes, and handsome in a sensual, full-lipped way. Unlike most of the Hispaniolans Valentine had observed in the boats, who either had a full beard or were clean-shaved, he wore a mustache.

"And some Spanish," Valentine said, then realized, as visitor, it would be best if he began the introductions. "My captain is more comfortable in Spanish. I am Lieutenant Rowan, of the Coastal Marines," Valentine said, turning to introduce Carrasca. She wore a combination of her own Jamaican attire and a coat liberated from Captain Saunders's chest.

"*Sí, bueno. Muy encantado,*" he agreed, then touched his chest. "El Capitán Boul."

"I understand you wish to make use of our market?" Boul asked, seated in the captain's cabin. Even with a table fan blowing, the air settled wet and thick on the three people gathered in the small space. "We have only a few liters of diesel oil, I am sorry to say."

"My captain has ample fuel, but some fresh food and, of course, water would be most appreciated. We can barter or pay in gold."

"Ours is a poor market, unless you count fish. Though once word got around that you wished to buy, the people would bring in chickens, eggs, pigs, fresh fruit, and vegetables. It would take only a day or two more, and your ship would be fully provisioned."

Carrasca exchanged a look with Valentine and shook her head.

"I must be at sea again. The damned pirates have too long a lead even now."

"In our mutual interest, I will ask the fishermen as they come in. They see ships, especially in the waters between here and Cuba."

"If you hear any news between now and when we leave tomorrow, we would be most obliged. A few hours are all we need to replenish our fresh water supply."

Boul put up his hands placatingly. "My friends, if you choose to stay, I can guarantee most advantageous terms for your barter in the market. Our people would have little use for gold. But tools, trinkets, even pencils and paper will get you much good food."

Valentine leaned forward in his chair. "Captain, do you have some special reason to have us stay here?"

Boul drummed his fingers on the table, but stopped as soon as he looked down and realized what he was doing. "I will lay my cards down, as you New Orleans gamblers say. Though we pay tribute to the cursed ones on the other side of the island, we still suffer their torments. Even now one of their Drakkar, a wooden vessel known as the *Sharkfin,* approaches. On it are the Drinkers of Death, the robed ones who come in the dark. A ship such as yours in the harbor will make them think again about anchoring. I saw your gun—it would blow the *Sharkfin* into kindling. Our market is poor because even at the rumor of one of the Drakkar, the Dragon-ships, my people fly to the mountains."

"We can't stay here forever," Valentine said. "And were we to destroy the *Sharkfin,* New Orleans would hear about it, and it would be trouble for us."

"But you may save us this season. This would not hurt your patrol, perhaps three days here. And I do mean what I say about making inquiries among the fishermen. You may buy what you will, and each day you stay your men will feast on what my poor town can provide. We make a very good rum, vodka even from potatoes."

Carrasca nodded. "So be it. We shall stay a few days. We'll anchor so our gun can cover the sea. And your town, in case of treachery, Captain Boul."

"Thank you, Captain. You are helping my people a great deal. Though I cannot blame you for thinking it, do not fear treachery."

Valentine escorted Boul off the *Thunderbolt* and asked about springs flowing into town. Boul pointed out a beach and assured Valentine the water was good there. Nevertheless, Valentine made a mental note to remind the party about the water-purification tablets. He returned to the captain's cabin, knocked, and entered. They sat down and talked about the watering and market party.

"Fresh food and time. We lucked out," she said once they'd decided which men would do what.

"Unless this *Sharkfin* shows up. Much as it would be nice to blow it into flotsam, our cover story would suffer. Even worse, one of your own ships could sail in."

"Doubtful, nothing on this side of the island worth going after," she said.

"Well, with your permission, tomorrow I'll take a few men into town and have a look around. All I need to do is make it easy for this man to find me."

He stood up, as did she. As he turned sideways to get past her to go out the door, their chests touched. She glanced up into his eyes and then away, as if afraid of what she might find there.

The watering party left under the supervision of one of Carrasca's petty officers. They used the *Thunderbolt*'s two boats, the smaller motor launch and a lifeboat, heaped with plastic ten-gallon barrels. It wasn't the most efficient way to water the ship, which had been amply filled before leaving

Jamaica anyway, but it gave the men something to do and added a touch of realism to the story.

Under further instructions from Carrasca, they also returned with planking torn from an old fishing boat. Some men fashioned it into a raft and attached a makeshift flag; then they towed the target out beyond the surf for gunnery practice. Carrasca made sure the distance was greater than that to the town, and she had her men lob a few shells at the target, to impress those ashore that the gun worked and they had shells to spare. She still didn't trust anyone on Hispaniola, no matter what promises came from below a handsome mustache.

Valentine was with Post when the gun began to fire. The healing lieutenant startled at the sound.

"Just gunnery training. I told you, remember?"

Post was red-faced. "Sorry, Val." He raised his arm on his wounded side. "Nerves might not be healed yet, but the shoulder's working great. Hardly a twinge." He flapped an elbow and smothered a wince.

Valentine went to the market the next day. Much of the town looked to be in rubble, victim to wave and war, storm or earthquake, and never rebuilt. What was still standing was gaily painted: blue-trimmed doorways looked out from whitewashed buildings, and elaborate designs like a child's drawing of men and animals decorated awnings and window sills. The widest street in Cape Haitian was crowded with straw-hatted food vendors, selling produce out of wooden carts. Valentine and his men would have been besieged by beggars and hustlers, except Captain Boul sent a set of navy-uniformed gunmen to act as escorts and intermediaries in the market. Which was just as well, because the Creole dialect of the streets was beyond Valentine's French. The acting-purser simply picked out items, and the strongmen passed out what looked like beaded ribbons to the people in the market.

Shouted offers for liquor, drugs, and even women

tempted a few of the sailors, but Valentine and the petty officer kept them at work filling the cart.

"Hey Lieutenant, you want a good drink?" someone hallooed in English. "Wine, me got some wine. I have friends up North, and I know what you like, what you want."

Valentine spotted the man waving to him from the crowd, a dark bottle in his hand.

"Don't buy anything from that one, sailor sir," the sergeant of the escort said in a mixture of French and Spanish. "There's better wine to be found. Off, Dog-boy, or you'll be sorry."

He looked like a man to Valentine, and he didn't see any dogs. The man's eager eyes implored him across the sea of straw hats in the market, and he held out the bottle again. "Have a taste—you'll want more."

Valentine reached for the bottle, and one of the guards rewarded Dog-boy with a crack across the wrist with a baton. It dropped, but Valentine's reflexes saved it from crashing to the cobblestones.

"You don't want his piss, sailor sir."

Valentine sniffed the open mouth of the bottle. His ears picked up the sound of something clinking against the glass within. Dog-boy had disappeared into the crowd.

"Maybe I don't. I've got a drain that needs unclogging on board—I'll use it on that."

Valentine kept the bottle in his hand for the remainder of the session in the market, using it as a pointer. The purser and his men hauled their acquisitions back to the dock, yet another set of round trips were ahead for the motor launch.

Once back on board, past the Grogs hungrily eyeing the supplies coming alongside, he took his bottle down to the cabin and emptied it down the drain. Whatever was within refused to come out, so he smashed the bottle against the steel sink. A wooden tube, lacquered and stoppered, had been stuck inside. He examined it for a moment, then pulled out the cork, and extracted a rolled-up note from the tube:

To officer with black hair and scar—
I will come to your ship tonight after midnight.
I will swim to the anchor chain.
Must keep clear of soldiers in boats.

—Victo

Valentine read the note twice, then got Ahn-Kha and took it up to Carrasca.

"Is he telling us there is danger from soldiers in boats? Or that he has to swim clear of them?" Ahn-Kha asked, after the note had been passed around in the cabin.

"The Oerlikon could sink any number of boats," Carrasca said. "I've looked around the harbor. They have a lot of those canoe fishing boats. I suppose they could put a couple hundred men in the water, but we'd sink them before they got halfway here. But we might want to shift anchorage, farther out."

Valentine shook his head. "He'll have a tough enough swim as it is. Let's wait until he's on board."

There was a rap at the door, and a teenager entered. "Captain, one of those rowboats dropped off a letter," he reported.

"Thank you, Lloyd," Carrasca said, opening it.

"Today is a day for notes," Ahn-Kha observed.

She handed it to Valentine. "An invitation to a dinner and beach party in our honor tomorrow night. However many officers and men as I choose to bring. I smell a rat with a nice mustache."

"We'll make some excuse tomorrow during the day," Valentine said. "A radio message. As long as this Victo is on board, we can take our leave of *El Capitán Boul*."

"You think he means to take hostages?" Carrasca asked. "Why didn't he do it today? There must have been ten or twelve men on shore at various times. He could have taken you and your party. That would have given him something to bargain with."

"He could be waiting for orders."

"*Huevos*. The man's a schemer—I could read his eyes," she said, touching the corner of her own. "He may be playing us false, but it's to his own purposes."

"I'm going to arm Ahn-Kha's Grogs and what's left of my marines. You might want to have the machine guns ready tonight."

"They'll be manned. I want everyone to have a chance at fresh food, though. There's an old tradition at sea to give your men a good feed before action." Her expression softened into that of the woman he'd played mah-jongg with in Jamaica. "Would you care to have dinner with me in the cabin?"

"Far be it from me to break with tradition," Valentine said.

The food tasted better in the cooler night air. Valentine put on a plain white shirt with his best pair of pants fresh from the laundry and went lightly up the stairs to Carrasca's cabin. Askin, her only lieutenant, answered the door. A handsome young Jamaican with hair cropped so short it made Valentine think of peach fuzz, Askin was dressed in a trim black uniform decorated with a heavy silver whistle on a thick chain. A linen covering added a formal note to the table in the wardroom. The *Thunderbolt*'s best plates and cutlery lay upon it.

"We really should have asked Post, as well," Carrasca said. She wore the same blue uniform Valentine remembered from the dinner at Commodore Jensen's, though now it bore an epaulette on the right shoulder.

"He's only just started walking," Valentine reported.

"The Chief doesn't care for formal meals, and Ahn-Kha—"

"Just wouldn't fit in," Valentine finished. "I don't mean with us, but in this cabin."

"It would be a bit like having a horse in here for dinner," Carrasca laughed. She sat, and the men followed suit.

Carrasca began uncovering dishes. "Askin, you did wonders with the birds."

"A sugar glaze from the beets on this island," the lieutenant explained. His diction held only a hint of Calypso.

She took another cover off. "The bean-and-rice dish is mine. Sweet potatoes. Crab cakes with goat-milk butter, and a fruit platter."

Valentine took a bite of a buttery crab cake, feeling guilty that he hadn't brought anything. He turned to Askin. "The captain tells me you've landed here before."

"Farther along the north coast, near the Samaná Peninsula," Askin said. "We were chasing some little trading ship. They beached it and waded through the surf to escape us. It took us forever to take off the cargo. Something must have scared some of them worse inland, because they came scampering back."

"Did they say what it was?" Valentine asked.

"I think they got a look at one of the mines. Bauxite, maybe. Those and the sugar plantations—they're hell on earth. Hispaniola is the worst island in the Carib."

"The Kurians have a knack for doing that."

"That old Specter by Kingston, he was a saint compared with the creatures running Santo Domingo. They don't even try to keep their people alive."

Unspoken agreement turned the three to their dishes, further conversation might spoil their appetites. Valentine had seen his share of cruelty in his years facing Kur, and worse, recently participated in it as part of his assumed role as a Coastal Marine.

The meal ended with fruit for dessert and a single glass of wine chilled into sangria. There were no toasts this time. Askin excused himself, carrying two green bananas out with him.

"He has the bridge as soon as it gets dark, even though we're at anchor," Carrasca explained. "I told him to be extra careful tonight. I warned the watch to keep an eye open for our swimmer. Now we wait, David."

Valentine sipped at his sangria, enjoying the sound of his name from her lips. "I have no complaints. I'm left alone with a beautiful woman."

Carrasca smiled, her teeth gleaming against her dusky skin. "Captain Valentine, I'm shocked. A breach of etiquette. But for God's sake, don't stop."

Valentine's innards warmed to the wine and the spark in her eyes. "I haven't had a woman to talk to in a long time, Malia. When all this is over, when we can both relax and take off our respective hats, so to speak, I'd like to spend some time with you. You're someone I can talk to."

"So that's what you'd do with me? Conversation?"

He met her gaze. "Yes, long, in-depth conversations. Late into the night."

"Really, David?" she asked. "How long has it been since your last good conversation with a woman?"

"Over a year. In New Orleans I was tempted to pay a woman to talk to me, but I resisted."

"It's better to wait for a decent conversationalist," she agreed.

"Yes."

"I'd like to talk to you, too. I'm sure you'd enjoy it. Women with any Cuban blood in them—well, they make great conversational partners. You'd be amazed at how many different topics I'm familiar with."

"I'm sure," Valentine said, smelling her femininity in the confines of the dining cabin.

"It's a shame, now that you've got me thinking about it, I've been lacking in decent conversation myself. The only problem is, we're both married to our duty. We can't have the men thinking anything else."

"Maybe if we whispered—"

"I tend to shout at the top of my lungs, when I'm really interested in the subject."

Valentine laughed. "We couldn't have that."

Carrasca bit her lower lip. "You speak French. Perhaps we could have a short—"

The ship's Klaxon went off. They froze. At the second screaming blast of the alarm, they hurried out of the cabin to the bridge, just a few steps away.

Carrasca killed the Klaxon and picked up the ship's squawk-mic. "Battle stations, battle stations." Aspin spoke to the engine room, asking for maximum revolutions.

Valentine stepped aside for men rushing to their stations. He looked to the shoreline from the wing of the bridge. Five great bonfires lit up the beach outside Cape Haitian. Wide fishing boats with double-banked oars approached like giant water beetles, men crammed inside. Pot shots from shore zipped through the air or *ting*ed harmlessly against the steel sides of the ship.

Why would they approach with the bonfires behind them, making them perfect silhouettes for . . .

He went to the opposite side of the bridge, heart in his throat, and searched the darkness. The stars went right to the horizon in the clear tropical night. No ship sailed out there; that much could be seen. He heard Carrasca shouting orders for the anchor cable to be cut. Valentine went to a searchlight and threw the switch. He began a slow sweep of the seaward approaches of the harbor, the searchlight's electric buzz filling his ears.

He probed the darkness with a knife of light. The beam fell across something small and gray, approaching like a sea monster with part of its snout showing. Orange light flashed, and a shell howled as it landed just in front of the ship. Water fountained into the air. But the cannon's flash told him what hunted the *Thunderbolt* from the sea.

It was not Boul's wooden Drakkar, but a submarine! The commodore had mentioned some old diesel ships in the hands of the Haitian Kur. It had a low profile like something from the Second World War. He hardened his ears in that direction even as the second shell approached and picked out the sound of churning engines.

He grudgingly congratulated Boul for a clever poker game. The thought stayed frozen in his mind as the second shell hit forward, beneath him. Time faded; the next thing he was aware of was a disembodied floating feeling.

David, I'm not going to hold you up anymore, his mother said. *You'll have to swim for yourself.*

Cool, slightly slimy Minnesota lake water engulfed him as she let go. Fear . . . He kicked hard and spun his arms like wheels until he broke the surface and felt air on his face again. The panic changed to triumph.

Swimming, Mom! By myself! Look! he sputtered.

His mother's bronze face split into a smile under its wet tangle of glossy black hair. *You're a regular motorboat.*

David Valentine spat out a mouthful of Caribbean as he came to his senses, disoriented. Distant and muted sounds echoed over a roaring in his brain.

He bobbed in the ocean, the waves adding to his sensation of drunkenness. Woolly-brained, he watched the *Thunderbolt* cut her cable and get under way. Someone had the presence of mind to turn the Oerlikon from the shore boats to the attacking ship. Red tracers crossed overhead, seeking the exposed figures on the bridge of the submarine. The deadly fireworks played across the deck of the submarine, tearing the conning tower's men and machinery to pieces. The submarine's gun fired again, and its shell detonated in the wake of the now-moving target. The Oerlikon's tracers shifted, and this time tore through the thin shield of the submarine's cannon. The thirty-millimeter shells blasted the gun's crew from the deck in a series of whipcrack explosions.

Valentine noted, rather dully, the *Thunderbolt* turning to escape the harbor—leaving him behind. She and the submarine traded machine-gun fire; the bullets scrabbled against the respective port sides of the two ships. The ineffectual fire reminded Valentine of a pair of crabs battling with their oversize fighting claws, both too well armored to be damaged by the exchange.

Hard hands grabbed him by the shirt and hauled him into a boat. He looked around at a mass of black faces, eyes and teeth shining in the night. A few pointed their guns at him. He could make out voices now.

"Put those things down, you fools," Valentine barked in French. "I'm not going anywhere." He consoled himself with the sight of the *Thunderbolt*'s churning wake as she escaped the harbor.

They landed and trooped up the beach and past the wounded Haitians. The soldiers' screams and lamentations struck Valentine as surreal, with soft sand beneath his feet and a breeze licking his skin as though he were just back from a pleasure swim. A few of the women from the town tended to the men in a haphazard fashion, caring only for the faces known to them and ignoring others.

The soldiers moved him along with words and gestures rather than the blows he expected, especially after the brief, intense fight. They escorted him to the stoutest building off the market square, a cinder-block three-tiered structure with a collonade and a few friezes that reminded him of an elaborate wedding cake he'd once seen back in New Orleans. They brought him into the basement by way of an exterior stairway and metal door broken only by a narrow gun slit. A navy-uniformed warden led him to a cell. Its ten-by-ten concrete floor supported no furniture, and only a drain hole and dirty ring on the floor around it hinted that there had once been plumbing fixtures.

Cockroaches scuttled for the corners at their entry. What light there was came in through the face-size window in the door, where tiny shards of reinforced glass and wire still stood in the broken pane like the teeth circling a lamprey's mouth. He stood in the holding cell, wet and uncomfortable, while they searched him. Finding him weaponless, they took only his belt.

He waited what he thought to be an hour or so, and a familiar eye appeared in the circle of jagged, stained glass. It widened in surprise.

"My God! So it's true—the bargainer himself," Boul exclaimed in French.

"That sounds like the man who told me not to fear treachery."

A melodious chuckle came from the hall. "I know which side of the bread my butter rests on, my friend. Or in this case, on which side of this door I wish to be standing."

"Funny thing, buttered bread," Valentine said, emotion facilitating his command of his mother's tongue. He sat and rested his back against the wall. "If it is dropped, life always arranges for it to land butter side down."

"My bread is brought to me, so I wouldn't know. Listen, my friend. You'll have buttered bread, decent food, as long as you stay here if you'll tell them the whole truth. That through me your captain was convinced to stay."

"Are you sure you want to take credit for tonight's fiasco? Your prize got away."

"Your sailors were more alert than we thought, for all the illicit rum and tequila they bought today. But your ship was damaged, my friend, damaged. Whatever you sought to do here is at an end. The Lords of Santo Domingo still rule, and they know now that you play a false game."

"Thanks to those who would sell their countrymen's lives. For what? A uniform? Someone to bring you your buttered bread?"

"I must put an end to this pleasant exchange, though in the future we'll have freedom and leisure to talk. Well, just leisure in your case. But first a comrade of yours will join you. It seems he wished to see you again a great deal, so much that he risked his life to be in the harbor tonight. One moment please."

So they had Victo, too. Valentine waited, and rested. *So close, and you blew it at the end.* He closed his eyes and his mind and tried to reduce his lifesign. Not that it was necessary in this particular heart of darkness, but the mental discipline would calm him for whatever lay ahead.

A heavy tread outside the door, and a rattle of a key in the lock made him open his eyes again. He readied an apology for Victo, whose life had also been on the table in this mad gamble. Valentine felt a flash of resentment at the superiors, Lifeweaver and human, who pushed men to their deaths, sacrificed like pawns. But it wasn't Victo who stood in the doorway, glowering at him.

Captain Saunders.

"By Kur and the Catastrophes, I owe the devil his due. It *is* you," Saunders rasped. His skin was darker, his hair lighter, and the wattles on his neck more pronounced with weight loss. He wore loose butter-colored cotton clothes and rope sandals.

"Good morning, Captain," Valentine said.

"Stow it, renegade. Boul, put this man in shackles. He's slippery."

Boul yelled something to his men outside the door, who rushed to comply with the Haitian Creole. Valentine submitted to his boots being stripped off, and his wrists and ankles being clamped in steel. A second chain linked the upper and lower segments of the restraints.

"That's better," Saunders said, looking over the fittings with a careful eye. He snickered. "So young, so sure of himself. Plotting behind my back. I found you out still, clever man."

"Shouldn't you be getting back to the *Thunderbolt*, sir? It is your command, after all."

A paroxysm passed over Saunders's face, and he reached into his shirt. Valentine saw a sheathed knife under his arm. Saunders clutched the hilt with a trembling hand, then relaxed.

"You should be congratulated for being in the right place at the right time, Captain," Valentine admitted. "Was it dumb luck or evil fate?"

"It took some doing," Saunders said. "I got away from those bastards off Jamaica by only the thinnest margins. I jumped in a raft with Peatwo and my pistols while the fighting was still going on. We rowed for shore." Saunders still enjoyed talking about himself, and he began to pace the cell.

"Nobody noticed a missing raft. But we've been busy killing a Kurian," Valentine said.

"I rowed for shore, but it turned out there was a third ship there. Didn't know that, did you? A little fishing boat, just a wheelhouse and a deck really. From the other pirates in Montego Bay. The scoundrels on board were hoping one or both of the ships would be so damaged by the fight, they could get in on some salvage.

"Their sailing master, for he wasn't fit for the word *captain,* was a crafty one, lurking there. Pointed a bunch of guns at us, bobbing there in the raft. I saw him watching Peatwo with a look I'd seen before, so I took my pistol and put it to Peatwo's head. Promised to blow the boy's brains out if they didn't put down their guns, but I'd trade the boy for my life. The sailing master chuckled and brought me on board.

"He meant to murder me, of course, so as soon as I got on deck, I shot him and another who moved clean dead. I made the others throw their guns overboard, and between me and Peatwo, we got five into the raft. That just left us with three, enough to handle the ship but not too many to watch.

"I couldn't go back north, but I knew the only Kurians with ships nearby were here. We made for Santo Domingo. I ended up shooting another of those Montego dogs on the trip. I stayed awake two days at one stretch, promising myself with every breath that I'd see you again and avenge myself. I offered the Devil my soul for this moment."

"Not much of a bargain for either of you."

"Hold that tongue, or I'll cut it out—by Kur, I will. We got to this island, and I found the local Lords. I gave them the Jamaicans, and Peatwo for that matter, for the promise to let me serve them at sea. That came hard. Felt a bit like that guy in the Bible who had to sacrifice his own son. I couldn't have made it that week at sea without Peatwo. The Kurians didn't know what to make of me. But they had that subma-

rine working; they used it at sea because it was almost un-
sinkable. The cannon's sights were wrecked. I fixed it up for
them, and they gave me the command.

"We heard about what happened in Jamaica. At first I
thought you had ideas about setting yourself up in style
there. When the good Boul radioed Santo Domingo that you
were seen off the coast, I knew the Devil had kept his part
of the bargain. You'll rot here until I get the *Thunderbolt*
back, and then what's left of you will go back to New Orleans for disposition. Dispossession, more like, of your trai-
torous hide. As slowly as I can make it last."

In a way, Valentine was relieved. He wouldn't be killed
outright, and so far no one had bothered to wonder just what
he was doing off the shore of Hispaniola.

"Better get that gun fixed, sir," Valentine suggested.
"Otherwise the *Thunderbolt* will sink your pigboat under
you."

"I intend to. The damage is repairable, within even the
capabilities of the joke of a machine shop they have here in
Haiti's wet asshole. But help is on the way."

Valentine feigned disinterest and said no more in the
hope that Saunders would brag out further details. But his
former captain turned to leave.

"Oh, Captain, one more thing," Valentine said. "Suppose
you do get the *Thunderbolt* back. Are your new masters here
just going to let you sail off in an armed ship that size? Our
mutual friend Captain Boul, he may just have orders to
shoot you in the back of the head once the *Thunderbolt*'s
safely taken."

"A traitor judges all others by his traitorousness," Saunders sneered, as if he had hit upon an important point of phi-
losophy. "Kur keeps her bargains with those useful to them."

"What about with those who are no longer useful to
them? What happened to Peatwo when you didn't need a
second set of eyes, Captain?"

"Boul, have him beaten!"

Saunders stormed out, letting his stomping feet do his

cursing for him. Boul's lips curled into an uneven grin, and two heavyset Haitians entered, wooden clubs in hand.

An hour later, Valentine consoled himself with the knowledge that this pain would not be forever. Pain never was; the body either died or healed. In either case, the pain subsided.

But for now, he had an existence of seeping blood and throbbing pain. Blood stinging his eyeballs—the sting coursed up the side of his face like a hot circuit. Blood in his mouth, blood in his urine from the hammerlike blows to his kidneys, he fancied his toes were bleeding where one of the jailers had stood on them with thick-soled boots. And pain underneath, pain as deep as the Cayman abyssal. Vomit covered his shirt, and worse filth stained the inside of his pants.

He felt a callused yet gentle hand rock his head. Some kind of leaves went into his mouth, and the hand worked his jaw. He chewed with loosened teeth and swallowed; it seemed important to the hand.

"*Oui, oui,* my child. This will help, yes," a woman's voice said in Haitian Creole.

Valentine opened one blood-gummed eye and looked up into a black face. Warm dark eyes looked down at him, a tenderness glowing there thanks to some inner light. He felt he must be resting in a lap—though the arrangement of her legs seemed wrong—but he only had a moment to enjoy the sensation before fading out.

When he awoke, he was in clean cotton ducks of the same kind he had seen under the straw hats in the Cape Haitian market. Something had woken him, and a sniff of fresher air made him turn to the door, which the breeze told him was open.

A figure slid in, moving mostly with its arms like a chimpanzee. It was the same woman who had cradled his head in her caressing hands. She was disfigured: two fleshy stumps were all she had left of her legs, and one arm ended in a leather-covered knob at her wrist. She had a wide nose, so wide it seemed to touch every other part of her face, below a cheerful yellow bandanna tied tight around her head. Swinging on her arms, like a cripple using two short crutches, she was at his side in two strides. She pivoted on the wrist-stump as neatly as a ballerina en pointe.

"Feeling better, child?"

"Yes. Whatever was in those leaves helped."

The door remained open. A lemon-sucking guard watched every move the woman made in the bare cell. Valentine noticed that she wore a man's wristwatch with a cracked crystal on her good arm.

"Food and water'll help more. I brought both. I'm Sissy. I tend to the poor souls in here."

"Sissy?"

"Short for Narcisse," she said, unrolling a bundle. A coconut and further food wrapped in bits of rag greeted him.

"Food doesn't sound that good, but that coconut—"

"As full of milk as a cow, child. You want me to hold it for you?" She sniffed at the air above his waist, like a mother wondering if a diaper needed changing.

"I think I can manage."

Valentine removed the coir plug and tipped the sweet, thin coconut milk down his throat. It tasted like pure honey.

"You're a good healer, child. I've seen men die from such a beating. Here you are with an appetite already."

"I'm grateful," he said, handing her the empty husk.

"You want the meat inside?"

"Maybe later."

"I understand, child. Been there myself."

"Sorry to hear that."

"Grateful *and* sorry." She chuckled. "That makes you two rungs up on every man in this town."

"Narcisse," Valentine said, not to his nurse, but to the ceiling of the cell. "That's a lovely name."

"Twenty years ago, I was a lovely girl."

"You still are. Nobody is more beautiful than someone who takes away pain."

She half snorted, half laughed. "Child, you're a charmer. Now you're three rungs up."

Valentine unwrapped a piece of cheese and nibbled at it with sore teeth. "Good of them to let you in here."

"Captain Boul's orders. I heard the men talking. They want you to live."

Valentine probed a loosened tooth with his tongue and refrained from comment.

"Ten minutes, and you'll need to pass water, bad," Sissy predicted. "I'll be back with a basin."

She swung herself to the door and glared up at the man blocking it. "Thank you," she said as he moved aside. Valentine almost felt the air chill at her tone.

Sissy helped him urinate at the end of the predicted ten-minute interval in such a matter-of-fact fashion, Valentine almost laughed at the procedure.

"Christ that burns," Valentine groaned.

"Pain means you're still breathing," she commiserated. "Told myself that before—and before that, too."

She put his head in her lap again and started to sponge blood clots out of his hair. "You're wondering, and you're too polite to ask. I'm like this from my own beatings, from trying to run away out of here. I started out in the sugar fields. Tried to get away once too often. I'd be dead, except I can cook better than anyone this side of the island. And they're afraid of my juju."

"Actually I was wondering about the watch. It doesn't fit you."

"Hmpf. Most people just see a woman with stumps. This belonged to my man, Robert," she said, pronouncing the name *Rowberr.* "He went to join the guerrillas, and I never seen him since. I think he's dead."

Valentine lay back, trying to fall asleep. There was no pain in sleep. "Do you ever think of running again?" he breathed, his voice hardly a whisper.

"Hard to run with no legs, child," she said, cradling his

head again and bringing her face close to his so he could hear.

"When you bring me dinner . . . ," Valentine began.

Narcisse listened, gently stroking his head. But Valentine felt her body tremble with excitement as he spoke.

Valentine lay down, and tried to sleep away the afternoon. He'd gotten up and walked around the cell. There was one final wall of pain to get through as he did so, and then he felt his strength coming back to him as though a dam had burst. He put his back to the wall where the guard couldn't see him and squatted and stretched and tried a few push-ups. The exertion left him as limp as water. He tried to sleep. He told himself he would never be able to rest: there were gaping holes in his plan, beginning with the necessity of him staying in this cell for another meal. He tried to relax, worried that a change in mood could alter his lifesign signature. He hadn't seen any Reapers on Haiti yet, or felt their presence, but that didn't mean they would not come for him. And with all those worries, sleep still ambushed him.

He woke with a start at the sound of Sissy's voice outside the door. "What, you on hourly wages? Food's getting cold, boy. Get this thing open."

The door swung inward, and Valentine rolled over to see Narcisse. She had changed into heavier long-sleeved clothes, and the yellow bandanna had been replaced by a blue-green one.

Valentine rolled onto his side and knelt, as a hungry man looking forward to his meal. The guards looked in Narcisse's bag, poking through the contents.

"Awful lot in here."

"You know the cap'n's orders. He wants him well fed. He didn't eat much earlier owing to the beating—he'll be healing-hungry now. I'm going to give him a wash, too. That's what the water's for."

The jailers exchanged a look. One stepped aside so she could pass. She executed a neat hop over his foot, but her trailing culottes caught on his boot. Something fell from between her stumps and clattered to the floor.

The guards and Valentine looked down. It was a filleting knife—with a razor-sharp blade and a sturdy handle.

The guard outside the door reached for his rifle. The one inside bent to grasp at the knife. Valentine took his chance. Excitement overrode the stiffness in his body.

He sprang, bringing his fist forward. The defunct but heavy watch that once belonged to Narcisse's lover was wrapped around his hand in an improvised brass knuckle. The jailer turned his head at the blur of motion. What was left of the crystal shattered against the bridge of his nose, even as he tried to bring up the knife.

The other raised his rifle. To Valentine it seemed as though the guard moved in slow motion, and a rifle is an unwieldy weapon for a close-quarters fight. Valentine whirled around the pain-blinded guard at the door and stepped past the long barrel. He brought his watch-covered fist against the second guard's jaw in a haymaker blow, trapping the gun under his other arm. The gun fired; its bullet went into the cell, splitting the air between Narcisse and the broken-nosed man at the door.

Sissy had the knife now, and stuck it up and under her opponent's rib cage. Valentine grabbed his guard's head and pushed it as hard as he could into the wall behind him. Two sickening, crunching thumps, and he let the man drop.

"Get the keys," Valentine said, blood and cordite in his nose.

"They ain't good for the outer door," she said, slamming the door to the interior staircase shut. "I got the captain's. Boul's asleep for the rest of the day, and not much use to anyone for a while after that. His chicken curry had a pinch of magic in it."

Valentine looked at both rifles and took the better of the two, an old Ruger Model 77/44. There were no spare magazines, but one of the guards had a handful of .44 cartridges in his pocket.

"Food and water?" Valentine asked. He took one of the guard's sandals off and put them on his bare feet.

"Got it," she said, throwing the bag over her shoulder.

Valentine knelt. "Okay, get your arms around me. We're out."

Narcisse wrapped her arms around his neck, holding on to her mutilated forearm with her good hand. Valentine came to his feet easily; she weighed no more than a loaded backpack. He went to the dead bolt on the basement exterior door.

"It's the shiny steel one with the longest barrel," she said in his ear.

The door opened, and Valentine brought the rifle barrel up the stairway.

"Most of the men that weren't wounded are behind sandbags in the harbor. They expect your ship to come back for you. The white man with the chicken neck wants to spring a trap once they land troops."

Valentine kept the rifle to his shoulder and ascended the stairs. Where his eyes went, the iron sights of the rifle followed. He heard banging on the door Narcisse had locked back in the cells.

A trio of navy-uniformed men approached the stairway, rifles held ready, hunched over as if trying to make themselves smaller. They hugged the wall, all in a row, like the three blind mice. Valentine ducked when he saw the rifle barrel come his way. The shot *ping*ed off the wall behind his head.

He popped his head and gun back up and shot the front man as he worked the bolt on his rifle. The other two dropped to the ground and fired without aiming.

Valentine ran, popping off another shot from his hip as he crossed the street, trying to keep the other two soldiers hugging pavement. His opponents looked more interested in getting behind the twitching body of their leader than in shooting at him. He made it into an alley chased only by the sound of a gunshot from the roof.

"You okay?" Valentine asked.

"You'd be running a lot lighter if I wasn't," she said in his ear.

"I want to get away from the waterfront, if that's where the soldiers are. You wouldn't have a suggestion on how to get to the resistance, would you?"

"We'll get out of town and head west. Hope you're feeling better and some kind of athlete, child. These mountains'll kill you if the captain's men don't."

Sissy guided him out past the standing buildings and into a mass of rubbled buildings. A shanty town of sorts grew out of the ruins, homes created from rebuilt walls and roofed with everything from corrugated aluminum to old doors to woven palm fronds. Gaping locals got out of Valentine's path. He was running with gun ready and Narcisse clinging to his back like a baby monkey riding on its mother. He ran to the canebrake beyond the rubble, then to the trees and momentary safety.

Valentine crossed the Plaine du Nord at a steady, loping run. Narcisse clung tightly to his back, Valentine's shirt tied around both their waists, to keep her from being bounced like a sack. They moved through the muted light of the forest, crossing old roads that were now only paths and the occasional overgrown foundation. During a break, he took a look to the south, at what looked like a tabletop mountain.

Narcisse panted: "How you run like that, child? Don't you tire?"

Valentine did not want to be reminded. "Oddly shaped mountain," he said.

"That's no mountain, that's the Citadelle. An old fortress. It took many years and many lives to build, they say. It belongs to him now."

"The local Kurian?"

She nodded.

"Why are we running toward it?" he asked.

"They wouldn't be expecting me to take you there. Once

we come near the ruins of Sans Souci, we turn west into the mountains. Then you'll be among friends."

The dead air of midday enveloped them. Sweat poured off the pair and mingled as it ran down Valentine's back. Narcisse mopped his brow and eyes as he ran.

By nightfall they hit a grade that made Valentine slow to a walk. Evening birdcalls and air flowing like a slow stream seemed to whisper a promise of relief from the day's heat. Valentine found a heavy tree trunk and set Narcisse down between two roots. He passed her water, and she spat out a beaded chain she had clenched between her teeth, and fingered the charm on it with her good hand.

"Those look like rosary beads," Valentine said as she drank.

"My favorite juju." She smiled, handing him the water. "They were blessed by the pope himself, in the long-ago, my mother told me. She got them from her mother."

"I thought you practiced voudou."

"Voudou's a bit of everything, child. Even the pope did it—he just didn't know he was."

Valentine emptied his gun and looked down the barrel. "Captain Boul's men take good care of their weapons."

"He dotes on that sort of thing. Every gun represents some piece of trading he did. He's just protecting his investment."

Valentine dried his chest with his shirt, eyes stinging with sweat. Even the thin cotton of his pants seemed to suffocate his skin.

"It's hot here. You'd think the shade would help." He bit into some kind of rice-flour bun from the sack of provisions.

"It is worse farther inland. The cool night is soon. Your name, Valent—Valenter?"

"Valentine."

"Oh, like the saint. And your first name?"

"David."

"Dav-eed," she said. "The king who danced. Your name is strong with magic."

"The only dancing I'll be doing is at the end of a rope, if we don't find the guerrillas." He looked east, where a long string of mountain feet ran down to the ocean. "Are you up to it?"

"There is a road along the coast. They will catch up soon on horses using it, once they know what direction we go. But perhaps they will not come this far. No man can run as you. This is a race for a story."

"Where is the finish line?"

"I cannot say for sure. They move. There are guerrillas to the west is all I know. Not many kilometers, I think. Their area begins at a place of good magic, and we are near it."

"So close to Captain Boul?"

"They have . . . an understanding, perhaps you would say. You do not know Haiti, David. The Kurian on this part of the island, he is more concerned with appearances than results."

"The one in the Citadel?"

"Yes."

"Do his . . ."—Valentine searched for a phrase— " 'drinkers of death' visit Cape Haitian often, or use the road?"

"Monks of death? You mean the Whisperers? He does not use them much. Again, appearances."

Valentine thought for a moment, wondering if he was losing something between his barely adequate French and her Haitian Creole. A Kurian who did not use his Reapers much?

"I don't understand."

"Knowing that is the first step on the path to wisdom."

"Hope the path isn't as steep as this damn hill," Valentine said. He picked her up, retied his shirt, and carried her onward.

The next day, after a long mix of jogging and walking the rugged mountains of the coast, Valentine heard the sound of a hound's cry. It brought back memories from five years ago.

He was tired, hungry despite emptying Narcisse's store of food, and still sore from the beating in the Cape Haitian jail. Evening was well on its way; the sun had disappeared behind the mountainside. Picking a path through the tangled growth would become a blind, exhausting flight for a normal man. Valentine's gift of night vision would help, but he needed a modicum of light, and without some moonlight penetrating the clouds that gathered above the canopy, they were as good as lost among the lianas and creeping vines.

"We're being tracked."

"Yes, we are," Narcisse agreed. Her strong good hand still locked the ring of muscle and bone around his neck and shoulders that allowed him to bear her.

"You wouldn't have some hot pepper somewhere in that food bag, would you?"

"I wasn't planning on cooking, child."

Green *cotorras* screeched at them from the trees above. The noisy parrots mocked them.

"How did they catch you, when you ran before?" Valentine asked, pushing up yet another steep hill. Perhaps he could outlast the tracker, if not the dogs. Talking to Narcisse might get his mind off the pain in his legs and back. Exhaustion was an enemy that could not be beaten, but it could be delayed if he kept his mind from giving in to it.

"The first time was when I worked in the cane fields, in Santo Domingo. I hitched a ride on a taptap—"

"What's a taptap?"

"One of those painted trucks. They are still running after all these years. The only thing on them that isn't forty years old is the tires. The driver of this taptap turned me in at the first station we came to. There's a standing reward for runaways; he was a poor man.

"After that I met my lover; he was one of the guards who came for me. Kinder than the rest. After punishment, a whipping, he got me a job cooking at a waystation for the guards on one of the highways. They would stop, and I would cook and wash. I had time on my own when there were no soldiers to take care of. I went into the woods, and at a waterfall met a juju-man."

"A witch doctor, you mean?"

"Yes, Dav-eed. When I touched the stream to drink or bathe, he said I made writing in the water, which told him I could practice voudou."

Valentine set her down next to a great mahogany tree, looked downslope, and set the sights on his rifle. He worked the bolt and chambered a round.

"So he taught you?"

"People think voudou is all fear and hate, but there is love and healing in it, Dav-eed. There is a bad side—like anything, it can be used to destroy. Those who work their magic with both hands can cause much sadness. Have you ever heard of a zombie?"

"Yes."

"On the east side of the island, there are many zombies, slaves to the Evil Ones. They hardly need their Whisperers to feed from them. Such a sad thing, to have the *gros-bon-ange* taken, and the poor soul standing there, with no chance to even run."

"The 'great good angel'?"

"It is the spirit that enters you at conception. It animates you."

"I learned it was called the 'vital aura.' "

"One word or another—it is all the same. Didn't I tell you that already?"

"Yes. Seems different when it comes from a Lifeweaver."

"Still think there's nothing to voudou?"

"I never said that. I've seen enough to know not to laugh off anything."

Valentine settled down behind a thick tree root, stomach against the moist earth, with a good view of the slope. "Our *gros-bon-anges* may be packing for a trip. I'm going to see if I can't take out a couple of these dogs before the light fails. I smell a rain coming. That'll throw them off if they don't get here first."

"Wait for me to tell you to shoot," she said, sliding next to him for a better view down the hill. She removed her bandanna, and Valentine saw more scars going up the side of her head. They had a stretched-over, half-healed look to them: burns from long ago.

"Why, are you going to work a charm to make me aim better?" he asked, tearing himself away from the tales told by the scar tissue.

"Don't know one, or I would, Dav-eed."

The occasional barks and yips grew louder. Valentine tucked the rifle closer to his shoulder. He wished he had had more time to get familiar with the gun; it felt a little nose-heavy. Too late to fill the stock with lead weights now.

Slathered dogs came out of the gloom, towing a ragged black figure up the slope. Valentine listened for the hoofbeats of more men behind with hard ears. He heard nothing.

Valentine looked down the barrel and put the foresight square on the man's chest. He placed his finger on the trigger, then startled with recognition. He put up his gun.

"That's the man who sent me the message in the market."

She squinted. "Yes, I thought so when I heard the dogs. His name's Victo, but the captain's men call him Dog-boy. He hunts wild pigs with those things. He's a character. Come into town just to trade, though I've seen him around more lately."

"Monsieur Valentine," Victo hallooed up the hill in English, waving. "Have no fear." He held up a pair of boots. "Look, I have your shoes, sir."

Valentine stood slowly, his aching body fighting him. "Thank you, Victo. You know what a good pair of boots means." He put on cotton socks, another gift from Victo, and slipped the familiar boots back on his sore feet. The sandals had chafed his skin badly during the long run from Cape Haitian.

"I thought you'd be on the *Thunderbolt*," Valentine said.

Victo showed a healthy set of teeth. "No, soon as we knew you were missing, I put ashore."

"Where's the *Thunderbolt*?"

"Down the coast, off a little island. They won't be seen, unless another ship from the other side of the island comes looking. That's Roots land." Valentine took a good look at the man who rescued his boots: Victo was handsome, with coal-black skin stretched tight over lean muscle.

"Roots?"

"The guerrillas."

Narcisse interrupted in her Haitian Creole. "Men, we need to be moving now. Sun is going down, but that doesn't mean they can't follow us still. There's more dogs on this part of the coast than just yours, Victo."

"Yes, woman. He carry you all this way?"

"Like an empty sack. Up and down these hills, never knew a man could run like that. What do they feed you up north?"

"I'll tell you, if you'll tell the story of why the guerrillas are called Roots. Do you hide in tunnels?"

Victo laughed in the slow, easygoing manner of the Caribbean. "It's an old saying, *blanc*. When the old hero Louverture was taken from us, he said, 'Overthrowing me, they have cut down the trunk of the tree of black liberty. I will shoot up again through the roots, for they are numerous and deep.' We aren't numerous, my friend, but we are deep. Deep in the mountains, deep in the forests. Though for once, all men wear the same yoke."

Valentine took up his human backpack again, and swallowed a grateful mouthful of Victo's water. It seemed almost futile; the water left him as fast as he took it in. He thirsted as if the last time he had water was yesterday. "Never been so thirsty," he said.

Victo pulled a metal tin from his pocket, an old breath-mint logo in red and white still visible on the lid. He opened it. "Salt pills. Take two now. Two more later."

"There are springs soon. Don't worry, child," Narcisse said.

The Cat led the way, and the dogs circled as they hiked.

It began to rain, one of the enervating downpours of the Caribbean summer. They made a queer procession, Valentine toting his human load, the rainsoaked dogs crisscrossing first in front, then behind, and Victo's long-legged tread at the rear.

They slogged through the night with an hour of fast walking along the hillsides, a ten-minute break, and then another hour of walking. By the time Valentine set Narcisse down again, he had lost the battle with exhaustion. His time in the KZ and life on the *Thunderbolt* had softened him from his years of run–walks with the Wolves and long treks with Ali Duvalier into the Great Plains. He had to take his mind off his legs, which felt like someone had shot them full of sulfuric acid.

"So you ran away from the station again?" he asked Narcisse. He put two more of Victo's salt pills on his tongue; they tasted almost sweet.

"Oh, yes. I heard you could get away if you reached the coast. There were boats, men who would take you across the waters to safety. But of course I was caught again. Brought to a coastal village, under a plantation owner. A terrible man, this one. He had four strong men hold me down, and he broke my legs with an iron rod. *Broke* is not a good enough word, he made it so the bones inside were nothing but splinters. You should have seen them—they looked like two run-over snakes. After that, there was nothing to do but take them off. The beast of a man gloated over me, said something about my not running anymore. He got his face too close. I tried to put out his eye. He chopped off my hand with a machete. For some reason, they let me live, perhaps as an example to others. For a while I went from plantation to plantation, and they would set me in the sun with a sign around my neck where the workers would walk by every day as a warning to others. Then Captain Boul found me. He had been a friend of Rowberr, in a manner, and he took me to his station on the cape."

"What ever happened to your lover?"

"He just vanished. I think that is the worst part of this time. You do not even know if people die. They just disappear. Perhaps they ran; perhaps they were killed. You don't know."

Valentine's legs no longer bothered him. He tried to imagine what it would feel like, to have the bones so broken they were nothing but pieces, and had to shift his mind to the trees towering overhead.

"My brothers and sisters, too. Just gone," Victo added.

"I'm sorry," Valentine said. It wasn't enough.

Victo nodded. "Let's sleep. It is safe—we are far enough into the Roots' lands that anyone after us will come slowly."

"Can you find them?" Valentine asked.

"They will find us."

Valentine would have slept through the dawn were it not for the birds. The parrots hollered back and forth between the trees like argumentative neighbors, while thousands more greeted the morning with song and call. Victo and the dogs slept in a snoring mass, and Narcisse lay with her back pressed up against his. He felt something disquieting in his crotch.

"Sissy," Valentine whispered.

"Yes, Dav-eed?" she yawned.

"I think a bug or something crawled up my leg."

"That is bad, especially if it is a centipede. Turn yourself so it rests in your trousers, rather than against your skin."

Valentine shifted, wondering if after all the hazards he faced he would finally be brought down by an insect. Whatever it was decided to cling to his thigh.

"It's still there."

"Take down your pants."

Victo woke up and looked at the operation. Valentine got into a position as if he were doing a push-up, and Narcisse helped him take down the loose cotton pants.

"It is a centipede," she said, smiling. Valentine looked down. It was long and black, with painful-looking pincers waving back and forth. Narcisse maneuvered her head and blew on the centipede. It didn't care for the breeze and began crawling down his leg. Still blowing, she herded it onto his lowered trousers, and from there used a stick to encourage it to return to the debris on the floor.

"They can kill, though for a man as healthy as you, it might just be very painful."

"The same thing happened to a friend of mine," Victo said. "It bit his sack—he said it swelled up like a mango. Oh, how he howled."

Valentine grimaced. "Thanks for waiting to tell me that."

Valentine heard the guerrillas first as he cast about that morning with his hard ears. The dog-led trio was following a game trail west up yet another hillside. Five or six men, keeping concealed, paralleled their track up the slope. He picked out their step from the cacophony of the Haitian forest: birdcalls, creaking trees, and wind in leaves.

He called a halt. The dogs startled at the sound of the guerrillas' approach down the hillside. Two came down to greet them; the rest observed from above. Valentine was relieved to hear glad words of greeting rather than a challenge when they caught sight of Victo. They were well fed if scantily dressed, with rifles tied across their shoulders and short wooden spears tipped with metal and thorn-bristled clubs. They embraced and descended into a bantering conversation Valentine couldn't begin to follow.

Victo turned to him with a smile. "They were sent to find us, Captain Valentine. Word of your escape reached the hills. They are also in contact with your ship. It is waiting off Labadee not far from here."

Valentine's growling stomach asked the next question. "Do they have food?"

"Soon, soon. Their company watches the road out of Limbe at the river. They have a camp there. It is a downhill walk."

"Thank God."

"But soon you will be climbing mountains again, my friend. You must see the keeper of the weapon against Kur."

"So you do know. What is it? Don't tell me I traveled a thousand miles for an old voudou curse."

"No. Papa Legba will tell you more. I do not know much about how it works. A very old magic, they say. But even the Whisperers fear to cross into this part of Haiti."

"Where do I find Papa Legba?"

Victo's eyes furrowed. "They did not tell you? You must go up to the Citadelle. To meet the Kurian there. We call him Papa Legba. He will show you the weapon."

Chapter Seven

La Citadelle, Haiti: A black revolutionary known as "the Tiger"—who earned his reputation by sawing people in half—dreamed of Haiti's Citadelle as one of a ring of forts to guard Hispaniola against a return of the white slaveholders. The work of two hundred thousand laborers, of whom twenty thousand perished and, according to island legend, had their blood used as mortar to cement the stones, reshaped the top of the mountain with battlements faintly resembling a giant ship. This grim monument looks out on eroded mountains, now being reclaimed by the lush forests of the days when Christopher Columbus viewed them.

Set in walls a hundred feet high and fully thirty feet thick at their base, gunports like shaded black eyes look out on the north coast of Haiti and the steep track leading to La Citadelle. It is exactly the kind of cyclopean monument the Kurians make their refuge as they order the affairs of men. Behind walls of cannonballs piled like banks of skulls, there are storerooms and cisterns enough to feed an army for a year, space for troops, and catacombs beneath ready for untold horrors. The Kurian Lord has perches aplenty to stand, brooding at an altitude of three thousand feet while the stars whirl overhead. He could contemplate his domain in security, knowing that even a United States infantry division of the twentieth century would have a tough time blasting his men from the mountaintop, but their like no longer exist on Vampire Earth.

Were the Citadelle's lord looking out from his sun-

*bleached battlements one bright April morning, he would
have seen a strange column ascending the switchback trail
to his door. A black man hikes in the lead, being helped up
the hillside by his sniffing dogs. Behind him a muscular
mass of apelike Grogs, using their arms as much as their
legs to negotiate the slope, followed by a taller, fawn-
colored relative carrying a gun with a six-foot barrel. Behind him a handsome, dark-haired man with a slight limp
uses a staff to get help up the worst parts of the trail. Ragged
black soldiers, all wary eyes and ready weapons, follow in
single file. The Kurian might think it a strange, pathetic assortment to challenge the stronghold atop the* Pic La Ferriere, *let alone the entire Kurian Order.*

David Valentine's second thoughts collided with third—
and fourth—thoughts on the long climb. He had thrown the
dice with his life lying on the table on more than one occasion, but never on such a strange gamble as this. Were it not
for Ahn-Kha's steady presence beside him, locking his long
toes around tree roots and rocks as he helped him over
washouts on the trail up the mountain, he would have returned to the *Thunderbolt* days ago and quitted his task. Despair had never struck him when the bullets were cracking
all around, but waited to infiltrate once he had a full belly
and a decent night's sleep.

He had rejoined the *Thunderbolt* after a morning with
Victo spent following the Limbe River to the coast, and
from there a short canoe trip to her anchorage off Labadee.
Following a freshwater shower and a change of clothes, he
held an open-air meeting on the stern, telling his story to the
Jamaican pirates and New Orleans mutineers, and explaining what would happen over the next few days.

As sunset fell, the officers and men decided that Carrasca
and Post would stay with the ship, and a few members of the
crew would join Grogs and the Haitian guerrillas on the next
step: making contact with the "Kurian ally" in his mountaintop fortress. This stirred the interest of the crew; they

had more questions than he had answers. The *Thunderbolt* would be safe enough. Her main armament had been repaired, and she was as ready to face a seaborn challenge as the day she sailed into Cape Haitian.

With that finished, the Grogs and men took their arms from the locker, and such provision as the NCOs could force them to carry. A beach party of sorts welcomed them to the mountains of Haiti, with comic sign language and a babble of English, French, and Spanish along with island patois the method of intercourse. Two mornings later, Valentine found himself sweating up *La Ferriere*'s escarpment with his odd conglomeration, guided by Victo.

Two silent sentries in tiger-striped uniforms stood in the lot before the main gate to the fortress. A rusting wall of aged jeeps and trucks was the first, and least impressive defense of La Citadelle, blocking the last few feet of what was left of the road up the slope.

A circle of Haitians Valentine took to be porters lounged in the shade of the high point looking out over the path like the prow of a massive ship. Some slept, some talked, one or two eyed the visitors with interest when a pair of sailors lit cigarettes. Valentine thought of the thousands of their forefathers it must have taken to build this castle among the clouds.

The guards and Victo exchanged more singsong words in their Creole. Valentine caught "Papa Legba," and *"oui"* but little else. A man in a clean white uniform appeared at the main gate and led them to an inner courtyard. There did not seem to be many inhabitants in evidence, just a handful of sentries keeping watch on the approaches to the fortress. The faint cry of a baby came from a high, narrow window. Below it the sound of the visitors echoed between the courtyard's stone walls.

"Papa Legba awaits," Victo translated. He looked eager, like a child about to be taken to Santa Claus himself on Christmas Eve.

The majordomo in the white uniform had the rest wait,

then led Valentine and Victo deeper into the fortress. The air inside the thick walls was cool and still. They went up stone staircases, past small galleys which once held cannon, and into some kind of common room. Shafts of light came in from openings in the roof to splash yellow on the high walls. A sizable fireplace dominated one wall, fronted by chairs and tables of mahogany, roughly finished as if the resident eschewed form for function. An old man sat before the fireplace. Nothing but dead ashes filled the hearth. He stood, his back still to them, and took a crutch from the wall.

"So they sent a Valentine to see me. My cousins to the north do have a sense of irony."

Victo fell to his knees, hands clasped under chin, and began to weave back and forth.

"I really am old. It's safe to say I'm the oldest sentient you shall ever converse with, unless you touch one of the minds encased in what you call a touchstone. But I hardly think they'd count."

Father Max used to talk about the touchstones, cryptically carven rocks containing a world's worth of information. Touching one caused what the old priest called a "revelation of sorts"—if it didn't drive you mad. Valentine had never heard of minds being encased in them.

Papa Legba turned around. He was a hunched-over, wizened figure, resembling a Haitian great-grandfather, right down to toothless gums. Weariness colored his every movement and expression.

"What's your game, Kurian?" Valentine asked.

"Show some respect," Victo interjected, his prayers over. "Papa's been protecting you since you came to this island. If you don't see that, you're a fool."

"You have no reason to love us, Valentine the younger. And I have even less reason to love you: I was once a Great One in the north. My mind-mates—what you would call a 'family'—are dead at your father's hand. From the perspective of my years, it hardly happened yesterday."

Valentine kept his face a mask, confusion and suspicion and interest all warring within.

"But that is war, and I hardly blame your race. I returned here to forget. Out of my sorrow came thinking, and from thinking came wisdom. After all, you've been supplanted out of your birthright, and you're being consumed even now. It is no wonder you struck back, though many said you'd be happy with Kur setting the parameters of your existence."

"Came to play god? I'm supposed to kneel before you and thank you for your divine intervention?"

The Kurian sighed. "One definition of man: a biped who is ungrateful."

He looked Valentine in the eyes. The Cat felt the same vertigo that he'd felt in Jamaica when he met the Specter's gaze across the sights of Ahn-Kha's rifle. He shifted his eyes away, feeling a little like a cowed dog.

The Kurian's toothless mouth turned up. "Let us turn from dark thoughts. Have a seat. Would you care for refreshment? No? Very well. To your duty, then."

"My duty is to bring back this weapon you claim to have. What is it?"

"A powerful one, a tool that can stop my brethren's avatars."

"What's it do? Shut down the connection between you and your Reapers, maybe? That would be handy."

"All in good time. You're an impatient race. Excuse me, I must sit. I tire easily," the Kurian said. "Valentine, surely you know that the first Door opened in the Western Hemisphere was right here on Haiti. There was a rich, rich harvesting of auras during the revolts against the colonial powers. I, and one or two others, encouraged some of the excesses. Papa Legba is the keeper of doors and gates, according to local legend. In this case, they were right. The door to the 'other world' was in my care. It is in my care now. The 'other world' just happened to be Kur."

Valentine bit his tongue. He envisioned what was beneath

the mask the Kurian wore; a shriveled, blue-skinned bat-winged octopus lurked behind the grandfatherly fakery. But to see one of the legendary doors—

"You'd like to see the gate, wouldn't you? I will show you. It's safe enough. This island isn't important anymore—my cousins do not use it. They have others, bigger and better located. Those hungry for their own principalities go through the newer ones on the larger continents. Asia is popular at the moment: they're much less troublesome than you North Americans. I'm 'just minding the store' as your kind used to say up North."

Valentine pushed at the old ashes in the fireplace with the toe of his boot. "You want to aid us against your 'cousins'?"

The Kurian shimmered for a moment in thought or emotion. "This is a beautiful world, with a gifted though primitive people living on it. I don't care to see it become a corpse, like Kur. Sad. Kur is a husk. The surface has been cleaned of all life save lichen. The same could happen here. That's why I stopped feeding on your kind."

"You aren't afraid of discovery?"

"I keep up appearances with the help of my scoundrel friend on the Cape, and a few others. Though it might be hard to say with whom the good Boul really sides, just as he does not know all my devices."

"I don't believe you," Valentine said in English, to prevent another outraged ejaculation from Victo. "How do you stay alive? I thought you needed to feed to live."

"I do feed, off vital aura, as you call it. Though you might say I just wet my lips, rather than drinking great drafts as my cousins do."

"You kill only once a month, I imagine. I'll write the Vatican and nominate you for sainthood."

"Your letter would be laughed at. There is still a powerful figure at Saint Peter's, true, but he comes from Kur, and his cardinals are to be feared. I will show you how I feed. No one dies. No one is hurt. I shall give you a tour, starting with the Door to Kur. Then you'll see me feed."

Valentine took his hands from his weapons. "You have me curious. 'Curiosity killed the cat' is another saying we have up North, though I hope it won't prove out today."

A pair of Haitian servants—"Voudou priests," Victo whispered in his ear—emerged at a wave of Papa Legba's hand. One had a small chair, like something a child might be carried in, on his back. The Kurian slid into it and crossed a seat belt across his chest.

"I have a litter for going outside, but this works better on some of the stairs, as you will see."

The priests led the way, through narrow corridors and down shoulder-width stairs. Valentine's sensitive nose noticed a change in the quality of the air, and he knew himself to be underground. The priests lit and took up oil lamps. They came to a wider corridor. A heavy door stood at the end, and Valentine startled when he saw two pinched-looking Reapers slumbering in alcoves to either side. The skin was stretched tight over their bony faces, and lips were rolled back from black pointed teeth.

"They sleep," the old Kurian said. "Have no fear."

Valentine found his heart beating in the vicinity of his Adam's apple as he passed the motionless robed figures. If they came around, they would make a quick end of him and Victo.

"I wake them once or twice a month, when sacrifices of goats and cattle are brought to Baron Samedi," Legba said in English, winking at Valentine. "I'm not the only one using that convenient charade. I would suspect there are a dozen or so Baron Samedis on the other side of the island, though the ceremonies may be a little more gruesome. Religion is useful. Don't think it applies just to ignorant Haitians. When we took your country in the days of your father and grandfathers, many of my cousins appeared as Jesus, and his supplicants were taken to Rapture in the embrace of the avatars. Dressed in white they look like tall, thin angels, and their serene eyes held many a Christian spellbound."

Beyond the doors was a well-room, less finished than the rest of the fortress, built around a pit, perhaps two and a half meters across. The stones lining the walls were not cut and shaped, but irregular, larger at the bottom and growing smaller as they neared the curved ceiling. The priests lit two more torches standing in brackets, and the room quickly filled with an oily reek. The Kurian slid off his chair-backpack. Thanks to the torchlight, Valentine could see that the wall stones formed a vaguely unsettling mosaic of light and dark rock, rather like tentacles reaching from the dark well.

"That leads to what is purportedly a cistern, Valentine. Care to climb down?"

Valentine looked down the granite-walled well. A series of metal rungs descended into the bottom. Only a single row of bricks acted as a warning of the depths beneath. Valentine's sharp eyes picked out a bottom lit by a dim red glow. He looked at Victo. The spy shrugged, wide-eyed—and kept clear of the pit.

Valentine felt a curious pull from the depths. "Why not? I've always wanted to see one of these Doors."

"If you hear anything on the way down, or while you are there, climb up quickly," Legba advised

"You can count on it."

Suppressing a shudder, Valentine clambered down the ancient metal rungs, testing each with a foot before resting his full weight on it. As he neared the bottom of the cistern, he felt it grow a good deal warmer. *Appropriate enough for a descent into hell.* The rungs gave way to handholds carved into the stone, placed closer together than the rungs on a regular ladder. Feeling for the holes with his feet, he descended until he stood inside the cistern.

Clammy sweat coursed down his back, but its source was not the heat. He loosened the machete in the sheath strapped to his thigh and touched the automatic at his hip. Three rings of characters resembling Chinese ideograms surrounded him, melted into the rock and lit from within. Curious, he probed one with his foot. His eyes adjusted, and he peered

at the walls. Several tunnels, also circled with the
ideograms, emptied into the room, the letters glowed red,
like the heating coils on an electric burner. He walked over
to one and looked more closely. It gave off no heat, and reminded him of an old present from the Lifeweaver who
oversaw his training as a Cat. He walked back to the ladder
and looked up.

"There are different doors down here. Do they all go to
Kur?" he whispered up the shaft.

"In a way, Valentine. You're looking at me from Kur itself. The gate is in the middle of the well."

With two hands and two feet again on the ladder, Valentine looked around. "You must be joking. How can that be?
I didn't feel anything when I descended. It just got warmer."

"The Doors work just like that. They are literally doors,
joining one world to another. When you pass from a dining
room to a kitchen, you do not feel anything save the heat of
the stove. You haven't crossed thousands of light-years,
you've just gone a few feet. I'm not a scientist who can explain it, but two pieces of space have been joined like a but-
ton joins two pieces of material in a garment."

Valentine sniffed the air, tasted it. It seemed drier than the
air of Haiti, and it had a metallic tang like a blacksmith's
shop when the forge is working. A whisper sounded from
deep within one of the tunnels, and he heard a dry scrape
like a snake shedding its skin on a rock. Valentine heard the
shuffling gait grow nearer. He did not bother with a last look
around, and shot up the ladder. A sudden, not-so-irrational
fear of things reaching for him, grabbing him to pull him
away from Earth forever spurred him in his climb. He
sprang from the mouth of the well.

He was trembling.

"I thought I might skip the grand tour for now. Just out of
curiosity, what does come up that ladder?"

"No one for thirty or more of your years, Valentine. And before that for a long march of years, much more disappeared

down it than came back up. Remember, there were hungry minds on Kur for centuries before we seized your planet."

Valentine's imagination, always too eager to supply visions at the wrong moment, visited him with images of bound Haitians being thrown down the well to blood-smeared shapes below. The torchlight's dancing shadows turned to a magic-lantern show of human souls in torment.

Valentine's eyes met the Kurian's, and he felt that sinking sensation again, not unpleasant this time, for it calmed his pounding heart.

"You're a sensitive man, young Valentine," the Kurian observed. "What leaps your mind makes."

"I've seen enough," he said, sniffing at the substance clinging to his clothing. It smelled like flour. The procession capped the torches and took up lanterns and the aged Kurian and left the well-room. From his seat on the bearer's back, the Kurian smiled at Valentine's relief.

"We leave the Citadelle tomorrow morning, and I shall take you to my true home, the palace ruins. I invite you to share my hospitality under these austere roofs, but somehow I think you will prefer to sleep outside the walls tonight."

"You read my mind," Valentine said.

"What I could. Your father was—what is the expression—an 'open book.' You keep more of yourself under lock and key. Afraid of what's in there?"

Valentine backed out of the room before the Kurian could say more.

They strung mosquito netting between wrecked trucks. Valentine and Ahn-Kha bedded down inside a defunct tap-tap, still brightly painted where the encroaching rust had not yet touched. Faces, slogans, depictions of food, and animals adorned the old shell.

Ahn-Kha gnawed on the leg of something Valentine guessed to be a dog.

"My David, you saw a Door?"

"Yes."

"My father told me they were simple-looking things. Just an arch of stone, no different from the gate we used to go into the courtyard."

"This one was in a well. It couldn't have been one of the original Doors of the Interworld Tree—those were supposed to be huge. They were built by the race that came before the Lifeweavers."

"I did not know this. I thought the Kurians built the network between worlds."

"Yes, but it's built on an older one, or they learned how to do it from an older race. Some kind of creatures made out of pure energy. The man who told me about it called them the Pre-Entities. They go back hundreds of millions of years. They were the original beings that existed on vital aura. They left behind their science when they finally died out, and the Lifeweavers found it. There was some kind of schism, and a bunch of Lifeweavers on a planet called Kur learned how to live off vital auras, becoming vampires, in effect."

"This word, *Lifeweavers*. In my tongue, they were called the 'prime movers,' I think it would be in English. Some of them use you, yes?"

"Help us."

"And the Gray Ones and other creatures who fight you, are they being 'helped' by the Kur?"

"Okay, use us. Change us even. You've heard people say they bred the Grogs. Maybe they did the same with us. Once a Lifeweaver told me that my species 'exceeded their expectations.' It makes me wonder. Lately I've felt like a pawn in a game of chess, but I can't see the rest of the board."

"Paw in chest?"

"A pawn. Chess—an old strategy game. Remember the Big Man's office in Omaha? You've seen the board. Eight squares by eight squares. The pieces are figures meant to represent different medieval icons. They move into an opposing piece's square, and it is removed from the game. The pieces are supposed to be kings and queens and knights and things. The pawns, well, they're the—"

"Cannon fodder," Ahn-Kha said, ears dancing, as they tended to do when he was pleased with himself.

"Yes. They tend to get taken off the board by the more powerful pieces."

Ahn-Kha crunched the bone between his teeth, like a ruminant with its cud. "Tell me, my David. In chess, can a pawn kill an enemy king?"

"Yes."

"Then be that pawn."

The next day, Valentine's party grew. A throng of voudou priests, porters, guerrillas, Grogs, and Valentine all shared a breakfast of rice porridge, ladled into wooden bowls from a larger pot. The unknown chef added texture by throwing in chunks of sweet potato, making three straight days he'd eaten it in one form or another. He had already grown tired of the endless parade of sweet potatoes and rice.

Papa Legba bobbed out the gate in a litter carried by four strong porter-priests. It reminded Valentine of pictures he had seen of Oriental monarchs being toted around in curtain-draped chairs. They left the walls of the massive Citadelle atop its mountain and made the descent northward on the landslide-broken road.

Valentine watched the sweating, straining back muscles of the porter-priests as they negotiated the trail. "You'd think a voodoo spirit could find a better way to get around," he muttered to Ahn-Kha.

On the way down, he had time to admire the view. Scattered clouds fled the coming sun. To the west, the Chaine de Belance and the Massif du Nord joined at the heart of the guerrilla country. To the north, partly hidden in morning mists, the old plantation plains stretched to Cape Haitian and the Caribbean, with further lower mountains to the east. New forests fought to make a comeback against soil weakened by erosion. He looked up at the fortress behind and above and tried to guess where the door to Kur was buried. *Odd to think that another world can be so close*, he thought. *As if you could climb the mountains to the moon by joining it at the horizon.*

Ahn-Kha glared at the sun, his ears drooping. "Too hot here, my David. It drains. The sun fixes itself to you like a leech."

"We won't be in it all day. They said it is only a few miles."

Valentine halted and let the men and Grogs walk by. The mixed forces had a sprightly step, though the Grogs panted in the heat. The new acquaintances, the feeling of being among friends—or in the Haitians' case, having allies off the island—formed a bond between the diverse groups.

The column plunged into new forest, vigorous young trees shooting upward, racing each other for the sun. As the land flattened out, they emerged into a field of palmetto, which in turn gave way to better-tended lands. Food crops and orchards surrounded them. In the distance, Valentine picked out the ruins of a mansionlike palace. A newer roof had been grafted onto old walls, though smaller wings of the old building still languished in disrepair.

Glorious gardens surrounded the hilltop half-ruin. Valentine had seen small decorative gardens before, but never anything on such a scale. Flowers representing each color of the spectrum stood in well-tended rows, clipped paths running around and between them, for a mile all around. A lake, shade trees, even a small fountain stood about the earthquake-ravaged walls.

Haitians in their eternal straw hats worked the fields and gardens. They had a sleek vitality to them: the healthy look that an ample diet and activity brings. Valentine had seen many farms and camps under Kurian rule, but never one where the occupants looked so hale.

Papa Legba, as Valentine was now willing to call him with grudging interest, descended from his litter. Valentine watched rib bones like oversize fingers spread and then close as the Kurian drank in the air.

"Come, come, Valentine, Victo. Walk with me in my gardens. Bring your giant guardian, if you wish. Francier, look to our guests, would you? Take them to a well, and let them pick their desire from the orchards."

Some of the sailors elbowed each other as they admired the lithe Haitian girls.

Valentine jerked his chin, and the gesture brought Torres forward. "Keep the men out of trouble," he said, before joining the Kurian. Ahn-Kha sang out a few orders to the Grogs and followed.

Legba made his way, slowly and painfully, to a bleached stone bench in the garden. Victo and Valentine each took an arm and helped him sit. Haitian girls, all muscle and gleaming smile, ran to his aid from the well, bringing water.

"Thank you, my children," the old Kurian said.

"You know what you are called up North?" Valentine asked.

"No. I'm sure my former cousins settled on something outrageous."

"The 'Once-ler.' It's from an old children's book by a man named Seuss."

Papa Legba shook his head. "I haven't heard of it. I don't read much human work. Some Dostoyevsky. A few lines of poetry, perhaps. I know a little Baudelaire."

Valentine watched it drink.

"So Kurians do live off of something other than fear and death," Valentine said.

"Yes, we eat. Though not as much as a human."

"The people here are so strong-looking. I was expecting a bunch of half-dead skeletons. I thought you were just taking their vital aura in doses rather than all at once."

"It is a hard thing to explain, Valentine. You know all life creates aura, even single-celled organisms. To a certain extent, this aura is also projected, just as your body gives off extra heat. The healthier a body is, the more it throws off.

I'm able to live off this part of the aura, though only just. It is a bit like osmosis. I have to be careful when I sleep, however. I was napping in a grove some years back, and when I woke, the grass was dead all around, and I had killed the tree shading me.

"It has not been easy, no. And again no. Perhaps it can be compared to giving up a drug addiction. Except the body does not recover after healing itself of the need for the drug. I live with it, fight with it, every day. A real physical need, like starvation, not the psychological one so familiar to those who give up a habit. I can control myself while awake, but in my dreams, Valentine, in my dreams. When I sleep, it is six thousand years ago, or thirty, and I swill myself into a coma on the sweet screaming auras of your kind."

Legba's appearance flickered for a moment, and Valentine got a glimpse of multipupiled eyes, but the black face returned, licking its lips. "Why does evil have such strength? The thoughts, they grow on you in a way that virtuous deeds do not." Papa shut his eyes for a long moment, and his face became as false as a death mask. He opened his eyes again.

"My children, I've seen evil not just at its birth, but at conception. I was on the councils when we first began to learn from the *Anciens* about the secrets of aura. I spoke for scientific inquiry, for reason, for knowledge. What harm lay in facts?

"Harm, indeed. It had been so long since our race knew evil, it was as though we had regained the innocence of your Eden. Though the weight of the Opinion went against us, we did not fail in our resolve, so we met in secret. We pieced together what we could, supplemented the rest with our own formidable science that had researched aural energies. We called the others *Dau'weem*, which has no precise translation in French or English. The closest I can come is 'back-thinkers.' We were the *Dau'wa*, the 'forward-thinkers,' and held ourselves superior.

"It would be easier to lay the finger on one evil being.

Say that this *Dau'wa* pushed us into what we became. But it was not so simple on Kur. We were scientists interested only in truth, and we were ready to subvert the Opinion even at the cost of our lives. The arrest of a *Dau'wa* galvanized us, and we began to plan against the day when there might be a more widespread persecution. We planned escape routes to other worlds, began to talk of weapons and plots. Sure enough, some of us, purely in the interest of science, tried out our theories on plants, animals, and finally a sentient. I remember the first time I fed on a sentient, some trembling wide-eyed creature from a long-nighted world of rock and ice. I consumed one and then another, and found that each aura was richer, as the terror in their pounding hearts mounted, knowing what was coming. I developed a taste for it.

"Some of them fought. We learned—what you would call the hard way—that it could be dangerous to drain the food ourselves, we turned to intermediaries, using our own DNA as well as others, to design the creatures you call Reapers. It took us ages to get the connections right, to get our animating guidance flowing out and the auric channels to us. In the midst of all this, we were unmasked. It was heresy on such a grand scale, I think the councils were unsure of how to handle it. They dithered, and we acted. Some fled to other worlds, including yours, and tried to carve out niches where we could live in hiding. A few recanted, but the rest of us used our avatars as weapons. We told ourselves lies, that it was us or them, justifying any tactics. They had forgotten war, but we took to it with a will, and our skill waxed.

"Kur was ours. During the battle, we made the most terrible discovery yet. A *Dau'weem* has the richest aura of all, like nothing we had experienced before. We began to openly boast of being connoisseurs of death, and we hunted our brothers up and down the tunnels of Kur.

"That proved to be a mistake. Had we pushed our advantage at that time, we could have owned every portal in the

Interworld Tree. But we were like pirates who, having seized one ship in a convoy, immediately drink ourselves into insensibility on the contents of the wine chests, forgetting all the other fat prizes to be had. When the orgy of death ended, we found ourselves shut off from the rest of the worlds. The Doors were shut, permanently it seemed.

"The *Dau'weem*'s strategy would have worked. We *Dau'wa* might have stayed trapped on Kur, gnawing at it until the world lay lifeless, and then turning on each other at the last. But the *Dau'weem* forgot that Kur was the library of the *Anciens*. We learned to live off minimal supplies of aura in that long dark time, thousands of your years. I found, somehow, that growing gardens, thriving fish, and happy sentient life could give me enough to exist. I guarded my estate, for there was no honor among us *Dau'wa* where auric energies were concerned. I even killed for it. We despaired of ever opening another door when we discovered an intact portal from one part of Kur to another. It was like having both halves of an equation, we realized how to go about it, and we began to open doors. Not to worlds with many of the *Dau'weem*, but to worlds rich in sentient life. Like yours.

"I believe you are familiar with the rest of the story."

"So you kept living off the living, so to speak?" Valentine asked.

"No, I slipped into old habits, like an addict who tries just one more injection for memory's sake. We took life from your world, consumed it, and I joined in with the rest. When the time came to make the move here, I was in the vanguard, so hungry for a world of fresh auras, I forgot that I could do with less. But we did it right, we laid our groundwork well, found allies amongst your own people— imagine a bull offering some of his cows to the meatpacker—and when the time came, your dominion collapsed easier than we had hoped. Of course there was error. Our earthquakes sank islands and coasts we had meant to leave intact. The viruses we used to break down your social order were more lethal than we planned. But perhaps it was to our advantage, after all. In many cases we came as saviors, not as conquerors."

"It's been done before."

"Yes, from what I've read, your race is adept at exploitation."

"Can you tell me one thing about the *Dau'weem*?"

Papa Legba looked into his eyes, but Valentine avoided the stare. Locking eyes with the Kurian was too much like sharing his mind from the inside.

"Yes, young Valentine?"

"Did they make us? Humans, I mean."

"Made you? I doubt it. You're too flawed. Shaped you? Perhaps. They needed the equivalent of our Reapers, you must remember, something to do their fighting. Both the *Dau'weem* and the *Dau'wa* are too canny to fight through anything but proxies."

"I had been told you were just bad at it."

"Bad at it? Are we? Who owns your planet, young Valentine? Or more important, from your point of view, that is— who keeps the *Dau'wa* from controlling all of it?"

Valentine felt a hot flush come to his face. "As long as we're talking about weapons, you're supposed to have one. I've come a long way to get it. I trust it's not just smoke and mirrors."

"You've seen it already, from a distance, Valentine, though perhaps no one told you. But I'll show you the source."

Papa Legba walked down a grassy hill, into a stand of taller trees. Victo and Valentine helped him down the path. The trees stood in a ring around a hollow, a bowl-shape in the landscape. A spring trickled out of a rocky overhang and fell into a rill that emptied into a pool.

"There are many springs in this area. Some of them run beneath the floor of the great house, a natural cooling system. Though this climate is to my liking. I was always too cold when I ventured outside in the cooler lands."

They entered into a pine woods. The trees had the twisted, tortured look of timber that grows on a windy coast, and short needles, like those on a balsam fir. The wind-warped limbs of the tree extended in the direction of the prevailing airs like a woman's hair blown in the wind. Ahn-Kha ran his hand over the needles and grimaced.

"Strange sort of pine, my David. The needles are like thorns."

Valentine touched the bark; it was smoother than most pines, more skinlike. It made him think of the beeches of the north. The smaller branches had thorns growing on them.

"It isn't pine, Golden One. It is quickwood, to translate it into English," the Kurian said. "This is your weapon."

"Trees? You can't—," Valentine began, then fell into a stunned silence.

"This is what you came to find."

All the miles, all the risks, for a stand of timber. He stifled a hysterical laugh. "Quickwood? A tree is the new weapon against Kur? Okay, walking through a thick stand would be like walking through razor-wire, but that's not much of a weapon."

Papa Legba nodded. "You are almost right. The *Dau'weem* don't think like men, you must remember. They create organisms to do their work, not tools. Quickwood takes different forms, and there is a variant that grows into thorny hedges."

"A hedge? Do you know how big a hedge we would need to keep the Reapers out of the Ozarks?"

"Where is the famous Valentine patience? You've no doubt already fought the Reapers. Why are they so hard to kill?"

Valentine called up his ugly memories. "Well, they're strong and fast, for one. They're on you before you can bring your gun up. Even if you put a few rounds into them, those robes they wear slow the bullets, and if you do get flesh, that black fluid turns gummy when it hits the air, they never bleed to death. Then there's their skeleton—"

"That 'gummy fluid,' Valentine. Their circulatory fluid. They use it to transport oxygen as you do, though inside them it stays as liquefied as your blood. Quickwood has chemicals in it, in the sap and pockets in the thorns, to be precise, that act as a catalyst. To you it is an irritant that makes you itch. To one of the Reapers it produces an effect similar to that which happens when they are wounded and the blood is exposed to atmosphere. When it enters their bloodstream—"

Valentine made the mental leap. "Holy Christ!" he said in English.

"Yes, but it kills them much faster than the wooden cross killed your prophet. It is most effective if the wood is still living or recently cut, the results are nothing short of spectacular. But even wood that is older, as long as it has some residue that gets brought into contact with their 'blood,' will prove lethal."

"Why is it here? Why haven't the Lifewe—the *Dau'weem* planted this stuff everywhere?"

"That is a story that would be worth telling, if anyone were in possession of the whole tale. It was grown on another continent, long ago. Quickwood was used in the first incursion against us. By *us,* I mean Kur, of course. A few tens of generations after the victory, your people knew only to worship these trees, and in the intervening millennia, even that practice faded. I imagine the trees were turned into huts or firewood. Once harvested, it does burn exceedingly well and makes fine charcoal.

"The next part of the story takes place in the shadowy years as Kur again opened doors to Earth. A *Dau'weem* named Sen living on Earth, or I should say who was trapped on Earth, for the *Dau'weem* had closed all the doors and destroyed the connections as best they could. Sen learned of the new one that had been opened here in Haiti. He tried to reveal himself to certain authorities, but was branded a heretic and threatened with death. With a few of his followers, he searched throughout Central Asia, hunting not for treasure or lost cities but for this kind of tree. They found some survivors, and not without a great deal of difficulty managed to get it to this island, where they thought a great battle might one day be fought against Kur.

"They planted seeds and saplings, but were discovered by Kur's allies. Somehow the fact that they had brought quickwood to the island remained secret. I can't say for certain that they all died, but I know Sen was returned to Kur. I remember the triumph when they brought him back. A diary one of his men kept, in Turkish of all things, stayed in a cave they were using. It was discovered only a few years ago. Haiti's charcoal gatherers destroyed most of the stands of quickwood they planted, so even the fact that the secret was kept from Kur was almost turned to naught. I happened upon the diary and managed to translate it. I realized there were quickwood trees living on the national preserve around the old ruins here, and I began to experiment with it. I've resurrected the hedge version of quickwood. You are welcome to take samples of that back with you, as well. Both variants are hardy. They will grow anywhere more mundane pine can exist."

Valentine began counting tree trunks. "How much have you grown?"

"More than you can carry. You can take back saplings, seeds, even timber if you choose. I've seen to it that more groves exist in the mountains you see west of here. That is why the resistance thrives here on Haiti. The Reapers who go into the mountains do not return."

"I'd like to talk to the leader of the guerrillas, find out how he uses it in action."

"Victo here can arrange it for you. He's one of them."

The conference was held on the first night of May, under a new moon. Valentine, Ahn-Kha, Victo, and Post met in one of the spacious old rooms of the partially restored estate at Sans Souci. Papa Legba slumbered in a hammock chair on a veranda, with two of his attending priests squatting at the foot, ready to do his bidding should he awake. Narcisse was nearby, sitting on a cushion and cheerful in a red dress, watching the conference and Papa Legba.

Three great guerrilla warriors attended, arriving with ceremony they found appropriate. A praise-singer entered first, regaling the attendees with a litany of virtues and victories of their warlord to a Caribbean beat. Bayenne, the Rock of Thormonde (among other titles), was from the south, with a thousand soldiers and ten thousand subjects under him. Jacques Monte-Cristi had men, his "sacred knives" scattered to the west, blocking any drive from the other half of the island along the north coast. Victo served one of his lieutenants, in charge of the area immediately around Cape Haitian, nominally under the control of Kur. And finally there was Anton Uwenge, the Blue Devil of the Three Rivers, who commanded "three legions, one for each river of the north"—though the "legions" sounded like undersize regiments when Valentine pressed Victo for details.

Valentine, acting as host after an introduction by Papa Legba, began the conference at a long table in what had once been a magnificent dining room. "Thank you all for making the journey to Sans Souci. Please forgive my French—it is poor, and my understanding of your inflections even worse. I may have to use my friend and rescuer Narcisse as an interpreter at times.

"We've heard about the successes you've had on this island up north. We know you fight here with few resources but courage. We think you can help us, by teaching us how you use quickwood when you fight. I mean to take some back in a ship, so that we can do the same in the North."

The guerrilla leaders exchanged a few quiet words and gestures.

Bayenne rose to speak. "My men dig traps in the hills," Bayenne began. "Some big enough to swallow a bus, some only as large as your foot. We line the bottoms with stakes cut from the branches of the sacred trees. They wound the Haitian soldiers forced to fight us, and many times a man with a bad foot wound is no longer forced to fight. The others, the Whisperers, they kill, as long as it is not a trap from last year. My men carry stabbing-daggers made of the sacred wood, as well."

Jacques Monte-Cristi spoke next. "Perhaps, *blanc,* you have seen the short spears some of my men carry? Except for the very tip, the blade is of wood, fashioned in such a way as to splinter and snap off in the wound. Sadly, it takes several men to get one of the cursed ones. They fight like demons. If you could get us better guns from the north, we would do more."

"We tried bows," Uwenge said, speaking in slow but clear English. "Blowguns, everything. Nothing will penetrate their robes. My men have wooden bayonets at the ends of their rifles now. But they still must get close. It takes a brave man to face one of the Whisperers. When they know a battle is coming, my men drug themselves with cocaine, sing songs, scream, anything to raise their courage. I never send out patrols of fewer than thirty men. If four or five come across a Whisperer, it is they who die. It is bad when they come from the sea in groups."

Valentine nodded. "It hasn't been for nothing. Your people are free."

Monte-Cristi nodded. "We sometimes think we are wearing them down. They do not raid into Haiti as they used to. But it grows harder and harder for us to go to Santo Domingo. They have established a chain of garrisons on the border in fortified posts, and they send out many patrols. Unless we use a small team, the garrisons send out columns. The men have to either scatter or fight as they retreat to Haiti. The columns corner them otherwise, it may end in brave battle, but they always win. Either way, we lose many men."

"That is the source of our guns," Uwenge added. "Without going into Santo Domingo, at least for me, there is no way to capture more. My men have wooden clubs and spears for reasons other than killing Whisperers. Boul in Cape Haitian smuggles a few to us, so we leave him alone, though he does terrible things to people trying to escape Domingo and then claims to be winning victories against us by pointing to the bodies. But he is useful to us, so we turn away and leave him to his games."

Post scratched the salt-and-pepper hair above his ear, extracted an insect, and dropped it to the floor, where he finished it with his foot. "We have a few extra guns on board, some ammunition."

"Anything would help," Uwenge said.

Valentine looked up from a map of Hispaniola. "Do you have friends, spies, anything beyond these garrisons?"

Bayenne nodded. "We have friends, through smugglers and traders. They pass us information."

"There are also the roadwatchers," Monte-Cristi said.

"Who are they?" Valentine asked.

"Spies. They watch the roads toward Haiti, let us know if many men go to one of the garrisons on the border. They also look out at the ocean from high points so we know when ships are coming."

"Do they have radios?"

"No, most rely on their children as runners."

"What about these garrisons?"

"We know that some have radio sets, the ones that are electrified. The rest use telephone lines."

"So most of their armed men are in the garrisons?"

Bayenne nodded. "Yes, or in the big cities on the coast."

Valentine thought for a moment, excitement building in him like a flywheel's electrical charge as it always did when he worked on a plan. "I'd like to see quickwood in action. I think we can help you get a new supply of weapons, but it would require men willing to go deep into Santo Domingo. I need to think this through with all of you. I can tell you this: We should be able to escape the pursuing columns. What do you say?"

"Tell us more, *blanc*," Uwenge said.

"First I need to know more about the interior of the island."

Chapter Eight

Santo Domingo, May: The Kurians outside the rebel territories of the Roots divide their subjects into a simple caste system. A young Santo Domingan is born into life as a peon, engineer, artisan, or soldier. The peons are the most numerous. They are the laborers who work the plantations, on the docks, in the fields, and within the mines. These establishments are known as stations, named for what they produce and for the man in charge. "Sugar Sanchez" would be a cane-sugar farm managed by a man (or infrequently a woman) named Sanchez. Peons are born, live, and die on the same plantation, though women are sometimes married off to other stations. The engineers are hardly worthy of the title—they are construction laborers responsible for maintenance of roads and buildings who enjoy a more varied life than the peons. Artisans can be found in the workshops doing tasks which take more expertise, enjoying enough comforts in exchange for their skill that they could be called "bourgeoisie" by the French-speaking Haitians. And finally, there are the soldiers, many of whom live in hope of distinguishing themselves in such a way that they are promoted to "Station Manager."

Being born into a class does not mean you stay there. An unenthusiastic soldier will find himself in a peon's barracks at a nickel mine if he makes an enemy of one of his officers. A young, vigorous peon may get into the soldier class through superior performance at the "trials," yearly con-

tests held at some larger stations or towns by the Kurian Order's recruiters.

Geography plays a role in Santo Domingo's organization. The Kur control the island from the coastal cities, and as a traveler goes inland, the visitor will see less and less evidence of organization. The Cordillera Central, the Caribbean's highest mountains, are comparatively uninhabited save for runaway peons and hunting Reapers. And the roadwatchers.

After the death of his parents and siblings, when Valentine filled the hours of youth in the Padre's library, he read a book about the space program. Though the astronauts were deservedly the heroes of the story, Mission Control back in Houston was the real nerve center of the operation.

As he stood at the roadside stop of La Miel at the unofficial border, a month's worth of planning came to a climax. He felt like the NASA flight director, receiving last-minute reports from the Haitians, the *Thunderbolt*'s crew, and even Santo Domingans before setting off.

He started off with Post, in charge of the core group of *Thunderbolt* marines and sailors who would use the machine guns brought off the ship.

"How are we doing with the ammunition for the belt-feds?" Valentine asked.

"I just finished checking it. The Haitians couldn't come up with any, or so they said. Leaving a supply on the ship, we've got a few thousand rounds, enough for one good fight unless we can pick some up."

"Let's have an 'alpha' gun and a 'beta' gun, then. Put the best gunner, by which I mean the least trigger-happy, on alpha. We'll just leave one belt with the beta team. The marines?"

"They're in good shape, plenty of rifle ammunition. I don't think anyone's got under sixty rounds—most have decided to carry over a hundred. About the same with the pack animals."

"Two canteens a man, at least, right?" Valentine asked.

"Yeah, some of the guys are carrying four."

"So far I haven't seen water being a problem, but we'll be moving fast. How are those pikes you came up with doing?"

Post shuffled his feet and looked down, but Valentine knew he was proud of his invention. Valentine had seen him working on them, and had a good idea of what Post was constructing, but he wanted his lieutenant to have his moment. Post waved a Coastal Marine over.

The man held an aluminum tube a good seven feet long. Valentine tested its heft.

"I wanted something light, of course. I found a bunch of aluminum pipe for electrical conduits in the machine shop. There was heaps of the stuff lying around in Kingston. It was easy to screw it together. Then we came up with the heads. It's that quickwood, threaded just like a pipe. Just a matter of screwing it in. It holds in well enough, but if we get a chance to stick it in a Reaper, it'll break off. Then you screw a new one."

He handed Valentine a sharpened cone of wood. It was perhaps sixteen inches long altogether, six inches of handle, threaded to go into the fitting at the end of the aluminum pole. The handle widened by an inch or so, before narrowing to a point capped with a sharp metal tip.

"I've seen those Reaper robes before. This'll penetrate," Post continued. "Material designed to stop a lead bullet doesn't do much good against a point like this. If things get dicey, you can grab a spare point by the handle and use it like a dagger. We've got an adapter for the rifles even, the men can put them on the end like a bayonet."

"The training with the Haitians?"

"We've got two pikemen to go with every rifleman. If it works like it is supposed to, the one with the shorter spear will stay in beside the rifleman. Then there's the man with the gun, and another with a long pike in back. Of course, that's only if we're up against a Reaper. Otherwise, the pikemen will be hugging dirt until they can get firearms."

"That's the whole point of this expedition."

Valentine met with Ahn-Kha next. The Grog held a mass of metal and wood the size of a ship's anchor in his arms.

"Practice with the crossbows?" Valentine asked.

"The new cords are holding better, my David."

"No shortage of nylon line on the *Thunderbolt*. Just a matter of weaving it together. We'll need Grogs for those. I don't think any of us are strong enough to cock a leaf-spring from a truck."

"Care to try?"

Valentine took the oversize crossbow. The wooden frame showed the usual Grog craftsmanship, from the reinforced trigger-housing to the heavy stock to balance the weighty span of metal at the front.

Valentine placed the crossbow on the ground, planted his feet against the reborn leaf-spring, and gripped the corded nylon. He heaved, and just managed to lock the cord over the trigger. He handed it back to Ahn-Kha, feeling sapped. Even a moment's exertion in Hispaniola's heat brought a fresh layer of sweat running over old accumulations of perspiration and dirt.

Ahn-Kha showed him one of the quarrels, also tipped with a metal point like Post's pikes. "See the wooden flutes? They will splinter in the wound. The quarrels are lacquered to keep the sap inside fresh."

"You're sure?"

"We shot a wild pig with one," Ahn-Kha said. "We dug inside, found half the shaft. The rest of the head shattered into splinters."

"How's it shoot?"

"Try."

Valentine lifted its weight with an effort. He tried to aim at a tree, but the weight of the crossbow defeated him.

Ahn-Kha snorted. "Try this." The Grog knelt into a three-point stance, and Valentine put the crossbow across his friend's back. Sighting on the tree was a good deal easier with a quarter ton of tripod. He tried the trigger.

The crossbow had more recoil than he'd thought, though it pulled forward rather than back into his shoulder. The quarrel spun oddly in flight; Valentine had only shot bows on occasion as a youth. The shaft buried itself into the tree trunk with a resounding *thwack*.

"We have four crossbows, and something even more interesting." Ahn-Kha threw a blanket off a lump on the ground, revealing something that looked like an old-fashioned cannon. Ahn-Kha unfolded a bipod at the nozzle, poured a measured amount of gunpowder in the muzzle, and tamped it down with a metal rod. Four wooden fins flared from the tip.

"It's a harpoon gun. Better range than the crossbows. The shaft might go clean through, but the fins will break off. We use loose-grain powder for this. The tight stuff launched it too fast—it didn't aim right."

"Seems a hell of a load to tote."

"The harpoon isn't the only thing it fires. We can load the head with explosives. It makes a good grenade thrower. I've designed one- and three-pound loads. We may find a use for them."

"We might at that," Valentine agreed.

He joined Jacques Monte-Cristi next. The guerrilla leader had an elongated face and deep hollows at his temples, as if a giant had grabbed his head as an infant and pulled his physiognomy into a new face. Gray frosted his shorn hair, and his eyes never rested. He had the lean, suspicious look that Valentine remembered from his years in the Wolves: that of a man who spent much of his time walking into danger.

"Have you heard from the others?" Valentine said. The French tripped off his tongue more easily with constant practice.

"My men reported that they are on the move. They will attack in the night the garrisons north and south of our route, and screen our movement into the central mountains."

"Rations?" Valentine had been asking the same questions

for weeks, then offering advice until he got the answers he wanted. Now it was a matter of routine.

"Each man has two days, and we have a further two days on packhorses."

"Let's take a walk."

Valentine took a turn through Monte-Cristi's campsite. Two hundred armed men, aided by thirty "pioneers" who carried extra supplies and tended to the pack animals, were gathered in chattering groups. Valentine expected more tension on this, the morning of the expedition. Instead he heard singing, joking, and laughter from the clustered men. There was little formal command structure to Monte-Cristi's "regiment"; some of the guerrilla leaders had eighty men under them—some commanded a dozen. Valentine knew the names of only the leaders, and the men under them were a nameless mass, though he knew many faces by now.

They looked at Valentine as he passed through, smiling and nodding. He caught a word in Creole and smiled as he silently translated it. Valentine had heard a few men call him "Scar," and it seemed that the moniker had become general.

"How did you become responsible for all this?" Valentine asked after they had passed through the men.

"My 'sacred knives'? Pure obstinacy, Captain. It is not well known, but I am Santo Domingan."

"Why shouldn't it be well known?"

"The two sides of the island have bitter feelings going back before the Kur."

"I see. How did you end up on this side of the line?"

Monte-Cristi walked him out of the village and up the hillside and found a shady tree. They sat on the ground side by side and looked down at the lounging soldiers in the village. War, as always, was endless stretches of waiting. Fingernail-sized wildflowers bloomed in the morning sun.

"I was in the Santo Domingo underground. And we were literally an underground. We lived in natural caves and tunnels. I was in the 'cadre,' which I suppose meant officers. Mostly we exhorted others to join, and our men to stay.

Eventually they hunted us down to our caves and blocked us up. Two times they went in after us. None ever came out to tell how strong we were. So they turned to words. The National Guard promised us good treatment if we would come out, and we refused. They tried to smoke us out with burning tires. There is not much gasoline on this island, but they even used that. Some died choking. Have you ever seen a body of a man who is air-poisoned?"

Valentine shook his head.

"We began to go hungry, and the next time they sent a prisoner in with food and more promises, I gave my men a choice. They could leave with honor—they had already been asked to endure more than any man could be expected to survive and remain sane—but I would stay and die. I asked only that they leave me their knives, so I would have something to remember them by as I stayed in the cave."

"How many stayed?" Valentine asked.

"Very few, perhaps one in eight. And you know, I was glad. I felt that no man should have to die as we were, like some kind of vermin. Even if they marched them out to a firing squad, I thought that a better end.

"Those that remained . . . became ugly. We stayed alive in there seven months. No food but what we could catch, water that tasted like sulfur. They sealed the entrance and made the cave a tomb though we were not yet dead. We sickened and died. Some of the men took their own lives. We kept alive in ways that only one who has been through it before would understand. I kept up hope by looking for other exits, or seeing if we could enlarge the air holes to get out. We did find a cave with bats and we ate them, and I remember those days as you might remember one of the finest feasts of your life.

"So how am I alive and out, you are wondering? Some of the very men who left me their knives had slipped away, and came into the hills to get our bones. Our remains were to be relics in a secret monument to the resistance, you see. When they found us, I had to be pulled up and out. We were walking skeletons. Sadly, three more men sickened and died eating too much when we got out. But I still had their knives, and offered them back to their families. When I was well enough, we slipped into Haiti. My heart is weak and sometimes I think I am a little crazy, for all I dream of is those days in the darkness. I keep away the desire to return and die in that cave by fighting."

"So you became a leader because you refused to give up? That's as good a way as any to become a hero."

"But I do not deserve it. There are legends already about our ordeal. In Santo Domingo they say I turned my men into zombies, and ate them. Here in Haiti they say Baron Samedi came and brought us food from the other world, and anyone who has eaten it is never the same again. Both legends are part truth and part falsehood. Ever since then I have been Monte-Cristi, the one who lives for revenge for all those who died in the cave. I fear I will return to the cave, either in body or spirit. Both would mean the death of me."

"Narcisse told me that you were the kind of man to fight to the last drop of your blood. Sounds like you came closer to doing it than anyone I've ever heard of."

Monte-Cristi did not smile. He was the only Hispaniolan Valentine had met who did not smile at the slightest opportunity. "The men are interested in you, too. Your ship, the Grogs, the Jamaican pirates, they already say you are a white Toussaint-Louverture. A man of cunning alliances."

"They say too much," Valentine said. He thought of adding a platitude, like, 'We all do what we can,' but decided it would be trite. The man sitting next to him was beyond aphorisms.

"I think someone looks for you," Monte-Cristi said, pointing down the hill.

"Lieutenant Post. Thank you for the story . . . err . . . do you have a rank? Colonel, perhaps?"

"I am just Monte-Cristi. I would feel happier if I were Jacques to you."

"Then I will always be David to you, sir."

"Your other responsibilities await. I should get back to my men."

They walked back down the hill. Valentine noticed that Monte-Cristi breathed heavily.

Post trotted up to him, showing no sign of wound or alcohol. "That bandy-legged fellow's back, sir," Post said. "He's asking for you."

"That 'bandy-legged fellow' is going to keep us alive in the mountains, Post. His name is Cercado, and we're counting on him to get us to San José."

"No offense, of course. He's just funny-looking, whatever he's good at."

Valentine found the funny-looking man in question at the village well, drinking. He was short of stature, potbellied, and naked from the waist up and knees down. Tangled hair covered his head, shoulders, and even something of his face. He was a "roadwatcher," the one with the most extensive network in central Hispaniola.

"Good news?" Valentine asked. He had learned in previous conversations with the roadwatcher that most items in his brain were categorized as either "good news" or "bad news." This valley was "bad news," for there were troops under an active officer. Another mountainside was "good news," because there were strawberries to eat and many honeycombs.

"Good news," Cercado reported. "The soldiers in the garrisons think they are going to be attacked along the mountain roads. They've sent out many patrols where the Haitians have gathered. We could take elephants over the mountains, and it would not be known for days."

"How about food reserves?"

"There could be much more, if you could let me go outside my personal network. And this business about putting caches everywhere—both north and south of the peaks— much of the effort will go to waste."

"Tell them if it is not eaten in four days, they may have it back. We could be forced to turn aside, or even back, and I want that food available. Also, just in case word does get out and they find some of them, they might guess wrong about where we are going because of the supplies."

Valentine missed his days on the *Thunderbolt*. Being on a ship eliminated many of the problems of food and drinking water, thanks to her available tonnage of stores. He was back to the days of commanding Wolves in the mountains, constantly worrying about how and where he would feed his men.

"You've done all that I asked and more. Take a meal and sleep while you can. We'll be setting off this afternoon."

"I can sleep while walking. I shall find you on the south slope of the Nalga de Maco tonight. If you hear hollow-log drumming, that means bad news. Turn back."

"Yes, I remember."

"But you will hear no drums, I am sure. Our friends will cause too much trouble for that."

Valentine made a noncommittal grunt.

The column was already ascending the mountainside when they heard the shots. Some trick of acoustics among the clouds and hills brought the faint popping sound of small-arms fire and deeper explosions from the garrison to the south, where Bayenne was making as much noise as possible. His feint against the garrison guarding one of the valley passages into Santo Domingo was crucial to drawing away whatever patrols might be out north of the garrison.

The raiding column moved with Ahn-Kha and his Grogs in the vanguard. Valentine hoped their unexpected presence would frighten, or at least confuse, any patrols they ran into. The heavier weapons, along with the sailors and marines of the *Thunderbolt,* followed behind, with Post in charge of making sure the main body did not lose contact with the Grogs. The Haitians were next with the packhorses, accompanied by a mounted force of Monte-Cristi's men watching the front, flanks and rear.

Valentine, astride a Haitian roan with a white blaze across its face, walked the animal along the marching column of Monte-Cristi's men. A runner from the forward column sought him out.

"Bad news, sir. The forward van ran into a patrol. They shot at each other—no one was hurt."

Valentine said a prayer of thanks that the men Monte-Cristi chose for his runners spoke their Creole clearly enough for him to understand.

So the Santo Domingans were no fools. He had hoped their forces would pull in around the garrisons, fearing an all-out assault. Instead they were probing.

Hoofbeats behind announced the arrival of Monte-Cristi.

"We're found out already. The screening patrol Bayenne sent out missed them," Valentine said.

"Do we turn back?"

Valentine fought the urge to swear. "They're your men, no matter what we decided about the command. The risk is greater now, but I say no. I won't make it an order, however. We can go with less. Detach a good number of men, fifty or sixty, under a capable officer. Have them chase that patrol south and make it look like we're a flanking maneuver to cut off the garrison's road. If they do cut it, so much the better."

"And if they meet greater numbers in turn?"

"Then they run like hell for Bayenne or anywhere they think is safe. I want the Santo Domingans to do the bleeding, not us."

"Agreed. Papa Legba said you were a man to be followed, despite your years. We go on."

After a brief halt that allowed Monte-Cristi to organize the detachment, they got under way again. The column trudged steadily and slowly uphill. The sun vanished in a crimson explosion, then turned the sky over to the stars. With the night complicating matters, Post called frequent halts to allow the column to keep in a compact bunch. At every stop, the men ate some of their rations meant to last for two days, but Valentine left that to Monte-Cristi. He had been warned that the men preferred to carry their food in their stomachs instead of in their bags.

Cercado appeared out of the dark, with two skinny youths he introduced as nephews. The boys did not take after their uncle in grooming: their scalps were shorn like merinos in springtime.

"We had some trouble near the border. A patrol."

"I am sorry, Captain. Always in war is bad news. Always."

You just summed up war almost as concisely as Sherman, roadwatcher. "We're pressing on. You've got more of your family spread out up the mountain, and then down to San José?"

"Yes."

"How many are there?"

Cercado frowned. "Were it not for the accursed ones, there would be sixty-seven or more. My father had five sons and three daughters, and I am the second oldest. My father and my elder brother both died. Every year more die than are born. There are twenty-nine of us now. In ten years' time, the family of Cercado will cease to be, unless some of the infants survive. They hunt us up and down the mountains, and sometimes they find us."

"Why do you keep on?"

"Why do you?"

Valentine nodded at the feral-looking man, for a moment feeling an affinity for him stronger than his battle-tested friendship with Post. "I understand. I'm the last of my family."

"You are still young. Find a wife, have children, go far from them. There are other ways to beat them than killing."

"My father tried that. I'm still the last."

"I see. So you stick to killing." It was a statement, not a question.

Valentine looked back at the men. "How long until we can rest?"

Cercado took the question literally. "At the rate you go? A few more hours. Say five at most. Then you will be safe among the heights."

* * *

They reached the heights, grassy meadows on the rounded tops of the mountains that reminded Valentine of some of the weather-rounded peaks of the Ouachitas. They had come up far. Far higher than the mountain that held the Once-ler's Citadel. It was cool, even for Haiti in June, at this elevation.

Valentine walked his horse backwards down the column. He nodded at Monte-Cristi. "We'll rest until dawn," Monte-Cristi announced. The men groaned in relief as they sat.

There was Post to see, and Ahn-Kha. The Grogs were already sleeping in a heap of limbs and broad backs, like pigs seeking the comfort of each other's warmth in a cold sty.

"Rest, my David. I will keep watch," Ahn-Kha said.

"I'll join you. I can sleep in the saddle tomorrow."

"You are limping. You always do when you are tired. Stop pretending you're a ghost and rest," Ahn-Kha argued, sotto voce. Ahn-Kha's rubbery lips came to a point like an accusing finger.

"Wake me in two hours. Then you can sleep. Two hours, old horse, and that's all."

"Agreed."

Valentine unsaddled his mount and wiped the sweat from its back and muzzle. By the time he hobbled it, gave it a nosebag full of vegetables ground with sugar, and checked its hooves, half an hour of his two was gone. He looked at Ahn-Kha, standing atop a rock with the patience of a tree, as if the rock itself would succumb to fatigue before the Golden One would. Comforted, he slept beneath the statue-like shape.

"Up. You've been asleep two hours," Ahn-Kha said, prodding him in the back with one of his crossbow bolts.

Valentine snatched the bolt and rapped Ahn-Kha on the shin with it before the Golden One could react. "Thanks."

Ahn-Kha responded with a playful swipe of his long-toed foot that Valentine ducked under even as he rose. There was a hint of something in the air, the early purple of the predawn. He realized he was chilled. "You lie down. My blanket's warm."

Ahn-Kha grunted and wrapped what he could of himself in the blanket. "Thank you, my David. That scout, Sera—"

"Cercado."

"Cercado kept awake. He moves well. I've never seen a man who can vanish among the rocks like that. Only you are more silent. But he hides even his shadow in his pocket."

"Speaking of silence . . . ," Valentine said.

The Grog snorted and closed his eyes.

Valentine watched the mists revealed by the dawn, admiring the craftsmanship of the crossbow quarrel while waiting out the light. The quarrel had chiseled ridges running down the shaft, creating an artful, air-guiding line from tip to flange. The Grogs put artistry into everything they made, even something meant to be fired once into an enemy.

The pink-and-blue of first light revealed his column isolated as though on the shores of an island, surrounded by a calm gray sea of fog. Everything was reduced at this height: the trees, grasses, and flowers were all smaller, as if imitating the foreshortened landscape below. He woke Monte-Cristi, who in turn woke his other chieftains. The soldiers gathered at a spring Cercado pointed out. Their guide's discovery was hardly more than a seep, but the men lined up as though it were a tiled bath.

Valentine wished for a moment he were one of them, joking as they waited for a washup. His thoughts drifted back, as they did with unsettling frequency, to the months of Quisling service on the Gulf Coast. Ordinary soldiers weren't asked to put on the uniform of their bitterest enemy, salute men they despised, organize more thorough sweeps of coastal islands and bays to capture auras for the insatiable Kurians. At the time he told himself, told Duvalier, that he just followed orders, didn't kill anyone himself unless they were shooting at him. Usually in defense of their families. Maybe Duvalier believed him. Trouble lay in that he couldn't convince himself. He could still hear the squalling of terrified children as his men shoved them and their mothers into pens, ready to be shipped—

"The mists are a stroke of fortune," Cercado said from somewhere on the other side of the world. "If we move now, we can be back among the trees before they clear. It is downhill from here."

Valentine boxed up his terrible memories. For now. "Good. We'll get off this ridge while it lasts."

He endured a series of vexing delays while the men took up their arms and equipment. Only the packhorses were ready, happily cropping mouthfuls of mountain grass.

Post came up the slope from the head of the column as Valentine mounted his horse. "There's trouble with the Grogs."

Valentine rode off the ridge and came upon Ahn-Kha, arguing with his scouts. The Golden One used a combination of barks and gestures to encourage his reluctant charges.

"What's the matter?"

Ahn-Kha's ears were up and pointed forward. "Fools! They take the mists for poisoned air. They remember their grandfathers' tales of chemical weapons of fifty years ago, and they're frightened of descending into the fog."

"Post, keep the column moving, don't worry about the Grogs for now," Valentine said, using the quarrel to tap the horse's flank. It trotted down the grassy slope toward the fog.

"I'll ride in and come out alive," he hollered back. "Tell them I breathe just as they do." The mist closed in around him. The sun winked white on the horizon.

When he replayed the incident in his mind later, Valentine rebuked himself for forgetting everything old Everready had taught him about moving alone, his first year as a Wolf. He had failed to lower his lifesign and his anger at the delays kept his senses from knowing the Reaper was near until it leapt out of the mist.

It wanted him as a prisoner, not as a corpse, for it killed the horse with a kick that caved in the roan's skull. Man, beast, and Reaper crashed to the meadow grass. Man fell beneath beast; Reaper landed on its feet beside Valentine with feline poise. It turned, its bullet-stopping cape cracking the air like a whip.

Valentine reached for his holster, but the Reaper was faster. It planted a foot on him, and knocked away his automatic faster than his eyes could follow the motion.

His arm went numb. The Reaper reached behind him and removed his machete from its sheath across his back. Pinned as he was, he could no more grasp the machine gun strapped across his saddlebags than he could the mountaintop.

"Hel—," Valentine managed, before the Reaper's long-fingered hand closed over his face. Fingernails like steel talons dug into his cheek.

The Reaper dragged him out from under the horse by his head, its baleful yellow eyes staring into his from an unkempt tangle of thin black hair. Its mouth was open in a theater-mask grin, revealing pointed black teeth. It looked upslope at some motion Valentine caught out of the corner of his eye, and pulled its captive to its chest, putting the other arm under his knees, like a muscular hero taking up his lover. The Reaper turned to run.

Valentine struck. In pulling him free, the Reaper released his trapped hand holding the quarrel. He gripped the wood near the point and struck the Reaper in the pit of its stomach. The Reaper staggered, gripping him so tightly to its chest, he thought his back would break. Valentine fought the crushing embrace and lost. He could not draw breath.

Suddenly Post was in front of them, one of his pikes barring the way. Valentine looked up at the Reaper's face. Its mouth yawned open in a terrible grimace, fighting some inner seizure. It dropped him, and sank to its knees.

Valentine rolled downhill. He turned three full revolutions before stopping himself. Vision wavering from pain and dizziness, he looked up at the Reaper. Its eyes rolled up into its skull. Post stood frozen, staring at the thing in astonishment.

Ahn-Kha appeared in the mists, his crossbow cocked and

ready. The Grog circled the Reaper, and saw the bolt protruding from the stomach, the wood swollen where it touched the avatar's flesh. Ahn-Kha came to Valentine's side, keeping the weapon ready but his attention on Valentine.

"My David. You are hurt?"

Valentine shook his head, cradling his right arm. "Not seriously. I think my hand . . . or my arm is banged up good." What he wanted to say was that it stung like a son of a bitch, but Ahn-Kha never complained of discomfort, so why should he?

"I heard your horse fall, and feared for you. I readied the crossbow, for only one of those would get the better of you, and came. Post, too."

"Stupid," Valentine grunted, flexing his fingers.

"For leaving the column?"

"No, stupid of me. My apologies, my friend, I put us in danger because I wasn't thinking."

"There can be no apologies between us. Come! Let us see how this quickwood kills."

The Grog pulled him to his feet with burly ease. They walked up the hill, Valentine feeling like a Sioux version of Richard III, limping along horseless and with paralyzed fingers. The head of the column appeared out of the mists, Grogs among the Haitians with weapons at the ready.

Valentine inspected the dead Reaper. Propped up on its knees, it seemed to be howling at the waxing sun rising from the Santo Domingo mountains.

"Tell your great friend that he hit it square," Monte-Cristi said. "A good shot, near enough the heart to kill it in a few seconds."

"No, that was me. I barely stabbed it. The wood went in an inch or two at most, that thing has muscle like armor plating."

Valentine thought back on those "few seconds," which seemed to his pained remembrance to be hours at least, and looked into the empty yellow eyes of the Reaper. He tried to imagine what it would feel like, having the heart harden into a solid mass. Did the Kurian at the other end feel the pain, as well? He found himself hoping so, before shrinking back from the sadistic speculations.

The men would waste the whole morning admiring the dead Reaper if he didn't move them along.

"Post, let's tighten the column up in this mist. Ahn-Kha, you and your Grogs will get a break for a while. Take a place at the rear."

As the various groups got themselves organized in four different tongues—counting Grog-speech as a language—Valentine retrieved his weapons and saddlebags. Monte-Cristi offered him his horse, but he declined. Penance for his foolishness would be being on foot for the rest of the long journey. A pair of Haitian pioneers retrieved the saddle and added it to the pack animals' burdens.

The Grogs looked at him, sniffing and pointing at the still-warm cadaver and muttering to each other. One licked its chops. Ahn-Kha growled something, and they turned abjectly away.

The Cat intervened: "Oh, belay that. They can dress and quarter it, as long as they do it quickly. But they have to share with any of the men who want a piece of horsemeat."

Valentine squatted in the hills looking down at the armory, which in turn stood in the hills above the dilapidated town of San Juan. Behind him, the serration crowned by Pico Duarte purpled the dawn's horizon.

His column had covered close to fifty mountainous miles in three nights and two days, and had once again been reduced when he detached Post to cut the valley road leading northwest out of San Juan to the garrison on Haiti's border. What was left of his command was hardly larger than the garrison inside the armory, if Cercado's estimation was to be believed.

Their march had been uncontested, if not uneventful, as they descended from the high mountains, following paths staked out by Cercado and his family. Until they ran into a trio of Santo Domingan soldiers on patrol.

Monte-Cristi's horsemen had finally run the scouts to earth this morning, and the hunt ended tragically, with the shooting of all three scouts when they came to bay among some rocks. Valentine seethed at the loss of vital information even as he congratulated Monte-Cristi's men for their coup.

He examined the armory from higher ground. It was built more to withstand thievery than assault, though inside a perimeter fence of barbed wire the buildings were linked by a series of walls and wooden towers. The whole edifice had the slapped-together look endemic to the Kurian Zone.

"The defenses are strongest to the town side," Monte-Cristi said, agreeing with Valentine's estimation. "If we can get through the wire before they know we are here—"

"See all the dog kennels?" Valentine said. "They'd start barking while we were still fifty feet outside the wire."

"So we turn around?"

The temptation was strong. He'd seen the quickwood work, up close and far sooner than he'd expected. Valentine had no desire to burn the lives of Monte-Cristi's soldiers, who had come so far so fast without letting fatigue wear down their spirits. Valentine couldn't take all the quickwood he could carry and then leave Hispaniola no better off than the day he arrived.

But there was more than duty and orders at stake.

If the Roots accomplished something to make the march worthwhile, won a victory, it might bring more numbers to their cause. A successful raid that didn't involve being ignominiously chased back across the border would hearten the Roots as much as it would dismay the Santo Domingan Kurians. But it had to start somewhere.

"No. We can't blow them out of there, and I can't ask your men for an assault. We'll have to do it another way."

"I cannot imagine how."

"With parley."

*　　*　　*

An hour later Valentine, Ahn-Kha, and Cercado walked out of the hills to the wire, a white flag in Ahn-Kha's hands. Again and again Valentine blew a small officer's whistle, drawing attention to their movements.

Behind them, Monte-Cristi's men and the Grogs flitted from tree to tree, appearing in as many places as possible. They appeared at the tops of rises, then sank into the long grass to show themselves again behind a tree. Even the bodies of the three Santo Domingan scouts were impressed into the action; they manned a wooden machine gun from the crotch of a branch while leaning behind a tree. Ahn-Kha's Grogs called to each other from a wide semicircle around the armory; their otherworldly voices echoed ominously between the hills.

The multicolored flag of Santo Domingo hung from the flagpole, its white cross visible now and then as the breeze took it. A small house stood before the flag. From it an officer with a braided hat emerged and observed them. Calling a few men around him, the officer strode up to the wire fence, looking toward his towers to see that he was properly covered. As he approached, hand on the pistol at his hip, Valentine took the safety off his drum-fed submachine gun.

"Translate for me, would you, Cercado? My Spanish may not be up to this."

Cercado nodded.

"What is it? Who are you men?" the officer called to them.

"We represent the free forces of Hispaniola," Valentine said, and waited for Cercado to translate. "We do not come to fight, but to find friends among those who would oppose Kur. Much of Haiti stands free of their menace, and we look to our brothers on this side of the island to join."

"Your men have been beaten in battle at the border. You are misguided. It would be best if you surrendered to me, not the other way around," the officer said.

"Do your generals always tell the truth?" Valentine asked through Cercado. "We give you an hour to decide. You do not have to join us, just leave us this place, intact, and you may go in peace. Though we would prefer for you and your men to join the movement which will see Hispaniola rid of them."

"Thank you for your terms. Here are mine. I will take your heads, or you will take mine. San Juan has many men, and others will come and drive you out of these mountains. The garrisons at the borders still stand. Two days ago they asked for more ammunition."

Valentine yelled in Spanish, as best he could: "Have you heard from the garrisons since then, my friend? And was the ammunition delivered? Or did it fall into our hands?"

The officer pursed his lips, but to his credit, he did not look doubtful. "We shall use the hour given to make ready for you. Come at your peril. If I were you, I would leave. Remember what I said about your heads."

"You can be sure of it," Cercado called, not waiting for Valentine's answer.

Valentine had his group back up, still facing the fort, and the officer did likewise. The men said something even Valentine's ears could not catch, but their tones were anxious.

Valentine returned to the shadow of a battle line. He would be reluctant to attack the alerted garrison even if he had the men he was trying to feign that he had. Was the officer bluffing as much as he?

He paced for a moment or two, as Ahn-Kha stared down at the armory.

"If they are expecting battle, there is not much sign of it. I've seen the same men go in and out of the center building three times," Ahn-Kha said.

"They might have sent some of his men to the forward garrisons."

"Perhaps they need another push."

Valentine nodded. "He said he'd come for our heads, I believe. Give them a push . . . good idea, old horse. I think I know how to do it. Come with me."

He climbed up the grassy slope, crunching through strawlike growth burnt by the dry season's sun. Monte-Cristi was at the edge of a steep ravine cutting the side of the slope, urging his men to move the unburdened packhorses down at a noisy, jangling trot and then up again at a walk.

"The hoofbeats echo well, do they not, Captain?" Monte-Cristi asked.

"Very well. Jacques, I think I have a better use for those poor scouts we shot this morning. I need a tent spike out of the baggage. Is there a bellows with the farrier supplies?"

"No, no bellows. Nor an anvil. But we do have tent spikes." Monte-Cristi got one of his pioneers to retrieve a spike, and joined Valentine as the Cat and Ahn-Kha went up to the stand of trees with the dead bodies.

"Let's get out of sight. Get a good hot fire going," Valentine said. He looked at the dead bodies, faces peaceful in death. Rigor mortis would soon alter their attitudes.

A couple of the Haitians gathered, looking on with interest. Cercado joined the group. Once the fire had grown, Valentine thrust a tent spike in the center of the fire, and Ahn-Kha blew through one of the hollow pipes used as a haft for Post's pikes, handing it to Cercado when he could do no more. The Grog's capacious lungs aided by Cercado applied enough wind to get the spike hot enough, when held with a piece of leather, hot enough so that when Valentine spat on the point, the spittle jumped off the metal rather than make contact.

Sweating from the fire's heat, Valentine crossed over to the bodies and shoved the spike into the eye sockets of each corpse. He was rewarded with a gruesome sizzling sound and the smell of burning flesh.

Valentine heard the Haitians mutter to themselves when he, evidently not satisfied with the disfigurement, drew his knife and sliced the ears and lips from each skull. He then ordered Ahn-Kha to sever the heads with an ax. Three hearty chops from the Grog and some knife work left the marred objects grinning in the sun.

Still not satisfied, Valentine took up the knife and looked at the three heads for inspiration. The frightening thing was how easy all this was. He expected to feel revolted, but something akin to exultation coursed through his veins. He remembered some lines of Nietzsche about how easily man reverted to savagery. Inspired, he knelt and loosened the uniformed culottes.

"My David, are you sure?" Ahn-Kha asked quietly.

"If I'm going to do this, I'm going to do this all the way," Valentine said. He took up the first man's genitals in his fist, drawing them as tightly as he could from the bodies. He sawed through the skin under the scrotal sac and in a moment held the awful result in his hand. He returned to the head, and placed his bloody trophy in the dead lipless mouth.

Monte-Cristi looked sickened. One of the Haitians backed away, fingering a crucifix, but Cercado squatted and rubbed his hands in delight.

"We can't attack them where they are," Valentine growled. "This'll do one of two things. Enrage them so they come up after us, or send them running." Valentine continued his depredations. He finished by putting the three heads in a sack, and shouldered the bloody burden.

"Their hour has passed. Will anyone come with me?"

Ahn-Kha and Cercado, followed by a Haitian or two, walked down the hill, again covered by the white flag and blasts of Valentine's whistle. Valentine saw rifles pointed out of loopholes in the sides of the buildings, tracking them. Machine guns in the guard towers pointed ugly flared mouths in their direction, ready to spit fire. Valentine spoke into Cercado's greasy ear.

"Far enough!" the officer shouted. "If you seek death, you may come farther."

"You spoke of heads earlier, my friend. Here! These men served a Whisperer, who now is dead on the mountainside. We will come tonight for the rest."

Ahn-Kha took the sack in his hands. The Golden One spun like a hammer-thrower and released the sack to fly up and over the wire wall. It landed with a knocking thump before the walls of the armory.

The emissaries scattered, followed by a shot, then a second, from the walls.

"So much for white flags," Valentine said to Cercado, as the pair took cover behind a hummock of earth. He searched for Ahn-Kha. The Grog lay concealed at the base of a tree.

"You fight as they do," Cercado said.

"Maybe," Valentine replied. "Actually, the whole reason I'm doing this is to prevent a fight. But if we have to face them, I want to do it with the advantage."

"Only two shots. Why not more?"

"Why not, indeed."

The skirmish line hit the wire after sunset. All through the afternoon and evening, Valentine rested and fed his weary men. He watched and waited. The town of San Juan, like most he had seen on Hispaniola through the eyes of his binoculars, was a patchwork of earthquake ruins, banana-leaf huts, and surviving architecture. A few women came to the gate, bearing baskets, but were turned away without admittance and wandered back down the six-mile trail into town.

The Haitians avoided his eyes as he moved among them, disturbed at his treatment of the corpses. Valentine tried to shrug it off as the natural uneasiness of superstitious men who had seen social taboos broken. The bodies had been beyond pain and as dead as Julius Caesar, whatever animating spirit they possessed was gone; their souls could be prowling the happy hunting grounds or barking in hell—he would never know. But their corpses might have saved some of the lives of the men now shifting their eyes whenever he looked at them. In a fit of ill-mood, he considered presenting Ahn-Kha's Grogs with the bodies as a feast—*that would give them something to mutter about!*—but discarded the idea.

With the moon still down and full dark upon the armory, Valentine hit the fence with Ahn-Kha and the Grogs. They threw hides over the wire, and bodily pulled up the posts of the nine-foot-high fence, tearing away a twenty-foot section. The Grogs covered the gap with shotgun and crossbow, and the Haitians poured through. Valentine signaled Ahn-Kha to let the Grogs start their howling. The Haitians screamed like demons as they crossed the compound and made for the buildings.

Not one shot was fired from the walls.

The Haitians poured up and over the stone battlements linking the buildings, using loopholes as footholds or boosting each other up by having two men launch the third over. There were a certain amount of mishaps to the attempt on the wall, but without bullets flying, the bumps and falls were comic rather than tragic. Axes and fence-post battering rams made short work of the wooden doors once the men made it inside the compound, as Valentine and Ahn-Kha's Grogs secured the perimeter and main gate, which gaped open. He heard shouting, splintering wood, and assorted whoops of victory from beyond the peaked roof of the main building.

Valentine was glad to see a corral with animals still in it, but judging from the way the gate was left ajar, only lame animals were left by the departing garrison. As he patted a dejected-looking mare nosing her empty grain bin, he heard the main doors to the armory swing wide. Monte-Cristi and two panting soldiers bowed elaborately.

"The Citadel of San Juan is ours, *mon capitaine*," Monte-Cristi laughed. "Not a shot fired. Most of the garrison has evacuated. What is left is inside."

"Send a few men down the road, where they have a good overlook on the trail, but I want them still to be able to see these buildings. Get organized for a quick pullout, I'll blow my whistle, and loud, three times if I want us out of here. Is there electricity?"

"No, just fat lamps."

"Be sure no one goes looking in the dynamite shed with one, would you?"

Valentine left the gate to Ahn-Kha and passed the main

gate into the compound. The hollow-eyed officer lay there, bound hand and foot, with two of his former subordinates holding on to lines tied to his limbs. An old charwoman sat on a step, smoking cigarettes rolled from newsprint as she watched events; a pair of Haitians clubbed the officer who had offered an exchange of heads with their rifle butts.

"Stop that!" Valentine yelled. Another guerrilla squatted before the officer, laughing and taunting the wretch.

"Stop that!" he yelled again, putting his hand on his pistol. The men stood and turned, and backed away, hiding behind each other like children caught at mischief.

"We join, we join, we fight the Capos, you see," one of the erstwhile Santo Domingan soldiers holding a rope said in French.

Valentine looked at his new recruits—they had probably been bad soldiers for the Santo Domingans, and would be bad soldiers in his Cause, but he had to make do with what he had. Valentine tried to put words together in Spanish.

"Thank you . . . give him freedom," he managed.

The Santo Domingans looked at him blankly, either not able to understand why he would want to free an enemy or confused by his Spanish.

Valentine drew his knife and took a step toward them. They dropped the traces in alarm. He realized that he was snarling. He knelt by the officer.

"My eyes! For the love of God shoot me, but don't burn out my eyes," the man said.

"I won't hurt you," Valentine said, doing his best to soothe the man. "You won't be hurt at all. Have you left any surprises . . . booby traps?"

The man shook his head.

"You'll remain among these buildings until we've found out for sure. If you speak the truth, you'll be let go. Do you still say there are no booby traps?"

"No. No, sir."

Valentine turned to Monte-Cristi. "Jacques, put him under guard. Guard, not torture. God, I'm thirsty. Is there a well?"

"Between the barracks and that house your friend stayed in."

"See if you can find any carts, wheelbarrows, anything, to begin with. I saw a wagon by the corral. Start there. Then start loading, medical supplies and machine tools first, then hand tools, then good-quality guns, and finally ammunition. Put the best cart you can find outside the walls but inside the gate. Load any explosives on it. No nitroglycerin even if you find it—I don't want to mess with that stuff. Dynamite would be best, if it hasn't sweated. Nothing heavier than a grenade or a small mortar. We'll use bigger shells and any nitro to bring down this place later. Then we'll start looking for food."

Valentine climbed a ladder to look out over the walls on Ahn-Kha, and then moved to the well. After a generous water break, he moved inside the officers' house. He checked the radio first. It was smashed, and there were no notes on the clipboard hanging next to it.

He wondered how long Bayenne and the other Haitians would be able to keep up their facade of an attack on the border garrisons to the northwest. Even now the Kurians could be mobilizing. He took up one of the smelly tallow lamps and checked the bedrooms; he decided that three officers shared the quarters. Strange that only one was still present; no wonder the man looked harried and his troops were on edge.

Valentine broke open lockers with a crowbar until he found a supply of cigars. He heard someone else investigating the dining room and saw Cercado rooting through a liquor cabinet. Once the roadwatcher had satisfied himself that nothing alcoholic remained, Valentine asked him for his translation services. He walked out of the house and went to the officer, who was drinking a cup of water brought to him by the charwoman. He offered his prisoner a cigar and a light.

"Now things are easier between us that the ugliness is over," Valentine said through Cercado.

The man drew on his cigar and looked at Valentine through narrowed eyes.

"You have nothing to be ashamed of," Valentine said, and waited for Cercado to interpret. "With the troubles you've been having on the borders and elsewhere, we knew you would have only a handful of men."

"Men!" the officer said, his eyes filled with disgust. "If only. I was left with the stupid and the incompetent. I, I— whose father was at the storming of Monte Plata. Left with the imbeciles and cowards."

"I understand. It is the same on my side. These Haitians, they look formidable, but they are hardly better than animals. I would trust a horse to have more sense."

"Mine forgot what sense they had when they saw the leavings of those scouts."

"With your best men away, what could you do?"

"Yes, first they called up the militia for the assault on the island in Lago Enriquilo. It is time we took it back from the Kurians of Haiti. Some of my underofficers went with them. Then when your guerrillas started trouble at the border, our Capos ordered that every man be scraped up and sent to reinforce the garrisons. Otherwise, you would not be sitting here."

"Undoubtedly. The fortunes of war, sir. One moment while I find out if you keep your word about the booby traps, and then you'll see that I keep my word about letting you go. I suppose it is too much to hope for that you would join us."

"No. In the end, you will be hunted."

Valentine smiled. "We shall see." He jerked his chin at Cercado and had him follow. When they were safely out of earshot, he stopped the guide.

"This Lago Enriquilo—it's southeast of here in another valley, yes?"

"I do not know much about it. An island in the center of a lake that lies in the pass to Port-au-Prince. The Kurians here have feuded with the Kurians there before. This island is fortified, it has guns that command the roads in the valley."

Monte-Cristi moved about the courtyard, shouting orders to his men. He joined the two. "Not a great bounty, I fear. The tools yes, but few weapons. Some explosives, some ammunition."

"That's disappointing, but it will mean we can move faster," Valentine said. "Can we be out of here by dawn?"

"Even before. The men are looking for food now, but so far have little that is good for travel."

"If that's the worst luck we have on this trip, I'll take it," Valentine said. "We can raise some hell behind this Kurian's army on our way out."

Monte-Cristi nodded. He looked pale and weary. Valentine was about to tell him to get some rest when a call from the gate brought them to the walls.

A runner came in through the gate. "Engines, sir, coming up the road. Headlights, too."

Three trucks ground up the irregular road from San Juan, judging from the lights.

"Ahn-Kha," Valentine called, "get the Grogs out of sight." Then to Monte-Cristi: "Hell, we should have had someone put on a uniform. Where have our new 'recruits' gotten to?"

"Too late to find them now."

Valentine got a better look at the trucks. All were variants on the sturdy two-ton military model, the backbone of the world's former armies since the 1940s. So beat up were these that Valentine would have believed they had seen service with Patton's Red Ball Express. Metal panels had been replaced with bamboo and canvas, and instead of headlights, oil lamps hung from the front and sides like a nineteenth-century carriage. Each had a perfect set of off-road tires and spares, however, thanks to the abundant rubber trees on the island.

Valentine waved from the walls, hoping that he would just be a silhouette.

"Don't shoot, don't shoot," Valentine said to the men now gathering at the walls and main gate. "We'll need these trucks. Let everyone get off. Jacques, pass the word. Lower that gun!" he said, the last to a Haitian who was sighting on the driver's side "window," which consisted of corrugated aluminum with a triangular view-slit cut into it. "Nobody shoot until I do! Nobody shoot!"

The driver of the first truck dismounted, with not a few glances into the passenger cabin. He opened his mouth, as if summoning words, before ejaculating in Spanish and throwing himself to the ground, butt in the air and arms crossed over his head. Faces looked up from the beds of the trucks.

"I didn't catch that," Valentine said.

"'Shoot, shoot, it's the Haitians,'" the fallen driver said." Monte-Cristi translated, raising his pistol.

"Wait," Valentine bellowed in French. "Don't fire!"

A familiar figure swung himself out of the cabin of the first truck. "I told you not to be a hero," he said, planting a boot in the upthrust Domingan's behind. "Don't tell me I'm late to the party again?" Lieutenant Post called up at the walls, a broad smile on his face.

Post looked as exhausted as Monte-Cristi, and Valentine was determined to allow everyone a couple hours' sleep in shifts while they loaded the trucks and assorted wagons. Monte-Cristi and his men looked after the few animals able to pull a load while Valentine spoke to Post.

"We found the road easily enough, sir," Post said. "Overgrown, deadfalls everywhere, mudslides . . . so picking a good ambush spot was simple, too. We let a rider or two pass before these trucks came running back from the border garrison. Full would have been better, but I figured you'd need either kind soon, so we hit these. There wasn't much of an escort, some men on horseback. The men went crazy with the machine guns—there wasn't an unwounded horse. I ended up pistoling three. Hated to do it. I don't know what's worse, screaming women or screaming horses. We got the dead and hurt off the road, bandaged up the wounded as best we could in the time it took to turn around the trucks and get things organized, and drove down here. I think we got into third gear once—it was mostly first and second. First in one of these is crawling, second is a quicker crawl. Only one checkpoint outside San Juan. I don't know if word that we were heading that way got out or what, but it was empty."

"Losses or wounded?"

"None, unless you count dysentery. Some of the men got gut-sick from eating the Santo Domingan's rations, I think. Or maybe it was from drinking lamp oil. That kid from Cercado's family, he knew every bend in the road, I'll give him that. You know, we could do worse than to give the road-watchers the weapons we find."

Valentine nodded. "We've both been lucky."

"From the stories the kid told me, there's a lot of discontent on the island. If some of the peasants here could just get their hands on enough guns and mortars—"

"That's the first thing I'm going to tell them when we make it back to Mountain Home, my friend. Get some rest: find a mattress and use it."

"Aye aye, sir," Post said, licking his dry lips as he eyed the well.

The rest of Valentine's evening/morning was an excursion into the curse of Babel. He found himself giving orders to work details in French, English, and Spanish, all of it reinforced with hand gestures and a constant struggle against exploding into profanity. He had to stop men from putting ammunition into weapons meant to be transported, and piling their own weapons in stacks to be carried on the trucks. Groups of men occupied themselves by removing food from one truck and placing it in another, and others, after having made three trips in and out of the armory, decided they had done enough and crawled under the carts and trucks to sleep. Men lit cigars by striking matches on the side of the explosives truck, tossing the matches into the sawdust used to cushion the cases of dynamite. Some of the *Thunderbolt*'s sailors and marines worked drunkenly, reeling and reeking from Haitian-soldier-supplied rum concealed in their canteens, before passing out from dehydration or dropping to their hands and knees to vomit. He caught the Santo Domingan deserters stuffing block after block of chocolate into their mouths, and briefly considered making an example of them. In the end, he put them under Ahn-Kha's supervision, and after they saw their new supervisor pick up a napping Grog by his ear, half-tearing it off so that blood ran down the side of the derelict's head, they took to their duties with a will. Valentine tried to comfort himself with the thought that he had been on more disorderly expeditions into the Kurian Zone.

Somehow, the sun found the armory above San Juan empty and the trucks and carts loaded. Behind a vanguard of cavalry was Post's "battle truck," piled with sandbags and fitted out with the *Thunderbolt*'s machine guns. Then came the other two trucks, towing carts filled with food and water. Behind that were horse-drawn carts and the packhorses, hardly burdened now compared with the loads they had brought over the Cordillera Central. The engines gunned to diesel-fueled life. There was not room for everyone to ride, so the convoy would have to move at the pace of a walking soldier, though the walking men enjoyed the rare treat of moving with only their arms and a small amount of ammunition.

Valentine placed himself in the third truck, the one hauling the explosives, with the most experienced driver: one of the Chief's mechanics from the *Thunderbolt*. He was an aging, bald Asiatic, with the pulp-Western name of Handy Sixguns.

"Actually it's Hardy, and the family's real name is Chen," Sixguns explained when Valentine asked him his last name. He had always known the man as Handy, until he sat in the webbing that served as the passenger seat in the truck cabin. They made conversation while the vehicles inched forward out of the gate. "My father carried four pistols everywhere, he was a 'wheelgun man' he used to say, just like the old old cowboy books. Trucker in the old times with a Mobile–Birmingham run, jammed gears for the Kurians, too. I wanted more variety, so I went to sea. Ended up in the *Thunderbolt*, going from Galveston to the Florida coast line once a month or so."

"You know Galveston?" Valentine asked. "I've been there, but never had a chance to get off the ship."

"Spent some time there, the old *Darcy Arthur* got wrecked in a storm, and I was living on the streets there for a while. You grow up fast under *them*."

"What ever happened to the elder Sixguns?"

"I never found out. I went back once, when I was in my twenties. The house was just deserted. No note, no nothing. The neighbors couldn't or wouldn't tell me anything. Funny, I still look for his face everywhere I go. Bad not knowing."

Worse than knowing the worst? Valentine wondered. At least Sixguns could imagine a future for his father. Valentine had the sorrowful memory of a crow pecking at the hole in the back of his father's skull, his dead siblings, his mother's violated corpse.

A long mile down the road, the convoy halted. Post and two sailors trotted down the road from the fort, where wisps of smoke could already be seen coming from the armory.

"When it hits that black powder . . ." Sixguns said.

Post trotted up to Valentine's truck. "We probably have another thirty minutes, sir," the lieutenant said. "I didn't want us to get caught in the explosion."

"Release the prisoner, not much he can do about it now," Valentine said. Post nodded and went over to the two Haitians escorting the captured officer. They cut the corded knots around his wrists and ankles. The officer looked back at his post, ashen-faced.

Valentine climbed down from his truck. "We're looking for good men, sir," he said in Spanish. Emotion gave him the eloquence to get through the semirehearsed speech. "I once served the Kurians, too. But now I'm with those who resist.

It's not a lost cause, or a sure death." The part about serving the Kurians was not strictly true, Valentine acknowledged to himself, but he thought it might help the man.

"No, they have my oath. They have my sister in Santo Domingo. All I need from you is a pistol with one bullet."

"That's not the way—," Valentine began, but the man lunged at him. Valentine sidestepped, stuck out a foot moving one way and a hand moving the other, and the officer went sprawling to the dirt. A Haitian raised his gun.

"No! Bind him again—he's coming with us," he said in French. Then in Spanish to the officer: "I'm sorry, I won't have you hurting yourself."

When they thought they were out of Valentine's hearing, some of the Haitians grumbled that a prisoner would ride while they would walk. Valentine shrugged it off. Soldiers that didn't grumble were thinking about something else, like their fears.

The trucks rattled into gear, and the men got to their feet, and the column was on its way.

The first stragglers appeared as they crossed a bridge south of San Juan. There had been some kind of skirmish at the bridge. Monte-Cristi's horsemen lit out after a few sentries who took shots at the column. After Post determined that it was safe to cross, Valentine ordered the men out of combat positions and back into the march order.

Valentine walked with the rear guard as the column headed south. He had heard riders somewhere to the east, and was not sure if they were some of Monte-Cristi's scouts or a Santo Domingan's. He saw six or seven ragged people, bundles over their shoulders or in woven baskets, following behind.

He found one of Monte-Cristi's subchiefs. "Who are they?"

The man shrugged. "Don't know. They attached themselves outside San Juan. There are two or three more now."

"Let me know if they try to catch up. I don't want one of them throwing a grenade into the explosives truck."

Monte-Cristi joined him at the rear of the column. "We ran into some soldiers from one of the sugar plantations. The riders treed one of them."

"Did they tell him the story and let him go?"

"Yes, *mon capitaine*. He is running even now, with the story that we are marching on Santo Domingo. But implying that we are stronger than we are—"

"We've got to play the role of . . . this reminds me of a lizard. I can't remember what it is called, but I know it lives in Australia. When it's threatened, these flaps of skin open up like an umbrella, and it opens its mouth and charges on its hind legs. It couldn't hurt anything larger than a bug if it tried, but the appearance of aggression makes a predator think twice," Valentine said. "Frilled lizard, that's what it's called," he added, his capacious memory coming to his aid. "We've got to look like we're charging, when we're really getting set to run."

"You are a man of strange interests," Monte-Cristi said.

"After I was orphaned, a teacher raised me," Valentine said. "I lived in his library. You were speaking of the militia. Where were the soldiers from?"

"A sugar plantation. From what I hear, it is a big one. It is on this road ahead, we will reach it soon."

"Good. I've heard of these plantations. I'd like to see one."

Valentine had seen many work camps in his years traveling in the Kurian Zone. Yet the worst the KZ offered in the lands familiar to him was only a shadow of what he found on the riverbank of the Yaque del Sur.

In the north, Kurian cruelty adhered to a certain logic. When it was time to kill, the Reapers usually performed the task in the dark of night, away from human eyes. Only certain auras were taken, and none wasted if possible, for infusions of vital aura were too valuable to whatever band of

Kurians were in charge. Perhaps this green valley was only loosely controlled, or perhaps the island's people were fecund enough for auras to be in oversupply; whatever the reason, death worked overtime in this part of Santo Domingo.

Dead, leaf-stripped palm trees along the road presented the first horrors. Valentine saw bodies, some nothing but rotting corpses beneath a mask of flies, tied to the trunks. Above the tormented figures bleached skulls were tucked into nests of pepper trees, threaded onto smaller branches. On some, the branches had grown through or around the skulls, swallowing them behind bark and bursting them asunder.

Valentine locked eyes with one victim still alive, atop a magnificent body bleeding at the tight bonds around his chest; the man was crying, but had exhausted his tears. Flies clustered at the raw sores where the rope cut into him. Crows and vultures feasted on what was left of the man just to the left of him, and the one to the right had fallen apart, only the upper half of the skeletal structure remaining attached to the tree.

To their credit, the Haitians did not wait for orders. The trucks stopped and men left their places in the column and rushed, knives in hand, to cut those still living free. Valentine kicked a bloated vulture out of the way and walked up the turn-off leading to the station. The vulture squawked and dragged its distended body to the culvert beside the road. It paused in the shade of a white-painted sign reading AZUCÁR D VARGAS. The Spanish word for "sugar" was peeling, but beneath the stenciled letters of Vargas's name were several layers of old primer.

Valentine looked down the cane-flanked lane.

A cluster of wooden buildings stood between two sets of high bamboo fence at the end of an unshaded gravel road. Valentine guessed them to be separate housing for the men and women of the plantation. Sugar cane stretched out to either side of the road, which was built up high enough to give a commanding view of the fields for miles. Cast aside at the gates of the establishment, like litter thrown along a highway, were more corpses long since rotted into a jumble of bones. Valentine saw a rat scuttle for cover among the bones.

Ahn-Kha appeared at his arm, showing his uncanny sense of knowing when he was wanted.

"I see a truck back there," Valentine said. "Get your Grogs together, and Post with his marines. Take whatever we need, animals, weapons, the truck if it will move, and some sugar. We're going to burn this place to the ground. Anyone carrying a gun or whip you shoot."

Valentine turned on his heel and went to Post's battle-truck. Post was helping carry one of the plantation hands to shade.

"Will, we're going to burn this place," Valentine said. He thought briefly of Duvalier and her various tales of arson in the KZ. She had been right. There were atrocities that only burning would cleanse. This was one of them. "I want it to look like it was never here, just a bare spot on the ground. Understand?"

Post pressed a canteen into the hands of the newly freed man. He stood, jaw set, stinking blood and pus from the peon spattered on his shirtfront. "Yes, sir."

Sailors and marines readied their weapons. Valentine chambered a round in his PPD and hopped up on the front bumper, holding on to the German logo on the grillework. The driver revved the engine, and turned from the line of torture-palms to the station road.

The truck roared down the lane, fast enough to kick up dust. A figure or two appeared in the doorway of the main building, rifles in their hands. The principal building of the plantation was a two-story brick house encircled by a wide shaded veranda. Post loosed a burst from a machine gun, and the men ran. Sharp rifle cracks brought them down, the fall of their bodies kicking up puffs of dust from the gravel surrounding the main house.

The truck braked before the house. Valentine released his grip, letting the final momentum of the aged Benz throw him forward. He landed nimbly and followed his gun barrel through the double doors. A man in a uniform similar to the ones he saw at San Juan stood at a glassless window, gaping at the men dismounting from the truck. He threw his hands forward, palms out, as if hoping to halt the men by body language.

"Qué?" he managed to get off, before Valentine cut him down with a burst from the PPD. The old, awful thrill ran through his body as he smelled the gunsmoke and the man's blood.

Valentine walked into the kitchen and looked out the open back door. A woman in white rags ran, carrying a baby in her arms, a naked boy alongside her. He ignored her. He passed through an empty dining room and into an office. An electric fan whirred atop a paper-strewn desk. One window was shuttered and the other window stood open. Valentine looked around, a smashed gun cabinet showed an empty bracket between two shotguns. Whoever occupied the office hadn't had time to get the key. Or get his footwear, Valentine noted, seeing a set of high military-style boots by the door.

Valentine moved away from the window, not wanting to give a rifleman an easy target. Outside he heard Grogs hooting amidst the tearing crash of wood splintering. He returned to the front veranda.

Post had the *Thunderbolt*'s marines backing up the Grogs as they stormed the barracks. The Haitians were at the gates of the worker compounds, breaking bamboo posts with crowbars and axes. The *Thunderbolt*'s men stayed at the battle-truck, training their weapons on the unoccupied buildings. A rifle or two popped from the cane fields, but wherever the shots were aimed, they caused no damage.

"See if there are any animals in the stables," he told Post, the sight of uniformed bodies lying here and there turning his bloodlust into revulsion. At the Kurian system. At himself.

An hour later the plantation was in flames, and Valentine had almost a hundred more charges. Before burning it he had turned over the contents of the station house, barracks, and storerooms to them so they could carry off what they would. The problem was that they carried it off in the trail of his convoy.

By the time they camped, still on the banks of the river flowing out of the mountains of the Cordillera Central, Valentine guessed those following his trucks, wagons, and animals to number in the hundreds. Some of the refugees drove pigs and goats, or pulled donkeys along with children or the aged perched on blanketed backs. He found Cercado warming some beans and rice on the battle-truck's radiator.

"A good day," Cercado said, between spoonfuls.

"We've picked up a lot of stragglers, though."

"Who would blame them?"

"Please, go among them. Find out what their plans are. Tell them . . . tell them we are marching toward battle, and we need young men who would use machetes or guns."

"You can't be serious, Captain. I doubt if one among them knows one end of a rifle from another. They'd be safer using it as a club."

"Perhaps. If this keeps going on, by the time we get to Puerto Viejo, we'll have thousands of them. It would be—"

"Unfortunate," Cercado finished.

"Agreed. Go among them, talk to them, see what they plan to do."

Cercado spat. "That I can tell you already. They want to get away."

"Let them know that's not an option. If they want to be free of the Kurians, they'll have to do it themselves. I'm not Moses. I can't bring the multitudes out of Egypt."

The next day, the caravan crawling southwest along the old highway was outnumbered by those following it. The

Santo Domingans never interfered with the soldiers, though Valentine expected that his men dropped back into their mass to distribute food and water, especially to the children. If they made it to the coast, it would be with an emptier belly and a tighter belt around it.

If there was a bright side, it was that from a distance, his column would be mistaken for an army moving down the road, occupying miles of trail. With Monte-Cristi's riders and the Grogs leaving the column on excursions to set fire to roadside police stations, gather weapons and ammunition, and cut down telephone wires, the Kurians farther east might be convinced their border garrisons had collapsed, and an invading host was pouring out of Haiti. In the intervening days, he might have a chance to slip away in the confusion without further battle.

Adding to this belief was the fact that the Kurians had already instituted a "scorched earth" policy as he moved east. They found fewer and fewer stations and plantations intact. Villages were burned and supplies destroyed or removed, adding to his logistics worries. They were beyond the zone where Cercado's roadwatching network had stashed food, and while water was plentiful grain was running out for the horses, and food became short for the men.

He reduced some of his problems by ordering the slaughter of a few broken-down pack animals when they camped that night, the second since leaving the armory at San Jose, sharing the ample meat out to the cooking pots of those trailing the convoy.

Cercado joined Valentine and Ahn-Kha at their cooking-fire, appearing as he always did with his mixture of good news and bad. Their guide smoked a cigar, sending satisfied puffs skyward with his back against a palm.

"The rumors you spread about an attack on Santo Domingo have come back to bite you, Captain Valentine," Cercado said. "Yes, it has scared the Kurians for now, but they are mustering forces west and east. These people have heard that the campaign against the island under Port-au-

Prince has been called off, and their general is marching east to crush you. Even larger forces will come soon from the west."

"How soon?" Valentine asked, grateful that Cercado was keeping his voice down.

"Impossible to say. You must travel faster once you make the turn for the coast. They may move to anticipate you."

Valentine looked into the fire. There had been delays almost from the first minute—how many were due to his faulty planning? How many to bad execution? His quick raid into the Kurian Zone, to test the quickwood weapons and get more arms for the Haitians, had succeeded in the first task: he had seen how effective the wood was with his own eyes. The second, while not being a total failure, had come far short of expectations. And now it looked as if the column would be swallowed entirely.

"You've done all we asked superbly, Cercado. We're almost to the road to the sea. You and your family members should slip away now and go back to your mountains. Take whatever weapons you wish, even some of those from the *Thunderbolt*. It is the least we can do for you."

"Captain, Santo Domingo has not seen the like of this in many years. Such a rising will come to a bad end, or a good one. Either way, it will be the subject for tales and songs that the peons of this island will tell long after I die, even should God grant me a life a hundred years long. What man, if he is a man, would not want to be a part of it? Even now, the poor peons on the road call you Revenant. They say that a Reaper had you in its arms, but before it could bite you, you bit it, killing it. They say when you are wounded, you cut the body parts from your enemies and meld them with your own. Such tales are told of you—it curls the hair on my toes.

"I will tell you something else. The smokes you saw on the horizon today, they are not just Jacques's riders—they are the peons fighting on their own, or the Whisperers burning and saving us the trouble of doing it. The countryside has risen. They've borne evil after evil too long. The men are sending their women and children to you for safety while they take to the hills."

"I thought it odd that there were so many women among them, my David," Ahn-Kha said.

"This has been a long time coming," Cercado continued, scratching his hairy potbelly and puffing away on the cigar. "The Domingan rulers left a hollow egg when they called away so many to fight against Kurian Haiti. It only took your footsteps to break the shell. Who knows, maybe in other parts of the island, as they gather men to crush you, other peons can take their chances. At the very least, the trade in sugar and rubber to their brothers in the north will be reduced for some time. Both require many men. If the Kurians kill those who rise, who will take their place in the cane fields and tapping rubber trees?"

"We're already overdue at the coast," Valentine said. "We should have been there today. At this rate, we will be two more days on the road."

"Do we dare travel at night?" Ahn-Kha said. "A final sprint, tonight and tomorrow, and the devils get the hind end?"

"Devil take the hindmost is how we usually say it, old horse," Valentine corrected. He pictured the island in his mind, the various forces moving. "We'll get to the coast, all right."

He rose from the fire and went to find Post.

In the end, the Grogs' skill as pig-hunters saved the column. The stations along the road relied on pig flesh to feed their soldiers, and to a lesser extent the workers, and as Valentine's columns approached, they emptied their pigpens and drove the pigs into the brush. The Grogs had noses to rival Valentine's own, and they tracked the future chops and sidemeat to their hiding places. The dust-raising column developed a system in which the front end would take the meat and begin boiling it or roasting it, and by the time the tail of the column passed the fires, the meat was ready to be eaten at the next rest-halt by those hundreds upon hundreds bringing up the rear.

Men, some of them armed, began to join the column from east, west, and north, telling tales of horsemen closing on the column from the barren stretches in the more arid regions of the island neighboring the well-watered river valley. More formations followed, bearing artillery and armed vehicles according to some of the tales. Valentine put Monte-Cristi in charge of adding the best-armed and healthiest of them to his own units, though there wasn't time for anything other than teaching them the system of moving for an hour, and then resting for ten minutes. Valentine was grateful for the additions; Post had gone pell-mell to the coast with the *Thunderbolt*'s marines and sailors in the battle-truck to prepare for the column's arrival.

By midday they turned south for the coast, moving on a smaller, less-used road. Valentine hoped that the change in direction would throw off any designs for the column's destruction.

He managed to get his charges a few miles south of the old highway by moving on into the evening. When he finally called for a halt, the men dropped in their tracks under the bright Caribbean stars. Few of his soldiers rode; Valentine had turned space in the trucks over to the ill, weak, and pregnant of the column. Even so, there were those who turned off the road throughout the day to rest in the shade, and they would probably never catch up now. Smaller bands of Santo Domingan horsemen had appeared as it got dark atop the distant hilltops, marking his turn to the coast.

He found Monte-Cristi in the center of a circle of his chieftans.

"Ever fought a rear-guard action, Jacques?" Valentine asked.

Cristi's eyes lit up. "My men have performed many an ambush. We run all the better afterwards, knowing we've hurt them."

Valentine smelled the pork being roasted by Monte-Cristi's cook, his mouth watering, but he ignored his hunger. This was the final sprint, and there was too much to do.

"Just hit them fast, and keep moving for the coast. I'm afraid they've guessed we've changed direction, and they might try to cut us off from the bay. We have to beat them to it."

"We could, if we could empty the trucks of everything but the supplies. My men could march through the night."

Valentine looked out at the sea of Santo Domingans sheltering behind the pickets. "A lot of these people can't. They joined us out of belief in some stories we spread."

"You did not ask them to come. They must accept the fortunes of war. Not one in five of them will fit on your ship even if they do make it to the bay. They will be no worse off than if we had never come here. Otherwise, you will be asking my men to die for nothing."

"You've seen how things are run here, Jacques. They've thrown in with us. We're their only chance."

"They knew the risks when they ran away."

"But that's just it, they haven't run away. They've run toward something, the chance at a free life. I would no more leave them behind than you'd leave those men you were stuck in the cave with."

"I will tell you something, Captain. There were times— yes, there were many times, in that hole, after it was sealed, that I would have turned them all over to the Kurians for fresh air, sun, and a real meal. I . . . I prayed for the chance."

Valentine made a show of fishing around in his bag for a strip of dried beef, so that he would not see the tears on Monte-Cristi's face. "The important thing is that when you had a real chance to give up, you didn't. How many of the legends on this island had the same doubts? Louverture, Pablo Duarte, I'm certain they had their moments when they questioned themselves." Valentine did not add that he had learned long ago that the only way he could live with himself was if he acted according to conscience, rather than orders or even military necessity. Usually his conscience and his duty asked the same things from him, but on the few occasions where their needs had diverged, duty lost.

The moon rose, and the drivers loaded their vehicles once more with those who had to ride.

Monte-Cristi handed Valentine his horse's reins. "Ride today, Captain. I'll be afoot with my men in the rear. It will do everyone good to be able to see you. His name is Luc, and like me he is a defector from the Kurians; he is strong enough to bear even your oversize friend on these mountains. Take care of him should I . . . should I fall."

Valentine read the expression in Monte-Cristi's face, and nodded dumbly. He cinched the saddle on the speckled gray gelding. He slung his submachine gun, grabbed a handful of mane, and mounted. Luc heaved a sigh and pawed at the earth, eager to be off.

"Any sign of our pursuers?"

Monte-Cristi shook his head. "No. For now they just watch."

"Build up the fires as we go. I want them to burn for a few more hours at least. Take care of yourself. Dinner tonight with me on the ship?"

"I look forward to it."

"Let's get everyone moving. Quietly."

Valentine rode at the head of the column, just behind the rear guard. He had contracted the mass of soldiers and civilians as much as possible, but the troops at his disposal could hardly watch the front and flanks, let alone defend them with so many men detached for the rear guard.

They made good time despite the dark. When his sensitive nose picked up the smell of the sea, Valentine's heart leapt. He began to trot his horse up and down the column, urging the weary walkers on as best as he could.

Everyone seemed to sense that it was time for the last sprint. The Grogs at the head of the column scouted, and helped the pioneers with the worst parts of the road by cutting down trees into washouts so the trucks could cross.

Valentine followed with a vanguard of armed men watching at all times as the others worked. He needed at least a small group of disciplined men to be ready for any emergency. Then came the overloaded trucks, the valves on the aged engines clattering in complaint. A few men traveled to either side of the road, visible through the scarcer vegetation in this more arid region of the island. Interspersed with the trucks, ready to give a shove, came the masses of Santo Domingans with their children and bundles in tow, hardly a goat remaining. Somewhere behind, more refugees followed, covered by Monte-Cristi's rear guard, composed of his most reliable men with the best weapons.

Valentine had enough on his mind, worrying about how he would find space, not to mention food, for perhaps two thousand extra mouths on the ride home without the Kurians intervening.

Which of course they did, just short of his goal.

A Grog shrieked a warning, and the dark of the road ahead burst into muzzle flashes. An automatic weapon swept the road, scattering both his men and the formation of pioneers. The Kurian soldiers were dispersed on the crest of a hill ahead.

Valentine could see the vast night out there, between the folds of the earth, and cursed. *Stopped!*

The Grogs came stumbling back, one wounded. Valentine got off Monte-Cristi's horse, led it into a gulley sheltering his soldiers.

"They must have just beaten us there, my David," Ahn-Kha said. "They are not dug in—they stand behind rocks and trees, or lie on the ground. It is just a screen, I think."

"But it's a well-placed screen, and we're the bugs."

"If the pioneers charge too—"

"There'll be that many more dead men. Any idea where their flank is?"

"No."

"Another hour, and I bet they have twice as many men. Give me your rifle. If we can at least get the automatic weapon . . ."

Ahn-Kha took his submachine gun. "Give the word, and we will go, my David."

Valentine's own men began shooting back at the soldiers ahead, and a slow, popping firefight took place and grew as both sides' soldiers gathered at the gunfire. Neither side seemed to have ammunition to waste; with no targets, the automatic weapon was silent.

"Ahn-Kha, I have a great favor to ask," Valentine said, adjusting the slide on the gun's rear sight.

"I know, my David. I will break for those rocks."

Ahn-Kha ran forward in the low, loping run of the Grogs, using his hands and feet. The machine gun fired, and Valentine's Cat eyes picked up the source. He placed the flange of the front sight on what he hoped was a head. He squeezed, and the heavy Grog-gun kicked out its .50-caliber shell. He slid back into the gulley.

"You got him," the Haitian at his right said, lifting his head.

"Keep—," Valentine began. Valentine saw the man's hair rustle as if a brush had been run upward through it, and he slumped. Valentine slid over to the corpse, and passed the rifle to a sheltering pioneer.

Valentine heard a whistling sound; then an explosion lit the night at the crest of the enemy hillside. He slid sideways for a better view and was rewarded by the sight of a second shell bursting on the crest, right in the middle of the road where the machine gun had been placed.

Naval gunfire, by God!

"My David, it's the *Thunderbolt*," Ahn-Kha shouted from his hiding place ahead. The sky began to turn orange, and somewhere in the distance, a rooster crowed. He heard shooting far behind; the rear guard was contesting the road with their pursuers.

Valentine took to his horse. They would not be ringed in.

"Over the hill and to the sea, men. To the sea!" he shouted. *"Sur la mer!"* the hills echoed. Valentine handed the Grog-gun to one of Ahn-Kha's warriors.

The Golden One let loose with a battle bellow, a blood-freezing sound. His Grogs answered, and went up and over the edge of the gully, their shotguns and rifles flaring in the half-light. There were no bayonets to glint in the rising sun, but the ivory in their oversize teeth shone.

The trucks gunned their engines and kicked up gravel from the road. Valentine passed Ahn-Kha. His friend sprayed the roadblock ahead with bullets from the PPD. The charging Grogs to either side made for an odd sight, going forward with two legs and an arm, almost like horses cantering. Valentine considered drawing his blade for effect, but the Haitians and Grogs needed no urging. He pulled his Colt automatic instead and briefly wondered how he would work the slide and keep atop of the galloping horse. . . .

The Santo Domingans did not wait to meet them. The sight and sound of charging Grogs amidst the *Thunderbolt*'s shell-fire proved too much for the thin line of riflemen. The cheering sight of knapsacks bobbing in the tall grass of the hillside as the Santo Domingans ran brought a victorious whoop from Valentine. The horse gathered itself to leap the roadblock, and Valentine gripped the mane. He saw dead men heaped by the machine gun as the horse jumped the felled tree.

Valentine heard shots from the fishing village at the base of the hill and saw the *Thunderbolt*'s marines deployed in a skirmish line advancing up the hill. Post, evidently trapped with his little contingent in the seaside fishing village, had heard the firing and acted.

The Santo Domingan soldiers surrendered or scattered, and the rout was complete.

Valentine swore to himself that he would see Post made into an officer in Southern Command if they ever made it back to the Free Territory.

As the column got moving again, Valentine reproached himself for jumping his horse into the most likely spot for another shell from the *Thunderbolt*. But in his later years that was forgotten when he remembered the pure glory of that moment, his first battlefield victory in eight years of soldiering.

Valentine saw boats drawn up on the beach, to either side of the village, under the guard of a sailor or two. Valentine had dispatched Post to the rendezvous with orders to gather every available craft, using the *Thunderbolt*'s forbidding bulk if necessary to confiscate a flotilla of fishing boats. Using all the *Thunderbolt*'s deck space, and a few large boats in tow, he hoped to get his charges along the coast.

It would be another long day while they loaded and supplied all the boats, but he had learned to expect nothing less.

By sunset, after an endless afternoon spent turning chaos into order, he stood on the *Thunderbolt*'s bridge in clean clothes with a hot meal inside him. The Santo Domingan refugees were crowded on board every seaworthy vessel. Monte-Cristi's rear guard had tumbled down from the hills into the *Thunderbolt*'s motorized boats, covered by cannon and Oerlikon. Last of all came Post's marines, setting fire to the huts of the village to add covering smoke to the debarkation.

But new worries replaced the old. Their cockleshell flotilla could fit the Haitian soldiers and Santo Domingans, just, but any kind of bad weather would lead to the possible loss of the boats, and perhaps the overcrowded *Thunderbolt*. The Kurians in Santo Domingo had a few ships, as well, mostly armed merchantmen that ran sugar and rubber and ore north. Any exchange of gunfire would be fatal to many of those crowding on the *Thunderbolt*'s decks. Waiting in the bay while they captured better vessels from other villages was out of the question. The Kurian forces had already gathered, lobbing mortar shells into the water as the *Thunderbolt* towed the boats out to sea.

Two single-masted fishing ships plodded alongside, reeking holds filled with mobs of huddled people. Dozens more stood forlornly on the shoreline.

He unburdened his concerns on the one who knew the waters best.

"Don't worry about the weather," Carrasca said, her hair blowing out in the fresh Caribbean breeze, just as it had that first morning taking the captured ship into Jamaica. The helmsman ignored them. "We have a few weeks left before worrying about real storms."

Valentine took the sea air into his nostrils like a drug. "We have to get farther off the coast. Two or three miles at least. They might have guns mounted."

"Let it go, David. We're at sea. My element, remember? Let me do the thinking for a while. You've done brilliantly. Maybe not what you set out to do, but it was the right choice in the end."

"I should—"

"Sleep. That's an order."

"Captain's word at sea is law," he said, turning up a corner of his mouth.

Her mock-serious attitude vanished. She glanced onto the bridge and stepped into his arms. He couldn't tell who started it, but they were kissing. "Sleep with me," she whispered. "Soon. When we get back to Jamaica. After we see this through." She broke off the embrace, leaving his body tingling. "Enough. You see, I take my duty as seriously as you. Tempting as the thought is," she added, looking at his crotch and then returning her eyes to his. She no longer watched him with that wary hint of fear that his pupils might be glowing.

Valentine, too aroused to feel embarrassed, saluted. "It's a date," he said, moving past her to leave the bridge. "I'll be in my cabin, if there's room to sleep between Post and Ahn-Kha, that is." He allowed his hand to trace the firm course of her buttock and thigh as he passed, puckishly wanting her to be as aroused as he.

Sure enough, Ahn-Kha lay on the floor, still smelling of gunsmoke. Post occupied his cot, having fallen into bed still in uniform. Post reeked of sweat and woodsmoke, blood and gun oil, tidewater and pig fat. Valentine did not even have to hypersensitize his nose to smell the story of his lieutenant's day. Valentine stepped over Ahn-Kha and managed to get his boots off before falling into a dreamless sleep.

A hand shook him awake. Valentine's nose told him it was Cercado before he was even partly awake.

"Captain, it is Monte-Cristi. Come, please."

Valentine rose out of bed, wide awake, but with the weighed-down feeling of a rushed awakening. Post and Ahn-Kha picked up on the alarm and stirred.

He followed Cercado out the door and down the short companionway to the officer's mess. Monte-Cristi sat up, held in the arms of one of his chieftans, some of his soldiers clustered in the doorway.

"Make a hole, dammit," Valentine growled, pushing into the compartment.

Monte-Cristi's breathing was labored.

"Jacques, what is it, a seizure?" Valentine asked.

Monte-Cristi looked up, wincing. "My heart, I think, David."

"He fainted away twice," the chieftan holding him elaborated. "We gave him some wine to ease the pain."

Valentine dashed back to his cabin, forcing his way past Ahn-Kha's companionway-filling bulk. He tore through his footlocker and came up with a bottle of white tablets. He rushed back to the mess.

"Water, someone," Valentine said, putting four white tablets into Monte-Cristi's mouth.

"It is ironic, David," Monte-Cristi said, after swallowing a drink of water to wash down the aspirin. "Hours of bullets flying around me, shells even. I've been on the run all day, and the moment I get to rest"—he shrugged, forcing a smile—"my heart chooses to kill me." He shut his eyes, and Valentine patted his hand until he opened them again. "We fooled them, going to sea like that."

"The Kurians forgot that the ocean is also a road."

"A good joke," Monte-Cristi managed.

"Yes, and we'll be laughing about it for weeks, over rum in your mountains."

"I—," Monte-Cristi began, but he simply faded. Valentine thought he had gone to sleep, but when he felt for a pulse there was nothing.

"Fuck!" Valentine said. He lowered Monte-Cristi to the deck. "It's a good heart, Jacques. It just needs some help. Ahn-Kha!" he shouted. "Get out of here, everyone, clear the floor," he yelled, forgetting to speak French, but his gestures served. Ahn-Kha entered. Valentine pounded on Monte-Cristi's chest and put an ear to his breast, listening for a beat. Nothing.

"Push on his chest, like this," Valentine said, demonstrating.

Ahn-Kha's thick shoulders went to work, the Grog's four-fingered hands on Monte-Cristi's breastbone. Valentine pinched off his nose and breathed as Ahn-Kha worked. A long, long minute went by, and Monte-Cristi heaved and gasped on his own.

" . . . think . . . perhaps . . . ," Monte-Cristi said. His eyes fluttered, and he looked more alert. "Why am I on the floor?"

"Relax," Valentine said. "Don't try to talk."

The rest of the voyage, Monte-Cristi's health consumed Valentine's attention to the point where he actually forgot about the *Thunderbolt*, Carrasca, the Santo Domingans in their flimsy boats, and the weather. He knew time passed only from the growth of his beard, and an occasional look out the window. He fed Monte-Cristi aspirin at each small meal and watched a little of his strength return.

"I feel . . . used up," Monte-Cristi confided, sitting in a canvas chair on the shady side of the deck as the coast slid by. "More so than before. But I will say this: Life is sweet now. It wasn't before. The past died the other day. Now I make my own future free of it."

"Your days carrying a rifle are over. Sit on a beach from now on, learn to fish," Valentine suggested.

"Why all this concern for a worn-out old man?" Monte-Cristi asked.

"Perhaps . . ." Valentine struggled for the right words, and would have struggled no matter what language he was using.

"Perhaps what?"

The man was beyond pretense, in himself or others. "Perhaps because I see you as one possible me in thirty years. Also, I didn't want an old enemy to lay his hands on you."

"Who? I thought you had not been to our land before."

"Death. The Grim Reaper, chief of all the others. When we got on board, I figured we left Death back on shore. Turned out He followed. The bastard's never satisfied. He wants more every chance he gets. So every chance I get, I kick him in the teeth. Sooner or later one of us is going to give up. It won't be me."

Chapter Nine

Free Haiti, July: It is easy to believe in spirits in the mountains of Haiti, when the misted woods press close all around. Groaning sounds that cannot be birds yet should not be trees echo through the night air. Even a trained ear finds them impossible to place. According to voudouists, waterfalls and streams are favorite haunts of the spirits. When you come across a mountainside waterfall, cascading down a rocky cliff like a splashing staircase, you get the feeling of being the first to lay eyes on it since the forming of the world; it becomes easy to imagine it consecrated by apparitions dancing in the mists as the shafts of sunlight strike them. Then a dragonfly with a hand-size wingspan whirs by or a parade of ants crosses a root in a chitin stream, and the spell is broken. The forest is just a forest, and the water is just water again — until later, when the body is elsewhere and the beauty of the place weaves its magical spell, knitting memory and imagination.

The Roots rejoiced at the return of her warriors in sacred ceremony and profane revelry.

Valentine watched the sacred portion from a moss-hided rock, dew-dusted ferns brushing at his frame. Soldiers and civilians gathered at a waterfall in the forested hills, led in singing by their priests. Narcisse sat on a rock in the swirling waters at the base of the waterfall, like the statue of the little mermaid, calling the men to her one at a time to receive a cleansing dip in the river. Other voudouists escorted the supplicants into the water, or sang hosannas in the background. Part baptism, part absolution, and part bath, the ritual moved Valentine. There was none of the solemnity of Father Max's traditional Catholic ceremonies: the participants and audience laughed and encouraged each other through catcalls.

The Grogs sat high on the hillside, chewing fruit and watching the human performance below as if from balcony seating. Further above, Ahn-Kha stood sentinel with crossbow and gun, a watchful set of eyes allowing the humans to relax below.

Valentine, by nature an observer rather than a participant at this sort of display, sat on his rock with Carrasca resting on a patch of grass beside him, dappled sun setting her hair agleam. By nature scientifically minded, a few years ago he might have thought the whole performance silly animism; but he had seen too much of the inexplicable since beginning his journeys to laugh anything off. He applauded when Monte-Cristi waded into the stream. Narcisse took extra time over him, either through concern over his frailty or giving the spirits ample opportunity to work their magic. The aged hero was the last of the spiritual bathers. Some of the *Thunderbolt*'s sailors and marines shuffled forward, and finally Post went through the ceremony. He emerged from his dunking and beckoned Valentine to join him.

"C'mon, Val," his friend said. "It's cooler than the jungle."

Valentine and Carrasca exchanged shrugs, and he stripped to applause from all. A few pointed at the white pock left by the old bullet wound on his leg.

Narcisse laid her hands on him, reciting something that sounded like mixed French and Latin. He lowered himself at her command to hoots of approval.

"I knew you had a strong *ti-bon-ange*, my boy. Ogun himself told me so just now," Narcisse affirmed. Valentine felt refreshed, if not strengthened or healed. He waded back to the shore. He reached for his clothes, but Carrasca snatched them up.

"I don't think you're through yet. Do you see anyone else getting dressed?"

There were more singsong chants, and the returning warriors lined up to walk naked back to the village. Valentine joined in the lines. The Grogs scrambled down from their rocky balconies to follow.

"How'd you get the leg wound?" Carrasca asked, falling into step next to him.

"Up in Nebraska. Acting like a damn fool."

"A damn fool who saved my people," Ahn-Kha added from behind.

"Your people saved themselves," Valentine demurred. "But it was years ago. I'll take sea duty any time. Fewer forty-mile days."

"You'd cover forty miles in a day? On horseback?" Carrasca asked.

"On foot. It was common in the Wolves. We weren't so special. Two hundred years ago, Zulu armies in Africa could run fifty in a day. And they weren't even trained by the Lifeweavers."

They came to the village near the spirit-spot, a trailside cluster of shacks painted and decorated in bright colors. Dancing red figures, green snakes, blue birds, and less recognizable patterns wound around doorframes, roofs and windows in the Haitian style. Tables and barrels heaped with food and drink stood in the doorways and alleys; musicians drummed a tattoo on hollow logs and ancient plastic pails, calling all together. The spectators ate and drank with enthusiasm. Handsome Haitian women poured rum and juice into wooden tumblers, which were emptied as quickly as they could be filled.

Just outside the village a rivulet emptied into a field of clay-colored mud. A shaman brought them to the edge of the water. He began to shout imprecations to Haiti's enemies. Valentine understood just enough to know he called on the warriors to be armed and shielded in new spirit. Monte-Cristi yelled a response and belly-flopped into the mud; he rolled around until he was well coated. His men followed, eager as overheated elephants to go into a cool wallow.

"Go on, boy," Narcisse said. "Take on Ogun's armor."

Valentine bit off a response about Ogun's armor not doing pigs a hell of a lot of good. He stuck a foot in the mud; it did feel cool and inviting between the toes.

Post gave him a shove. Valentine fell into Napoleon's fifth element facefirst, rolled over, and let out a whoop.

"*Thunderbolt!*" he called.

The men shouted the name of their ship and dived in with the Haitians. Soon it was almost impossible to tell black skin from white—or Grog skin, for that matter, as all were covered in the grayish plaster.

Valentine, grinning behind a mask of mud, rose and advanced on Carrasca in a threatening crouch.

"Oh, no!" she said, backing away. "I'll never get it out of my—"

He vaulted out of the mud, landing beside her before she had time to turn. He clasped her around the chest and dragged her, shrieking and kicking, into the mud. He flopped into the morass, and she landed astride him.

"Bastard!" she laughed, flinging a wet handful of soil down at him. "At least you were undressed."

"I'll wash them myself."

Valentine watched her bind her partially despoiled hair up in a bandanna, and pull off her shirt with muddy fingers. Her shorts followed. She pinned him into the wallow with a knee, her eyes wide and hot. He felt her take his head in her hands and she kissed him, pressing against his body tightly enough to squeeze mud out from the join where their bodies met. When she came up for air, he saw her nipples hard beneath their gray coating.

Sailors, marines, and Haitians followed his example, grabbing women out of the hooting crowd and pulling them into the mud. A few ran or struggled, laughing all the time, but the only screams were ones of delight as the men planted muddy kisses on flushed cheeks, necks, and breasts.

Valentine rolled Carrasca over and kissed her, and then she returned the move. When their lips finally parted, she was on top again. She looked around at the muddy figures, dancing, playing, and making love.

"You've started an orgy, Captain," she said. "I don't know what I think about an officer that lets his men get out of hand like this."

Valentine cupped her buttocks. "I'll let them be, my hands are rather full of something else at the moment."

"Is that some kind of crack?"

He explored further with his fingers. "No, but this is."

She giggled an un-captainish giggle. "Another bad joke like that and a certain marine of my acquaintance won't get his brains fucked out momentarily."

"We'll talk some more in the bushes." Valentine picked himself up and offered a hand.

"Your tongue's going to be busy elsewhere."

He slapped her mud-covered buttock and followed her into the forest, first running and then walking, until they splashed across the stream and found a clearing, a field next to an abandoned hut, perhaps a former garden. Long grasses and palmettos had supplanted the rich soil's food crops. Valentine was in no mood to search for the perfect glade, especially with Carrasca exploring his hardness from behind, using it like a divining rod to find a spot to make love.

They sank to their knees, tongues exploring one another's mouths.

He found mudless patches of her body to kiss, and explored the rest of her coated skin with his hands. "Val . . . ," she began, and then trailed off into a Spanish–English murmur that grew more and more feral as he pressed her into his arms. She sank limp to the ground. He lay next to her, cradling her and running his hands up and down her body, lingering at her inner thighs. His mouth explored where his fingers left off, and she again took his head in her hands; she pressed her mons up to his mouth. The salty-sweet feminine musk hardened him beyond self-control, and he rose up from her sex and positioned himself between her legs.

He felt her open for him and he moved inside her, everything inside her warm and wet and magic. Her face grew contorted as he moved in her, ever deeper and faster as their passion waxed. She raked at his back with her nails, sending chips of dried mud flying like a sculptor working with ten tiny chisels. He shut his eyes, lost in his own sensations yet still aware of her. He felt an irresistible, toboggan-ride rush of pleasure, and the draining spasms came.

They drowsed away a few moments in each other's arms, tingling as if joined by a low voltage circuit.

"Another kick in the teeth," he mused, feeling the matted-down grass beneath his back.

"Huh?"

"For Death. There's more than one way to strike a blow for life."

She furrowed her brows, and then evidently gave up trying to figure out what he was talking about. Her hand explored him.

"Blow for life . . . and they say men don't come with instructions."

She moved downward, and took his limp penis in her mouth. Tongue and mouth, passionately applied, worked a resurrection.

"That's the spirit," she said, straddling him, coming up for more than air.

The Haitians showed their gratitude when it came time to fill the *Thunderbolt* with quickwood and provisions. Ahn-Kha and his Grogs supervised the cutting and milling of some of the trees into usable lengths. Smaller saplings were gently extracted by shovel, placed in clay cauldrons or wrapped in layers of dirt and burlap, and ported down to the beach one at a time. As a final gift during a visit to the beach, Papa Legba gave the entire ship's crew each a leather tobacco pouch with a handful of seeds for new quickwood trees.

"Kur is a dry place," the renegade said when Valentine asked about the seeds. "These will remain dormant for years if kept out of your sun, until placed in moist soil. They grow slowly, so have patience. Let the wood mature, and take only branches if you must."

"We'll see that they end up in the right hands," Valentine promised. "Perhaps someday you'll come north and see the groves yourself."

"No, I'll stay in the warmth and the growing gardens. In a cold climate, I doubt I could survive a winter without . . . a different means of support."

"Maybe cows would do, or pigs."

"You still do not understand, do you, Valentine? It is the sapient mind that gives us the kind of vital aura infusion that truly satisfies. Each aura has a different flavor: a man enduring hideous tortures, a woman desperate to save her offspring, a terrified child taken in the night all have a distinct feel when absorbed. The 'rush' as you might call it varies— an aura can be consumed in the time it takes to scream, or over the course of many painful hours. There were times when my—"

"Point taken," Valentine said, instinctively balling his fists.

"I forget my manners. Would one discuss cuts of meat or beef stew recipes with a group of cattle? Forgive me, son of mine enemy."

Valentine relaxed, but wanted to end the interview. "Perhaps when I'm old and the winters feel too long, I'll come back to the islands." He met Carrasca's eyes across the glare of the sand, and she cupped the leather pouch suggestively. "I'd like to hear more about Kur, and the other planets in the Interworld Tree."

"A strong mind is a blessing when the body grows frail," the Once-ler of many names agreed. "May fortune walk with you, for you'll walk into many lands bereft of it." He waved in his weary fashion and let his bearers carry him off. "The debt is paid," Valentine heard him say.

At the time the phrase was just one more curiosity from the enigmatic Kurian. It would be years before Valentine learned its significance.

He took his leave of Monte-Cristi, sitting at the edge of the beach in a hammock chair fanning himself.

"Did the river and mud cure take, Jacques?"

"Not as much as Narcisse's cooking. She's a gifted woman, something for the body, something for the *ange*. You were wise to offer her a trip north, it is something she has long dreamed of. I also have a message from our friend with the dogs at the Cape. They've fixed the holes in that old submarine. I wouldn't be surprised if your enemy comes looking for you. Though Boul is chafing, he may throw in with us in the end. The Santo Domingans have trouble keeping the last road along the north coast open, with these new guns the Roots have been shooting up their convoys. He senses a change in the wind."

"Then I won't worry about Haiti any more, Jacques. If my old friend Boul is thinking of throwing in with you, you must be sure to win."

"Some of our mechanics are making crossbows like those your ape-men use—but smaller. Better against the Whisperers than spears." Valentine walked among Monte-Cristi's chieftans and soldiers, thanking them as best he could in Haitian Creole, before returning to Jacques. Their conversation moved on to military technicalities, smothering the good-bye in trivia.

Narcisse arrived with an assortment of potted dishes for the officer's mess, bags of provisions, and a chest full of Haitian spices. "Fried plaintains, fried pork, a bag of mushrooms—they're good on everything," she said, lifting lids and pointing with her mutilated arm. "Enough fruit to last a long while, fresh and dried. Now the spices—" She contin-

ued checking over the contents of her baggage like a marine
preparing for a landing on a hostile shore.

"I'd have never left that cell if it weren't for you, Narcisse."

"And I'd still be getting stains out of Boul's underwear.
We help each other, *blanc*."

He stepped on to one of the *Thunderbolt*'s launches, Narcisse once again riding in her place on his back, and as it left
the beach Valentine felt sadness, and some relief. Relief at
the fact that he found on Haiti what he spent over a year getting to, and sadness in saying good-bye to so many of those
who risked everything to help him. He turned his body toward the ship, its outline changed by the potted trees lashed
everywhere on the decks. The old *Thunderbolt* looked like a
floating forest.

The launch hove alongside, and Valentine climbed
aboard and reported himself present to the mate on watch.
He and some sailors helped Narcisse to the galley, where she
sniffed suspiciously at the Jamaican pepperpot the cook's
mate was creating in celebration of leaving Hispaniola.

Valentine went up on deck and watched the preparations
for departure. The motor launch was swung up, and a last
few sailors and marines came out to the ship with the
Haitians. There were friendly exchanges of cotton ducks
for pigskin utility vests, earrings for copper bracelets, and
so on over the side of the ship. There would have to be a
strict search for smuggled alcohol, and the wearisome task
of getting rid of lice and bedbugs which undoubtedly
hitched a ride from the shore. But Valentine could leave
those details to Carrasca and her mates. He and Post had to
make sure the marines and Grogs were ready to fight if necessary.

The last lap. He needed to get the ship to the Texican
coast. His superiors would handle the rest; he would be back
to being a cog in a larger machine, rather than the axis
driving the various cogs. Would he miss the taste of inde-

pendent command he had been given? Being on his own was a banquet of endless servings of stress and headaches, but the freedom added spice to the dishes.

Thankfully, for this last voyage he would not have to turn into Captain Bligh on the *Bounty* and ask his crew to sacrifice for the cargo. The saplings were hardy enough to survive the short trip across the Caribbean, assuming the *Thunderbolt*'s aged diesels held out, without taxing the ship's freshwater resources. After the challenges of the late months, Valentine was ready to spend a week supervising potted saplings.

Ahn-Kha again quartered his Grogs in the forward well deck, their old tentage replaced by a grove of quickwood plants, their crossbows and pikes stored below, shotguns and rifles cleaned and put away in the arms lockers. He wandered among the bunks of the marines. His complement was already displaying souvenirs acquired on the island, hung upon bunk and locker. Hispaniolan voudou charms wrought from wood and bead swung with the ship's gentle motion.

He returned to the deck for a last look at Haiti. The mountains, so green that the color deserved a richer word to describe it, stood out against the azure blue of the sky and the argent blue of the Caribbean waters below. It was an island of extremes: beauty and hideousness, laughter and despair, freedom and slavery. But from this island that had known an almost endless series of sorrows for the past six hundred years, a new world could spring.

Narcisse's dishes made a superb dinner, once the cook and his mate let her take over supervision of the meals. Valentine had the galley busy, and treated Post and the rest of the *Thunderbolt*'s marines to a feast. Good food and plentiful tobacco—all as night fell after an easy day's duties—made the men lively.

"How's life in the Ozarks?" a stout corporal with a stand of red hair asked. "I've heard the winters pass hard."

"Irish, I know a lot of stories get passed around the Kurian Zone about that," Valentine said. "There's enough to eat. Sometimes it isn't what you'd like as a first choice, or even a second, but we don't starve. You'll find out there's a lot of ways to cook chickpeas, and you'll get sick of dried fruit, I can promise you that."

"Women?" Hurst called, and the men snickered.

"That's one thing we're not short of. Fact is, there's so many, you'll find a few in uniform. There are a lot of lonely widows, too, which makes a man think, but if any of you have a mind to be a second husband, you'll have your pick. We've got schools, roads, there's a gambling boat, show-boats, and I'm even *told* of a floating whorehouse or two on the Lake of the Ozarks. Being an officer and a gentleman, I wouldn't know details, naturally."

The men snickered and passed around comments under their breath, like kids in school, and Valentine heard Carrasca's name mentioned.

"Enough of that," Post growled.

A shout echoed from above. The collision Klaxon sounded. Something thumped against the ship's hull, a grinding jar that had everyone reaching for a table or a bunk brace to steady themselves.

"Vampir—," the squawk-box sounded, before falling silent. Valentine listened with hard ears, trying to shut out the bleating alarm, and heard the icy shrieks of Reapers.

"My God, they followed us!" Post said.

"Take arms, men—anything!" Valentine shouted. He didn't have so much as a knife on him.

"Quickwood, anyone have some?" Post asked.

The marines were already grabbing rifles and shotguns from the beckets in the wall of their quarters; a corporal coolly gave out bullets as the men took arms from the wall.

"Sir!" one marine shouted, running up to him with two of Post's screw-in pike-points. A scream, then a second, came from above—along with a smattering of gunfire.

"It'll have to do."

"Post, take Wilde and his team and get to the Oerlikon. Ignore anything else, I don't care if she's on fire, get that weapon manned. Irish, you and the rest of the men follow me! The forward stairs, we have to get to the bridge. Hand me that machete, Torres."

Post shoved a speedloader into a heavy .44 revolver with a trembling hand and gestured to his assigned men.

"Marines, you see a Reaper, shoot until it's down if you can. They'll have the advantage up close like this. Let me get in and get its head off, or stick it with the quickwood. If I catch it, get up to Post. Any more wood down here?"

"Here's a pike," another said.

"Take the tip off—it's too hard to use on the pole. Ignore any wounded, don't pay attention to anything, we go to the bridge. Now, with me!"

They moved at his order into the night's chaos. Valentine rushed out into the next compartment forward and gained the stairs leading up to the main deck. A marine caught his rifle going through the doorway and tripped, but the rest jumped over him and up the stairs in a steady stream.

The compartment above opened onto the deck from doors on either side of the ship, and Valentine led his men to the door opposite from the side of the grinding collision. If he could just get them out in the open as an organized team, rather than as frightened individuals, the ship might stand a chance. The deck door on the collision side swung open, and the men brought up their guns.

"Wait!" Valentine rasped, holding the flat of the blade of the machete against the man behind him. "It's Owens."

A sailor made it in and slammed the door shut behind. "They're everywhere—we have to get below," he said.

"You'll come with us," he said to the unstrung man. "Bellows and Gomez, Owens goes between you two. C'mon, the rest of you."

They burst onto the port side of the ship, running for the stairs to the bridge. Shots and piercing Reaper screams filled the night. As Valentine hit the first step, a caped figure appeared at the top of the stairs.

"Shoot it!" Valentine shouted, throwing himself down on the stairs so the men would have a clear view.

The Reaper lunged. Shotgun blasts flashed blue-white. Even the awesome strength in the Reaper's pounce was no match for buckshot at close range, and the wounded thing cried out as it was blown back. It recovered and vaulted over the rail to drop to the deck, but Torres swiveled the mouth of his shotgun and blew it into the darkness.

It splashed into the water, and Valentine ascended the stairs. He ducked without thinking, and heard the *whoof* of a Reaper's hand cut the air where his head had been. Valentine lashed back up, driving the quickwood pike-point in his hand up like a striking cobra. It caught the Reaper under the arm and drove through fabric built to stop bullets but not an old-fashioned point. Valentine felt sticky fluid hit his hand, and he got out from under the wound.

"Marines," he called down at the men and across the ship. His team was leaning over the rail to shoot at the Reaper that had blown into the sea; he had to keep them going to the bridge. He ran up the rest of the stairs. The wounded Reaper stood up, its jaws open in painful spasm as it clawed at the quickwood point buried in its armpit. It lost its balance and sagged against the upper deck rail.

Valentine paid it no more attention. Another Reaper, its back turned to him, tore away the metal door to the bridge, peeling it like a painter removing wallpaper.

"Aim for the face," Valentine said to the men who joined him on the upper deck. The Reaper whirled. Valentine heard screams and shooting from the stairs below. Torres, just behind him, fired at the Reaper at the door, throwing it against the bridge-cabin. Valentine circled as the others continued to shoot, pumping round after round into the thrashing creature.

He took a good grip on the machete and gathered himself.

The men stopped shooting, hurrying to reload. He dashed forward like a cricket-bowler, catching it in the throat with the heavy blade. The head did not come off, but he damaged the nerve trunks and vertebrae enough for it to go limp. It continued to snap at him with gleaming jaws, its yellow eyes dimming.

The wound closed over the blade.

Valentine left the machete wedged in its neck and went to the rail to look at the gangway below. The Kurian death machine at the back of his men had taken its toll in the seconds it took him to deal with the other. Twisted bodies and pieces of bodies lay on the deck. Three survivors fired pistols as it advanced. The Reaper used Owen's corpse as a shield. Valentine vaulted over the rail and landed behind it.

It ignored his presence, continuing forward toward the marines. Valentine lashed out with a foot, catching it in the small of the back, but he might as well have kicked the *Thunderbolt*. He took his other pike-point in both hands and drove it between the thing's shoulder blades.

The point struck near enough to the Reaper's heart to stiffen it instantly. The Reaper arched its back, its whole body bending like a bow, and hit the deck, still clutching Owen's bullet riddled body.

He was out of quickwood and had no time to look for the other pike-point among the bodies. "Everyone to the bridge," he said.

Irish hauled the Reaper out of the way of the damaged door. Valentine heard the welcome pounding of the Oerlikon from aft; Post must have gotten it into action. He went to the starboard rail and looked over the side. Kurian sailors were taking cover as the Oerlikon's fire moved up and down the deck of the submarine. Valentine saw a strange, thin smokestack at the rear of the ship. A snorkel on a submarine? Perhaps that was how it had crept up so close to the *Thunderbolt* without being seen. A quick rise to the surface, Reapers ready at the hatches, and all there would be to do was leap on board, an easy matter for the superhuman avatars.

There was still fighting forward. Valentine heard the Grogs screaming and a gunshot or two from the rear. "Torres, take two men and cover the men at the Oerlikon from here. They'll go for that if they get organized. Who had the other pike-point?"

"Hurst, sir. He's dead below," Torres said. "I'll check—"

"No, everyone stay together up here."

The bridge door opened, and Carrasca stood at the portal, a shotgun at her shoulder. "What is it?"

"Kurians, on the *Sharkfin*. They tried to board us. Too greedy. They could have just put a big limpet mine against the side and sunk us. But Saunders wants his ship back."

"What do we do about the Reapers still on board?" Carrasca said. "The Chief says there's some of them hammering at the engine room door. They'll get through."

"Tell the Chief to pour it on. Let's get to the wheel," Valentine said.

They went to the bridge, lit by a single red bulb over the map table. The instrument lights had long since gone out and never been replaced.

Valentine saw the sub making off, gathering speed as it ran. Post's Oerlikon bursts riddled the stern as it sought safety beneath the waves, explosions and smoke flying from the impact of the thirty-millimeter shells.

"We've got to get to the main gun. What a target! The Oerlikon is tearing it up," Carrasca said.

"He's just scratching its back—the real vitals are under water. We can still get them. The prow's reinforced, you know. Icebreaker."

"*Jesu,*" Carrasca said. "If we get enough speed . . ." She went to the engine room squawk. "Chief, everything she's got. Maximum revolutions!"

"Aye aye, sir," the Chief crackled back. "Do something about those bastards on the other side of the bulkhead—they're tearing the rivets out."

"You want the wheel?" Carrasca said to Valentine.

"You're the better helmsman."

Carrasca took the ship into a gentle turn, letting her gain momentum.

"Ramming speed, Hortator," Valentine said.

A Grog lept up to the bridge window, howling in fear. A pale arm plucked it back down. Valentine heard a thud on the roof and more shots from outside.

"What's that?" the Chief said. "I—"

Carrasca hit the collision alarm again as the *Thunderbolt* knifed through the water. She aimed for the conning tower but didn't hit it square; at the last moment the submarine must have known what was coming and turned away. The impact threw Carrasca against the wheel. Valentine hung onto the instrument panel. The Reaper on the roof of the bridge fell forward into the cannon mount.

The *Thunderbolt* ran up and over the submarine, to the sound of tortured metal breaking up. Valentine saw the stern of the sub burst from the water like a breaching whale.

"*Madre de Dios,* snapped in two!" Carrasca said.

The Reaper on the gun deck jumped from the side of the ship, plummeting into the water by the crippled sub, perhaps summoned to the aid of its Master Kurian in its final need. Valentine had one more thing to do. He took Carrasca's shotgun and went to the door.

"Stay here, and keep the doors locked. The Reapers'll be disoriented—they won't work together once their Masters are dead, but they're still dangerous. Wild animals in a trap: all confusion and pain."

Valentine glanced down to the Grog deck, but saw no sign of Ahn-Kha or his Grogs. Just bodies. Grogs, Jamaicans, and the *Thunderbolt*'s sailors were strewn in broken pieces everywhere on the deck like mannequins run over by a tractor-trailer, under blood-splashed quickwood branches. He ignored the gruesome tableau and went to the starboard arms locker, where he retrieved out one of the aged machine guns. He placed a belt into the receiver and hefted the weight. It was a more suitable weapon for Ahn-Kha, or a tripod, but it would have to do.

Another Reaper, its form misshapen by a missing leg, jumped from the stern into the water. Valentine moved forward, down to the Grog deck, and then up to the bow. He leaned over and winced at the damage to the front of the ship. Hopefully just her forward compartment was flooding. The ship could absorb this kind of damage and still proceed under her own power, were she fresh from the dockyard. Was she still sound enough to float?

The submarine was gone. All that remained of her on the surface was a fuel-oil slick, spreading across the water like a bloodstain at a murder site. And debris. And bodies. Swimming men struggled to stay afloat amidst the floating wreckage.

Valentine spotted one odd shape, a long thin tentacle with a heavy membrane attached. A Kurian, forgetting to disguise himself in his distress. Valentine loosed a burst into the struggling form. He swung the smoking barrel to the next swimmer, an oil-coated man in white, and killed him with another burst. A heavy form floated on a life preserver, perhaps dead, perhaps faking it. Valentine could not make out the features for certain, but the hair looked as though it might belong to Captain Saunders. He fired a burst into the body, which twitched at the impact of the bullets before disappearing under the oil. Another swimmer burst through the oil, taking a deep gasp of air, having miraculously escaped the sinking sub. Valentine shot him before he could draw his second breath.

The gun grew hot, and he had to slow his rate of fire. The brass casings dropped onto the deck, and hundreds lay at his feet when a hand touched his shoulder.

"It's over, my David," came a familiar bass.

"Oh, dear God," Post added, looking at the casings scattered on the deck. Valentine met his lieutenant's gaze, looking for understanding. Instead he saw disgust. Post could see only pitiful figures in the wreckage being murdered for no reason. Several Kurians had to have been on board the submarine for that many Reapers to attack at once, and it would be easy for one of them to pose as a sailor. As long as the Kurians lived, the Reapers that might still be on board the *Thunderbolt* could kill, plant a bomb, or otherwise sabotage the ship. He could no more risk a Kurian deciding to achieve a Pyrrhic victory by destroying the *Thunderbolt* that he could have let Alistar live back in New Orleans.

Valentine tossed the gun to the deck and left the bow. Ahn-Kha trailed him. Valentine was thankful for his comrade's silence. Ahn-Kha would listen and give his opinion sometime in the future, but now there was too much to do. He did not look over his shoulder to see Post, but he heard him unload the gun and pick it up.

"How many of your Grogs are left?" Valentine said.

"A hand-and-two." Ahn-Kha had forgotten himself in the crisis and used Golden One phraseology for six. "It was desperate, even with the crossbows and the quickwood. There were many of them. We hunted the last of them from the stern with the pikes. When we wounded one in the leg with a pike, it managed to tear its own limb off and escape. They've learned to fear wounds from these weapons."

"So the ship is clear? Will she be able to continue?" They descended to the Grog-deck.

"I do not know. That is for the captain and the Chief to say. I was thrown off my feet by the collision, but I was belowdecks and saw no water. She does not seem to sink."

"Mr. Post," Valentine said when Post joined them on the well deck. "We have to get the guns manned and ready while we're motionless. The submarine wasn't the only ship the Santo Domingans had. You'll be in charge of that. But leave me enough for a party to search the ship. Ahn-Kha with his crossbow, a couple of pike men, men with shotguns, four should do it. We'll look for any of our people who are wounded, of course, but we have to be ready for a fight. A Reaper or two may still be holed up somewhere on board. We'll check every corner big enough to hold a dog. Once we know the ship is safe, the Chief can go to work and see if she'll be able to move again.

"After that, we'll clean up the dead, and the ship. I don't want everyone walking over bloodstains for the rest of the trip. Any questions?"

Post shook his head. "No, sir. I think they already pulled up a sailor from the submarine portside, sir. Shall I shoot him, just in case?"

Valentine ignored the rebuke. "Let me talk to him."

The sailor was a Cuban by birth, but his mother had been taken to Santo Domingo when she and her family were captured in a raid. He sat by the entryway, trembling and wet from head to toe, with a blanket around his narrow shoulders. Valentine's Spanish wasn't up to the dialect, so Carrasca translated his story.

"I served on the *Sharkfin* four cruises, as a mechanic. I had just been called forward to get gas masks, because the damage from your gun was filling the engine room with smoke, when the collision came. Some of the men tried to get out through the old torpedo room, but those doors long since quit working. I made it out through the forward deck hatch—" Carrasca quit translating when the submariner howled in pain as Valentine grabbed his wrist and twisted it, dropping the wretch to his knees. The prisoner was human. A Kurian's disguise would have flickered.

"Val, stop!" Carrasca said. "He's just telling us what happened to him."

"I'm making sure he is who he says he is. Tell him I apologize. See if he'd like to join up with us—we could use him."

The Santo Domingan sailor seemed willing. Through Carrasca, he relayed why.

"The White Captain of the north, he was a madman. He convinced the Kur that if they got this ship, they could take over all the islands south of here. He promoted men he trusted, and to gain his trust they had to treat us badly. We worked like mad and were still punished. I had planned to swim away the first chance I could get, let the Haitians castrate me and use me as a slave in the fields. At least I would live."

"What about this last trip? Who was on board?"

"Seigneurs from the Samaná Peninsula. They had their eye on the lands west of Cape Haitian, and with this boat they could have ruled the coast. I had no love for them, I am glad they are dead."

Valentine silently commended the dead Saunders for his final throw of the dice. With the right men under him, he would have been able to snatch the *Thunderbolt* away from the Hispaniolan Kurians in the manner Valentine took it away from the rulers of New Orleans. A man of strange contradictions. Long ago he had quit asking himself why so many talented men chose to devote themselves to serving the enemies of their blood.

After the ship had been searched and re-searched, Valentine returned to his cabin, feeling an itchy burn from the Reaper-blood. He'd wiped it off quickly enough, but needed a thorough cleansing with pumice.

Post was rinsing his mouth out with baking soda in their cabin. Ahn-Kha had moved forward with the ship's remaining Grogs.

"Do you want to talk about it?" Valentine asked, scrubbing hard and working up a lather.

Post did him the courtesy of not playing dumb.

"Sir, you've pulled this whole thing, the ship, the quick-wood, the Jamaicans and the Haitians together like a . . . like a magic trick, something out of nothing. I respect you for that. I'm not sure I can serve under you anymore. When we get to Texas, it's good-bye."

"It's what happened at the bow?"

Post nodded. "I can't stop thinking about the bodies in the water, sir. When you got those Santo Domingans away from their plantations, I thought that you pretty much walked on water. Woulda died for you then, if it meant accomplishing something you were trying to achieve. Never thought I'd want to die for anything or anyone. Maybe to get away from them, but not for anything."

It took Valentine a moment to regain his equilibrium. "You shouldn't have to die for anyone. Least of all me. Risking your life, weighing it against what you are trying to do—it's something any man does."

"Any man worth the iron in his blood."

"But you feel differently now."

Post waited a moment, but Valentine made no gesture to hurry him. The words would come when his lieutenant was ready.

"If your idea of the right thing to do is machine-gunning sailors who've had their ship sunk from under them, I want no part of it. You can cite precedents all you want, wrong is wrong."

"I had to make sure all the Kurians were dead. For all we knew, there was a Reaper squatting in the magazine with a hand grenade, just in case the *Thunderbolt* got the upper hand in the fight. If a Kurian has his puppet pull the pin and hug a couple of shells in his arms with the grenade under its chin, it's going to do it. Sometimes it is just as dangerous to beat the Kurians as it is to run from them. They'd rather destroy than let another own something that was theirs. The Reapers were clawing through to the Chief in the stern. I had to disorganize them, quickly, and that's the only way I had to do it.

"Remember, Post, they were serving the enemy. That's war."

Post shook his head. "I was serving the enemy. As soon as you gave me a chance, I switched. I bet a lot of those sailors would have done the same as that fellow we pulled out of the water. When you were shooting them, it was like you were shooting me."

"I understand. But I don't know how I'm going to get along without you. But go with my friendship. Shake on it?"

His lieutenant pursed his lips, then took his hand. "Could be you have what it takes for the kind of war this is and I don't. Sorry, Val, but I can't see death like that again. I'm afraid I'd shoot you, or myself, or maybe both."

"Drop it, Will. Serving our side's different from working for the Kurians. I'll give you your choice, and wish you well when the *Thunderbolt* sails away. One thing, though: even if I did the wrong thing, the quickwood has a better chance of getting back to Southern Command if you come with it. Having it could turn things around, make a difference in a lot of innocent lives being saved. What happened at the bow was wrong, I'll grant you. But weigh it on the right scale. How wrong is it when a Reaper takes a six-year-old girl, because the Kurian running the show wants a different-flavored aura?"

Post shook his head. "That's a maybe. I'd rather deal in certainties, and those bodies floating in the diesel fuel were real, not supposition." He turned away.

"Will, if you're going to hate me, hate me for a good reason. Ask me sometime how I became a captain in the Coastal Marines."

Post would not, or could not, see that Valentine would have preferred to rescue the *Sharkfin*'s survivors. But the risk to the mission, to losing all their lives and even more time in the quest to get the quickwood into the hands of Southern Command required him to act as he did. Valentine had learned long ago not to second-guess himself where matters of life and death were concerned, or he would never be able to make a decision again. He had made right decisions and wrong decisions, and sometimes had to bury the bodies of those who died for no other reason than his bad judgment. Like Gabriella Cho, the night he left her alone and wounded in the confusion of a battle, or his old company's Master Sergeant Gator, lying in a hilltop grave in eastern Oklahoma.

Struggling with his own memories as much as he had with the Kurians, David Valentine went to bed.

Carrasca, Valentine, and the Chief decided the ship should be refitted before exploring a potentially hostile coastline, and two months in drydock at Jayport would allow the Chief to consummate a long-desired overhaul. There was the added incentive of replacing the losses from the encounter with the *Sharkfin,* so in the end Valentine agreed with yet another delay in his return to El Norte.

They returned to the harbor to a mixture of cheers and curiosity over their topiary. There were the inevitable problems with safely storing their precious cargo and finding living space for the crew during the refit, hampered by the occasional tropical storms and hurricanes brushing the island.

Valentine, Post, Narcisse, and Ahn-Kha were left with the leisure to recruit Jamaicans to join his marines, reduced to a bare handful in the fight against the Reapers. Valentine was shocked to see a soccer field filled with Jamaicans who wished to follow the Crying Man to sea, off their sunny island and into peril. In the end, he selected fifty for the short run to the coast; the *Thunderbolt* would be cramped, but it gave him a core of willing men to accompany him on the long trip back to the Ozarks.

There was also time with Carrasca as the Chief worked on the bow. Long rides into the countryside, talks with the locals, trips to sporting events and lunches made of market-square purchases filled the mornings. In the afternoon when the rains came, they talked or laughed or made love as the mood struck, and waited for the cool of the evening to walk back to the ship. Sometimes they spent the night at the commodore's house, joining him for mah-jongg or cribbage depending on the availability of players. The weeks passed like a dream. Valentine had never known so many idle days in all his years serving Southern Command. There was time to know another person, not as a comrade, superior, or underling, but as a friend and lover.

He learned her moods, and in turn she learned his. They pretended that the respite would never end by not discussing it, talking instead of the perfect hillock for a beach house or whether Valentine would make a better fisherman or planter.

Valentine was more than half-willing to take these conversations at face value.

Reality intruded when the Chief refloated the ship, and they had to make ready for the last voyage. Then the idyll was over.

"You're a wanderer, too," she said as they lay together.

"What's that?" Sex always made him wool-brained.

"You wander. Is it so you don't have to put down roots?"

He rubbed his eyes. "I'm not blown around. It's more like a current."

"Even coconuts wash up, by and by. What keeps you at sea?"

"Same as you. Duty." He would have added something about his dreams of a better future, dreams made almost realistic-sounding thanks to the quickwood, but his lover sighed.

Valentine turned on his elbow. The whites of her eyes caught the night sky coming through the window. They looked wet.

"Are you saying I should wash up here?" He half hoped she'd say yes. He'd get the quickwood back to the Ozarks and return.

She didn't say anything for a moment, but her mouth twitched.

"What then?" he insisted.

"Nothing. Nothing important. Important as our duty."

Chapter Ten

The Texas Coast, October: South of Corpus Christi, the southernmost Kurian city in what had been the United States, the coastline is a collection of fishing villages hiding among ancient concrete resorts, suffering under the depredations of both the Kurian Alcaldes of Mexico and the Texas variety farther north and inland. The long stretches of the thin, sandy island running the coast of Texas provide a protected inland waterway that sees little commerce under Kur other than smuggling. Stopping this was one of the gunboat's principal duties in her cruises under Captain Saunders, when her crew spent years losing fugitives in the thornbushes and grassy hummocks of the half-mile-wide, seemingly endless coastal sandbar where once vacationing college students lost their underwear along with their virginity.

This part of Texas is typical of most of the state not under the direct eye of the Kurians: independent and isolated, asking nothing from the outside world and trusting no one.

The *Thunderbolt* followed her new prow into South Bay on a rainy dawn. A few open shrimp boats bobbed in the bay, and beyond them, some beach fisherman could be seen, their oversize rods hanging out over the lapping surf of the bay.

Valentine had never seen this part of Texas in his time on the *Thunderbolt*, though Torres had visited this coast on occasion in his days with the Corpus Christi Kur. Torres was the sole surviving crewman who knew Brownsville, so he stood on the bridge with Carrasca and Valentine.

Valentine fingered the leaves on a quickwood sapling; Carrasca had taken a fancy to one and installed it on the bridge. A few others had been planted near Kingsport, bordering the graves of the Jamaicans and Louisiana *Thunderbolt* crew who had died defending the ship from the Reapers. After explaining to the commodore the importance of the quickwood saplings, Valentine had placed further seeds in the dirt covering the bodies as they lay in their graves. He hoped one day trees would sprout and be used as weapons against the slayers of the sailors.

"Why no Kurians around here, Torres?" Valentine asked.

"Can't say. Seems that they never managed to get installed here. Not really free territory, so to speak, but there's a resistance here. I've heard of a Kurian or two coming to the area, but anyone going to work for them winds up with their throats slit pretty soon. Their Reapers can't travel much either, the resistance assembles and smokes them out of anywhere they hold up. Every now and then a bunch sweep up from Mexico, or down from San Antonio or Corpus Christi, but when they're gone, the resistance pops up again."

"What did the resistance think of the Coastal Patrol?"

"We never did much inshore except try to chase down smugglers so the resistance didn't object to us, I guess. But that's just what we heard when we came into the bay. There were only one or two safe places to visit, right up against the shore where the *Thunderbolt*'s guns could cover. The old hands told us to sleep on board if we knew what was good for us."

Valentine looked at the overgrown ruins. Palms stood up through roofs, bougainvillea sprouted everywhere, covering the ruins along the bay further.

"Looks like the work of hurricanes," Carrasca said, examining the coast through a pair of binoculars. While on Jamaica she'd dyed and recut one of Saunders's uniform coats, adding shoulder padding so she could fill it. The middle still hung a little loose thanks to the dead man's potbelly. "What now, Captain?"

"According to plan, I'm supposed to be contacted here, and failing that I need to go inland to Harland. Southern Command has a liaison officer here. He was supposed to stay around the bay, but I'm so overdue, he might have gone back to his base. That's where I need to get to if I'm not met here."

"Anything special we're supposed to do?"

"Act as if this were an ordinary patrol," Valentine said.

"Very well," Carrasca said, turning to the old hand. "Torres, what was the procedure? Do they have pilots?"

"No."

"So how would Saunders handle it?"

"Cruise the bay. Anything that looked oceangoing, we were to sink, unless we could board it and were satisfied it belonged to the Corpus Christi Kurians. Their signet was a crane over a sunrise, I think Asian-looking, only with Mexican colors. Stood out like a sore thumb in Texas. But if there was any doubt, we'd seize it and bring it back to New Orleans, and let the Kurians haggle it out."

"Then that's what we'll do. Helm, let's take a look at that inlet to starboard. After the check?"

"If the captain felt like it, he'd let us dock. There's a concrete wharf by the old Brownsville channel, and some of the harbor joints traded with us. Good place to pick up crabs, lice, and the drip from the whores. We were always under orders to go in groups of four at least, armed with rifles and sidearms. Don't try the chow—they give coasties rat meat."

"Shall we dine on board tonight, Captain Valentine?"

Valentine found himself smiling. "I've eaten rat any number of times. I'm sure Narcisse could spice it up into a state dinner, if she had to, Captain."

"Torres, what would the Captain do if he didn't want to give the men liberty in the port?"

"We'd raid a shrimp boat for food and leave, sir."

"It would be best if the captain decides to grant liberty. It can buy us some time."

They wasted the morning cruising the bay, but saw nothing larger than open fishing boats. Valentine was relieved. He didn't want to arrive at a strange port and start burning local shipping; especially when the success of his mission could depend on the aid, or at least noninterference, of the natives. With that out of the way, the *Thunderbolt* tied up at the pier near the stagnant channel. A few blocks of cracked concrete buildings leered out at them, garish—and misspelled—advertisements painted over doorways in a mixture of Spanish and English.

An afternoon rain soaked the men tying her up, and the gangway guard took shelter under the stairs to the top deck.

Carrasca, her new lieutenant, Valentine, and Post decided to dine one last time in the wardroom. With their combined coaxing, they got the Chief to join them. The Chief sat uncomfortably at the cramped table, awkward in his civilian clothes.

"They're the only ones that weren't oil stained," he explained.

They heard Narcisse's voice shout orders from the galley. With the crew now mostly Jamaican, the dishes reflected that island's preference for spiced chicken and pork dishes, leavened with rice, vegetables, and fresh fruits.

"Captain," Valentine began, as the eating slowed, "you, your officers, and the men have more than carried out your part of the bargain. I'm happy to leave the *Thunderbolt* in the Commodore's Flotilla. I know Mr. Post and the Chief will serve you ably."

Post elbowed the Chief. The Chief had met a woman in Jamaica, a beauty who could have appeared in one of the old tourism posters in her yellow two-piece bikini, and had decided to stay with the ship.

"Happily ever afters," Post said, lifting a glass of lemonade to the Chief.

Carrasca shifted in her seat and rearranged the rice on her plate.

Valentine's stomach did flip-flops as he looked at her. "Just see me and the cargo into the hands of my contacts here. You'll take my promise to do anything I can to help you in our common Cause. I'll never forget the *Thunderbolt* and her captain."

The object of his thoughts and memories smiled. "You'll always have a berth on any of our ships and a bed in Jayport."

Carrasca stared levelly into his eyes as she spoke, but he saw her jaw tighten after the last sentence. Valentine felt his throat go thick.

"Ah—thank you for the offer."

The table sensed a tension and covered it with technical talk about improvements in the ship since the overhaul. It lasted until the Chief and the two lieutenants excused themselves. Post closed the cabin door behind him.

Carrasca reached out and took Valentine's hand.

"Sorry," she said. "I've been preoccupied since we refloated. We've had no time alone."

"We're not the first couple sacrificed to the Cause."

"I'll miss the sound of your heartbeat." Her skin lost some of its usual glow.

"I wish we could say a proper good-bye."

"I know, and I agree. Discipline. It'll be lonely without you."

"You have your grandfather. The Caribbean, this ship."

"And you have your duty. We're both married, in a way, to both of them."

He lowered his voice. "It was a wonderful time, Malia."

"You'll always be a part of me, David."

Discipline or no, he kissed her, long and hard. It was agonizing to let her go, knowing that his lips might never meet hers again.

"Forgive me," he said, stepping away.

*　　*　　*

A full day passed, and no one from the shore tried to make contact with the *Thunderbolt*. A few idlers gathered to watch the sailors on the *Thunderbolt* go about their daily duties, but no one requested permission to come on board, and the men who went in groups off the ship claimed no one spoke to them but bar touts.

"I'll have to go inland after all," Valentine decided at the end of the second day. Carrasca looked at him from beneath her black brows, pulling a wet bang out of her eye to do so. They both were plastered with sweat. Even with the windows wide open, the bridge was stifling in the windless harbor. The afternoon rain had succeeded only in dampening the heat.

"Have the Chief send some people in to look for a critical part," Valentine said. "Claim we have a breakdown. Maybe that won't incite too much comment. I don't like the idea of her sitting here, tied up to a dock, with the cargo on board. The people on shore have got to be wondering why the ship looks like a topiary."

"You're not leaving tonight."

"I have to. I've got a better chance moving at night."

"Alone? Can you pass as a native? From what Torres says, they don't like strangers poking around here. You don't want to be strung up in a tree by your own allies."

"They're only allies in the 'the enemy of my enemy is my friend' sense. Southern Command never had any luck getting Texas guerrillas to work with us, except right on the borderlands, where we could arm them—and shelter them if they had to run. Not that a Texan ever called it running."

She nodded. "Any orders while you're gone?"

"I hope to be back, or at least send word, in a couple days. If you don't hear from me in five, go back to Jamaica, plant the trees, and wait for the next Southern Command agent to head south."

"Somehow I don't think there are too many David Valentines to be found. Some woman needs to make more."

Valentine squeezed her arm as he passed out of the bridge and went to his cabin. He smelled the musty odor of wet

Grog and found Ahn-Kha waiting, cleaning out his pointed ears with a delicate wooden implement that was part spoon and part chopstick.

"I needed a wash," Ahn-Kha said. "I've put out your things."

Valentine looked at his bunk. His dyed-to-black fatigue pants lay spread on the bed with matching moccasin boots (he'd made them last month of Jamaican calfskin) and topped by his combat vest and pistol. A canvas knapsack was already loaded with food and water flasks. A felt-brimmed hat with a beadwork band stood atop the pile.

"I don't wear hats," Valentine said. "Unless it's winter, and even then I like the stocking kind, or a coonskin."

"Start, my David. You'll blend in better. You want your drum-gun?"

"No, I'm going to travel light and fast."

"Then I cannot accompany you?"

"Sorry, old horse. I will take one of those pike-points though. Just in case."

Valentine went down the gangway with a group of sailors going to one of the wharf-side cantinas. He wore a rain poncho to conceal his lack of uniform, a borrowed gold earring pinching his ear and the hat rolled up in a pocket.

The men, under Carrasca's lieutenant, pushed two tables together and ordered the inevitable chicken, rice, bean, and tortilla meal. The cantina provided an outhouse for the comfort of its braver—or desperate—guests, and after a light meal and a lot of boiled water, Valentine excused himself. Feeling a bit like Superman from the old comic books, he exited the outhouse wearing a light leather vest, the knapsack, his weapons belt, and the hat. The poncho was in his knapsack and the sailor's earring in his pocket.

He hiked down what used to be a main street, walking just off the nearly worn away center line of the road and trying to look like he knew where he was going. Once clear of the harborside, he turned west out of town, coming to a line of shacks bordering the marshy flats, picturing a map of the Brownsville area in his head.

There were many palms above, some delicate limbed trees, and groves of thick kunai grasses and palmettos. His nose picked up the faint salt smell of the ocean, but the moist, just-overturned-rock smell of the marsh was far stronger. In the interest of speed, he stayed to the road, hoping that he would sense trouble before it found him. He fell into a steady jog. When his body warmed to the pace he fell into his old wolf lope, with hardly a twinge from his leg wound.

He stopped when he hit the old interstate, crawled into a thick stand of grass and napped after emptying one of his flasks and eating some dried fruit and fried bread. He took in the landscape as he rested. The sea had its beauty, but it was refreshing to be on land again with its confused breezes and variety of bird and animal life.

Valentine woke himself when the moon rose. He knew little about this area beyond the large scale map, and even Torres had been no help. According to his orders, the center of this part of Texas's guerrilla activity was supposedly near the old airport at Harlingen and somewhere called Rio Hondo.

The guerrillas saved him the trouble of finding them by finding him. As he trotted up the overgrown interstate running northwest, two men on horseback pulled up on a little rise above him. They had rifles pointed at the stars above out and on their hips, and reins in the other hand, ready to shoot him down or ride him down as circumstances warranted.

Valentine stopped and bent over, panting and rubbing his aching left leg.

"Yo down thar," a dry throat called. "You're the damnedest runner I ever saw. You'd think the devil himself was chasing you, but there's nothing behind you but empty."

"Keep your hands away from that gun, stranger," the other said. Like Valentine, he wore only a vest and had a gleaming Western tie at his throat.

Valentine was too tired for the good cop–bad cop routine. "I hope you're Texas Rangers."

"You do?" Dry Throat said. "Well, there's some that say that, and it turns out they hoped the opposite."

Valentine walked up the man-made hillside, hands above his head. "You'll find out if you give me a chance to talk. My name's Ghost, out of Southern Command in the Ouachitas. I'm looking for a place called 'the Academy,' and your colonel. I don't know his name, but I know the man I'm looking for, a friend of his. Patrick Fields."

"Seems to me if that were the case, you'd be well north of here, heading south."

"I came by sea."

"Haw!" Western Tie said.

"Handcuff me, hog-tie me, whatever, just bring me to either Fields or your CO."

"I'm Sergeant Ranson," Dry Throat said. "This is Corporal Colorado. Colorado, climb down and take his weapons, pad him down. We're on patrol, and we can't just quit whenever we feel like it. I'll send Colorado back for a guard, and they'll take you north." Valentine warmed to Ranson as a man who made up his mind quickly and correctly.

"Should I get out the irons, Gil?" Colorado asked as the young man unbuckled Valentine's weapon harness.

"No, man seems straight enough. If his story isn't true and he is a spy, he's going about this a mite odd."

Colorado rode off north. Ranson had Valentine walk ahead of him to an old roadside stop on the southbound side of the interstate. It seemed like any other decayed husk of the Old World, save for a ladder up to an empty platform where a gasoline sign once stood. Valentine decided it must give a commanding view, day or night—if the moon was out. He smelled water.

"Colorado will be back in a couple hours. Let me go up and take a look around. Do me a favor and walk my horse, would you? A few times around the building will be fine."

Valentine complied, as Ranson made a slow climb to the

perch for a long look-round. When the Ranger returned Valentine handed the reins over.

"In the mood for some coffee, Sergeant?"

Ranson's lean face lit up. "You have coffee out of Mexico?"

"Better. Jamaican."

"Holy Moses, why didn't you say so? I ain't had coffee from anywhere east of Padre Island in years. There's a mortar and pestle we use for corn inside, and a coffeepot."

In three-quarters of an hour, they were sharing the coffee, the Jamaican beans campfire-toasted and stone-ground.

"Lord, that's good," Ranson said, sipping appreciatively. He was lean as a winter wolf and sat in an old wooden chair with long legs stretched across a pile of cordwood.

"You aren't worried I drugged it?"

"Naw. I'd kill you before it got me. Besides, you drank first, and I poured. So you've been to sea."

"Yes."

"I didn't want to say anything to Colorado, but a few of us have been told to keep an eye out for a stranger calling himself Ghost. Seems to me you're mighty overdue."

"It wasn't a pleasure cruise."

"Delays beyond your control. I know what you mean. I was on a patrol once on the Rio Grande. It was supposed to last a month. They ended up chasing us west—we didn't make it back till Christmas, five months overdue. My wife was collecting death pension already."

"So the Kurians have the river?" Valentine asked.

"The whole damned valley. Mexican Kurians, they call 'em the Alcaldes, like they was old aristocracy or something. Good farm land, some of the best in the world. The folks there smuggle us out what they can. How are things up north? We don't get news unless it comes roundabout."

"Hard, but Southern Command is holding out."

"And what were you out for? Intelligence?"

"I'll be happy to tell you if your colonel or Mr. Fields okays it."

Ranson winked with one whole side of his face. " 'Loose lips,' whatever that means. My dad used to say it when he was playing his cards close to the chest. Personally, I like a set of loose lips. 'Specially if they're attached to a genuine redhead."

Two more riders arrived with Colorado at the dawn. "Sergeant Hughes says we're supposed to cut our patrol short and see this man back to the Academy."

"Kind of him," Ranson said. "Switch to the relief horse. I expect they want him there pronto. Wish we had a spare for you, young man."

"I expect he can run some more," Colorado said. "He did pretty well there at the end on the road. I'd like to see that trick again."

While the sergeant passed on his report on the patrol, Colorado readied the horses, placing the saddlebags and rifle sheaths on the patient animals. Ranson mounted, still chewing on a snatched breakfast.

They set off, Colorado in the lead and moving his horse at a brisk walk, quickly enough so Valentine had to force himself to hurry at a pace just below a jog, which he found increasingly annoying.

"I'm going to run, it's easier than walking like this," he said, breaking into a trot.

Colorado kicked his horse to a trot, and Ranson followed. The sergeant smiled at some inner joke. Valentine set his jaw, and ran faster, passing the trotting horse at a steady lope.

"What the hell?" Colorado said. He touched his heels to the horse's flanks, and it broke into a canter.

Valentine had to pour it on to keep up with the cantering horse, but he did so. His whole body seemed suffused in warmth, a warmth that slowly grew uncomfortable. Even a Wolf couldn't move at this rate for long. His legs filled with a fiery ache, and his heart beat like a duck's wings. The sweating horse tired of the race, as well, and kept trying to break into a gallop.

"Cut it out, Colorado," Ranson yelled from the dust-trail. "You'll kill the damn horse or our friend."

Perspiration crusted with dust coated Valentine's face, but he kept pace until Colorado halted, fighting the urge to lean forward to catch his wind. He slowed back down to a walk matching the horse's, controlling his breath as best he could.

"Sheeet," Colorado said. "They shouldn'ta called you Ghost, it shoulda been Shanks. I never seen—hell, never heard of a man able to run like that."

Valentine concentrated on breathing.

"You done treating our ally like a bastard?" Ranson asked.

"Ally? We're taking him under guard, ain't we?"

"If them Reapers showed up, he'd be guarding us, not the other way around. Don't you know a Hunter when you meet one, you damned fool?"

"Ha! My pa used to say those Hunters were just good liars, is all. There's nothing to that story."

"Apple didn't fall far from the tree." Ranson said under his breath. But his eyes shared the joke with Valentine, knowing the Cat heard.

The Academy was easy to find. It bordered on a defunct airport whose runways now served as a rifle range. The airport's concourses and some of the hangars had been demolished, but the control tower still dominated the camp, reinforced with a pyramid of sandbags and timber all the way to the top. On the other side of the old military education campus there was a cemetery, graves arranged facing a giant statue that seemed familiar yet out of place to Valentine. "It's the model of the one that stood in Washington, Marines raising the flag at the top of Mount Surabachi on Iwo Jima," Ranson explained, and Valentine realized he had seen the photo it was based on. "It was a helluva fight in the

Pacific in 1945. The men who finally got up there and planted that flag were from Texas."

Valentine remembered it differently, but he was in no mood to discuss military history minutiae at the moment. Ranson brought him through the rows of barracks, one lot vacant like a missing tooth, and took him to the brick head-quarters. Like the control tower, it was layered in sandbags and barbed wire, with hard-points guarding both entrances.

"Don't worry about washing up," Colorado said as Valentine retied his hair when they moved through the door past a sentry. "The colonel likes to hear news first. Every-thing else waits, unless you're bleeding. Bleeding badly, that is."

Spurs clattering in the wood-floored hallway, they approached a reception desk. It was a beautifully carved piece of wood, like many of the items decorating the entrance hallway. Valentine got the impression every square foot of wall space was covered by a painted portrait or photograph. The only ones he recognized were Sam Houston and the Texas United States Presidents. The woman at the desk wore a cheerful Mexican print blouse and a ready smile, but Valentine saw a pistol lying right next to the phone.

"Courier for the colonel," Ranson said. "Tell him it's Longbow Resolution. The Ghost is finally haunting us."

Another Ranger walked down the hall and out the door, saddlebags hung over uniformed shoulders. Valentine found the contrast between the rough, tanned, mustachioed men and the ornate furnishings interesting.

"Map room, second floor," the receptionist drawled, looking at Valentine from under curled eyelashes.

"Colorado, you can go get yourself fed," Ranson said. "I'll see things through from here."

The younger man took the dismissal well. He hesitated only a moment before saying, "I'll see if I can snag us some bottles of beer for when you're finished, Sarge."

"You do that, Colorado. Thanks."

"Good luck with the colonel, Shanks," Colorado said, offering his hand. "Hope there's no hard feelings over our little race."

Valentine shook it and thanked him. Ranson lead him to a white-painted staircase, and they ascended past photographs of cities filled with pavement, glass, and steel.

Valentine loved maps, and the map room captivated him. A four-foot globe stood by one wall-spanning bookcase, but the other walls were covered with maps. A long library table dominated the center of the room, placed on an oriental rug spread on the polished wooden floor. Tall windows lighted the room. Chairs stood beneath the mounted maps on the walls. One of the maps, showing the Rio Grande region of Texas, was festooned with pins and colored ribbons. Valentine walked up to an older, glassed-in map of the state, which looked to date from Texas's earliest days.

A handsomely dressed Latino opened the door and held it open for the colonel. The Colonel of the Texas Rangers, Officer Commanding the Academy, had undoubtedly been a tall man in the days before his confinement to a wheelchair. Valentine guessed he must have stood close to six five at one time, judging from how high he sat in the wood-and-metal contraption he wheeled himself around in. He was gray haired and clear eyed, and gave the impression of lively vitality from the waist up, like an alert prairie dog whose hind legs are hidden in his burrow. He wore a bronze star enclosed by a circle, pinned over a frilly white-and-blue ribbon.

"Col. Steven Hibbert, Texas Rangers," the colonel said, extending his hand. "Glad to meet you."

The Texans were devoted hand-shakers. "Thank you for your hospitality, Colonel Hibbert. My name's Valentine, but I'd prefer if you just referred to me as Smith, or Ghost, in your paperwork, if I end up being mentioned."

"We generally call him 'the colonel,' " Ranson said.

"Whatever you're comfortable with, young man. This is my chief of staff, Major Zacharias."

After another handshake, the colonel moved on to business. They sat at one end of the long library table, so all eyes could be at the same level.

"Well, Ghost, your contact here went back north a month or so ago on a courier run. He didn't have much choice—he told us about you and asked for our assistance. Fields is a good man, about all he ever asked us for in the past was information about the state of things in Texas and on the Mexican border, and a couple of times he brought us warning of troop movements that saved lives. I'm willing to do whatever I can to help Southern Command. He said you'd have something needing to get north."

"Yes, sir," Valentine said, relieved at their accommodating attitude. "I'm to give you part of my cargo in exchange for your assistance. It's a weapon. Deadliest thing I've ever seen used on a Reaper." Valentine showed the colonel the quickwood pike point he'd brought, and explained the catalytic action the wood had in a Reaper's bloodstream.

The colonel and his chief of staff exchanged looks. "Well, now," Zacharias said. "That's good news. Some kind of silver bullet, huh?"

The colonel shifted his weight in his chair. "And you've seen this work with your own two eyes."

"Yes, Colonel."

"Because I've heard tales of big medicine against the Kurians before, and every one of them turned out about as effective as the bulletproof vests made out of old sticks and beads the Indians wore."

"Not just me. Others, too—you don't have to wonder if I'm crazy. I'll leave you with what I can spare, some saplings you can plant and some lumber you can turn into weapons. We've found that crossbow bolts and spear-points work best."

"Our armorer will take a look at what you've done," the colonel said.

"It's a lot easier than trying to go in and behead them, that's for sure. Time is important, Colonel. Every day the ship waits in harbor—"

"Easy, now, son. South Bay isn't really our ground—not that it's Kurian. If we ride in armed for Reapers and offload you, someone will talk. If this stuff is important as you say it is, we might want to keep it as a surprise for the bloodsuckers. Major, let's put Harbormaster into effect."

Zacharias made a note on a clipboard as the colonel spun his wheels back to Valentine. "You get back to your ship and bring it across the bay to the entrance to the old intracoastal shipping channel. There's a white lighthouse there, manned by some of the Corpus Christi crew. We've got a spy there, and this sounds important enough for him to break his cover. He'll knock out their radio and make sure our Rangers grab the place. We'll make it look like a simple hit-'n'-loot. When you see two blue lights burning, one on top of the other, bring your ship in as close as the tide'll let you, and we'll start loading up your cargo. This will happen twenty-four hours after you get safely back to your vessel. Questions?"

"Two blue lights vertically." Valentine sagged into his chair in exhausted relief. The colonel's quick mind relieved him of his last few worries about getting his prize to the Rangers safely. He shook himself back to the present.

"No questions, Colonel. Some food and a few hours' sleep, and I'll be ready to go."

"You'll get more than that. There's still some things we have to organize. You'll have until dawn tomorrow to eat and rest up. That okay by you?"

"Better than okay."

"Major Zacharias, you'll have operational command. Put Flagstaff in charge of trains and logistics, use Three-Feather's reserve riders for the main force. I want plenty of scouts, too. Send two couriers now and get Harbormaster going. Ranson, you'll take our friend back to his ship and go onboard as liaison."

"Can I bring Colorado along, Colonel? 'Bout time he started working on a longer line."

"Sure, how often does a man get a chance to go to sea

nowadays—even if it is just a ride across the harbor. Mr.
Valentine, we'll meet again when your cargo is here, safe
and sound."

Night on the harbor. The old lighthouse near the wrecked
causeway had two lights burning.

Valentine watched from his familiar bridge-perch as the
ship's boats, and a commandeered shrimp boat, moved
quickwood, men, and material from ship to shore. There was
nothing for him to do on shore, save hear Flagstaff give
gruff orders to the Rangers and contingent of laborers he
commanded. Oxen stood in their traces, and smaller horse-
wagons held supplies for the two hundred riders Zacharias
brought to guard the precious cargo. The eight-man garrison
of the lighthouse was under lock and key, though five of
them expressed an interest in moving inland with the
Rangers. Valentine idly listened to the sound of waves lapping against the ship as he pulled his tiny collection of books
from its railed shelf, lulled by the hint of motion as the
Thunderbolt rocked at anchor. He felt melancholy. The
Thunderbolt had become a home.

And it was time to leave.

He would miss the sound of the sailors talking as they
washed down the decks in the morning, the smell of good
coffee, the wide horizons of the sea. He thought of his father, and his description of the charm of naval service:
"Duty at sea, especially when you were out months at a
stretch, sounds like you're away from everything, that you'd
be lonely and homesick, but you aren't. To a sailor, the ship
is a home he takes with him. It's like traveling with your job
and all your neighbors. There's nothing like it." His father
had been right.

He also liked being able to hit the Kurians where he
chose, instead of spending all his time parrying blows. Moving men, their food, and equipment was simplified by the
tonnage a ship could carry. A real navy, well handled, could
make the Kurian seaboard spend far more of its time gar-

risoning harbors and seaside towns, out of fear that a occupying force would appear over the horizon. The Free Zones
in the Appalachians, the Ozarks, and the Rockies would be
given breathing room. But he was just one officer, a spy-
saboteur trained to work inside the Kurian Zone. Putting together real sea power would take combinations of time and
resources the Kurians took pains to prevent. The great ports
of the world were solidly in Kur's grip. But with quickwood—

"The quickwood beams are going now, Captain," Post reported. "These Texans are organized."

Valentine nodded. "They have to be. This pocket doesn't
have any Lifeweavers. They're going up against the Reapers
with small arms and guts, and a lot of people on farms and
in towns slipping them news and supplies. They're smart,
they don't fight over the Rio Valley or the coast, nothing
that's important to the Kurians. Texas is a big place, they've
got distance on their side as long as they stay mobile."

"I'd always heard they were just bushwackers in uniform."

Ranson, who'd approached and caught the tail end of the
conversation, cut in to elaborate. He described how the
Rangers would go into some one-horse village and relocate
the residents. "Then a few Reapers and Quislings come riding in, lifesign reads normal, they think it's just another
town. But it's a town armed to the teeth with men who know
how to use their guns. We've got a heck of an intelligence
network, most everyone between the Rio and San Antonio
city limits knows what to do if they see a column coming
into the area. We use a lot of heliographs, since the sun's almost always shining. The Kurians have been burned too
many times—now they only roll through with big pacifica-
tion raids. When that happens, the Rangers scatter."

"How much do you know about the quickwood?" Post
asked. Farther back on the ship, proof of the efficacy of the
weapon stood on the upper deck. A dead Reaper, frozen as a
statue with skin hard as tree bark, stood gripping the ship's

rail and canopy—though not truly lifeless, at least in the vegetable sense. The Reaper was beginning to sprout tiny green leaves.

"Everything," Valentine said. "I'll give another briefing to their weapons people. I'm going to leave them some lumber and saplings. Want to throw in your seed-pouch?"

"They'll need it more in the Ozarks."

"I'll carry it there for you, Will."

"You've got enough equipment, what with that ugly-assed gun you tote, Val, and there's still a lot of miles ahead of us. I'll bring it myself. You'll need somebody around to carry out your godawful plans anyway, won't you?"

Valentine felt his eyes moisten. "Why the change of mind?"

"More of a change of heart. When I was watching the Chief and his girl on Jamaica, and you and—well, I got lonely for a woman. The beach beauties were willing, but I want to find my wife. Tell her I was wrong and she was right."

"About the system?" Valentine asked, remembering their conversation before the mutiny.

"When we first got married, we didn't know each other that well. I was in uniform then, but it was for the food and the security. Gail was a sharp girl, and figured out I didn't really like *them*, or my job. We talked about us getting a posting way out on some frontier, and running for Arkansas. We used to talk like that a lot.

"Funny thing was, after I got married to her, all of a sudden I wanted to do better, have better housing and better food for us, or her really. I went officer, mustanged up from a sergeant to a junior lieutenant. Part of the process was indoctrination, of course. Lectures at the New Universal Church building—you know the routine. Then I had to spew the same stuff to my men: all about mankind poisoning and ruining the Earth, crime and overcrowding and starvation and homelessness. Then the shit that came down in '22 and how the Kurians came to restore 'natural order,' all that Darwin stuff they come up with about men needing control. Of course, the Kurians never admit that they probably started it all—they make it sound like they saved us from extinction. But anyway, I started to believe it. You probably can't understand—"

"But I do," Valentine said. "I've heard a few speakers for the Church. While they're talking, it seems reasonable enough. It takes the next drained body you see to set you straight again."

"Well, Gail and I grew more distant. She didn't like my talking about making captain, or joining the Coastal Marines to advance faster. I was drinking a little too much on days off with the others. But it was the baby that did it."

"Baby?" Valentine asked. "You never said anything about children."

"It would have been a baby, I guess," Post said. "Gail didn't want to have it, she 'couldn't bring a child into the world for *them*.' She aborted it—I hate to think how. I found out and said something stupid. I think I quoted the New Order's law on abortion like it was Scripture. She took off, I don't know where. Left me a note with her wedding ring: 'Maybe you can replace this with a brass one.' At first, I was actually glad to be rid of her. I thought her opinions might be preventing me from getting promoted." He ran his hands through his multitoned hair in frustration, gripping the locks at the back of his head as if trying to tear the memories out before continuing.

"I only realized later, after she was gone, that she was the thing that kept me going. All of a sudden I was ashamed every time I put on my uniform. I hated the job—I hated the people. Drinking helped me forget . . . let me go to sleep. Pretty soon it helped me make it through the day. Then wake up. Thanks to you, I got a part of my life back. I owe you that, whatever your methods. Now I want the rest of me."

Valentine stood on shore with his volunteers: a smattering of Jamaicans, many of the *Thunderbolt*'s remaining

marines, and a few sailors who decided to go back to the
Ozarks to look for their families. The group said their
farewells to their comrades from the *Thunderbolt.* Narcisse
sat atop a wagon, distributing voudou amulets and cheek-
smacking kisses.

Captain Carrasca, dressed again in the looser pirate
clothes Valentine had first seen her wearing, said good-bye
to each of the men as they walked down the gangway. When
she got to Ahn-Kha, she hugged him, her outspread hands
making it just to the other side of his armpits. When that was
over, she gave him a wooden tube that Valentine thought
looked like a bamboo flute. Ahn-Kha bowed.

Valentine stood at the entry port last.

"I'm glad Will is going with you," Carrasca said. "I'd
give almost anything to keep Narcisse in the galley. Won't
be sorry to see the Grogs go. We can do without their unique
odor. But the two of you will be missed."

"Torres will make you a fine officer of Marines."

"Yes, he's already polished those railroad tracks three
times, and it's only been a day.

"One more thing." Carrasca stepped forward and embraced him in turn. Post tactfully drew the men away from
the gangplank, and the pair stepped behind the lifeboat davit.

"If I ask you to do something for me, will you do it?"

"You shouldn't have to ask that question, my love.
You're the best thing that's happened to me in years." He
kissed her, softly and lingeringly.

"When you're back safe in your mountains, write me. We
used to get courier pouches every now and then from Southern Command, years ago before the Kurians set up their in-
tercoastal patrol chain. Now smugglers get newspapers and
pamphlets to us through your logistics men. The commodore would like to see more, and so would I. Maybe you
can set up a new mail run. From your stories, it sounds like
you have the experience. Anything. Just let me know that
you're okay."

"It's a promise. Write me, as well."

"I will."

They stood looking at each other, neither sure of what to say. She smiled.

"Almost forgot. I made you something." She reached into the baggy pants and pulled out another leather pouch. Stitched into the leather was the legend: THUNDERBOLT / JAMAICA-HAITI-TEXAS 2070 / CAPT. MALIA CARRASCA.

Valentine took the pouch. It felt as though it were full of a lot of coin-sized objects, only lighter. "Your quickwood seeds?"

"Look."

He opened it and extracted a handful of mah-jongg pieces. The bamboo pieces were delicately painted.

Valentine finally said, "Your work?"

"Of course. Should be rainproof, I lacquered them enough. You and Ahn-Kha and Post and Narcisse can play."

"Thanks, but . . . damn. I feel like I should send you away with something," Valentine said.

"You have," she said. "More than you know." Her eyes glistened with tears.

"How's that?"

"Hope. Someday we'll have ships going up the Mississippi to your Ozarks. I have a feeling . . . things are about to get better."

Valentine felt a pleasant thrill at the latest example of their minds following similar trails. If it weren't for the quickwood . . .

"Hope for someday, then."

" 'Someday.' That's all our generation has: hope." She raised her chin. "Texas is waiting. I don't wish the men to see me teary-eyed. Back to hard-nosed captain, Captain."

"Yes sir," Valentine said, saluting.

She returned the gesture, her emotions under control again. Valentine felt the old wall go up. It was as if they had never kissed. As if they were strangers. Inspiration came to him.

"I left that old Coastal Marine uniform coat in the closet in my room. You're welcome to that. It doesn't mean much to me, and won't do me any good where I'm going. All I'm keeping are the boots and the pants I dyed."

The wall vanished. "I'll make earrings out of the buttons," she said with a smile.

"Better and better." He caressed her cheek with the back of his hand. Carrasca . . . caress. He smiled to himself. "Good-bye, Malia."

"Adios, David. You can always find a home with us on Jamaica, you know that."

"I do." He hurried off the *Thunderbolt*. Valentine couldn't let his mind dwell on the idea.

Four days later, Valentine and Post sat in the Academy Map Room. A pair of electric fans fought a losing battle with the lingering summer heat. Ahn-Kha stood behind and in between them. His bulk wouldn't allow him to do anything but demolish the antiques in the room, and the Grog had declined the offer by one of the Rangers at the meeting to go seek out a piano bench.

"We've accomplished part one," the colonel said from the head of the library table, after hearing the reports from the various Rangers involved. "Now comes the hard part, getting those wagons up to the Ozarks. Zacharias, before my encounter with that piece of shrapnel, you used to be in charge of our northern areas. What's your suggestion?"

Zacharias's dark eyes studied the map, as if looking for something that would appear if he just stared long enough. "With the kind of men we'll need to guard the wagons, there's no question of slipping it through the San Antonio–Austin–Houston belt, though I bet we could get north of Corpus Christi. We're going to have to swing west of San Antonio. Not too far west, we can't be moving across the desert, either. The hill country could shield and water us."

"That means crossing the Ranch."

"The Ranch?" Valentine said. "What ranch?"

"You've never heard of the Ranch?"

Valentine began to shake his head, then stopped. "Wait,

you mean what I think you mean? That's a legend in a lot of places. No one's ever proved it true."

"What's this?" Post asked. "I've never even heard the story."

"The Ranch," the colonel said, "is a real place. Maybe elsewhere sometimes it is and sometimes it's not, but I'll tell you it's true in Central Texas. We've seen it. The Ranch, Mr. Post, is kind of an experimental farm the Kurians run. According to our sources, they use it to come up with new life-forms. Biological servants. Even something other than humans to squeeze the juice outta. Intelligent, but easier to handle."

"There's a lot of strange sights to be seen in those hills," Zacharias said. "The Kurian settlements give it a wide berth, there's a huge stretch of empty ringing it. The Ranch gives us our best chance of getting up to the Dallas area and past it. Then it's into the pinewoods of East Texas, and you'll be home. Getting back will be easier with no cargo to guard. We can either break up and get home in small groups the direct way or trace our route back."

"It's your part of the country," Valentine said. "If that's what you want to do, I'll support it. Whatever gives us our best chance of getting through without fighting."

"Colonel, if we're going to try to get across the Ranch, I'd like to have Baltz along," Zacharias said.

"I'll send word."

"What's his specialty?" Valentine asked.

"Her specialty," Zacharias corrected. "Back in the cattle-drive days, they used to have one or two old bulls to lead all the other cattle, especially for things like river crossings. Baltz is kind of like that, except she ain't a bull. Bullheaded, oh yeah. She grew up in the Ranch, worked there. Not in the secret buildings, on the outside. She knows the land. We'll need her and her staff, sure as a hot summer sunset."

Chapter Eleven

The Ranch, Central Texas, November: Texas, at 266,000 square miles, is larger than any country of old Europe, and could fit a few Eastern states within her expanse. The same could almost be said of the lands around the Ranch, which stretch from the hill country west of San Antonio in the south to Abilene in the north, taking up the Edwards Plateau in the west and ending at the old I-35 in the east. Why the Kurians wanted such a vast expanse for their experiments can only be guessed at; perhaps the research stations they established on the Colorado River and the San Angelo area needed isolation.

The thorough depopulation of the area supported this theory. It is one of the few parts of the Kurian Zone run without the aid of Quisling forces. Its borders are watched by Grogs, either hardened to or oblivious of what goes on in the hinterland of the region.

It is one of the most beautiful parts of the Lone Star State, a land of limestone bluffs over twisted rivers, of rolling hills dotted with wildflowers and fragrant of sage. Longhorns, wearing no brand at all, roam the valleys alongside buffalo, with antelope watching from the hilltops and white-tailed deer sheltering in the cedar and oak forests. Cypress grows in the river valleys, and zone-tail hawks drift above the southern tip of the American Great Plains. If the wildlife could talk, they could tell of new, strange inhabitants wandering the hills.

David Valentine scratched the bristle on his chin in thought, raking his memory. Only one animal on earth looked like that, and they were called . . . "Zebras, by God."

"Yes, that's right, zebras," Amelia Baltz said.

She was a square-built woman, a thick, tough-skinned German as solid as a Gothic cathedral. She rode with Valentine and her staff at the front of the wagon train when she wasn't driving her buckboard or conferring with the Ranger-scouts on the best path for the column to take. Her "staff" consisted of a towheaded thirteen-year-old girl named Eve, a walking suntan who was all scrawny limbs under a face that twitched like a rabbit when she thought. There was also an assortment of animals ranging from riding and pack-horses to dogs, cats, and the only chickens Valentine had ever known to lay eggs while traveling.

"The zebras, David, come from an old—I guess you'd call it a zoo—near Kerrville. It was home to ostriches, too, and they're thriving in the hill country. The damn things'll kick your head clean off if you startle them, so don't wander into the brush to take a shit without looking for something with a feathery white ass. Funny thing is, you come up on 'em head-on, they turn and run. You sneak up behind . . . *swish-whack*."

Baltz had a direct earthiness that came from better than forty years of life in the open. She wore bandannas over hair, mouth, and neck when the dust kicked up and settled on the broad brim of her hat, and an ancient pair of curving, head-wrapping sunglasses.

"Are we on the Ranch lands yet?"

"We're just skirting the edge. We've left the Grog-pickets behind. What they do if they cut our trail I don't know, they don't go into the Ranch proper, at least not anymore, even following an enemy. They ain't that dumb—no offense intended to your big-assed shadow there. The Ranch has its own security. One relief: the Hissers don't wander these hills, so we don't have to worry about lifesign."

"No offense understood," Ahn-Kha said. The Golden

One walked alongside Valentine's horse, his long rifle protected from the dust by a soft leather sheath. "Perhaps the unusual animals are the reason people think this place is used by Kur for experiments."

"We don't think, we know. I worked their lands, when I was nearer your age, David, or even younger. I was an electrician; I handled the lines running between the stations. Being a specialist means you see some things they don't want you to tell about, so they made me live on the Ranch, with some of the other people they couldn't do without. About twelve years ago, they decided to clean house and bring in some new people. They showed up, and I didn't like the way they were rounding us up for a 'meeting.' I got Eve, jumped in a Hummer, and rode it till the oil ran out, then ran south on foot.

"I never saw much of what was going on inside the stations—I just worked the lines outside. When I had to work a box indoors, they blindfolded me until I got to the utility room. But even outside you saw things. Once I heard some kind of muttering in the underbrush and I looked down and these two pigs were nosing through some scrub. They weren't grunting, they were forming something like words, I just didn't understand.

"They've had a lot of trouble with breakouts. Keeping a pig in a pen and keeping a pig that thinks like you do is something else entire."

"I can imagine," Valentine said. He could imagine, too much. The hills felt as if they were waiting for him to turn his back. He would have almost preferred to hear that they were stiff with Reapers.

"Can you, boy? I wonder. There was a rumor that once something got out; they blasted a whole quarter of the place with nerve agents. Hold 'em up here a minute, me and the dogs are going to scout that tree line."

The wagon train always got under way before dawn. Each move was a two-segment effort. The mounted screen of ranger scouts moved a day ahead of the column under Zacharias's lieutenant, charting the course for the wagons and choosing the best spots for stream-crossings, resting places, and the next night's campsight. The convoy of fifteen wagons and the rest of the escort made up the second segment. The convoy spent only about six hours a day in motion. The oxen pulled better with frequent rest stops and out-spans, and those always meant at least a couple of hours of delay while teams were unhitched and then reorganized.

Valentine left much of the management of the column to the Texans, and he and Post worked at getting their men to patrol effectively alongside the rangers. With their baggage in the wagons, the mix of former marines and sailors had to carry only their arms and ready ammunition, and perhaps a canteen or walking stick. There was some grumbling about marching while all the Texans got to ride, and there was some comment by the Texans about having to guard and support "foreign mouths"—though there was no complaint about the quality of Narcisse's chuckwagon cooking. Ahn-Kha and his surviving Grogs stuck close to Valentine as he moved about, like children keeping close to their parent among strangers.

"If we run into anything, our men will be glad the horsemen gave them warning, and the Texans will be grateful for all our rifles," Valentine said to Post, when they talked over the men's adaption to the trail and their new allies. They both agreed that even after days in the wagons, sweeping wide around San Antonio, the column was still moving like a balky horse.

Steak on the hoof followed the wagon train, driven so as to muddle the wagon tracks and footprints. Regular barbecues in the evening gradually brought the two camps together, until Texans were teaching Jamaicans to play horseshoes and guitars, and the mariners were enthralling their hosts with stories and music, and dances and songs from the other side of the Gulf.

By the time they entered the lands Baltz identified as

being on the Ranch proper, the column was as cohesive and
cooperative as Valentine could have hoped, due to habit
more than leadership or training. At rest halts, Valentine's
soldiers took over the picket duty, fanning out to gather
some of the seasonal crops growing wild: plentiful apples,
squash, and pumpkins. Their foraging made a difference to
the barbecues, and with the nights growing longer as October waned, the evening meals became more leisurely. Narcisse contributed her own ideas about cooking to the drive.
Some of the Texans began to anticipate the nights when she
cooked Creole dishes—the variety was welcome with night
after night of slaughtered beef and preserved food.

It was at one peaceful camp, as Valentine walked the
picket line with Post to make sure the sentries were under
cover with good fields of vision, that a pair of the *Thunderbolt*'s sailors, one Jamaican and one former Coastal Patrol-
man, came running down from a grass-covered hill.

"Captain, there's some kinda big animals the other side
of this hill. They're making a hell of a noise," the old New
Orleans hand reported, moving from one foot to the other
like a schoolkid asking for a trip to the toilet.

The Cat hardened his ears. It sounded like construction
work, or logging. He thought he heard a tree being pushed
over.

"Post," Valentine said, "find Baltz, please. Tell her to
meet me on top of that hill. Let the camp know we've seen
something, but I doubt there's immediate danger. They
wouldn't be making so much noise if they meant to cause
trouble. Take my horse back, would you?" Valentine dismounted and placed a drum in his submachine gun, and
shouldered the weapon.

"Let's have a look," Valentine said to the men.

"Sir, that gun ain't gonna do much against what's on the
other side of this hill."

"We can always outrun it."

"Two of us get away, then. The two fastest," the Jamaican
predicted.

They filed back up the hill and began to crawl through the grass and brush when they reached the crest. Valentine looked back toward the camp and saw Baltz and Eve trotting toward their observation point.

"Losey, go back down a ways and show 'em where we are," Valentine said to the Jamaican, who nodded and crawled backwards out of sight.

Valentine heard the sound of another tree tipping and looked into the valley.

They were huge quadrapeds. More strange wildlife of Central Texas, he really couldn't —

"You've got to be kidding," Valentine said. "Those are elephants, but with two trunks. Or is it one trunk cut in two?"

"Can't see too well, sir. My eyes have been fadin' since I turned thirty. See how they're using tools?"

Valentine did see. The gray giants were using picks and shovels to dig in a clearing they had enlarged in a patch of woods. Other elephants used their foreheads to knock trees over, facing outward from the clearing.

"What did I tell you, boy?" Baltz said, creeping up on her haunches. The girl watched silently from behind. "Don't that beat all? Them 'fants, looks like three or four families down there, they're getting set for winter. They're making a windbreak, some of the trees they're leaving up will be pushed together to make sort of a roof. They don't like the cold. Don't use fire, though. They talk, and you can hear them a long way away, the dogs pick up stuff below our hearing frequency. I knew we'd run into some 'fants in the next day or two—the dogs signaled it."

"Why are they digging?" the sailor asked.

"Food storage. That's an old riverbed, and they're going to put stuff they gathered in the clay. They've figured out how to dry fruit. You'll see apples all over the place lying on stones."

"The Kurians thought they could feed off those? They look like they could stomp a Reaper."

"Nah, the Grogs hunt them with tranquilizers from horse-back, or vehicles. The 'fants haven't really worked out for them. I don't think they did much research on elephants, the wild things had a family loyalty they didn't count on. Up-ping the intelligence a couple of degrees was one of their dumber moves. We'd best get away from here soon though, if there are 'fants around, there might be hunters. Though the tracks I've seen today don't show it."

"You want us to move at night?" Valentine asked

"Just for a couple more hours."

"Light'll be gone soon—let's get moving, then. Eve, don't you ever say anything?"

"No sir," Eve said, eyes wide on the elephants.

"You'd better go pack up the menagerie," Baltz said to Eve. The girl took one long look, then scampered off. "C'mon boy, sightseeing's over. We should get away from here."

"Is she a relative?" Valentine said.

"She's been with me since she was a babe in arms. The Kurians had a research station in a crossroads town called Eden. I never found out what they were breeding. There was a fire, and they called in everyone with two arms and two legs to help fight it. Well, for some reason there were human babies at this station, most of 'em died account of the smoke, they dragged them out in this cart-cage contraption. Looked to be five, or maybe six infants in this cage. I saw her fingers moving and got her out. She started coughing up a storm, and even with all the noise she was making, I snuck her to my truck. I didn't know who to trust, so I started liv-ing out of my truck with her in it. Whenever I had to deal with anyone else, I put her in a tool case, with air holes, of course. She seemed to pick up on the danger, even though she was barely crawling—she'd keep quiet for hours until I opened it up again."

*   *   *

The next day it was Baltz who summoned Valentine. She sat her horse beneath a steel tower, a pair of power lines hanging from the arms.

"This is funny, Captain," she said. Valentine startled; it was the first time she had ever called him anything other than his first name, or boy.

"You don't mean funny 'ha-ha' I take it."

"No. Funny-scary. This is a main source line. It runs back up to an oil-burning plant in Abeline. It's dead, and I mean long dead. I haven't been this deep into the Ranch in years, but I'd say this hasn't carried current in two or three years, judging from bird and insect activity. I climbed the tower and had a close look."

"Maybe they found a new power source," Valentine said, but it sounded wrong even as a guess.

"You know the Kurians, son, they don't bother with something that's working. Civic improvements are the last thing on their mind. You're talking about a shutdown to at least half the Ranch, probably more, if this line is dead."

"Maybe they gave up on these experiments. Found them unproductive?"

"That might be. They have the patience of Job, though, which makes sense considering they don't die. What's wrong, guys?"

Her assorted mutts were whining worriedly and slinking around behind her horse. Valentine's horse began to toss its head. He dismounted and soothed the animal.

"It's coming from that brush over there," Baltz said, her horse under better control.

Valentine unlatched the flap on his .45's holster. He handed his reins to Baltz, and pulled his machete from its saddle.

"That's what I call a pig-sticker," Baltz said.

"A Grog would have shot by now. This isn't the right time of day for a Reaper, but I'm not taking any chances. Maybe he's got a motorcycle helmet on."

Valentine cursed himself for not carrying one of Post's

spearheads. He took a few cautious steps toward the brush, every nerve alert.

He heard grass move, and whatever was crawling through the brush changed course at his approach. Valentine made ready to leap forward or back, gun in his hand and machete held ready to swing.

A sound like fifty castanets came from the brush. It sounded familiar, only too loud; he hadn't turned up his ears that much. What kind of rattler would make that much noise?

He found out when the snake struck from cover. The king of all rattlers, its head as large as a melon, lashed out with mouth gaping and fangs pointed down and forward. It aimed for Valentine's thigh.

A blur of reflexes saved him from a strike moving faster than the eye could follow. He spun, pulling his leg out of the way as he brought the blade around and down as fast as a propeller. The fine steel edge severed the neck of the rattler two feet below the neck, and the head flopped to the grass, biting at nothing. The decapitated body thrashed back and forth, rattle still buzzing angrily.

"Jesus, that's a hell of a snake," Baltz said as the serpentine body slowed and stopped.

Valentine breathed until his heart slowed and the burning above his kidneys faded.

"You moved faster than the damn snake, boy. I didn't know what happened till it was over. You touched by God or something?"

"Or something," Valentine agreed. "Don't tell me the Kurians made smart, venomous reptiles."

"I don't think it was smart. Creeping up on all of us like that."

"If it wasn't smart, then why did they bother? Breed a few thousand of them and drop them on farmland in the Ozarks from planes?"

"I wouldn't put it past 'em. But they're new here. Dead lines, big snakes, no Grog patrols away from the borders. It adds up to something. I'd say the Ranch is under new management."

"Anyone see a sign that said 'Animal Farm'?"

The reference was lost on Baltz.

That night Valentine worked with the snakeskin. He found something in it appealing and with Ahn-Kha's help he turned the hide into a bandolier. He didn't intend to be without a spearpoint or two in the future. After the camp trooped past the hide to whistle, gape, and ask the same questions over and over, he and Ahn-Kha went to work. They stretched lengths of snakeskin from wagonwheel to wagonwheel on one of the supply wagons, peeling off the remaining muscle and salting down the skin.

"The Gray Ones like snakemeat, my David. Even better than beef."

"They're welcome to it—there's enough to last them a week."

"This is good skin. Very light and strong. I think I will try layering it, so the scales go different directions. Make armor for the chest and shoulders. Better than sharkskin."

They ate and drank as they worked, with the other two Grogs squatting by the campfire, toasting snakemeat on sticks and watching their every move.

"Whatcha makin' boy?" the familiar voice of Baltz called in passing. She approached them with the rolling walk of someone constantly at sea or on horseback.

"A conversation piece, most likely," Valentine said. "There's some coffee left."

"No, really, looks like a big-assed belt. New clothes, Uncle?"

"It's for me," Valentine said. "Thought I'd keep a couple of spearpoints in a bandolier."

"Ah, yeah, your precious wood. Word around the campfire is that you've got some kind of weapon against the Hissers."

"Reapers, we call them."

"Hissers is more accurate."

"Depends on if you're describing what they do or what they sound like."

"So these spears kill 'em?" she asked, eyes narrowed.

"I've seen it more than once, more than twice. If the wood is fairly fresh, when it hits their bloodstream, it kills them. Fast."

Baltz laughed, a barking sound more suitable for one of her dogs. "'Bout time we found something that did. Can I have one of your stickers?"

"Take a couple. It's the least we can do for your help. Help yourself to some seeds and a sapling while you're at it. When you get home, you can plant it. Maybe someday it'll be a liberty tree."

"A liberty tree?"

"Something old, so old it's forgotten. Has to do with the founding of the old United States. It's an idea I've been working on ever since I found out what I had to bring back. I picture these trees growing in all the freeholds."

"Pretty much everything worthwhile in life started out as somebody's dream, boy. This one's worth a chase."

An orange explosion of teeth and claws shot out from under Valentine's snakeskin-adorned wagon. Ahn-Kha dropped his blade in alarm, and Valentine jumped.

"That's Georgie, my cat. Wonder what spooked him?" Baltz said, squatting to look under the wagon.

"Shit!" she screamed, falling backwards in alarm.

Valentine knelt, hand on his machete and ready to jump, and looked under the wagon. A chimpanzee form hung under the wagon, glaring at him with red eyes and a rat face. But the oversized back legs were all wrong, and the tail . . .

"Nusk!" Ahn-Kha bellowed, and his Grogs grabbed cooking implements from the campfire.

"Hey, it's—," Valentine said as the creature dropped from its inverted hiding place, spun like a cat, and hit the ground running. The Grogs howled and ran around the other side of the wagon in pursuit. Valentine jumped up into the driver's seat of the wagon for a better look.

The oversize vermin shot like a brown bolt of lightning through the camp, startling and scattering men and animals. Someone managed to bring a shotgun up, but blasted only trampled-down grasses in the thing's wake. A flick of its cotton-tuft tail was the last Valentine saw of it, but his ears followed the scrambling claws through the darkness, northwest into the heart of the Ranch.

Valentine shook his head, wishing they were off the Ranch. He'd had enough of the Texas hills with creatures from an H. G. Wells novel popping out of the brush.

"Okay, so they made some cross of jackrabbit and rat the size of a raccoon," he said, turning to Baltz. "What else do we have to look forward to? Cockroaches built like armored personnel carriers?"

Baltz passed one of her assorted handkerchiefs across her face. "Boy, oh boy, I didn't know about those things. They must be new. Did you see those red eyes?"

Valentine sat down on the bench seat at the front of the wagon, rubbing the back of his neck under his black mane. "That might explain the rattlesnakes. To hunt loose rat-rabbits, whatever. Rodents. Snakes are the best rodent-killers on earth."

"My David, I think it is more than that," Ahn-Kha said.

"What's that?" Valentine asked.

"It was here to listen. Perhaps it understood us."

"Rats are smart, but English-speaking?"

"Smart at surviving, anyway," Zacharias said, coming out of the dark. "It got away. The pickets didn't even notice it."

Ahn-Kha pointed under the wagon. "It was here for some time. It got bored and started drawing, or gnawing."

Valentine looked at the scratchings. They looked like a cross between hieroglyphics and Indian cave paintings.

"Huh, an artist," a Texan crouching at the other side of the wagon remarked.

"My David, a hunted animal doesn't bother to doodle. I think the Kurians bred the creatures for their auras."

"I believe you've got it, old horse. Colonel Hibbert said something about that. Rodents breed like crazy, eat anything, and grow fast."

"True," Ahn-Kha rumbled. "The rat-things perhaps didn't like being eaten any better than you humans do. I think they fought back."

"Successfully," Valentine agreed.

Two days later, the Rangers riding screen for the convoy called up Zacharias and Valentine. They saw more of the "ratbit." The scouts had paused at the middle of a notch in the hills the wagon train would have to cross as they moved north. They were traveling through scattered trees, what in this part of Texas might be called a forest.

A smokehouse filled with cuts of meat Valentine guessed to be snake stood near a trampled out area that had the trodden-on look of a campsite. Tracks of wheeled vehicles, perhaps off-road bicycles, could be seen.

"The Grogs travel on four-wheelers and motorcycles sometimes," Baltz said. "Bicycles, too. Maybe this is a camp of theirs."

"Auntie Amy! Look over here," Eve called. They rode over and found a notch in the hillside filled with piles of apples, ears of corn, nuts, berries, and even alfalfa and hay for the animals.

"Hell, the Grogs didn't do this," Zacharias said.

"The ratbits?"

Eve gasped: "Look at the bark!"

Valentine saw a piece of bark tucked in the crotch of a sapling over the gathered supply.

TAK AND LEAV WOODS

"What is this, a bribe? They're afraid we're going to move in on them?" Zacharias said, after sounding out the words on the sign.

"Maybe they're trying to hurry us through. You think we're drawing something they're afraid of?"

"We don't know who wrote this," Valentine said. "It could be a bunch of well-read kangaroos." Valentine wouldn't have been surprised to meet Toad of Toad Hall after skirting the Ranch.

"Agreed," Zacharias said. "Nice gesture, to speed us on our way."

Valentine nodded, and turned his horse. "Something to tell your grandchildren about, Zacharias. The helpful ratbits of Central Texas."

Valentine heard the high, sputtering sounds of engines and reached for his binoculars. They were loaners from the Rangers. Carrasca hadn't been willing to part with any of the *Thunderbolt*'s optics. He brought up the lenses and searched the distant hillside.

A sharp-nosed head, no, two heads, were bobbing over the sun-dried grasses. The vehicle broke out of the tall grass and into the open. It looked something like a baby carriage with a single-bore piston-engine on the back. At the motorcycle-style steering controls was a ratbit, a second rider clung on behind, facing the engine. It appeared to be working some kind of lever. A throttle?

"Ingenious little fellers," Ranson said, pulling his horse up next to Valentine. Valentine passed him the glasses. "I wonder if they drill for their own oil and refine it."

"Easier to steal it, probably."

"They're paralleling us."

Valentine felt something was wrong with the picture. "It's plain enough to see that we're leaving. Are they making sure of it?"

The wagon train ground on to the squeal of wooden axles and the tramp of feet and hooves; the ratbits disappeared behind the hill.

"I think a tight picket line tonight is a good idea," Valentine said to Zacharias and Baltz as they began uncoupling the wagons and building the nightly laager around the oxen and cattle. "The ratbits have me worried."

"They seemed friendly enough," Baltz said, groaning and rubbing her back as she got off the horse. "Left us food, didn't they?"

"Nobody's dropped dead from poisoning," Zacharias agreed. "But it won't hurt to be in tight tonight. I figure on a brush with the Grogs when I set the pickets. I don't think we'll need eyes way out to buy us time to get set."

"Post," Valentine called.

"Sir?"

"New orders for tonight." Valentine stepped over and explained to Post what he wanted the sentries to do. Post made a circuit of the camp, passing on the instructions. He returned and idled next to Valentine, taking in the sky, until Valentine noticed his leg twitching.

"What is it, Will?"

"You okay?" He kept his voice down.

"Why shouldn't I be?"

"You look played out. I've never seen you this tired, even when we were crossing Santo Domingo."

"Tired of campfires and cold water, I think." Now that the journey was almost over, Valentine looked forward to turning over the quickwood and taking a leave. Saunders and the *Thunderbolt*, the Once-ler, Malia . . . He needed peace, a quiet room looking out over a lake, perhaps. He'd never work in the Kurian Zone again.

"You told me once to ask you about what you did to get your captaincy in the Coastal Marines," Post said, as though reading his mind. "You sounded unhappy about it. You said it would give me a real reason to hate you."

"Having second thoughts about not leaving with Carrasca?"

"No, it's not that. Val, if it troubles you, talk about it. If anyone's in a position to understand, it's me. I wasted half a life under the bastards. After talking to you about my wife that night back on the *Thunderbolt*, I felt better about myself than I had in years. Took the bottle right out of my hand."

Valentine felt uneasy. The Ranch was getting to him. Talking to Post was better than empty fretting. "Let's walk."

They walked, side by side, the summer-dried grass crunching under their feet as they circled the laager. At first, the words came slowly. He wasn't sure where to begin, exactly, and the events were vague as they came back to him, as disturbed mud obscures the features of a body being dredged from a lakebed.

He'd never even told Duvalier. So the story came hard at first.

"I came down from the north with fake papers saying I'd served on a cruiser on the Great Lakes. I talked right for the identity, and I'd been to some of the places in the background. They put me in this police boat on the Louisiana coast, looking for smugglers. There was a gunfight or two, but we had a pair of fifty-calibers on the patrol boat that settled most arguments when those opened up on the shoreline . . ."

The Coastal Marines had a tip about a big cargo going out of the west side of Lake Pontchartrain, in a red-painted barge. He and a squad of men took the barge easily. The tug captain tried to bargain his way out, offered Valentine and the troops money, liquor, tobacco.

Valentine had none of it. His job was to impress his superiors with his diligence and efficiency, not pluck tempting feathers for his nest. Within the hearing of his sergeant and men, he turned down the bribe, made a show of moving the captain and his mates along with a pistol to the ringbolts.

Then he opened the cargo hatch.

Six families, in the dingy yellow overalls of Louisiana rural labor, were rousted from hiding spots among the more legitimate loads of cargo. There was resignation, not lamentation, as they were lined up, counted, and put in steel restraints.

He had no choice. A Reaper met the barge when it tied up at the Coastal Patrol dock.

". . . and you're thinking 'So what?' It goes back to my first time leading men into the Kurian Zone. My first real responsibility. I took five families out of Louisiana after a raid. It was a hard march—we even had Reapers on us.

"When we got back to the Free Territory at the fort, each and every one thanked me. Hugs, kisses, tears. I even met one of them a couple years later. Her name was Theresa Brugen. . . . She was a nurse-trainee at a hospital where they looked at my leg wound. She cried when she saw me again.

"I've always been proud of that trip. Those twenty-six lives, twenty-six lives changed, saved—it was the first time I really thought I'd made a difference. When I turned the families from the red barge over to the Reaper—it was like that evaporated."

Post shrugged. "What could you do?"

The faces appeared in the darkness, this time accusing. "I could have got them out. It would have blown my cover. Someone else would have had to go get the quickwood. Maybe in a year, maybe in a month. There are other Cats. Other ships."

"Ships with me?"

Valentine said, "What do you mean?"

"I'm not a philosopher, so this is going to come out wrong. Hope you'll understand anyway."

"Shoot."

"Well, Val, sometimes you'll try your damnedest and everything will go to shit. Other times you'll be drunk off your ass, trying your damnedest to kill yourself, and you'll find an answer to your prayers through a haze of gin. If I'd been as squared away as Worthington, would you have trusted me with your friendship?"

"Possibly. Depends on how I read you at the time."

"For all we know, Worthington was unorthodox as an upside-down cross, and just kept it hidden. Why let it worry you? Cause and effect is slippery stuff. Forget about the 'what-ifs.'"

"Easier said than done."

"Remember, I've got my own set of 'what-ifs.' Do what I do. Keep thinking about the 'what's-nexts.'"

Valentine heard engines in the distance when he hardened his ears as they passed out dinner. Some of the horses shifted restlessly as the wagon train settled in to camp. The sun was setting, and the moon wouldn't be up for hours. It was the time he'd attack, if he were the ratbits.

The ratbits were intelligent, no doubt about that. If they were hostile, why leave food? If they weren't hostile, why would they not communicate their good intentions in person or simply leave them alone?

He heard a familiar heavy tread behind him. "I will be glad when we are clear of this land," Ahn-Kha said. "I feel watchers."

"Did you hand out the shotguns?"

"Of course. My Gray Ones are armed, and Post is speaking to the other men who will be on picket duty now."

"What will you use, if it comes to that?"

"A shovel, my David. You remember the *skiops* the Golden Ones used. It is close enough. This will be a tough-and-rumble fight."

"Rough-and-*tumble* is the way you usually hear it. Shall we meet it at the pickets, or back at the wagons?"

"The pickets would be better, give your hearing a chance. The sun is touching the horizon now."

Valentine left Post in charge of the inner ring of sentries. Valentine had placed extra men at the wagons, reserves of weapons and ammunition ready just in case, and every bucket filled with sand or water. He wasn't about to have his cargo burned by ratbits, with a few hundred miles to go. He and Ahn-Kha, with the other two Grogs to either side, walked just behind the line of sentries.

"Excuse, sir. Where the sun swelled up. Hurts to look, but

I think some of that grass might be moving," one of the Jamaican recruits said.

"Wind?" Ahn-Kha asked.

Valentine listened with hard ears. The brush and grassland were alive with the sound like bacon on a skillet.

"They're creeping up on us, right out of the sun," Valentine said. He had to admire the ratbits. The men brought up their guns.

"Don't shoot until you see them coming for you," he added, but worked the slide on his .45 and chambered a round just in case. "Maybe it's an embassy."

One of the Grogs hooted, and a Marine added, "Oh, my God."

A brown tide surged out of the heavier growth toward the strip of trees that marked the western pickets. The spaniel-size ratbits ran with little bounces, almost bounding as they approached, covering a yard of sun-dried Texas grass with every hop.

At least the ratbits weren't using guns. The pickets fired a few shots, making no more of a difference than they would if fired into one of the gulf's waves. The ratbits did not slow at the gunfire.

"Back to the wagons," Valentine yelled. "Just run!"

The men did not need the encouragement. There was something terrifying about the brown wave undulating across the Texas countryside like a carpet unrolling. A few threw away their weapons in mad flight. Valentine saw one marine catch his feet and fall. Before he could rise, the ratbits were up and over him.

"Gettayahiiii . . . ," the stricken man cried.

A few ratbits, farther ahead than the rest, were already beside Valentine, looking up at him as if to gauge whether he was worth jumping. Valentine leapt into one of the circled wagons. Ahn-Kha halted in a gap and stood behind interlaced trek-tows, swinging his shovel in warning.

All along the wagons, gunfire broke out, high rifle cracks, booming shotguns, and the snapping sound of pistol shots. Wounded ratbits squealed as bullets tore through their small bodies. Valentine emptied his pistol into ratbits climbing the wagon wheels, then drew his blade. He cut air again and again as the ratbits jumped onto the wagon and jumped off just as quick as he swung his blade. He saw a ratbit fly backwards, thrown by a blow from Ahn-Kha's shovel. The men caught on the ground did not last long—five or six ratbits would leap onto the unfortunate's limbs, slowing him so two or three others could jump on the back and bear their opponent down. He saw one man rise again, choking a ratbit with both hands, but another tore into his ear, bringing a scream of pain before he fell again. The air filled with high-pitched squeaks and squeals as the battle raged.

The ratbits drove the men from the wagons. Valentine could see them grabbing things and running off out of the corner of his eye. A trio of ratbits were making off with a sapling, grabbing it by the burlap that held the dirt and roots and—

He felt claws on his legs, and another rodent leapt on his arm. He punched at it, but it grabbed his wrist in wiry little claws and buried its sharp front teeth in the flesh between thumb and forefinger. He felt another running up his back. He dropped his sword to reach for the beast, desperate to stop the crawly feel on his body. A ratbit caught up the sword and waved it threateningly. But it did not slash at him.

A ratbit in the back of his wagon held up one of Post's spearpoints, and another made off with a quickwood quarrel. Something in his mind clicked. They were after the quickwood. *Quickwoods! Woods!*

"Cease firing!" he bellowed. "Cease fire! No shooting! They're not trying to kill us—they just want quickwood."

Already the ratbits were leaving. Valentine saw more saplings disappear, but the ratbits didn't seem to be taking any food, weapons, or other tools from the convoy. Nor were they stealing all the quickwood. They seemed mostly interested in the saplings, perhaps because that was the easiest thing to identify. While the ground was littered with dead ratbits, most of the men had just been held down and relieved of their weapons, to stand, as Valentine did, rubbing painful bites and watching the quickwood being taken. Even the first marine to fall came out of the tree line, holding his hands up, now avoided by the ratbits as he was no longer a threat. From beyond the tree line Valentine heard the sound of the small motors of the ratbits. He hopped out of the wagon and found a first-aid kit. With a cotton dressing pressed to his wound, he walked to the west, following the last few ratbits checking the bodies of their comrades and helping any who weren't beyond hope.

One wounded figure appeared to be of some concern, judging by the number of ratbits clustered around it. Valentine approached the circle of rodents, and a few turned, baring their teeth at him and reaching for small knives.

He held out his hands, hoping to make himself understood, and stopped. He pointed at his bandage, then at the prone ratbit. The teeth went away, but the ratbits gave no other sign that they understood. He tossed them the bandage. They jumped away as it landed, then returned, sniffing it and squeaking.

Valentine ran back to the circled wagons. "A medic! I need a medic!"

The closest thing he could find among the confused men was a pharmacist's mate from the *Thunderbolt* named Speere. He was young and awkward, but had performed his duties well enough on the ship. Valentine had him grab a first-aid kit and follow.

"What, are you kidding, Cap? There are hurt men back at the wagons," Speere objected when they came up on the ratbits.

"This fight wouldn't have happened at all if we'd made an attempt to communicate with them. I want to make amends."

"I'm not a vet, sir," Speere said, but stood up when he saw Valentine's face. "But I'll do what I can," he said.

The two humans slowly approached the ratbits. Fifteen or

twenty were around their stricken comrade, squeaking and chittering. The ratbits made room, and Speere knelt beside the wounded ratbit. A ratbit was pressing a piece of cloth into a wound on the other ratbit's back. Judging from the gray around the eyes, ears, and mouth, this was an older specimen.

"Looks like a bullet across the back," Speere said, looking at the wound. "Might be some nerve damage, even if it didn't clip the spine. Doesn't look like he can move his back legs."

"Can you give it . . . him anything for the pain?"

"I dunno, a drop of laudanum might help. I don't think it would kill him, but you never know."

"Do it."

Valentine and the ratbits watched as Speere used an eyedropper to add medicine to a capful of water, then refilled the empty eyedropper with the mixture and shot it down the ratbit's throat. The ratbit seemed to understand oral medication, and after a minute's allowing it to take effect submitted to Speere, who was sprinkling antiseptic powder in the wound and then sewing up the tear in the skin. "Maybe it's worse than it looks," Speere said. "Didn't go too deep. Looks like this guy had some subcutaneous fat. It might have cushioned his spine."

"Let's get him back to the camp."

"You think they'll let us?"

"We'll find out," Valentine said, and turned his head back to the wagons. "Hey! We need a stretcher here."

The wagon train did not move on the next day. Valentine thought it would be best to let his wounded rest. Narcisse took over care of the gray-haired patient. She unrolled a sheet of leather; glass jars filled with powders and herbs stood in neat sewn-in pockets. She began to work her Haitian medicine and steamed something in a ceramic mug.

The next morning the old ratbit was doing better. It could move its legs, a sign that met with approval from the four other giant ratbits who accompanied it to the human camp. They all shared a thin soup cooked up by Narcisse.

A strange ratbit visitor came into camp with the dawn. Another oldster, this one with an eyepatch over its left eye, to match a torn-off ear on the other side. The wounds were from long ago, however. It bore a container over its shoulder. Valentine realized it was part of a rattler-tail. Its parcel clinked oddly as it moved.

It approached the other ratbit, and they chattered at each other. Ratbit-speech was a strange *yeek*ing sound, and whatever was said was over with quickly. The eyepatch ratbit dumped its sack on the ground, and Valentine smiled when he recognized Scrabble pieces.

"Can you understand us?" Valentine said.

The ratbit hunted with its eye in the pile.

Y E S

"We are sorry about the deaths. You should have tried this earlier."

The ratbit removed the three chips from the dirt and arranged more.

W E D I D S H O T B Y H O R S R Y D E R S

"We didn't understand what you meant when you said 'leave woods.'"

N O M U C H S P E A K M E N

The ratbit removed that and started again.

N I E D W O O D F O R K I L
M O N S T E R S

"The thing is, you took quite a few saplings. We need them. Understand?"

Y E S

"We can leave you a few, and some wood, and some seeds, to grow more trees. Good enough?"

The ratbit did not rearrange the letters. It just pointed to YES again.

"Deal. Someday I'd like to hear about what happened. How did you drive the Kurians out of this part of the land?"

WREK THE ALL SO WE NOT DIE

"Do your people have a name?"

BATCH FIVETE EN

The ratbits put on a feast that night, in the center of a wide half-crescent of oaks and elms. Traces of a foundation stood in the yellowed grass, smoke-darkened conduit pipes and junction boxes stood among the wildflowers like scarecrows. Later Valentine learned that beneath the soil there was a thriving town of tunnels and dens.

The humans only nibbled from the Batch Fifteen banquet. A proper feast, to the hundreds of gathered ratbits, meant piling anything edible—to a ratbit—in a great heap in the center of the clearing and then burrowing within the pile in a race for the choicest tidbits: a bone with a bit of marrow, still-ripe fall fruits and melons, an ear of corn still only partially eaten. It was a bit like dining from a restaurant kitchen at the end of the night, fresh food, leftovers, and garbage all for the taking.

The dinner looked to be a disaster, at least from the human point of view, until the ratbits dragged a series of still-sealed cartons from a clogged stairwell hidden in the grass. In them were candy bars and chips and fruit-flavored drinks in shiny plastic packets, only a few years old and therefore still edible. Valentine ate something called a Chocdelite that was almost eye-crossing in its sweetness.

Zacharias joined him, and they sat on one of the wagons, next to Baltz's orange tomcat, who was scrunched into a back-arched ball under the seat as he watched the ratbits go to and fro. Zacharias offered Valentine a taste of some orange-and-pineapple flavored drink.

"I'm thinking vending machines," Zacharias said, examining the label. "Says it's from Florida."

"Nothing but the best for the scientists. Or the honored guests."

A faint sputtering from the sky made them both look up. An arrow shape, like an oversize kite with an engine attached, flew overhead and buzzed away a pair of circling buzzards. Another aerial visitor, a hawk, flapped hard to gain altitude and avoided the airborne prowler. A ratbit worked the controls from a tiny seat.

"I'll be—," Zacharias began. "Clever varmints."

"That they are."

"Did you have any schooling, Valentine?"

"Yes. About as good as I could get in the Minnesota backwoods. An old Jesuit still ran a one-room schoolhouse. I lived in his library."

"I remember when I was learning maths from ol' Miss Gage. We were studying multiplication, and she showed us how one pair of breeding rabbits could produce—well, I don't remember exactly, but it was over a thousand—other rabbits once you counted their offspring . . . in just a year. Makes you wonder."

Valentine nodded, troubled by the evidence on the Ranch that the Kurians had gone to so much effort to find a replacement for the human race.

Chapter Twelve

The Piney Woods, December of the forty-eighth year of the Kurian Order: East Texas is covered with timber, a woodscape more extensive than all of New England. The pines stand as straight as Baptists on Easter Sunday, their evenly spaced branches ascending the trunk like ladder rungs.

Texas saw its first oil boom in this part of the state, but before that a timber boom brought white men to sculpt the land with its first roads and towns. After mankind's fall, the gently rolling landscape went fallow, and vigorous young forests have sprung up again from the old ranches and farms scattered around Lake Texoma to Sabine Lake in the Gulf.

The Texas Rangers are active here, as well, raising hell all along the informal border with the Kurian Zone that runs the length of the Neches River and along the road-and-rail "Sabine Corridor" the Kurians maintain from Shreveport to Dallas. The Lifeweavers are present to help the Texans in this part of the country. The Rangers have organized their own teams of Wolves, Cats, and Bears to hunt the Reapers, passing material and information to and from Southern Command through the network of Logistics Commandos.

The far north of the region, between the Red and Sulphur rivers, sees the least guerrilla activity. There is little human habitation to speak of. Southern Command proper patrols this area from its forward bases along the Red River. A few hunter-gatherer communities—usually Native American or Louisiana Creole—wander the area, pulling up stakes every few months to avoid the depredations of the Reapers

and Quislings raiding out of the Dallas Paramountcy. With
fall in its death throes and winter coming, a wet, muddy
hush falls over the land. Snowstorms are not unknown to the
Piney Woods, and man and animal both retire deep into the
woods to wait out the cold.

The pines smelled like home. The crisp aroma in the chill
breeze of an East Texas December tickled his nose and
brought back memories of winter camps in the Ozarks and
Ouachitas. It marked his first breath in the lands of the
Ozark Free Territory in over two years.

Half his wagons ground along almost empty. The stores
and supplies within had long since been eaten up, and with
the ratbits of "Batch Fifteen" having taken better than a
wagonload of quickwood to fight their own war against the
Kurians, the remaining wagons were traveling light.

Leaving the Ranch was not as easy as entering it. They
had fought two nighttime skirmishes against the Grogs in
the borderlands and hurried into the empty lands north of
Dallas and Fort Worth. A team of rangers turned southeast to
confuse the pursuit, and the Batch Fifteen rodents did their
best to muddle the trail.

Valentine had some of the quickwood lumber turned into
spearpoints and crossbow quarrels anticipating an attack
from the Reapers, but the hunt never began. They broke into
the cattle-drive routes running up from Texas and into the
plains without incident. Valentine put a moratorium on further slaughter of the dwindling cattle, so from a distance
they might look like another wagon train bringing beef and
trade north to the railheads in Oklahoma and Kansas for
shipment east. The Kurians in northern Texas, never thick to
begin with this close to the Free Territory, seemed quiescent.

It was as though their enemies were hibernating out the
winter: they did not send patrols or Reapers to trouble them.
There was a nervous day at the Trinity River crossing when
some riders observed them from a hilltop. They did not stay
to identify themselves, but rode away before the Rangers on

their worn-out horses could catch them. But as this area could be considered no-man's-land between the Free Territory and the Kurian Zone, they could have been anything from smugglers to robbers to scouts from some fearful community hiding in a river valley, wishing for nothing more than to be left alone.

"How are you planning to get back?" Valentine asked Zacharias as a team of Rangers went out to ride an old highway running northeast out of the ghost town of Paris, checking for signs of human habitation. Valentine hoped to find one of the Southern Command Guard garrisons or a Wolf patrol somewhere near the Red River.

"We'll head south. Hell with the wagons—there's plenty more where they came from. Ride slow down south until we hook up with the Eastern Rangers. They'll fix us up with remounts, and then we'll slip through somewhere between Houston and San Antonio. Won't be that hard this time of year. If the story of the Rangers in this century ever gets written, this'll make an interesting chapter. Bargaining with ratbits over magic trees."

"Don't forget the elephants with two trunks."

"The elephants we'll never forget."

Valentine laughed tiredly. It was good to be able to laugh again. *Just a few more days to tote the weary load*—the line from *Gone with the Wind* had been running through his mind of late. "I hope you know how much the help you've given and the risks you've run mean to the Ozark Free Territory."

"Well, young Captain," Zacharias said, from the vast age difference of five years, "you want my advice, the first thing you use the quickwood on is a campaign with us. You saddle up every man who can hold a gun and every cannon that's got a shell, and hit Dallas from the northeast. The East Texas Rangers come in from the southeast, and we'll hit 'em out of the Ranch, since the Kur no longer seem to be running things there. Once we've got Dallas cleaned up, the rest of Texas will be pieces just waiting to be picked up. Then we've got enough country to really live. Hell, old Kirby Smith held out against the whole damn Union that way, till the surrender. I expect we could do the same."

"I'm one of the squashed guys at the bottom of the totem pole, Major," Valentine said. "The idea sounds fine to me, but it's for men and women above my rank to decide."

They watched the wagon train go by. Narcisse waved to them from the back of her horse, and Valentine moved to put himself between the trail and a fallen tree trunk. A Texan admirer of Narcisse's cooking had rigged a saddle so she could put her stumps into a pair of cut-off rifle-sheaths, and Ahn-Kha fixed a quirt to her "short arm." Sissy had turned into an admirable neck-reiner in the last month, but had developed a taste for jumping—though often she ended up plummeting to the earth despite the horse mane gripped with her teeth. Valentine wanted her to arrive in the Free Territory with neck intact.

Zacharias stripped a handful of pine needles as he rode. "We gotta start winning somewhere. This is as good a place as any." He handed the needles to Valentine like a bouquet.

"Southern Command has grown into something that's like an egg. It can resist pressure as long as it's evenly distributed from all around. But if you rap it too hard in any one spot, it cracks. Your plan would mean all yolk and no shell for us in Missouri and Arkansas. I'll tell the brass—the Lifeweavers, even—everything I can about the state of things in Texas. I'll let them know you're ready. Napoléon once made a comment that you can't make an omelet without breaking eggs. Maybe they'll follow his advice."

"Yeah, I heard about that guy. Confederate general from out East, right? Rode under Bobby Lee?"

Valentine just chuckled again.

The scouts came back, signaling that the road was clear. The men of the convoy went about hooking up the oxen to the wagons one more time.

* * *

Valentine would always associate his return to the Free Territory with the old Shell Oil emblem. Three busted-up tankers were parked in a triangle blocking the road a few miles out from the Red River. The tankers had been turned into hollow forts, firing slits carved into the sides and sandbags mounted on the top. It was a typical forward post for Southern Command: easily created, transported, defended, and abandoned.

The watchpost stood on the reverse slope of a hill in the old highway. The road cut across the countryside; a long, straight ribbon placed over the hills and hollows as a testament to the days when engineers treated the topography as if it did not exist. The garrison must have thought them a column of Quislings, for they did not wait to greet them, but promptly retreated out, hustling down a culvert running along the road. Valentine watched five or six men run, with the bent-over stride of men keeping their heads down, appearing and then disappearing in gaps of the brush running along the road.

"So much for the valor of Southern Command," Valentine said dryly. Baltz coughed up something from deep in her chest and spat.

"If only the rest of our meetings were so simple," Zacharias said. "It would have been a faster trip. Perhaps your tall companion frightened them off. Shall I run them down?"

"No, spare the horses," Valentine decided. "They'll be off calling on higher authority. Suits us either way. But I'd better ride ahead from here with just one or two. I hope they don't shoot before trying to identify us. Interested in meeting some animals from Arkansas, Baltz? They're a unique brand of razorbacks."

"Sure, son. I've done my job: got you across most of Texas. If I catch a bullet, it's no loss."

"Ahn-Kha," Valentine said, "better take your Gray Ones and sit in the wagons. They might take a shot if they see you."

"Understood, my David. Be cautious, I am more worried

about you. Frightened soldiers do strange things. It would be ironic, but undesirable, to have all your efforts end with one of Southern Command's bullets."

The vanguard of the column reorganized itself. Valentine and Baltz, with Ranson a horse-length behind, holding a white flag, rode a half-mile ahead of the wagons. Groups of Texans rode before, interspersed with, and following the teams, with long files of Valentine's soldiers marching alongside the rattling wagon wheels, all moving at the patient pace of the plodding oxen.

Valentine looked at the rusting monument to the Texas oil industry. Weeds grew in the rotted tires; rust ran down the marred sides like red icicles. He smelled a fire smoldering inside the fort—they had caught the men at dinner, something even crackled in a pan—

"Ride. Ride like hell!" Valentine shouted, thumping his spurs into the horse's flanks. His horse leapt down the road, and the others caught its panic and joined in the flight.

A flash lit up the Texas countryside, followed by a boom that came up through the horses' legs and shivered him in his saddle. Valentine looked over his shoulder and saw one of the tankers rear up on its back axles, and another rolled forward into the ditch at the edge of the highway. The base of the triangle, facing the rear of the fort, stood intact.

"They fired whatever they had in their arms locker," Valentine said.

"Must have been underground. Looks like most of the blast went up. Dynamite, I'll bet."

"Handy for engineering or sabotage. Just as well we weren't in the fort at the time," Valentine said. "That's not like the Wolves. Usually they're cleverer with booby traps."

"New standing orders, maybe," Ranson said. "Destroy whatever's going to fall in the enemy's hands."

They camped that night next to an old marker that indicated the state-line border was a mere two miles away. A chilling drizzle began just after sundown. Valentine sat underneath a tarp in front of the shielded cooking fire just off the road, part of the farthest-forward pickets with the convoy. He listened to the drops evaporate against the flaming wood. He felt drained, utterly and completely empty. Just a few more days, he told himself, and he could finally lay down his responsibilities and rest. His young body seemed as old and battered as the faded mile-marker.

"They are taking their time on the other side of the river," Ahn-Kha said. The Golden One had wrapped himself into a horse blanket. When wet, Ahn-Kha's fawn-colored hair matted down into a rain slicker, still keeping a precious layer of air in between the wet hair and his skin.

"They're watching us. There are two men with their horses about five hundred yards off, just east of here. I heard them come up once it got dark while I was circling the camp. Wind's blowing the other way, or you could smell them. I'll go out again with the white flag tomorrow— maybe they'll have worked up the nerve to talk."

The rain grew heavier. Valentine considered returning to the wagons, but it would be crowded enough under the beds. He had slept out in the wet before. It wouldn't hurt him to do so again. He threw a blanket over his head and did his best to ignore the rain.

He awoke with a sneeze. A Texas-size cold had come upon him in the night, and he blinked the gum out of his eyes. One of the pickets had a fire with a pot of hickory-nut coffee going under a piece of corrugated tin. The ranger handed him a cup without a word. Valentine drank, nodding gratefully and passing another cup to a second ranger on watch, and looked down the road. It was a sunless dawn. A sea-gray sky washed the landscape of its color.

Two men approached the picket line, keeping out in the open, guns across their shoulders like yokes. A few Texans recognized the attitude. In this part of the country, that meant parley. They wore charcoal-gray uniforms, mottled with streaks of pale yellow and brown, the winter camo of the Southern Command's Guards. One had a set of sergeant's stripes on his arm.

"You with Southern Command?" Valentine called when he felt they were close enough. His throat felt like it had a rough ball of twine lodged in it.

The sergeant narrowed his eyes. "You all smugglers?"

"No. Identify yourselves, and I'll do the same."

They exchanged looks. "Third East Texas Regiment, Noyes Brigade, out of Texarkana."

"I'm a Cat coming in with priority cargo."

"That so?"

"You call me *sir*, Sergeant."

Valentine cocked his head, and the man with the stripes added, "Sir."

"Code name's Ghost, requesting immediate radio or telegraph contact with Southern Command GHQ. Can you assist?"

"That'll be for Captain Murphy to say . . . sir. He's on the other side of the river. What's this cargo? Hadn't heard logistics were out on a raid hereabouts."

"I've got a dozen wagons back there that need guarding once we're over the Red. What's Captain Murphy's command?"

"We'll let him talk to you, sir, once your bona fides clear."

"Are there any Wolves around?"

"Not for us to say, sir. Even if we knew, asking your pardon."

"I hope you have more to say when your captain tells you to talk. Please inform him I need rations for a hundred eighty men when we get across the river. Thank you, Sergeant."

Valentine went back to the fire and let the Guards return to their command. He could get the wagon-train to the river, at least, and turn it over to Captain Murphy and his Guards. He had asked for a lot of supplies, but filling the Rangers' saddlebags was the least he could do before they parted. He took his shivering horse from its place beneath a pine tree and rode back to the wagon train, saddle-sore muscles protesting at the effort.

*   *   *

The crossing went slowly. Every bridge on the Red was down for miles, according to the Guards. Without a swing south to Texarkana that would eat precious days, they would have to cross at Two-Skunk ferry.

Valentine was sure there was an amusing story behind the ferry's name, but he was in no mood for fireside yarns. He wanted the psychological safety of the river behind him, and a warm drink in his belly. Then he would quit seeing Reapers moving between the trees at night and imagining converging columns of Quislings racing to cut his convoy off from the Ouachitas. The ferry was a small one pulled across by rope strung along the ruined pilings of an old bridge, and it could manage only one wagon and unhitched team at a time. At the rate the ferrymen—Guards doing labor they had little enthusiasm for—progressed, it would take all day to get the column across. He went over to Major Zacharias, who was sharing a cold meal with his men as they waited to push the next wagon onto the timber float.

"Zacharias, you've helped work a miracle. I can't ask you to do more, so feel free to go back south once we've crossed."

"Texas is as grateful to you as you are to her, Captain Valentine. Mission accomplished once you are across the river?"

"Yes. I'm told the captain of this company is finally arrived. Let me speak to him first, but I'm sure we don't need to bring you much farther. I'll arrange to have feed for the horses and rations for the men sent back on the ferry. There should be some supplies available here."

"Thank you, Valentine. I'd be grateful."

Valentine stood, idly scratching the ears of one of the oxen as the ferry pulled him across the Red River. The winter rains had raised its level.

"What kind of priority-one cargo is this, suh?" the ferryman asked, shifting his quid to a sagging cheek. "All's I sees is plants."

Valentine tightened his jaws in frustration. If a laboring

ferryman knew there was important cargo in the wagons, then word would spread to every housewife and postman in thirty miles in a day or two.

"New kind of food crop. Like the heartroot."

"Heartroot?" The ferryman looked at one of the Guards.

"That mushroom stuff. Not too popular around here, sir," the Guard said.

Three years ago, Valentine and Ahn-Kha had brought the Grog-staple from Omaha, and Valentine was surprised Southern Command wasn't still distributing the mushroom-like growth. It grew a breadloaf-big hunk of protein, fats, and carbohydrates out of any wet garbage from a pile of leaves to a slop pail, and it preserved well if properly dried.

Valentine stepped onto the east bank, nursing a headache that spoiled what should be a feeling of triumph. He had done it. He was finally to the Free Territory with what he set out to get nearly two years ago. He looked around. A few Guards stood at their posts around the ferry, watching the teams get rehitched.

Ahn-Kha joined him. "My David, I made a promise to Captain Carrasca. When we were back in the Ozarks, I was to give you this." Ahn-Kha extracted the flute she had given him from between his football-size pectorals and untied the leather thong that kept it around his neck. He upended it and gave it two vigorous taps. A waxy envelope appeared. "It is a letter for you."

Valentine trembled at the memories brought by her hand-writing.

Ahn-Kha withdrew and left him alone under a riverside sycamore. With rain running down the back of his neck and soaking his shirt, he could hear the creaks and groans of the ferry ropes in their wheels, the calls of the rivermen, and the wet pot-iron smell of the Red was in his nostrils. And he'd remember it all for the rest of his life.

He opened the seal and took out the sheet of Captain Saunders's stationery.

Dear David,

If you're reading this letter it means you're home and safe. I wish I were there to congratulate you. You have two things to congratulate yourself about, actually. The first is the success of your journey. The second I kept a secret so the first would be completed. I'm sorry you have to find out about it this way, but the fact of the matter is you're going to be a father.

David, deep breath and keep your perspective. I'll be fine. I'm not the first woman to have a baby, and I'm in a better position than most. We have a wonderful hospital with all the equipment, and what passes for trained doctors these days. Jamaica will be a safe place for our child (and many others) thanks to you. I hope it's a boy with your hair and eyes, but I'll take whatever comes, knowing that he or she'll be pointed out as the child of a brave man who helped my harbor.

Right now, knowing you, you're thinking about how soon you can get down here. Put this letter away and read the above again when you've had a few days. It would be good for me to have you here. It would also be very selfish. They wouldn't have put you in charge of the quickwood if they didn't think a lot of you, and I doubt your Southern Command would be the better for you coming down here. Someone like that loud-mouthed fool Hawthorne would probably replace you up there.

If the war ends, come. If you are badly hurt, come. If you grow old, come, and we'll warm our bones together under the palms. But don't come out of duty to me. We're alike enough that I know you have a more important duty you must be true to, or you will never be happy.

Love,
Malia

Valentine swallowed. His cold disappeared in a flood of emotion. He could leave the wagon train with Southern Command, take Post and Ahn-Kha and his Jamaicans, and go south with the Rangers. A boat wouldn't be that hard to get, they could sail with the prevailing winds—

A rider trotted past the ferry and turned toward the sycamore. A Guard in an officer's uniform with captain's bars and MURPHY stitched above his shirt pocket peered out from under the cowl of his rain slicker and pulled back the hood. The rider had tight-curled brown hair that reminded Valentine of a dog he had once known in Minnesota. Eighty or so men on winter-fat, shaggy horses sat their mounts behind him at the wagons. Valentine carefully tucked the letter back in the envelope and thrust it in his shirt.

The rider dismounted. "You must be this Ghost," Murphy said, offering his hand instead of a salute. "I'm Alan Murphy. They said you had the blackest hair this side of hell. It's an honor—I don't get to meet many Cats. Do I salute you, or what?" Murphy eyed the new snakeskin bandolier with its three quickwood stabbing-points across Valentine's chest.

"In theory, I hold the rank of captain, but I don't use it much, Captain Murphy. I'm going to need escort either to Fort Smith or Arkadelphia, whichever works better for your men."

"My company is at your disposal, Captain—"

"Just *Ghost* will do, if you have to put anything on paper."

Murphy explained he had already been in touch with Southern Command. He was expecting a delay while other troops could be brought up to escort the convoy. Southern Command couldn't pull troops away from a river crossing, even if it was the time of year when they did not expect action. Valentine made arrangements to have the Texans resupplied, and he saw to it that bags of oats, sides of pork, and a generous quantity of beans returned to the south side of the Red with him on the ferry.

As he moved through the Texans, saying good-bye, trying to forget what he had just read, he felt a tug at his sleeve. He turned to find Eve behind him.

"Yes, Eve? Going to finally say something, are you?"

"Mr. Valentine, the man who works the lines on this side, he's bad."

Valentine groaned inside. He hoped the man hadn't done something reprehensible to the pubescent girl. "What did he do to you that's bad?"

Her face contorted in adolescent exasperation. "No, he didn't do anything to *me*. I said he's a bad man. Bad inside."

"How do you know a man can be bad inside?"

She shrugged. "I'm not sure. When I touch your hand, I know you're good. I can feel caring. That you do things to help people. I touched him while we were moving horses onto the ferry, and I knew he wasn't like you. He's done bad things to people."

"Sometimes soldiers have to do bad things. Sometimes they don't have a choice."

"Maybe," she said, as if turning the idea over in her mind. "But I do know I can tell who is good and who is bad in his secret heart. He's a bad man."

"Thanks for telling me, Eve. I'll watch myself. Just in case, take this," he said, reaching into the leather tobacco pouch he wore around his neck. "Here's a quickwood seed. You know what it can do, right? Plant your tree somewhere safe, where you can take care of it. Where only you know about it. Your people in Texas may need it. I need to talk to your aunt now before I go over the river again. Let's find her."

Baltz stood with Zacharias underneath a thick-limbed riverbank willow, eating plums from a jar of syrup. Valentine interrupted a conversation about the best route south.

"I'd feel better if we'd of run into some local Rangers. I don't want to be riding through the country blind," Zacharias was saying.

"They stay more to the south," Baltz said. "This patch is

close enough to the Ozarks that they don't need to waste their time here."

"The wagons are getting across, slow but sure," Valentine said. "It's time for a last thank-you." He sneezed. Between the cold and Malia's letter—he was already desperate to reread it—he could barely stand to go about the formalities. He wanted the good-byes over with so he could think.

"Too bad all that rum's gone," Baltz said. "Sounds like you could use it."

"You have a supply of quickwood for the East Texans, right?" Valentine said, wiping his nose.

"Wish it were more," Zacharias said. "But this is good tree country. In twenty years, they'll have lots."

"Watch yourselves. None of the Free Territory boys are mixing with ours like they usually would. Maybe the Jamaican accents are making them skittish . . . but I get the feeling there's something wrong."

"Maybe Southern Command's had a setback," Zacharias said. "Or the Quislings have tried ambushes by posing as incoming Logistics Commandos."

"Wouldn't be the first time," Baltz said.

Valentine wiped his nose. "Losses in battle somewhere else, possibly. That might be why we didn't run into any Wolves. Without their patrols here, you're going to have to be careful. Could explain why these Guards were so quick to hightail it."

"You worry about yourself, Mr. Valentine," Baltz said. "We'll be fine."

Valentine shook hands all around. Texas style.

The sign outside town said BERN WOODS. Their destination stood in a farmland clearing a few miles from the river.

It was a widening-of-the-road town: two lines of buildings facing each other with a few houses scattered along the side streets. Like many old towns, the uninhabited buildings provided spare fixtures, glass, and shingles for the others.

The outbuildings had a pulled-apart look where they had not been demolished entirely.

This close to the borderlands, the towns were walled, and Bern Woods was no exception. The plentiful pine provided makings for a tall stockade. Gaps between the brick buildings were filled with sharpened tree trunks and earth, with corrugated aluminum adding a fireproof layer to the outside. A tower stood at each end of town at the gates, looking out over scratch farmland and pasture.

Murphy waved to the guards in the tower, and the gate swung open. They passed one of the last outbuildings, a house with a faint piggy smell coming from it. Wire at the open doors and window showed that the old house was being used as barn.

Valentine hardened his ears and nose. His now-raging cold interfered with his sense of smell and hearing, but he could still tell an occupied pigpen from an abandoned one. This one was empty. It was hog-killing time, but why slaughter all the livestock? Did a family pull up and move? Were logistics punishing the town for hiding supplies?

He looked back at his men. Post, curious to see what Free Territory looked like, walked at the head of files of former Jamaicans and *Thunderbolt* marines, at least those who hadn't taken the Texas teamsters' places at the wagons, to either side of the transport. The men shivered in the winter wind. The men had a good chance of seeing their first snowfall that night if the temperature continued to drop.

The gates came to a rest with a thump.

A gallows. The sight of it froze him before his brain processed the structure. It stood in an open spot, like a broken tooth, between two buildings on the left side of the main street. Hangings were rare in the Free Territory, and only a few capital crimes merited them. Even Quisling officers faced the firing squad rather than the noose; the hangings that did take place went on in a prison, not a town square. The sight of a gallows was all too common in the Kurian Zone, however. Valentine's memory raced back to a story his first captain had told him, of a town secretly seized by the Kurians to trap the Wolves in his command.

"Kenso," Valentine said to Ahn-Kha. The word for "danger" was one of the few in the Golden One's vocabulary that he knew. Ahn-Kha's ears shot up in surprise, then flattened against his bullet-head.

Valentine held up his right hand. "Ho," he called, keeping the horse moving to allow the wagon train to come to a stop without collisions, even as his feverish mind raced.

"What's the matter?" Murphy said. If it was an act, it was a superb one.

"We can't outspan in town. You want all these oxen milling around people's porches? Could get smelly," Valentine asked.

"I'm headquartered at this town. There's two corrals and a barn or two. They'll fit."

Post approached, ready as always for orders.

Valentine ignored Murphy. "Mr. Post, we'll circle the wagons in that clearing there, if you please. Downwind from the town, as a gesture to the civilians. Thank you." Post stiffened at the formal tone and elaborate pleasantries. "That is, if you have no objections, Captain Murphy?"

Murphy looked around at his men, then up the road to the town. "Well . . . no, of course not. Why would I?"

Valentine got off his horse and led it to Post. "Mr. Post, let's snap to it," he said, and then lowered his voice, tilting toward Post with his chin jutting out, as if upbraiding him privately. "I can't explain, but I don't like the look of this. Keep your gun handy, and alert the men. I hope it's nothing."

Post nodded and turned to give orders to the sergeants in the wagons. If the lieutenant looked upset to Murphy, he hoped that the feigned reprimand would explain the startled eyes and stiff backbone. Valentine turned on his heel and led his horse toward the clearing, Ahn-Kha falling in behind like an obedient dog. Ahn-Kha made as if to loosen the saddle on the horse and instead loosened Valentine's submachine gun in its sheath.

The wagon wheels resumed their noisy journey, squealing their axle-joints as the teams turned off the road and bumped to the clearing.

The captain came to some kind of decision. Murphy herded his men to the rear of the column. When he turned them one more time, to face the tired men bringing up the rear, he extracted a wide-mouthed pistol and pointed it at the center of the column. Across the distance, the Cat met the mounted man's eyes and read his fixed expression.

"To arms!" Valentine bellowed.

The hammer fell on Murphy's gun, and a flare arced out, sputtering through the sky in slow motion. The former *Thunderbolt* men threw themselves down from the wagons, pulling rifles and pistols. Post vaulted into the bed of the front wagon, where men were already loading a machine gun. Ahn-Kha brought up his long rifle, swinging the mouth toward Murphy, but the turncoat came off his saddle in a blur of horseflesh as his men dismounted and let their horses run.

The flare hit in the center of the column of wagons, and lay there, sparking. It spat out a chemical cough.

A wave of gunfire ripped across the convoy. Valentine saw heads appear at the walls of Bern Woods. The gate towers sprouted men as if someone had touched a wand to the platforms. He pulled out his PPD as a bullet smacked into the horse's flank. The wounded beast leapt sideways, knocking him to the ground even as it lurched, hind legs collapsing.

Smoke began to pour out of the flare, as if in landing it had opened some underground reservoir of purple steam.

The sound of shooting grew like the roar of an approaching wave. Machine guns added their deadly mechanical drum roll to the air-rending sound of gunfire. Panicked oxen bellowed and died. Other teams of horses ran from the explosions, throwing drivers from the runaway wagons.

Valentine smelled his horse's blood even as he tried to shut out the high, whinnying screams. Ahn-Kha swung the barrel, and his gun cracked. The Grog didn't shoot the horse; he dropped a figure in the gate tower firing an assault rifle. Valentine saw a Jamaican fall to earth, dying in a pose eerily like a Muslim praying.

The flare, after its brief fireworks, sputtered out.

Valentine sent a bullet into his wounded horse's head, then took cover behind the body. Ahn-Kha rolled to his side.

A hissing sound, and something exploded among the wagons. The blast threw a severed hand into the air, spinning it like a tossed daisy. Valentine squeezed off burst after burst into Murphy's men, emptying the drum on his gun. The turncoats were firing shotguns and lobbing grenades into the rear wagons; confused men got up to run, and died.

Another hiss and another explosion among the wagons. Pieces of a team flew as their wagon reared up on its back wheels, falling to pieces even as it overturned. Valentine saw something like a stovepipe pointing out from the stone roof of the town's tallest building. A recoilless rifle? More men poured from the gates at both sides of the town.

"Ahn-Kha!" he said, slapping his aiming friend on the shoulder. Valentine pointed. Heads appeared briefly over the barrel as the weapon was reloaded.

Ahn-Kha slid a finger-length bullet into the receiver. An ear twitched on the Grog as he brought the gun up and sighted with a rose-colored eye. Sighting in the time it took to draw a breath, the gun snapped and shot. Valentine saw a hat, or perhaps part of a head, torn away by the bullet.

The backblast of the recoilless flared in a gray cloud; and the shell exploded by Post's wagon. Old Handy Sixguns and the machine-gunners disappeared in the blast. Nothing but body parts remained. Valentine's marines were crawling out of the cross fire, or throwing away their weapons and sheltering among the stumps in the clearing.

The precious quickwood was burning. Two wagons flamed, putting oily smoke into the colorless sky. Valentine clenched his teeth until his jaws screamed in agony, reloading and firing his gun with tears in his eyes. He saw a Quisling rider grasp Narcisse by the hair and jerk her from her saddle, ignoring the blows from the quirt fixed to her arm. Post gone, his Jamaicans cut to pieces. Nothing mattered now.

"Away, David, away!" Ahn-Kha shouted, waving at the approaching troops.

"The quickwood," Valentine said.

"No choice! The smoke is blowing this way—it will cover us."

A bullet hit the limp horse, its impact causing still-warm muscles to twitch. Horses dragging a wagon came around the shattered front of the column. A Jamaican lay in the bed of the wagon, working the reins from the shelter of the bed. Ahn-Kha dropped his gun. The Grog pulled Valentine to his feet—grabbing him by the collar like a disobedient child—and ran in pursuit of the wagon.

Bullets zipped through the air all around: insects buzzing in their ears for a split second and then fleeing. Ahn-Kha caught the back of the wagon with one long arm as he hauled Valentine in tow with iron fingers. He swung up in an apish leap. A bullet caught the Grog at the apex of his jump. He dropped Valentine as he tumbled into the wagon. The wounding of his friend brought Valentine out of his mental maze.

Valentine felt something pull at his sleeve. The bullet that cut through his clothing hit the back of the wagon with a splintering *thwak*. He locked eyes with Ahn-Kha as the Grog's ear flaps fell limp. His friend toppled into the back of the wagon.

He ran. He jumped into the wagon just as one of the team was cut down by gunfire. Ahn-Kha lay groaning in his native tongue, hand pressed against his buttock.

"Sir! Sir!" the wounded Jamaican said, pushing a machine gun lying at the bottom of the wagon at Valentine with a bloody foot. "It's still got bullets."

Valentine took up the weapon. He rested it on the side of the wagon and turned it against Murphy's turncoats still burning and killing among the other wagons. The chatter of the weapon attracted bullets from all directions. Valentine waited for the inevitable impact. He would die with his mission, with the men he'd misled. Another flare landed by the wagon, spewing more purple mist. Mortar shells dropped, seeking his position.

Valentine heard hooves approach through the smoke, and turned the gun. Only a short length of bullets dangled from the belt.

"David!" Valentine heard a familiar voice call. "Captain Valentine! Men, find Captain Valentine."

Post came out of the purple haze, leading two horses. His clothes were in rags, and his eyes were bright in bruised sockets. Blood ran from a cut on his thigh. Another mortar shell exploded and the horses danced in terror, but Post dragged them on.

"Take Ahn-Kha with the other horse. He's hurt. I'm staying with the men."

"No use!" Post said, bringing the animals beside the wagon.

"Can't—," Valentine began, but Ahn-Kha's bloody fingers wrapped themselves around the snakeskin bandolier and pulled him bodily out of the wagon.

"My David, we go. I shall run. There's nothing else to do."

"No!"

The Grog hauled Valentine to a horse. He hopped on one leg, supporting himself with his other tree-trunk arm as though using a crutch. Post handed over the reins and helped the Jamaican into one of the saddles, then held the horse for Valentine to mount. Valentine saw blood running from Post's ear.

"No," Valentine said tightly, slinging his empty PPD and grabbing the horse by the throat latch. "You're hurt, you ride."

Post and the wounded Jamaican rode hard for the woods. A handful of others, including Ahn-Kha and Valentine, followed the two riders.

As they fled, a shell found the wagon. More oily smoke rose into the winter sky. Valentine ran with the rest, half-hoping his heart would burst from the effort. He ran from his enemies, from defeat, from his dead and wounded men. He wished he could run from his failure, but it stayed with him all the way to the trees and beyond.

Behind him, the quickwood burned.

This ends the third volume following the career of David Valentine. His return to what had been the Ozark Free Territory is chronicled in the fourth, Valentine's Rising. *For more information on it and other tales of Vampire Earth, please visit the author's Web site at http://www. vampireearth.com.*

Valentine half dozed in front of the field pack with the head-set on. Like most Quisling military equipment, it was ruggedly functional and almost aggressively ugly. Late at night, the Quisling operators were more social, keeping each other company in the after-midnight hours of the quiet watches. Someone had just finished giving instructions on how to clear a gummed condensation tube on a still. Valentine twisted the dial back to a scratchier conversation about a pregnant washerwoman.

"So she goes to your CO. So what? She should be happy. She's safe for a couple years now. Over," the advice giver said.

"She wants housing with the NCO wives," the advice seeker explained. "She's already got a three-year-old. She wants me to marry her so they can move in. Over."

"That's an old story. She's in it for the ration book, bro. Look, if a piece of ass pisses you off, threaten to have her tossed off-post. That'll shut her up. Better yet, just do it. Sounds to me like she's—"

Valentine turned the dial again.

". . . fight in Pine Bluff. Put me down for twenty coin on Jebro. He'll take Meredith like a sapper popping an old woman. Over."

"Sure thing. You want any of the prefight action? Couple of convicts. It's a blood match—the loser goes to the Slits. Over."

Valentine had heard the term "Slits" on the Mississippi.

It referred to the Reapers' slit-pupil eyes, or perhaps the narrow wound their stabbing tongue left above the breastbone.

"No, haven't seen 'em. I'd be wasting my money. Over."

Valentine heard a horse snort and stamp outside the cracked window. The sound brought him awake in a flash. A pair of alarmed whinnies cut the night air.

"Arms! Quietly now, arms!" Valentine said to the sleeping men huddled against the walls in the warm room where they had enjoyed dinner. He snatched up his pistol and worked the slide.

Ahn-Kha appeared at his elbow. How so much mass moved with such speed and stealth—

"What is it, my David?" Ahn-Kha breathed, his rubbery lips barely forming the words.

"Something is spooking the horses. Watch the front with your Grogs. Post," Valentine said to his lieutenant, who appeared in his trousers and boots, pulling on a jacket, "get the Smalls and M'Daw into the cellar, please. Stay down there with them."

Valentine waved to the wagon sentry Jefferson, but the man's eyes searched elsewhere. Jefferson had his rifle up and ready. Two of the horses reared, and he stood to see over them.

They came out of the snow, bounding on spring-steel legs. Three of them. He and all his people would be dead inside two minutes.

"Reapers!" Valentine bellowed, bringing up his pistol in a two-handed grip. As he centered the front sight on one he noticed it was naked but so dirt-covered that it looked clothed. A torn cloth collar was all that remained of whatever it had been wearing. He fired three times; the .45 barked deafeningly in the enclosed space.

At the sound of his shots his men moved even faster. Two marines scrambled to the window and stuck their rifles out of the loophole-sized slats in the shutters.

A Reaper leapt toward Jefferson, whose gun snapped impotently, and Valentine reached for his machete as he braced himself for the sight of the Texan's disassembly. Perhaps he could get the Reaper in the back as it killed Jefferson. But it didn't land on the sentry. The naked avatar came down on top of a horse on the balls of its feet like a circus rider. It reached for the animal's neck, snake-hinged jaw opening wide. The fangs tore into the muscle of the screaming horse's shoulder. The horse dropped as the piercing tongue hit the beast's heart.

The other two, robeless and running naked in the snow-storm like the first, also ignored Jefferson, chasing the horses instead. The Jamaicans' rifles fired in unison when one Reaper came around the cart and into the open, but the only effect Valentine saw was a bullet strike into a mount's rump. The horse dropped sideways with a Reaper on top of it. Some instinct made the wounded animal roll. It turned its heavy body across the spider-thin form and came to its feet, kicking. As the Reaper knelt a pair of hooves caught it across the back, sending it flying against the cart.

The third disappeared into the snowstorm, chasing a terrified bay.

"Stay at the front of the house with the others," he said to Ahn-Kha, who stood ready with a quickwood spearpoint. He threw open the door—and held up his hands when Jefferson whirled and pointed the rifle at him, muzzle seemingly aimed right between his eyes. The gun snapped again.

Valentine almost flew to the broken-backed Reaper. It got to its feet somehow, swaying on the pivot-point of its shattered spine. It lashed out. Valentine slipped under the raking claw. The momentum of the Reaper's strike tipped it again, and Valentine buried his blade in it as it sprawled facedown in the snow. He ground the machete into the Reaper, pinned like a bug on mounting Styrofoam. It tried once to shrug him off, but with its back broken, its inhumanly strong muscles were useless. The Reaper twitched as the blade worked its way through cablelike nerve tissue. In five seconds it was limp.

The other one lifted its blood-smeared face from the

twitching horse and lumbered off into the night, its belly swollen like a starvation victim's. Valentine heard the annoying snap of Jefferson's rifle again, followed by curses as he worked the bolt.

"Jefferson, calm down. You might try loading your weapon. Don't kill any of us once you do."

"Sorry, Captain. Sorry—"

Valentine ignored him and listened with hard ears all around the woods, but all he could hear were the Reaper's fading footfalls. They had attacked alone and hit the biggest-warmest targets they could see. Evidently they were masterless; their Kurian had probably been killed or had fled out of control range, and they were acting on pure instinct. He looked at the broken-backed one.

"Lucky. So so lucky," Valentine said.

"And horsemeat for breakfast," Jefferson agreed.

"Get inside, Jefferson. Don't worry about the horses for now."

The Texan wasted no time getting out of the wagon. Valentine put a new magazine in his gun and backed toward the house, still listening and smelling. Nothing. Not even the cold feeling he usually got when Reapers were around, but his ears were still ringing from the gunshots inside, and the snow was killing odors.

He rapped on the door and backed into the house, still covering the quickwood.

"Anything out front?" he called, eyes never leaving the trees.

"Nothing, sir," Ahn-Kha said.

He heard a horse scream in the distance. The Reaper had caught up with the bay.

"Post," Valentine shouted.

"Sir?" he heard through the cellar floor.

"I'm going out after them. Two blasts on my whistle when I come back in. Don't let anyone shoot me." Valentine caught Jefferson's eye and winked. The red on his face faded and the Texan smiled back.

"Yessir," Post answered.

Valentine tore off a peeling strip of wallpaper and wiped the resinlike Reaper blood off his machete. He considered bringing a quickwood spear, but decided to hunt the Reaper with just the blade: it would be vulnerable after a feed. He nodded to the Jamaicans and opened the front door. After a long listen, he dashed past a tree and into the brush of the forest.

A nervous horse from the other team nickered at him. He moved from tree to tree, following the tracks, smelling the dribbled horse blood.

Valentine dried his hand on his pant leg and took a better grip on his machete. He sniffed the ground with his Wolf's nose, picking up the horse blood. He instinctively broke into his old loping run, broken like a horse's canter by his stiff leg, following the scent.

He didn't have far to travel. A half mile later, after a run that verged on a climb up a steep incline, he came to the Reaper's resting spot. Water flowing down the limestone had created a crevice-cave under the rocky overhang. An old Cat named Everready used to say that Reapers got "dopey" after a feed; with a belly full of blood they often slept like drunkards. This one had hardly gotten out of sight of the house before succumbing to the need for sleep. He saw its pale foot, black toenails sharp against the ash-colored skin, sticking out of a pile of leaves.

Valentine heard whistling respiration. He put his hand on his pistol and decided to risk a single shot. He drew and sighted on the source of the breathing.

The shot tossed leaves into the air. The Reaper came to its feet, crashing its skull against the overhang. A black wound crossed its scraggly hairline. It went down to its hands and knees. Valentine sighted on a slit pupil in a bilious yellow iris.

"Anyone at the other end?" Valentine asked, looking into the eye. The thing looked back, animal pain and confusion in its eye—a badger with a limb crushed in a trap. It scuttled to the side. Valentine tracked the pupil with his gun. "What are you doing out here?"

harrrruk! it spat.

It exploded out of the leaves.

Valentine fired, catching it in the chest. The bullet's impact rolled it back into the cave, but it came out again in its inhuman, crabwise crawl.

It moved fast. As fast as a wide-awake Reaper, despite its recent feeding.

Valentine shot again . . . again . . . again. Black flowers blossomed on the thing's skin at the wet slap of each slug's impact. It shot out from the crevice, slithering like a snake. Valentine pounced, machete ready. He pinned it, driving the knee of his good leg into the small of its back, wishing he hadn't been so cocksure, that he'd brought quickwood to finish it. He raised the blade high and brought it down on the back of the Reaper's neck, the power of the blow driving it into the thing's spine. He tried to pull it back for another blow, but the black blood had already sealed the blade into the wound.

It continued to crawl, only half of its body now working.

Valentine stood up and drove his booted heel onto the blade. If he couldn't pull it out, he could get it in farther. He stomped again, almost dancing on the back of the blade. The Reaper ceased its crawl, but the head still thrashed.

urrack . . . shhhar, it hissed.

Valentine put a new magazine in his gun. It was beyond being a threat to anything but an earthworm or a beetle now, but he wouldn't let it suffer. He brought the muzzle to the ear hole, angling it so the bullet wouldn't bounce off the bony baffle just behind the ear. He didn't want to risk the jaws without a couple of men with crowbars to pry the mouth open and a pair of pliers to rip the stabbing tongue out.

He heard sliding footfall behind and turned, the foresight of the pistol leading the way.

It was the other Reaper, blood covering its face but cruel

interest in its eyes. It squatted to spring. It had possessed instinct enough to approach from downwind.

Valentine emptied the magazine into it, knocking it over backward. Then he ran. Downhill. Fast.

It followed. Faster.